The INSTITUTE f

ANGRY
ROBOT

D0051746

THE BEAST OF NIGHTFALL LODGE

S. A. SIDOR

ACCLAIMED AUTHOR OF *Fury From the Tomb*

Incoming!

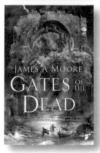

The BEAST *of* NIGHTFALL LODGE

"Pulp-fiction pastiches are hardly rare these days but few are as artfully executed as this one, which brings together ancient mummies, cursed tombs, loathsome monsters, and Mexican bandits. Narrated by a young Egyptologist blissfully lacking in self-awareness, it's tongue-in-cheek joy from start to finish."

Financial Times

"The greatest horror-adventure-Western mash-up imaginable to human minds."

Steve Hockensmith, New York Times bestselling author of
Pride & Prejudice and Zombies: Dawn of the Dreadfuls

"As Rom's mission grows increasingly wild – and increasingly dangerous, the book only grows more compulsively readable."

Barnes & Noble Sci-Fi & Fantasy Blog

"*Fury From the Tomb* is your cure for the pulp fiction blues you never knew you had. This tantalizing mashup combines supernatural horror, western and adventure in one shiny package."

Kirkus Reviews

"*Fury From the Tomb* is a full-on, red blooded assembly of dead things that should really be dead. In other words, the sort of thing you would sit down and gleefully watch at your local flea pit while your mates try to steal your oversized tub of horrifically sweet popcorn."

Strange Alliances

BY THE SAME AUTHOR

Fury from the Tomb

Skin River
Bone Factory
The Mirror's Edge
Pitch Dark

S A SIDOR

THE INSTITUTE *for* SINGULAR ANTIQUITIES

The Beast of Nightfall Lodge

ANGRY ROBOT

ANGRY ROBOT
An imprint of Watkins Media Ltd

Unit 11, Shepperton House,
89 Shepperton Road,
London N1 3DF • UK

angryrobotbooks.com
twitter.com/angryrobotbooks
If you go down

An Angry Robot paperback original 2018

Copyright © S A Sidor 2019

Cover by Daniel Strange
Set in Meridien by Argh! Nottingham

Distributed in the United States by Penguin Random House, Inc., New York.

ISBN 978 0 85766 764 9
Ebook ISBN 978 0 85766 765 6

Printed in the United States of America

9 8 7 6 5 4 3 2

For Emma and Quinn

1

"O" IS FOR OWL

New Year's Day, 1920
The Waterston Institute for Singular Antiquities
Manhattan, New York City

The Institute study was cold. The whole laboratory, the entire building, drank in the frigid weather and stored it up despite any fire raging in the fireplace. One had to sit close to the flames to appreciate the heat. I had arranged my reading room around the tidy, soot-black bricks. Here a person could survive the winter, close to a liquor cabinet, books at hand, a gothic window cut into the wall at the other end of the room in case you might want to see if the world still existed.

I never used that window.

Evangeline Waterston stared at me over her shoulder as she slipped a worm-eaten book from the lowest shelf of my private library at the Institute for Singular Antiquities. My library, *her* Institute. Since Montague Waterston had disappeared many years ago and left his fortune to Evangeline, his only child, she had decided to sink a good bit of that fortune right here. She hired me at the start of things, after my first Egyptian expedition to unearth a cursed sorcerer's tomb. Her father had financed the dig. Surprising everyone, including myself, I brought the sorcerer's mummy and those of his servants back to Manhattan, only to lose them on a train ride out to Los Angeles. Banditos robbed the train, and Evangeline and I, along with a bounty hunter named Rex McTroy, and a resilient Chinese boy named Yong Wu, went to Mexico to bring them back. Dead or alive was an apt phrase for that quest.

From the wreckage of the strange desert affair came the unlikely birth of the Waterston Institute for Singular Antiquities. Over our years together, we had built the Institute's rare collections to a level of both prestige and shocking notoriety. We offered no apologies for our artifacts or our unorthodox methods. People talked about us, and Evangeline said that was better than silent indifference. I think she enjoyed turning heads in the stuffy museum world.

Admittedly, I did too.

Holding the chunky old book in her right hand, as if testing its weight, Evangeline used her left hand to balance a brandy snifter of excellent Kentucky bourbon. I'd poured the drink for her earlier in the evening. We had dined together with our fellow adventurer, and now a distinguished medical researcher, Dr Yong Wu. But he left our company soon after the meal ended, expressing his regrets over his lack of sleep on New Year's Eve, before catching a cab to his hotel across town. Evangeline inhaled the aroma of her liquor, tilted the glass, and took a sip, rolling the whiskey around with her tongue. A dimple appeared beside her mouth and she tapped the book's well-bumped spine, her smile growing slyer by the second.

"Do you ever think about the Beast?" she asked.

"Which beast is that? We have encountered so many in our time." I flicked my gaze up and away, and sucked noisily at my pipe, emitting a perique-scented cloud. I attempted to obscure myself, trying to appear both uninterested and comfortably settled for the remainder of the evening on my chaise longue, facing the fireplace, eyes fixed upon the richly enflamed logs trapped behind the screen. But her question – indeed, Evangeline herself – made that all but impossible. Oh, how I watched her, always, and how she in return knew it. She straightened, emptied the glass, and set it down on a side table, then stretched and pressed a hand against the corseted curve of her lower back. Evangeline pointed the tattered corner of the book at me.

"Ah, but only one deserved the name," she said.

She squinted at me through the fruity smoke.

"*Deserve* is a moral word," I said. "Are we not scientists? And freethinkers?"

"Dr Romulus Hardy, you know the creature I mean. You're only playing at not knowing."

"How dare you accuse me of being a pretender...? Good God, woman!" I said, smiling.

Evangeline tossed the book – a sizable volume – across the library at me. It hit with a bone-drumming thud in the middle of my chest. An ember shower erupted from my pipe bowl. I feared a broken stem!

Fiery crumbs spilled down my vest. In a panic, I licked two fingers and snuffed out the spritely shreds of tobacco as they landed atop the buttoned soft green leather of my daybed. Evangeline's aim had always been precise. The book had expelled a significant degree of dust on me which I distractedly brushed away. I sneezed then and rubbed my eyes.

When my vision cleared, Evangeline was steps closer to me.

"Do you not want to talk about it because talking about it makes you sad?"

"It doesn't make me sad," I lied.

"Really? You have a tendency toward sadness even when matters do not trend that way. These events unfortunately do. So, I assumed your reluctance–"

"If anything, it makes me angry."

She paused to assess how my anger was doing in the moment.

"Well, I understand that too," she said.

"We went through a lot together on that frozen mountain. I have no wish to relive it."

"The four of us? You're talking about our team, our little hunting party?"

"You, me, McTroy, and Wu... we were hardly left unscathed. But there were more than four of us present at the so-called hunt when it all began. Do you remember that peculiar howling wind on the first night as Oscar Adderly laid out his challenge? I certainly do. A trick of the mountainous terrain, he said. But it was an unnatural sound. We should have run, there and then." I felt gooseflesh on my arms, a prickling of the hairs lifting on my neck. "The other hunters, the

Adderlys... what happened at Nightfall Lodge should never have happened to anyone."

"I know you were badly hurt," she said, her voice growing softer.

"I wasn't alone. We all received our wounds."

"And you blame me?"

"It was a long time ago, more than thirty years. I don't know what I think."

"But Romulus Hardy never forgets the past. That is what makes him such a renowned Egyptologist. You dust off your artifacts, you catalogue and ponder. You make certain nothing ever dies, even if it only lives in your head." There was a hard, bitter edge to her words. She was doing her best to draw me out by any means. To what end I was not sure. Even though I was wide awake, I was leery of being pulled into an all-night conversation I would eventually regret.

"This is not Egyptology. When it came down to it, the whole matter had little to do with my areas of expertise."

"The venture included an element of ancient historical significance, a prize that Oscar Adderly dangled. I recall you being excited once you were received properly in New Mexico. You were enthusiastic, charmingly so, if memory serves."

I thought about what she said. It was true, of course. I couldn't wait to get started after our bounty-hunting friend, Rex McTroy, provided me the details. Boosting my interest even further, Oscar Adderly made us an outrageous offer from his throne of manly luxury, Nightfall Lodge – a chalet he personally designed and had carved into the remote mountainside as a monument to, well... himself. How he strutted in front of a wall of antlers and beheaded wild creatures as he enticed us to track a most unusual, and dangerous, quarry. I see him still – that proud rooster puffing on his El Rey del Mundo Havana cigar. Who might've guessed his fate?

"I was baited. The Adderlys knew how to draw people's attention and how to make you believe their family's interests were your very own. It was their gift," I admitted.

"They had many gifts. Showmanship included."

Evangeline also had the gift of showmanship, though hers was less dramatic, and often more effective; at least it always worked when she used it on me. She retrieved the bourbon from the cabinet and refilled our drinks. The decades had been kind to her. From across the room it was difficult to guess her age. She wore her hair pinned in a coiled braid. Crisp silvery white, it brought out her agate-green eyes. Possessing a stronger chin than most men in their twenties, Evangeline moved purposefully, even when the purpose might be unclear. You could sense the crackling of her intellectual energy in the air. Her back stiffened to any challenge. Some women said she was handsome. Others called her haughty. Most men remained hushed in her presence, and that was no small accomplishment. As she passed me my glass, she smiled, and her fingertips lightly grazed my wrist, warming me more than any fire or liquor ever would.

"Why do you want to talk about the beast tonight?" I asked.

"The event is unresolved between us. I think you've

blocked it off."

"I agree, but what good will ever come–"

"Look at the book," she said, settling her hip on the arm of my chaise.

I had almost forgotten about the book. "Your weapon, you mean?"

I picked it up from the chaise. I gazed at the cover.

"Do you remember?" she asked. "You once told me the story of its acquisition."

"I can't say I recall that at all." I read the title: "*Odd & Ghastly Rhymes for Frightening Young Children*. Do you want me to read you a bedtime story?"

"You're good at bedtime stories. But I am not sleepy tonight."

"Is this in German? I'm only decent at dead languages. You'll have to be the reader."

"It's not German." She slapped at my arm playfully. "No, all the words are English. I don't need to translate it for you. But yes, I *would* like you to read it to me."

"All of it?"

"Just one rhyme, if you please." She cocked her head and looked at me curiously. "You really don't remember this book?"

I leafed through the old tome and shook my head.

"Wherever did I get this?" I mumbled in absent-minded amusement.

Evangeline walked over to the window and stared out at the steely moonlit night. "You know this book, Hardy. Read from 'An Eerie Alphabet Rhyme.' It's near the beginning."

I found the table of contents and located the page. The paper was heavy but brittle. I turned carefully to the nursery rhyme in question.

"You see how fragile old books get," I said. "This one's poor pages have been bent over, again and again, folded to save someone's favorite spot, no doubt. Now the folded piece is missing, the beginning of the poem is but a fragment. The letter 'A' might be Anaconda, given the *'tight squeezing'* that follows. 'B' was definitely Bat *'a-flitter in the' somewhere* – that bit's part of what's been lost. I'll have to start with the letter 'C' I'm afraid."

"C is fine," Evangeline said, staring out the window into Central Park.

"Very well," I said. "Here we go.

"'C' is for Centipede asleep on your cheek.
Stir and you'll wake her. Those legs! Shriek!
'D' is for Dung Beetle rolling 'round her ball.
Strong little scarab – she gives it her all."

I said, "Oh, I do like dung beetles. The Egyptians loved them. Scarabs are the most fascinating creatures. I once saw a specimen at the Field Museum as big and fat as a ripe plum. And the variety of colors is astonishing, not to mention the iconography. Without the scarab, I scarcely think Egypt would be Egypt..."

"Skip down lower in the rhyme," she said.

"All right, Miss Impatience." I dropped a few lines. "Things grow a bit darker farther along the alphabet, I see. The mood alters. Charm disappears. It is all grim business and rough shadows thrown upon the floral bedroom wallpaper." I tried to laugh, but my throat was dry. I sipped, or rather gulped, from my whiskey.

My heart was beating emphatically in my chest. I had
no conscious idea why that might be the case. "I'll try
this part. Tell me how you like it.

> "'O' is for Owl who hunts in the night.
> Silent and swift is his murderous flight."

Here I paused for a long while. Had the fire died? I
turned immediately colder, much colder, and my skin
felt tight across my nose, wind-burned. Every breath
I took smelled of musk and pine. My lungs throbbed
with an iron cold. I had the waking illusion I was
bundled in a weighted coat; I could hardly move, and
when I needed to leave here – *a great danger was coming,
I had to flee or die* – I would be too slow to escape.

"Hardy?"

I shook my head to clear the sensations. My eyes
skimmed over the page. It was as if I had scales on my
eyeballs; my tears were freezing. The roots of my teeth
pulsed, biting on ice.

I read the words Evangeline had been waiting for
me to find.

> "'W' is for ~~Wolf Wendigo~~ Wickedness in the wintery
> wood.
> Hungry and gaunt in the tall trees he stood."

The scratched-out "Wolf" – I knew who had done
that. The word "Wendigo" I had struck through myself.
The "Wickedness" substitution was in my handwriting.
I remembered this book now. So many years ago... but I
zoomed in as if I were twirling the knob of a microscope

and focusing on a slide squirming with fundamental yet previously invisible life. My head dizzy, I flipped to the first page. There was an inscription. The book had been a gift, half in jest, and half as a warning. *How had I forgotten?* I made myself forget. Obviously, Evangeline remembered better than I did.

> *To My Witty, Shy Rom –*
>   *May your nightmares end and your new dreams glitter like stars.*
>   *Eternally yours & a Kiss in the Dark –*
>   *Cassi*

When I looked up again, Evangeline had seated herself across from me in a wingback armchair. Those agate-green eyes watched me without judgment. My face was wet. I touched my cheeks. My hand trembled. I was gasping.

"How long have I been sitting here like this?"

"Too long," she said. "You need to get it out of you. You've bottled it up for too many years and it is killing you, Hardy. You're a smart man, and you know what I'm saying is true. However much it hurts, it must come out. We need to get it into the open to destroy it. Now. Tonight. You've been haunting your own thoughts for far too long."

I looked away from her. Sometimes she was like staring at the sun.

"What do you expect me to do?" I asked.

Her gaze was direct. So too were her words.

"Tell me what you think happened. The mountain adventure... the whole story."

"I can't. You were there too. Why should I have to tell you?"

"Because I think you have gone wrong somewhere in your mind. You're lost in the woods, terrified. It's eating you alive. I'm here with you and I'm staying no matter what happens. I'll help you. You need to know you're safe. I'm telling you that above all else. You are safe."

The fire glowed bright behind her, Evangeline, my partner, whom I trusted with my life.

"No one is safe," I said.

Then I began my story.

2

STEAM HEAT ON BEAVER STREET

Hallowe'en, 1890
The Waterston Institute for Singular Antiquities
Manhattan, New York City

In the early days of the Institute, the size of our collection dictated the size of our offices. We rented a single room above a tobacconist's shop on Beaver Street around the corner from the Delmonico brothers' Citadel restaurant. I worked there alone. I had space enough for a large desk, my bookshelves, a cot, and no more. I saw no reason for separate lodgings. My work was my life. I am a simple man, and in my young bachelor days I favored spartan, monkish habits. Books were my only extravagance. Also, a cane I had picked up in Mexico. The cane's knob featured the head of an ape, done in silver. I allowed myself this eccentricity, and a man walking alone in the city needs a way of defending himself from ruffians. Evangeline was busy, still settling her father's business affairs in Los Angeles. She promised she would join me once we had another project prepared, another great expedition in the offing.

To be truthful, we had been mired in this stasis for quite a while. After rushing through a burst of hectic activity finding the location for our new offices, Evangeline left New York for California. I went back to my study of Egyptology. We wrote to each other, first daily, then weekly. Finally, the letters stopped. I had not seen her in nearly two years. But she continued to pay the bills and my monthly research stipend.

I spent most days reading, poring over maps of the Nile Valley and contemplating my next dig. What were Egyptologists if not planners? I would like to say we were scholars. But were we astronomers and students of religious ritual, practice, and belief? Or were we historians, philologists, and classicists? Some claimed our primary job to be excavators and engineers of extraction. The discipline was undecided, changing daily, and not really that disciplined. To be sure, my comrades in Egyptology were all those things I mentioned and more. But what bothered me deeply was that in truth we were destroyers. Too often we seized the fruit of Egyptian culture and dropped the emptied husks behind us like so much refuse. We raided and went home.

I was no better. I had robbed a sorcerer's grave and left dead men in my wake. I took what was not mine to take, and I paid a hefty price for my transgressions. So I was more than a bit hesitant to get back in the game. I did enjoy the anticipatory act of preparation. All the mistakes were still waiting to be made. I was free of action, yes, but also free of guilt. Until I read that Flinders Petrie was planning an exploration into the Holy Land. My mind started to dream again, but in biblical proportions. I imagined myself leading an army of diggers in search of a pharaoh's undiscovered tomb, perhaps even a lost city. The Waterston fortune would pay my way. I had the itch to board a ship to Alexandria, ride day and night into the desert, and get my hands dirty.

One late October midday, Hallowe'en in fact, I was unpacking a box of ancient seals and rings. I had purchased them from a dealer I'd met at the American Natural History Museum in Central Park, after a discussion on the habits of the round-tailed muskrat. He invited me for tea and a look at his private items soon to be available at auction. The tea was weak, the seals were frauds – not even clever ones – but I asked him to throw in a four-chambered alabaster kohl vessel I spotted holding down a pile of unpaid bills on a nearby table, which I suspected was authentic and well beyond his knowledge. He agreed gladly.

I slid the rings off my desk. The cost of those fraudulent trinkets was a fraction of the value of the lovely Middle Period cosmetic urn used to sweeten the pot. As I carefully unboxed the artifact, I heard footsteps climbing up the stairwell.

I received no visitors here. Not even the landlord, or the jovial, sallow-faced tobacconist from downstairs with whom I chatted about the fates of the two New York Giants baseball teams over a morning pipeful. Those stairs were mine alone to tread upon. I pushed away from my desk in a state of genuine startlement.

Who can it be?

Three swift knocks on the door jolted the silence.

"Yes?" I called out.

"Delivery," the voice outside the door answered.

"You have the wrong office. I am expecting no delivery."

Three louder and more rapid knocks followed.

"Go away. I am an office for antiquities! Check your address!"

"I have coffee," said the voice.

"What did you say?"

"This is a special delivery coffee for... Dr Ramalass Hardcheese?"

"Oh, for the love of all that is holy... I am coming." I stood and straightened my vest before answering the call.

I opened the door, saying, "The name is Dr ROM-U-LUS HAR-DY."

My caller was a slim, older boy dressed like a cowboy in his Sunday church clothes and a long duster coat. He wore his hat pulled down over his face and carried no coffee of any kind.

"Where is this delivery, young sir? You have disturbed me at my work."

He thumbed the brim of his hat up and smiled.

I passed quickly from anger to confusion to recognition.

"Yong Wu! Is that really you? You've grown so tall!" I shouted.

I could not resist the urge to clap him on the shoulders. My heart surged.

"Hello, Dr Hardy. I am happy to find you well."

Here was a boy I first met on my doomed train ride

west. He had been the porter's assistant then, and the first time we introduced ourselves he was delivering coffee to my private train car filled with crated mummies. I frowned in mock sternness. "Ramalass Hardcheese?"

Wu blushed. "McTroy told me to say that."

"I have no doubt about that." I led Wu by the arm into my office. "If you don't have coffee, I certainly do. Come in and sit down. I'm afraid there's only one chair. But I sit all day. I have a fireplace and can heat up some water. Remember making coffee over the fire in the Gila Desert? We are a bit more civilized here. Now let me see if I have an extra cup." I dusted out the cup I found. "Take off your coat. We have steam heat on Beaver Street. It's boiling in the winter when it's not freezing and drafty. The summers are no milder, though I wouldn't trade it for a day riding the Camino Del Diablo wondering if I'd die of thirst or a bandito's bullet.

"Wu, it is *good* to see you. Don't tell me that scoundrel McTroy put you on a train and made you ride all the way out to New York City alone. Let me take your coat and hat." I hung his things on a wall peg. Wu kept his long hair braids tucked up under the hat. I shook his hand. It was rough, calloused.

"Remember, sir, I worked on a train alone."

"Yes, yes you did. Remarkable things are common for you, I forgot. How is McTroy?"

"He is the same. McTroy is teaching me to be a bounty man. To track and hunt..."

I nodded.

"And you are studying, I hope," I said. "I trust it

hasn't been all six-guns and cussing?"

This was Wu's turn to nod at me.

We waited for the water to boil. In the tiny office there were few places to look, especially when another person arrived. I chose the window pane. Wu stared at the floor. I opened the window a crack and observed a carriage passing below. I must have smelled horses every day, but today their animal smell transported me back to a different place, on the trail with my three friends in Mexico. Did I transmit this very thought to Wu? Who knows the uncanny powers of the human mind?

A sorcerer had occupied my psychic landscape for a time against my will, and his presence left a residual stain of strangeness I lived with, gifting me with expanded sensibility but also a muddled sense of where I left off and others began. Edges blurred. Other people's thoughts mixed without warning into my own. I glimpsed their hearts in glass cases, but the cases were often ill-lit or draped. The vegetable seller's youngest daughter had a cough that worried him in the night. (*All I did was buy lettuce from his stand.*) A tall, elegant woman at the New York Public Library disliked her dead husband's high-strung poodle but tolerated the canine because she was terrified of empty houses. (*We sat all morning at the same long table, in complete silence.*) It was something like remembering old conversations you've had with people that they've utterly forgotten. I was a benign spy, and I had no control over it. The clip-clop of hooves drummed. I shut my eyes to see a kaleidoscopic swirl of sunset colors and weird desert thoughts hanging there buoyantly, expectantly, in the depthless darkness. (*Look, Wu, horses!*)

I felt inseparable from my friends; we were parts of the same living organism.

"I have my own horse. A black and white pinto," Wu said. "Her name is Magpie."

"Is she fast?" I asked, pulling back into the solid world.

"Very fast, and very smart. She is the best horse. But she has a strong mind of her own."

"The best ones always do."

Independence is a valuable trait... within reason. But, like Wu, I found myself attracted to that which can never be tamed. He was too young for women; at least I hoped McTroy hadn't tried to initiate him into that arena yet, a boy of what? Twelve years? Even McTroy wasn't so imprudent. I guessed the bounty man's heart was likely as scarred as the rest of him. And having seen the women of Yuma, I suspected temptations were but few, and limited to dark, moonless nights and a momentary slippage of character. Wu was a child, an orphan practically. We owed him what remained of his childhood. His parents had saved our lives. Surely, McTroy would respect them enough to protect their son in matters of amour.

Here I was thinking like an old man when I had but journeyed midway into my third decade. Women evaded me – purposefully, I sometimes imagined. Not that their charms did not work – they did, but their actuality remained vexingly elusive. Perhaps if I left the office and talked to people I would find more success.

"What brings you to the city? Have you grown tired of dusty Yuma?"

"No," Wu said. "I like living in Yuma."

He got up from his chair and browsed through my books.

"Ah, I was hoping you'd say you wanted to join me at the Institute. I have need for an assistant, you know. And, if we're lucky, I think Miss Evangeline will visit here eventually."

"She visited us in Yuma."

"What's that you say?"

The coffeepot rattled.

"Dr Hardy! Your hand!"

I removed my fingers from the pot handle. The pain was coming now. It throbbed like a heartbeat of some small, fragile creature that was biting me.

"A minor burn, nothing more," I said, as I wrapped a handkerchief around them and using a small white towel, lifted the pot to fill our cups. "You've seen Evangeline in Yuma? On local mining business, was she? Just passing through town?"

Wu shook his head. "I don't think so. She stayed with us for two weeks the last time."

"Two weeks!" I nearly dropped the pot. "I see she's been checking up on you then. That's good. She must be as worried as I've been about you living with McTroy. You've grown very close to Miss Evangeline. I'm glad that your relationship continues."

Wu frowned at me. "Miss Evangeline did not seem to worry about McTroy."

"She masks her feelings, Wu. Women, like fine artifacts, are not so easy to understand. They have layers that must be peeled back. Depths, Wu... depths are contained in them."

Wu showed puzzlement, and I figured he was grasping at what I said.

"We went riding a lot. Magpie loves her. Miss Evangeline fed her apples out of her hand and would laugh at the way it tickled. She and McTroy would talk and walk, walk and talk. At night they would go riding again, but I would be too tired to go with them."

"Everyone loves Evangeline," I said. My coffee was too hot to drink. Still, I drank it.

Wu patted his jacket as a look of embarrassment overtook him. "I have a letter for you from McTroy. He said it was important and I should give it to you as soon as I arrived."

I took the plain, unmarked envelope from the boy and tore it open.

"I didn't know the brute could write."

Dear Doc,

Yes, I can write. Mama raised me up to handle wordy men. Listen to the news Yong Wu has to tell. He does not know the whole story. Not by a long shot. I won't lie to you. Danger is guaranteed. Sure as Hell the weather will be cold. There's money in this proposition and that's a fact. It's a snipe hunt as far as I can tell. The man making the offer is a museum type like you-know-who (you, Doc!). Fool's money spends as good as any other. Join us if you want. Leave the mummies out of this. – McTroy

P.S. The boy is turning out fine despite your soft influences. Ha! Unclench your fists, Doc, 'fore you hurt somebody.

Opening my hand, I flicked a stiff finger at the paper. Then I let it float down to my desk.

"McTroy's inviting me on some sort of speculative venture. *Humph.* I couldn't possibly go. I am too occupied with things; planning a new Egyptian expedition, for a start. I can see the disappointment in your eyes, Yong Wu. You might want to think about joining me on a trip overseas to Nile country. You'll learn about culture. See amazing sights in an ancient terrain."

"Isn't that where the cursed mummies came from?"

"Yes." I struggled to add a more positive note. "McTroy said you have news?"

"We're going to New Mexico Territory."

"All of you? Evangeline is going too?"

"Yes, she is there already, visiting a woman of dark interests like herself."

I guffawed. "I suppose this lady's a witch who's written a book of spells?"

Wu nodded vigorously, adding to my general confusion. "She talks to the dead. But Miss Evangeline didn't call her a witch. She called her a spirit medium. Miss E wants to record her 'dead talks' for the Institute. The witch lives in Raton. How did you know about her?"

I leaned my back against the cool brick wall. "At times my intuition astonishes even me. But why would McTroy make this trip?" I wondered aloud.

"To collect the bounty on a butcherer of nine men from Raton," Wu said, deepening his voice with manly seriousness. "The spirit lady's husband is offering $10,000 to the man who captures the killer."

McTroy could not resist cash. He would jump at the chance for making such a fortune. If Evangeline conducted some occult business in the same town, then all the better for him. Ah, he was a shrewd dog. But I decided to prove myself a shrewder one yet. "Wu, we are finally getting somewhere. The picture coalesces. This assassin must have quite a reputation. What's his name?"

"He has no name."

"People don't know his name? So, he is a mystery man," I concluded.

"The people on the mountain say he is no man. They have seen him on the forest slopes. In the Sangre de Cristo Mountains they hear his scream at night through the trees. His body is too tall to be human. His steps are long, and they disappear, leaving no track in the dirt or snow. He vanishes when they chase him. Something grows out of his head, like a crown. Like horns. He ate those nine men, Dr Hardy. They were all hunters. He killed them and he ate them. No one can stop him. We are headed there to catch him. They say he has no name because he is no man."

"No man? I don't understand what you mean."

"They say he is a monster."

"What kind of monster?" I asked, perplexed.

Wu shrugged and showed me his empty hands.

"They call him the Beast."

3
THE CASTLE RAM

The Streets and Grand Central Depot
Lower Manhattan, New York City

I was not about to let Rex McTroy ride into the mountains of New Mexico with Yong Wu and Evangeline lacking my company. I thrilled for adventure as much as any man. I would take a holiday and go to the Sangre de Cristo range. Mountains are notorious for meditation and revelation. Perhaps I would learn a thing or two about myself I did not know already. Chasing monsters, indeed. I was more baffled by McTroy's brief note than I was intrigued. The urge to deny him remained strong. But I think McTroy knew if he sent Wu in person I would not refuse his invitation – at least that was my interpretation of matters at the time – and he must have needed me, or my expertise, for something, although I did not know what it might possibly be. Does Egypt now lie on the border of Colorado and New Mexico? I felt guilty putting Wu back on a train when he'd just come off one, so we spent the rest of the day

sightseeing in Manhattan before heading west. Wu
had never seen the ocean. I walked him down to the
harbor where he informed me that he saw the Pacific
Ocean daily when he lived in San Francisco.

"Here is the mighty Atlantic," I said, sweeping out
my arm.

"It looks very like the Pacific."

"Well I don't know about that."

"You don't think so?"

"I have never seen the Pacific," I said, turning up
my collar to the damp salty breeze. "On the other side
of these waters lies Egypt. Just thinking of it makes my
limbs tingle. Amazing!"

Wu nodded. "This," he pointed to the gray wavelets
in the harbor and the ships and various tugs and small
craft bouncing up and down upon them, "is very like
the Pacific."

We left the waterfront, and I continued guiding
the boy on my "city tour," one I had often imagined
giving if I ever were to enjoy the occasion of an out-
of-state visitor. New Yorkers do love to brag about our
metropolis even if we complain to each other about
living here. The dirt, the crime, the crowdedness of
the place. But I wouldn't trade it. Wu must have been
awed by the experience as his silence spoke volumes
about the great sensations he was no doubt having for
his first visit to Gotham. Yet I might have negligently
overlooked his state of travel weariness, for he seemed
to be almost asleep on his feet; I cut my planned tour
short and decided to wind up our excursion with a
special surprise. We circled toward home, but veering
off my usual course, I stopped our progress at Mott and

Canal Streets. I spun on my heels, jabbing my silver cane tip at the surrounding buildings, and the hustle-bustle of passing strangers (almost all men) as if I were bursting balloons – POP-POP-POP – in a boardwalk arcade game.

"What do you think of it, Wu?"

Wu's chin was tucked down into his duster, but his eyes darted around.

Had his powers of observation diminished so under the tutelage of McTroy?

"This is Chinatown!"

"I am an American. I was born in California," he said.

Of course, I knew Wu had lived in San Francisco with his parents prior to their seeking employment on the railroad. His father had been a teacher, his mother a cook, before an unforeseen tragedy of a parasitic and vampiric nature infected his parents in the desert of the Southwest. Here I was embarrassing the poor boy with my misplaced enthusiasm.

"We are all Americans, Wu. You are wise beyond your years. Now let me take you to an American feast at the Citadel where we will dine on vol-au-vent financière like kings!"

Alas, I drank too much brandy at the Delmonicos'. Wu slept on my cot. I curled up on my desk, using a stack of reports from the Egypt Exploration Fund as my pillow, waking with a crick in my neck and bleary, unfocused eyes. My head ached as we met our train an hour later at the Grand Central Depot. I boarded unsteadily, my innards in locomotion before the train lurched from the platform. Soon my brain pounded in wicked rhythm with the clack of the wheels. I cannot speak of my memory of the whistle without feeling it piercing me again like a red-hot needle in my medulla. The eastern half of the country passed me through a pallid haze of pipe smoke and steaming cups of coffee dutifully supplied by Wu. I came alive again in Chicago as we changed trains to the Atchison, Topeka and Santa Fe line that would deliver us to our final stop in Raton, New Mexico.

"I went to college here," I told Wu, whilst grabbing a hasty meal between trains.

"You are not from New York?"

I shook my head and dove into a slab of ham, warm cornbread, and a pickled egg.

"Born in Peoria, Illinois. My father was a farmer. Nothing ever happened in Peoria, not for me in any case. If I wanted real adventure, I had to leave to find it, that much I knew."

"So, you left?"

"Take a lesson from it," I said with a wink and an encouraging nod. "Perhaps our fate and fortune lie in the mountains of New Mexico? One never knows until one goes. Remember that."

Wu promised he would.

I offered him half my pickled egg and he politely declined.

They say travel takes a person out of themselves, but I am never more myself than when I travel. For better or worse, I bring Romulus Hardy with me wherever I go. Here I was, with no mummy crates to worry about and only my bag to carry. My last train ride out

West began with anxiety and ended in tragedy. I was determined not to relive it. And tragedy did *not* strike.

Until we got to Raton.

November 5, 1890
Train station and the Castle Ram Hotel
Raton, New Mexico Territory

I often think that, if not for mining, Americans would have left the West unspoiled, but such speculation is moot. Raton was in mining country, thus Raton existed, and so did her railroad station. Wu and I disembarked, rumpled, and in my case, glad to be free of the confines of the narrow train car. I am not one who fancies tight spaces. I loathe them. The Pullman sleeper that Wu and I shared felt closer to a coffin than a bed, and I say this as a person who once experienced the real threat of being buried alive. Happily, I left that glorified crate in motion for a wide vista nailed to one place. I crossed the platform quickly. A snowy briskness trailed the high air blowing down from the mountains. It colored my cheeks and incensed the depot with a strong fragrance of piñon pines. My cane tapped the boards nervously.

"What is the name of the place where Evangeline is staying?"

"The Castle Ram Hotel," Wu answered.

I surveyed the town's main street. "There's not much here, Wu. And certainly not many inns worthy of lodging someone of Evangeline Waterston's caliber." I stopped a clayey gray-all-over gentleman wearing an old cavalry hat turned shapeless with age, much like the man himself. "Excuse me, sir, where is the Castle Ram Hotel?"

"Where it's always been, I suppose."

"And that is...?"

"Yonder." He pointed with his thumb. "It's got a big sheep on the sign."

I tipped my bowler to him.

"You a gambler?" the man asked, pulling all the wrinkles of his face up and to the right, inquisitively, as if an invisible fishhook had snagged the corner of his eye.

"Me? A gambler?" I shared an amused glance with Wu. "Hardly, my good fellow, I am only guilty of being a scholar, a historian of the ancient world, and chiefly an Egyptologist."

"That some kind of foreign gambling?"

"In a way, yes. But in the way you mean, no. I am a man of science, not dice games."

"Oh," the man said. "So it ain't like baccarat?"

I shook my head.

"How about you, son, you play *fan-tan*? Them's a Chinese game with buttons."

"I do not play, sir," Wu answered.

The man loosened his wrinkles and, slack-faced looked longingly off into some dreamy zone beyond us. "I was a gambler. Came here with a bundle. Lost it all. My hand too." He showed us the empty cuff of his sleeve, and then his pale wrist poked out, tied off like a sausage. "They was good times here, though you'd never know, seein' things now. Enjoy yourselves! Too bad ye ain't gamblers." He waved the hand he had and passed grayly up the street into a dim saloon.

"That was a strange man," Wu said. "And he is the only townsperson out today."

What Wu said was correct, though I had not noticed it on my own. The street was awfully quiet. Deserted, in fact. A few horses were tied to the hitching rail outside the saloon. There was a medicine show wagon parked in a tented lot across from the drinking establishment. Painted in sickly yellow letters on the side was: *Doc Spooner's Famous Elixirs and Potent Remedies*. A hungry-looking dog the color of boiled sweets trotted away from us, checking over his bony shoulder to see if we were following him. "We are the exception. Let us find this Sheep Castle."

"Castle Ram," Wu corrected me.

I was glad to see his attention to detail. "Castle Ram it is!"

The one-handed gambler had pointed us in the right direction. The sign outside the hotel soon came into our view. Indeed, there was a sheep painted on it, or, more accurately, the portrait of a ram's head.

"Will you look at that evil thing!" I grabbed Wu by the arm.

The ram's head did not appear painted as much as burned into a weathered, splintery plank suspended from twin chains. Huge, thickly-ribbed horns spiraled outward from an almost human face that appeared abnormally long with a wide, brutish anthropoid forehead; its mouth tilted in a sneer, a forked beard dangling from its chin. The eyes shone, catching the late afternoon light. As we approached, I saw a pair of glass orbs embedded in the wood; between them the woodgrain sketched a vague yet recognizable shape, something very like a star.

A thin, elongated star.

"I do not like it," Wu said.

"Agreed. What an eccentric building this is. One wouldn't expect to find it here."

The hotel façade gave every appearance of being an actual castle barbican, though the gateway was drastically reduced in size. The construction materials seemed rough and curiously stone-like to the point I felt the urge to touch them and verify their properties. Using my cane for leverage, I vaulted the muddy gutter. I knocked my cane's apish knob and then my fist against the castle wall. Hollow-sounding wood, as I expected. Above the entrance, my gaze climbed the heights of the battlements studded by turrets and two flanking corner towers. Darkly stained lattice strips were hammered to the doors. They represented a portcullis grill dropping down to bar intruders and guard whatever lived inside the Castle Ram's keep. The scene was like a stage.

"Time to cross the moat," I said to Wu.

He noted the flooded trench between himself and the boardwalk.

With a running start, a smiling Wu leapt the odiferous gutter to join me.

"Those are arrowslits," I said, indicating the vertical openings in the towers.

"What are they for?"

"Bowmen. Though I can't see how bowmen are needed here. These are decorations."

Wu whispered, "Who are the people inside?"

"Inside?"

I followed his gaze and saw as he did the flicker of quick movements and glittery black eyes peeking out. Too many eyes. I was backing away, tugging Wu after me and raising my cane defensively when an explosion of noise erupted from the left tower, and a mob of crows flapped through an unseen hole in the rooftop. The right tower roost emptied as well. Crows spilled forth, cawing, swooping, and circling overhead like black-feathered messengers announcing our presence to every citizen of sleepy Raton.

"A-ha! We have spooked ourselves. They're only birds," I said, but I was not calm.

Wu laughed, unconvincingly, and it is true the crows proved marginally less unsettling after they perched on the battlements, watching us as if we were a pair of trembling mice.

We entered the castle proper.

Candlelight. I have toured cathedrals with fewer candles than the Castle Ram Hotel lobby. One end of the room opened through an archway to a parlor furnished with chairs and settees piled with embroidered pillows of uncommon size and shape, ranging from bolsters and spheres to plush cubes and wedges; someone had arranged a few of the larger cushions in a heap on the floor. Ornate mythological creatures were carved into the settee arms, but none I recognized, which was curious since my knowledge of mythology covered ancient Eastern cultures and the Greco-Roman tradition. There were several colossal urns scattered about the lounge periphery. They contained no flowers but collections of dried branches like crude broomsticks.

I bent to inspect a pot and discovered a strong herbal scent. A medieval chandelier hung from the ceiling and yet, despite the abundant flames, shadows packed the room. But no people. The front desk remained similarly vacant. So quiet you might imagine no one had ever worked there. I dodged a candelabrum to lean forward and inspect a thick, leather-bound book lying on the counter beside a pen and inkwell. After checking the lobby again for any guests, I turned the book and opened it.

The hotel registry.

It was blank.

Not a single signature.

Empty line after empty line filled the pages.

"Unless this is a new ledger, we have quite a mystery to begin our adventure," I said.

Wu was about to answer me, to warn me, actually, when a bespectacled, bald man wearing a deep brown suit manifested himself from a doorway behind the desk and adjacent to the key and mail cubbies. With both hands the man seized the registry, sliding it away from me. His smile was a slow-acting poison.

"Can I help you?" he asked, in a most unhelpful tone.

"Yes, you can. I didn't see you hiding there."

"Hiding? I don't know what you mean."

"You were taking your afternoon tea, perhaps? No matter. I am Dr Rom Hardy, and I am meeting a guest of your hotel today. I may even be a guest myself. This is my assistant, Wu."

The front deskman said nothing. Did nothing.

"Miss Evangeline Waterston of the California

Waterstons? She is your guest?"

"I don't believe she is," he said.

"She *is* your guest. Evangeline Waterston. Check your book, why don't you?"

"I don't need to check my book. We have no guest by that name."

I shifted so Wu could stand with me, confronting the deskman.

"Tell him, Wu."

"She is staying here. The Adderlys made her reservation. They own this place."

The deskman was unmoved. "I'm afraid we have no guest by that name."

"Is there another hotel in Raton?" I asked.

"Not one as luxurious as ours," the deskman answered smugly.

"But there are others?"

"Rooming houses... the saloon offers sleeping rooms with such a ruckus below no man could sleep... Madame Champagne's Velvet Box has beds, but little sleeping goes on there–"

"You would agree that a fine lady would stay here?"

"Undoubtedly."

"That settles it then. Evangeline Waterston is nothing if not fine. Do please send a message to her that we have arrived."

The deskman was stunned. Without taking his eyes off me, he reached for a recess in the wall and jerked a beaded needlepoint bell pull. I did not hear any bell ring. But a hotel porter materialized behind Wu and me. We did not detect his approach and would not have noticed him standing there if the deskman had not addressed him directly.

"Marcus, inform Miss Waterston she has two visitors."

Marcus was stooped and slightly older than the Sphinx. He gave no signal to acknowledge his orders but slipped off into a draped area that I presumed concealed a staircase.

We awaited his return.

"Might I inquire if you have any rooms available? My assistant and I need lodging."

The deskman replied with no hesitation. "Sorry, we're booked."

I made a show of glancing around the abandoned vestibule.

"Crowded, is it?"

"A very busy time of year. Perhaps the saloon has accommodations."

I resisted the desire to rap him on the nose with my ape.

Marcus returned.

"She is not in her room," he told the deskman. "Her trunks are gone as well."

The deskman cocked his head toward me as if I had not heard. "Miss Waterston has apparently left the hotel premises. You may choose at this time to do the same."

"Surely she must have passed by your counter. Perhaps you saw where she went?"

The slim brown shoulders rose and fell with an indifferent shrug.

My rage was growing, and my ears felt hot. I wetted my thumb and forefinger and pinched out every wick of his candelabrum. Trickles of smoke drifted across his face. He removed his glasses and rubbed at his eyes. Then he put his glasses on again.

"Come, Wu. This dingy pit stinks of mold and dust. The employees fare no better."

I lifted my bag. Wu did the same with his. We swiveled away from the front desk. It was then I noticed the painting of a woman hanging opposite the desk. The woman in the portrait was an enchanting beauty. She was seated upon a black throne. Her eyes seemed to follow us as we marched back over the threshold and into the natural brightness of the outdoors. If I hadn't been piqued by the deskman's rudeness, I would've lingered for a deeper study of the pale, dark-haired woman done in oils. She had the kind of face that improved with further scrutiny. Who was she? Why did her likeness breathe more life into the hotel than the actual men who worked there? I had no answers, only more questions.

"I am starting to feel we are not welcomed here," Wu said.

"Most observant, my friend, but the question is why. And the other question is where."

"Where?" Wu asked.

"Where the hell is everyone?" I shouted in frustration. "I wonder if Evangeline ever checked into the Castle Ram. She would not tolerate such deliberate obtuseness and rude clerks!"

Gunshots rang out in quick succession.

"Where did those come from?" I asked, ducking and searching for signs of motion.

Wu pointed across the street. "The saloon. Where

the old man went."

"And where we might rent a room for the night." I jumped down from the boardwalk.

Wu hesitated in following me.

"We're going in there?"

"It appears to be where the action is. Therefore..."

Wu finished my thought. "Miss Evangeline will be there too!"

"Correct." I resumed my stride. Wu joined me. I smelled gunpowder and cigars. Men's voices shouted inside the saloon. I saw two giant eyes painted on the establishment, but I could not read its name, sliced in half as it was by shade. The evening sun dyed the peaks a crimson red.

"Now we know how the Sangre de Cristos got their name," I said, though I was unsure if the blood on the mountains would be the only blood we witnessed this night.

I never carried a gun.

Wu drew a pistol from his bag. Before I could stop him, he pushed through the batwing doors into the chaos of the saloon.

4
THE STARRY EYES PROPOSITION

Starry Eyes Saloon
Raton, New Mexico Territory

The man leaning over the bar, dripping blood from his jagged ear into a glass of whiskey, was laughing. Like a spiderweb, a crack spread across the mirror behind the bar, and in the center of the crack was a bullet hole. A second, older man wearing a flattened red flower in his lapel approached the bleeding drinker with a look of concern.

"Billy, let me see that wound."

"He grazed me. It's nothing," Billy said, as he drank his whiskey down.

The barman refilled the glass without asking him to pay for it. Patrons went back to their card games, cigar smoking, and drinking. Conversations resumed. The Starry Eyes Saloon was packed wall-to-wall with customers. The room was hot. I felt my cheeks flush. It was easy to imagine that all the citizens of Raton were here, crammed into this single business. It wasn't all men; I did spot some women mixing in with the crowd. Dancers, cardplayers, hired companions, but others too, women of apparent taste and distinction, like flowers growing in a field of pig manure. Every chair in the house was filled, and the standees barely left us enough room to blend. We tried our best given the circumstances. I did not see Evangeline. But most of the room stretched beyond my sight though a bluish haze of smoke.

Wu tucked his pistol discreetly into his belt before anyone noticed. I stepped in front of him and politely attempted to progress forward. Gradually we moved to the end of the bar, next to Billy, which was the only place where we could go, the crowd being bunched up so tight.

"Show me," the older man said to Billy sternly. "I have to keep you in repair, Kid."

Billy picked up his glass and turned, leaning his elbows back on the bar, allowing the other man to inspect his injury. The rest of the bystanders avoided looking at Billy.

"I told him, Pops," Billy said.

"Yes, you did." Pops pressed a soiled bar towel to the laceration. Billy winced.

"I gave the coward every chance. He got what was coming to him."

"You're going to need a stitch or two to save that ear."

I hadn't noticed it before, but the older man, Pops, carried a black Gladstone bag. He withdrew a needle and a loop of heavy thread. He began to reattach the lobe of Billy's ear. As the surgeon sewed, Billy stared into an empty space, reviewing the gunfight Wu and I had just missed seeing. I wanted to look away, but I could not force myself to do it.

"I said you won't draw on me if you have half a brain, you fool. Gutless *and* brainless, that's what he was. Did he know who he was dealing with, I wonder?" Billy shook his head in reply to his own question.

"Don't move, please," Pops sighed.

"He was damn slow. Got off a lucky shot. He could've killed somebody!" Billy slapped his knee, inviting the crowd to join him in a laugh. But they declined. "I put him down like the mangy bug-eyed cur he was," he said finally.

"Stop moving or you will have to learn to live with a damn crooked ear." Pops pulled his bloodstained hands away, leaving a long thread hanging loosely from Billy's cartilage.

"I don't care," Billy said, but he reined in his fidgeting. "Keep going. Sew me."

I was wondering about the fate of Billy's counterpart in the gunfight when a group of men emerged from the parting crowd carrying the limp body of a dead man on their shoulders. The man's head lolled, openmouthed, bouncing horribly with each step. As they began to pass, Billy stopped them. He stood up on his tiptoes, tugged at the dead man's dusty shirt, and smiled.

"Look here, Pops! Plumb through the heart! What would you call a shot like that?"

Pops tipped his head back. His lips pursed as he searched for the right word.

"Perfection," he decided.

"*PUR*-fection. That's what I'm talking about. He was

dead the minute he talked sass to me." Billy tapped the corpse's chest. "Only you didn't know it yet. But I knew it. I *knew* it!"

The grim procession continued out the batwing doors. A shift at the last moment of exiting the Starry Eyes caused the corpse's head to swivel toward me, and I was sickened to see the old gray man who had greeted us on our arrival and directed us to the Castle Ram. The *one-handed* man. He wore no holster. I conjectured that his left hand had not been swift to pull a gun.

"Crazy old coot," Billy said. "Asking if I'm a gambler... Damn if I ain't Billy the Kid!"

I perked up at the mention of the infamous gunfighter.

Billy saw my reaction and acknowledged me by raising his eyebrows gamely.

Now reader, you may not recall your outlaw history, but William H. Bonney, also known as Billy the Kid, died in 1881. He was killed by the famous lawman Pat Garrett. The original Billy the Kid was a cattle rustler and a murderer. While he had forged his reputation in New Mexico, he had also *died* there, in Fort Sumner, nine years ago. Rumors of his survival persisted, as the legends of bad men often do. From of the corner of my eye, while working diligently to conceal my interest, I studied the killer next to me. Slim, poor posture, cheap boots. I looked higher only to find him staring boldly back at me. Note here: his frosty blue eyes, a blond beard of sparse bristles, and small crooked yellow teeth like corn. This young gent propped against the bar would have been a scrawny boy of no more than ten, nine years ago. He could not possibly be Billy the Kid.

"You looking for something, mister?"

"Me? No... I am new to town." I added, "How is your ear?"

"Stings a little. But Pops will fix me. The man keeps me in fighting shape."

"Glad to hear it."

"You see the shooting?"

"No. I was at the hotel. I just arrived on the train."

"Then you missed yourself a great show. I'm a legend, you know?"

He drained his whiskey. Pops asked him to roll up his sleeve. The surgeon removed a syringe from his bag and filled the vial from an upturned little green bottle. He tied a cord to the muscle in Billy's arm and massaged the forearm searching for a plump vein. I noticed the arm was covered with bruises. Perhaps Billy ran into mischief often and needed his damage repaired on a routine basis. Pops pushed in the needle and depressed the plunger. Billy's eyes sparkled wetly.

"We finished here, Pops?"

Billy rebuttoned his cuff. He sucked air through his teeth as he combed his fingers through the lank strands of greasy hair that fell over his eyes before replacing his hat.

"Go forth and multiply," Pops said.

Billy caught a dancer's elbow and whirled her around, escorting her into the gathering.

Pops was putting his instruments away. I sidled closer to him.

"Is that young man your son?"

He shook his head, amused. "Everyone calls me Pops. I am no kin to that wild boy."

"Did I hear correctly that your friend calls himself Billy the Kid?"

"You did." Pops shut his bag and ordered a pink gin from the barkeeper.

"But Billy the Kid is dead." I offered a cautious half-smile. Stating the obvious had taken on an inherent danger within the present circumstances.

"Do not share that information with my friend. He is easily offended. You'll find yourself in trouble like that codger they carried out of here."

The surgeon appeared serious. Dead serious. I decided to drop the matter.

"Is the Starry Eyes always so popular a spot?" I asked to change the subject.

"I wouldn't know. This is my first visit here. New Mexico is Billy's terrain. We are travelers now, the two of us, bold and enterprising businessmen of the future. We sail wherever the winds carry us. Do you have ailments of the body or mind? I have the cure... in my wagon."

I could not gauge the irony in his statement though I sensed more than a small pinch.

"Are you here for business or pleasure?" I inquired.

"Pleasure is my business, Mr...?"

"Dr Romulus Hardy," I introduced myself, tipping my bowler.

"Dr Pops Spooner." He shook my hand. His was cool and jumpy as a sunfish. He withdrew it quickly. "A fellow medical man?" He shared a knowing glance with me, but I failed miserably at reciprocating since I did not comprehend what he meant by it.

"Doctor of Egyptology," I said. "Adventure is my

trade, you might say."

He smiled wryly. "Your geography needs improvement, Dr Hardy. The only pyramids you'll find in Raton reside in pairs at Miss Champagne's cathouse." His mouth opened slightly, and he sucked his lip. "If it's adventure you seek, look no farther than the Velvet Box's dungeon of amusements. I've never explored a better setup, apart from the Quartier Pigalle. Hard to see where Miss Champagne recruits her legion of such highly delicious girls, or where she finds the flow of clientele in this tiny mountain backwater. I am not complaining, sir. I have never been so thoroughly exhausted in my life. Yet my body craves the coming hour when I return for more!"

An electric shiver ran through him. I feared he might be having a seizure.

I checked to see if Wu had overheard his remarks, although I was not entirely sure I grasped the whole meaning of them myself.

Wu's grin told me that he understood enough.

"Wu, what is that you're drinking?"

"It's a beer."

I swiped the glass away from him. "This could be turpentine, tobacco juice, and mountain goat piss for all you know." I took a sip and then another. Then one more, for the sake of the boy.

"It tasted like beer," Wu said.

"How do you know the taste of beer? Is McTroy teaching you anything but the most unsavory habits?" Even to my own ears I sounded like a self-righteous prude. I finished the draft.

Wu was protesting to my right side when Pops

tugged at my left arm and pointed the edge of his glass toward a source of commotion in the barroom as the crowd began to part like a red sea of faces, and the wooden prow of a ship glided forward in our direction. The ship was only an elevated, wheeled pulpit that two men were pushing with significant effort. Following the men came two women, opposite in their looks, but both quite striking. The first wore a black lace dress, matching her dark eyes and darker hair and emphasizing her pale complexion. She was the woman whose portrait hung in the Castle Ram! I could tell she was tall though she wore gold braces on her long legs, and sat in a wheelchair, rather than the throne depicted in the hotel painting. The second woman pushed the wheelchair. I had traveled halfway across the country to see her face again.

She was Evangeline Waterston.

She did not see me.

Yong Wu jumped to greet her, but I held him back. And we watched and waited to see what would happen next.

A short, bearded man, who carried himself with authority and the gruffness of a natural leader, climbed the steps of the pulpit after it was pushed back against the bar and in full view of the room. Evangeline and the woman in the wheelchair stationed themselves on the other side of the podium out of our line of sight.

The man cleared his throat and raised a hand.

The crowd grew quiet.

"Now you all know why we are here this evening," he began. I did not know, but I kept that fact to myself. "I am Oscar Adderly. I own the Starry Eyes and the

Castle Ram Hotel, and, to tell you the truth, most of the land in this town either belongs to me now or it once did. There's coal in these mountains. The mines that bring up that coal are Adderly mines. But I am not occupied with the daily operations of my mines. I hire people to do that for me. What I do is travel this globe of ours. And I hunt. The more exotic a beast is, the more I desire to track it down, whether that means I must slash my way into a leafy green hellish jungle, roast my hide on the plains of dry grasslands, or freeze my feet, and nether parts–" here the crowd laughed – "...on a block of dirty polar ice. I will stalk my prey, kill it, and bring the body back here to America. I preserve these bodies with artistry. And the beneficiaries of my art are the museums in New York, Washington, and Chicago.

"The reason I tell you this is because we have a problem in the Sangre de Cristo mountains; we have a *dire* problem here in Raton, and that problem is a creature I do not understand. This creature is terrorizing our homes. He, she, or whatever it is, is killing our animals, and now it is killing us! Nine good men have died. Let me repeat, nine good men have died within a day's walk of where I am standing right now. I apologize to the women here tonight, but I am sparing no detail when I tell you these men were viciously ripped apart, de-limbed, beheaded, unmanned, skinned alive, and then eaten so that all we might recover were bones and ragged bits of clothing soaked in their blood."

Here one of the men who had pushed the pulpit into place retrieved a large burlap sack from behind the bar and spilled onto the floor a pile of bones that if my quick count was correct contained part of five of the nine victims. People in the crowd gasped. A buxom red-haired dancer screamed and fell backward, landing dramatically in the arms of a dapper card player.

Adderly continued, "I will not stand for this carnage in my town. That is why I am offering $10,000–" Another gasp went up, dare I say louder than the cry the bone-spilling elicited. "$10,000 for the capture of this Beast!"

The room erupted with cheers, and chair legs banged into the floor so that it felt like a locomotive had left its tracks at the station and was rumbling outside the very walls.

"Here! Here is my first rule. I do not want it dead. I want to study it and kill it and stuff it myself. If any one of you fine hunters kills the Beast I will pay you… yes, reluctantly I will pay. But I will only pay $1,000. So, wound me this creature, snare it, cage it, drop it ass over elbows into a pit, and $10,000 are yours. A good many of you are outsiders to Raton. Welcome. I have no time for longer pleasantries.

"Now I will give you my second rule. Do not hunt for the Beast on my mountain. Where is my mountain, you ask? Any local will tell you how to find the road to Nightfall Lodge. The lodge, my home, sits near the top of my mountain. I have not seen the Beast on my mountain, and I assure you it is not there. But if I find you on my mountain I will shoot you dead and drop your body down a hole where no one will ever find you, and your families will never know that you died here because you could not follow a simple rule. I say it again: capture, but do not kill the Beast, and stay off my mountain.

"I am finished talking, but some of you are lucky enough to know my wife, Vivienne, and you are familiar with her unusual gifts. Vivienne talks to the dead. And the dead talk back through her. She is an elegant instrument of secrets and enigmas. I am blessed to have her. As a favor to me, she has agreed to talk to one of these slaughtered men. Let him tell you what to look for as you go into the woods tomorrow. Vivienne, dear, will you please come up here and share your talents with us."

Oscar Adderly climbed down the stairs and, in a feat of some strength, lifted his wife from her wheelchair. He carried her up onto the podium, and there she was able to stand on her own, balancing upon two braced legs with her arms locked on the pulpit buttressing her in place. Any weakness in her legs had transferred power into her arms, for they held her steady; the muscles were lithe and rippled like peeled, smooth branches of white wood. She carried herself with self-assured elegance despite her infirmity. I had a better look at her now that she was above me. Her large dark eyes dominated her face; she wore her hair piled on the top of her head, the black curls held with a carved horn comb shaped like the moon.

Standing in the pulpit, Vivienne was taller than her husband by several inches.

Her smile was as dazzling as it was brief. Then she called for the lamplights of the bar to be lowered. A single black candle on an iron stand was placed in front of her, and lit. It made a soft, spitting sound as the wick burned.

She gazed into the dancing flame.

I felt myself growing lightheaded and realized I had not been breathing.

I took several deep breaths in unison with Vivienne Adderly. She swayed, and I swayed.

She grew still, and I felt the short distance between us shrink as if it were only us here, not a room containing better than a hundred strangers in the audience, just the two of us sitting across a table staring into the flickering candle together. I heard a clock ticking in a hallway.

Then quiet.

Her eyes widened as if she'd been caught by surprise. Her taut throat moved.

And when she began to speak I felt she was talking only to me.

5

FLOATING HEAD

"Who are you, friend?" Vivienne asked as her head turned slightly to the left. Her voice had taken on a singsong quality. Slowly her head pivoted back to the center, and this time when she spoke it was a shockingly different voice that came out. Deep, accented, and choked with fear.

"I am... I am..." The voice stopped.

Vivienne's head turned left again. "Go on, friend, you are safe here. Tell me your name."

"I am Gustav. Gustav Svensson. Where...?"

A woman sitting at the table nearest to the bar whispered, "He was the third man killed."

One of the drinkers at her table, a heavy man in a beaverskin cap, shushed her.

"Where am I?" Gustav asked. Vivienne's head quaked, so did the words she channeled.

"You are with me in the Starry Eyes Saloon," she answered. As she resumed her own musical voice the shaking vanished. "We are safe. We are only talking. The doors are locked."

The doors were not locked, but she meant to put the frightened hunter at ease, I supposed.

"Might I have a beer?" he asked.

A few in the audience laughed but most stayed silent.

"No, Gustav, you cannot. But you may talk with us. We need to hear you."

"I am thirsty." Gustav (Vivienne) nodded solemnly. "But I will…" He swallowed with effort, like a child taking a spoonful of cod-liver oil. "I will talk first."

"Thank you," Vivienne said. "We must ask you, Gustav, about what happened on the mountain. In the woods. You were hunting elk, were you not?"

"Mule deer," he said. "I seen a big buck. I was waiting for him to show again. I got down behind a rock. I had my rifle pointed where I thought he would come out of the spruces. The wind blew in my face but not too bad. I waited, watching a patch of shadow on the snow that I thought might be him, his shadow I mean. But he wasn't coming through them trees. I was hungry. I could hear my stomach growling. It was hard to keep still because it was cold kneeling in the wind that morning. I been out for hours. My face felt like a hard mask. I wanted to go home, but I wanted to take that big muley on the naked slope if he would only step out of them spruces."

The voice paused.

"What happened next?" Left-facing Vivienne prompted him to continue.

"Snow."

"Snow?"

"I seen snow falling. Big flakes floating down slow.

Like torn lace. The shadow was gone. *Where did my muley run to?* I wondered. The bigger shadow came then. But from the other side of me where I wasn't looking, where the trees bunched up real thick. Right by me this shadow stops. I could piss and hit this shadow."

Vivienne and Gustav looked at the barroom floor, but they saw the shadow too.

And I saw it with them. I don't know about the other patrons in the bar. I don't know about Wu. But I know the shadow was right there on the dirty pine planks, the shadow creeping over the knotholes, over a trail of blood drops that had fallen from the chest wound of the gray man Billy the Kid murdered, and red streaks smeared where boots had scuffed them. The shadow of a head bloomed like ink spilled in water. A huge head; not with curled horns like the ram on the Castle hotel sign, but the head was shaped similarly. There was a blankness to it, a uniformity, and a deadness that I felt inside me. And it had long crooked antlers branching off and mixing with the men and women sitting at their tables or standing around watching this medium, this black-haired occultist. I don't think the others saw the shadow like I did, because they would not have let it touch them. It was foul, this erasure of light. Worse than a stain. You would not let it touch you if you could help it. Well, I wouldn't. It kept stretching. Pulling thin so it wasn't like an elk or a ram or any animal but something new and terrible to behold.

Longer, longer, it pulled, and those branches reached out touching so many people.

I shut my eyes. But I saw it still stretching like black taffy.

"What did you do, Gustav?"

"I shut my eyes. I thought…" He laughed, but it was harsh, the way a man sucks air in and out when he's in pain to keep from crying out. Nervously he continued, "I thought maybe here's Gustav's lucky day. Maybe he gets an elk instead of a muley. I shift my rifle, smooth as new snow on the snowbank, because I know I got no time. One shot, I think. You make your shot, Gustav, and then you get to eat, drink, and tell everybody at the Starry your lucky day elk story."

He stopped.

"But it was not an elk, was it? Gustav?"

"I don't want to say no more what it was." He coughed. "I want my beer… so thirsty."

A noise started then outside the Starry Eyes. It was not far away. A kind of high whistle that hurt your ears like an icy stream of water pouring inside, like the point of a skinny knife tapping your eardrums. Every person made a face of discomfort and clapped their hands over the sides of their heads or plugged up their ears with their fingers or pieces of clothing, anything they could find to muffle it. And the whistle climbed higher, louder. There was another sound too, just outside the walls, like boots, or, better yet, *hooves* clopping on the boardwalk and punching holes in the mud around the back alley. This sound circled us. The whistle seemed right above us. *On the roof*, I thought. *It's on the roof.* Then the hooves were knocking up there too. Loud. One-two. One-two. A man, or some two-legged creature, walked on the roof. What creature except a human being walks on two legs?

"Gustav?" Vivienne asked. "What was the shadow?"

The whistle went silent, like it wanted to hear Gustav telling us what happened.

"Ooooooh…" Gustav moaned. "Can't tell you. My legs cramped from kneeling in the snow so long. I try to get up, but the snow is deep all around me, there in front of me it's deep, I don't know where to go that's not deep… I'm running trying to run but the snow is to my hips."

Gustav was chewing his lip.

She turned left to face him in the trance world where they connected.

"Did you see an elk? Or a bear? A cougar? Was it wolves, Gustav? What got you?"

"Wasn't no elk or bear or puma cat no wolf pack neither that took me down in the snow like a fawn like a fawn in the snow I was out on that naked slope in the deep snow running like a hare I was like meat running for its life but there's no running from a thing like that—"

"Why didn't you shoot it?" Oscar Adderly called out in his strong voice.

The question enraged Gustav.

"Goddamn you! It was a demon. Can you shoot a demon? Show me how!"

The branching, stretching shadow head on the floor floated up to the ceiling of the saloon. It was solid and charcoal black, not a phantasm or a ghostly vapor. I could not see through it. It stood on two legs in the middle of the room, and its head was too tall, so the body hunched forward to fit itself. It was a gaunt thing, stripped of fat, but it was not weak. The arms were sinewy and long. The face was a blank in which

I could see nothing but two glowing red eyes like pits of ruby fire.

I do not know if it was the result of the residuals that the sorcerer left in my mind years ago, but I felt that I was connected to Vivienne and Gustav. That she had sunk the end of a cord into my mind the same way she'd speared Gustav out of his wandering forever in the woods – or wherever it was his soul had traveled. We three were looped together in this vision of the day Gustav lost his life on the mountain slope. The patrons in the barroom glimpsed us, but I was *there*, with Gustav and Vivienne and that antlered demon stalking the hunter in the cold.

Gustav said, "I know I'm going to die. I'm slow and the shadow it's… I'm under it and inside it and I spin around and fire my rifle, but it takes my rifle and it throws it so far over the tops of the tallest pines so high it looks like a little bird flying and disappearing in the snow. I want to fall back into the snow and I'm not looking at the demon but it picks me up and I feel like I'm rising up so fast I feel the wind and my hat my coat they rip off of me and I won't open my eyes but I keep going higher like I'm flying like the demon's flying with me and we're over the treetops and I feel my boots hitting the tips of the trees and the snow fills up my eyes my eyes my hair is frozen to my head and then…"

"Then what…?" Vivienne and I asked him aloud at the same time.

Vivienne was looking at me now, from her vantage point up in the pulpit. She was Vivienne and not Gustav. I saw her curiously puzzling over me: *Who are you? Do I know you?* I heard her questions the same as if she had asked me while peeking over the rim of a teacup, seated beside a sunny garden window and a table with cucumber sandwiches. The rest of the people in the Starry Eyes were like statues, immobilized and unaware of our little conversation.

"I am Rom Hardy," I said, knowing she was the only person who heard me.

She smiled. Her lips were unnaturally red. Beautiful, but strange. "Rom Hardy," she tested how my name tasted. "Let us talk later, Rom Hardy. Gustav needs to finish his tale."

I felt I had no choice but to nod. She would accept no less from me.

"Hunter! Gustav!" she shouted. "What did this demon do to you after you flew so high?"

Gustav stared out of Vivienne's face. It was as if one photo lay atop a second, and their images bled together until all I saw was Gustav. His eyes were bleeding. He looked like one of those holy shrines crying tears of blood in a church somewhere in Central Europe, only there was nothing holy sharing this space with us. Gustav's arms and torso materialized in front of the pulpit. But below the waist he wasn't filled in yet.

"It threw me down the mountain. My back broke. I couldn't move. It started on my legs. *'The demon is eating me!'* I screamed. No one heard. Such a cold, lonely place. Only the wind in the pines answered. The demon beast put its face up against me and it licked me. I never felt the bite. My belly opened like pantry doors. It took what it wanted from under my ribs. Greedy thing, like it was starving. The red snow steamed. It looked up at me, a smiling face slick with my gravy. It ate the soft parts first. I squeezed fistfuls of snow until they were lumps of ice and they melted. I stared up at the sky. The pain changed me into something I never was before that day. I walked away from my body. Until you brought me back. I want my beer now. Give me my–"

Gustav was finished. His chin dropped, his unblinking eyes fixed on the floor.

Half of him was all they ever found on the slope.

Gustav's spirit lost its energy. He looked like ashes, cold ashes left in the snow. His face disappeared from Vivienne's. But the spiky antlered shadow crouched over the saloon folk, and this time they clearly saw it. A table full of cigar-smoking men bolted for the batwing doors. They might have made it outside if another gang sitting nearer the exit hadn't had the same idea. The two crews collided, and a fistfight ensued. Knives slashed blindly in the semi-dark, flickering room. Each one of them imagined it was the demon shoving them, and the demon claws grabbing; knife cuts were the demon beast's sharp teeth slicing their way to a hot meal.

I didn't see Vivienne's black candle topple from its stand, but, after it landed in a puddle of rotgut whiskey, I watched the flames pop up like little devils dancing. The barroom filled with evil energy. My ears popped at the sudden pressure change. Icehouse cold seeped up from the spaces between the floorboards. The rush of oxygen doubled the combustion. Above us, and everywhere around us, the piercing beastly whistle returned. The four walls shook with a thunderous rumble I imagined equal to a wild buffalo stampede, and already the panicking patrons were stepping on the drunks and the fallen among them. Trampling them in the sawdust. Without warning the saloon lamps burst, spraying a mist of hot coal-oil on the terrified crowd.

Women screamed, men screamed.

Fire!

I turned to find Wu, to tell him we needed to get out. The Starry Eyes was a matchbox.

But Wu was gone.

6

An Imperfect Reunion

A strong hand seized my arm and dragged me around the bar counter. The room filled so quickly with the blackest smoke that I could make out the shape of a man and nothing more.

"Duck," an oddly familiar voice said.

I had no time to decide, only to obey. I ducked, and we sped from behind the bar into a secret passageway that opened though two sliding racks of shelved liquor bottles.

Here was a narrow corridor.

My fear of tight spaces pushed a lump into my throat. But there was no time to entertain my private dread. We were moving now, straight back. I perceived no light whatsoever. But my companion and I were not alone in the passageway. Other footfalls were evident, and I also detected what could only be the rolling of wheels. Smoke followed us into the corridor. It was being sucked in, and its effect choked me. The sound of coughing told me the others had trouble breathing too. We turned ninety degrees left. I trailed the ape head of my stick along the wall.

"Cover your mouth. We're almost there," the voice said.

I tucked my face into the crook of my elbow. Truth be told, it was no easier to breathe in my woolen sleeve, but the choking was less severe. My eyes burned, but behind us in the saloon whole people were roasting alive in the fire.

"Watch your step." The hand jerked me up so hard, I had no choice but to rise with it.

Fresh air and light. We had arrived in the back alley behind the Starry Eyes saloon.

An old but well-kept Concord coach and a team of sturdy horses waited for us. The door swung wide. I followed my rescuer inside. The rather lovely burgundy upholstery appeared as supple as a maiden's hand. I dove into it. My landing was soft and well supported, as I expected. Two wide seats faced each other; between them sat an ample bench. A rubber wheel passed the coach window on an upward trajectory, and I realized it was Vivienne's wheelchair being loaded into the cargo area. Leather side curtains dropped over both windows, keeping out the smoke. There were other figures seated in the dark coach.

The driver cracked his whip, and with a jolt, off we went.

I heard the distinct pop-fizz of a striking match.

A face with glittery gray eyes filled the globe of match light. I knew him as both a rival and a friend, an honest hero and a hardened tracker of men he'd shoot in the head as soon as speak to; his name has passed into legend, no doubt because of our odd exploits together, as well as the blood-soaked trail he walked alone. This was the bounty man extraordinaire: Rex McTroy, sitting beside me.

"Hidey there, Doc. Long time no see. Why, you look paler than poor ole Gustav."

"I am not pale. It is the lighting."

"I never noticed this before, but you got a forehead on you that could crack boulders."

"The better to outthink you with, McTroy," I said, tapping my temple.

"Miss Evangeline, did you ever reckon the size of Doc's melon?"

"He has a noble brow," Evangeline said, from the seat opposite us. "I positively adore it."

Next to her the two Adderlys remained silent. Their expressions were masked partly by shadows. Oscar's mouth opened as if he were about to speak. I nodded to acknowledge their presence. Oscar thrust a hand out toward me.

McTroy passed me my bowler, which I had mislaid in the Starry Eyes inferno, filling the hand I had extended to meet Oscar's. "Cover your nobleness 'fore the coyotes mistake it for the moon and start howling. We'll keep the curtains down just in case."

Oscar took his hand back and folded his arms.

"No coyote can see me in here," I said, while understanding and immediately regretting the absurdity of my defense upon uttering it. Vivienne Adderly's big eyes crinkled in amusement. Oscar shifted in his seat and grunted softly.

"Good point, Doc." McTroy grinned.

"More importantly," I said urgently. "Wu is missing. He may be trapped in that fire."

"Fret not, my nervous compadre," McTroy said. "Wu's ridin' up top with the buggy driver. He tried to get you out of the saloon back there, but you were stupefied by Viv Adderly, which, mind you, is completely justifiable. However, the boy couldn't shake you out of it. He came and got me. Then I got you. You've stared some at the Adderlys, notably the missus, but you haven't been introduced yet. So, let's do it now."

His match hand drifted from Evangeline to the well-dressed couple. Vivienne touched a finger-sized red candle to McTroy's flame. When it lit she turned it upright.

"Thank you kindly," he said, blowing out his lucifer. "This here's Oscar and Vivienne. They invited us up to their mountain lodge to slay the damned Beast. We're in their coach. Adderlys, this fella is Doc. He's awful serious, but he don't mean it."

"I'm the reason you're here, Dr Hardy. The reason you are all here," Oscar said.

"Good to meet you," I said, feeling awkward for a myriad of reasons.

I re-extended my hand to Oscar, and he gripped it as if his intention were to crush the bones to dust. Vivienne then offered me her hand. I touched my lips to her knuckles. They were surprisingly warm, with a faint scent of roses and black licorice. My mouth failed to work; its connection to my thoughts grew choppy.

"You… you are… your abilities are quite…" I stumbled.

"Is that the first time you've ever seen a woman trance?" she asked me, eyes flashing.

I nodded.

"Well, it won't be the last if you're staying with us," she said. "I promise."

Vivienne and Evangeline laughed. McTroy slipped his hand behind the side curtain and peeked out. I leaned into his shoulder, gazing past him to see the Starry Eyes saloon and her neighboring buildings engulfed in flames. Our coach drove toward the mountains to the north. I could see men behind us forming a line to throw buckets of water on the fire. They would be lucky to save one side of the street. The smoke was a black cloud looming heavily over the town.

"I fear that people died back there," I said.

"I'll rebuild," Oscar Adderly replied.

"That's not the... ah!" I startled. McTroy had grabbed my knee and squeezed hard.

"My friend is sensitive to the perils of others," McTroy said to Oscar.

Oscar nodded, and then he turned to me. "They're flinty back there. They'll be fine."

I looked at McTroy, but he inclined his head toward Oscar as if the man had imparted a bit of wisdom. I decided to keep my comments to myself. Yet it struck me that neither McTroy nor Evangeline seemed concerned about the fearsome appearance of the antlered shadow creature and the subsequent conflagration which we had fled fortunately by way of a secret passage and a private coach. "I would've died," I said, adding, "if not for your intervention."

"I get a kick saving you, Doc." McTroy let the curtain fall back. He cocked a thumb in the direction of the town. "They broke the big front windows. Everybody got out. Right now the ne'er-do-wells are drinking free whiskey in hellfire's cherry glow. Almost wish I was with them. They have a drinking story they can tell forever 'bout the night the Starry Eyes burnt down."

"But what if everyone didn't happen to make it out?" I asked, hypothetically.

Oscar said, "A man should never let himself get so drunk in a bar that he can't leave when the time comes. I assure you, Dr Hardy, your sympathies are given to those who have none for you, or any other man, woman, or child. Rumors of my offer brought out the cutthroats and scoundrels. They will kill each other whether or not my saloon burns. It's the way of nature."

"What nature is that?" Evangeline asked. Despite her obvious conviviality with Vivienne, I detected that she maintained a certain guarded distance while appraising Vivienne's mate.

"The same nature that makes the hawk grip its talons into the squirrel's back. Or that sinks the lion's sharp curved tooth into the neck of a gazelle." Oscar reached into his coat, retrieved a stout, black-leafed cigar, and tore off the wrapper, dropping it to the coach floor.

He grasped Vivienne's wrist, guiding the candle nearer to light his tobacco.

"Must you?" Vivienne asked.

"I must," he said, as he puffed. "I entertain no illusions, Miss Evangeline. I see things as they are. In the desert or the jungle, no animal cries for another. Feed or be fed upon. Man is the same way. He cannot drive the survival instinct from his soul. I do not run from my nature. I relish it."

His cigar glowed redly, and the smoke stung our eyes.

"This is tiresome conversation, Oscar. I am already so tired," Vivienne said, rolling up her leather curtain to allow the smoke to clear. "Save it for tomorrow. May tonight be different?"

"As you wish, darling," he conceded. "I know how your dead talks exhaust you."

"But we did learn something. Talking to the hunter was worthwhile," she said, cheerfully nudging her husband. "Gustav gave us details!"

"Yes, he did," Oscar said. "Though I don't know how much I trust that Swede."

"You think he lied?" McTroy asked.

"He didn't sound like a man lying," I added. "I believed him. The creature killed Gustav."

"What creature, Dr Hardy?" Oscar asked. "He described no animal I know. And I know them all."

"The huge shadow on the ceiling? Wasn't that the thing that did for him?" I said.

Oscar waved his hand. "That was Gustav's nightmare. We saw a shadow puppet. A moving portrait of what he imagined was chasing him on the mountain. Do we take for truth every child's bad dream? No. And we shouldn't listen to a man who tells us a monster ate him."

"*Something* ate him," McTroy said.

"Grizzly bear." Oscar waved dismissively. "Maybe a big cat. It might've even been other men who did it. Maybe some of those you're so worried about, Dr Hardy. Don't look shocked. I've met cannibals. Supped with them, in fact. On an island south of the equator.

A lovely bunch. Yet I never sampled their stew." He chuckled and rubbed his hands delightedly, like a boy scaring other children with ghost stories at a Christmas party.

I have met cannibal monks and corpse-eating ghouls. It was my memories that changed my expression so dramatically, not my shock. I could almost smell the anthropophagites' stew.

"You're frightening him, Oscar!" Vivienne said. "Leave the man alone until we get a brandy or two in him, at least."

Evangeline and McTroy, who had met the same monsters I did, stayed silent.

"It is intriguing, gentlemen, and fine lady," Oscar said, with a nod to Evangeline. "I'll grant you that. This mystery is why you are here. Why I invited you. I have many clues, a puzzle, if you will, and no solution to satisfy me. Something is killing hunters in Raton. It is a strange and bloodthirsty beast. What do we know of its nature? Is it a new beast or a very old one? What is its origin? I want to see it. Up close. I want to have it locked in a cage where I might study it."

The coach wheels made an odd rhythmic change in their sound.

"Pardon me," I said. "Are those cobblestones?" I peered out the window to find gas lamps lit on either side of the lane. Indeed, I made out the cobblestone road passing beneath us.

When I looked back at Oscar, he was grinning widely.

"They *are* cobblestones, Dr Hardy, from the Paris *rue* where Vivienne lived as a child. I paid to have every one prized up, labeled, and re-laid here. I also paid the damned Parisians to fix their damned street. All to make her happy. To make my wife feel more at home."

"I do not remember *la rue*," Vivienne said, touching my knee lightly with her fingernails.

"But it sounds the same! Trust me," Oscar insisted. "I remember."

"When I lived there, I walked on the stones with bare feet," she said.

At the mention of *walking*, my eyes were involuntarily drawn to the gold leg braces she wore from ankle to mid-thigh. Underneath the gold, I saw dark wine-colored leather sleeves strapped around her muscles. Her dress parted enough for me to mark that the sleeves laced tightly up the front, along the shinbone, with cut-out circles for her knees. In the light from the gas lamps I noticed filigree decorations on the gold. The metalwork depicted astronomical symbols: the sun and moon, major and minor planets. Asteroids, comets, stars. Zodiac pictograms were there as well, and other markings unfamiliar to me, but the light was poor, and I could not study them too closely for obvious reasons.

Vivienne shifted her legs. I quickly gazed up. She smiled at me privately, as her husband continued to catalogue the expenses of shipping an entire French road overseas.

The coach slowed.

"We have arrived," Vivienne said.

"Where is the house?" I asked, as I stood waiting outside the coach. The gas lamps cast an orange glow over the snow-covered rocky terrain. Away from the mountain a string of lights lay like distant campfires: this was Raton. One campfire surged and flickered more brightly than the others; that was the Starry Eyes, still blazing. But on the mountain darkness ruled. The moon was a bone shard embedded in the clouds, mists haloing her silver aura. Starlight twinkled icily, but so far away. The coach driver was a small man, a dwarf, in fact, with a grim face and a long drooping black moustache. He carried both a whip and a Bowie knife on his belt.

"Step aside," he said to me.

"Which side?" I asked.

"Pick one."

I picked left. He walked past me and turned a large iron key set into the rocks. Then he removed the half-smoked cheroot from his mouth and touched it near the same rock. A tongue of flame filled a previously hidden gas globe set at my waist. The driver walked ahead, occasionally drawing on his cheroot as he lit a series of identical globes along a path. I could see now that what at first appeared to be the stony face of the mountain was, in actuality, the entrance to a mansion hewn into the mountain.

Nightfall Lodge.

"Remarkable," I said. A horizontal sheet of ice hanging off the craggy shelf became a row of large glass windows heavily draped against the cold but with an incredible view to the south.

"One of a kind," Oscar said. "I have a passion for rarities. Much like your Institute for Singular Antiquities. We have that in common."

"You've heard of us?" I said, sounding more surprised than I meant to.

"Miss Waterston has filled us in on her plans for the future. A most ambitious project. I am captivated by Evangeline's concept."

Was it the concept or the woman that captivated you? I wondered. *Her* plans, did he say? What of *our* plans? It seemed I was fated to struggle forever with one or another Waterston over the control of our mutual endeavors. Worthwhile? Yes, but nonetheless frustrating.

Oscar called his coach-driver back from Nightfall's doors.

"Hodgson, escort Mrs Adderly into the house."

The driver nodded to his boss. He climbed up the rear ladder of the coach and came down with Vivienne's wheelchair balanced on his shoulder. It was clear he had performed this task many times before for the chair did not bounce against the coach and he set it lightly on the ground beside the coach's step. McTroy moved to help get Vivienne down, but Hodgson halted him with a hand gesture and, gathering Mrs Adderly in one stout arm, pivoted, descending the step, and depositing her gently in her seat. Vivienne unclasped her arms from his corded neck. She nodded at the driver warmly, giving a quick squeeze to his thick forearm, and then looked away at the mountain.

"Thank you," she said. Hodgson tucked a fox-fur blanket across her lap.

He pushed her chair along the walkway to the lodge doors.

I felt someone standing to the side of me and turned,

hoping to find Evangeline.

"Wu? You scared me back there in town. I thought we'd left you behind."

"You scared me as well. I could not get you to move or talk. You were like…" Wu pulled an unflatteringly stricken face, halfway between a politician and a mule-kicked drunkard.

"Stop that." I swatted him with my glove. He did not stop. "Wu, please, enough!"

"See? It was making me feel strange too," he responded.

"I understand. But I was in a trance of some kind."

"We all been there, Doc. You were black-haired lady-tranced. Witchified." McTroy smirked and wiggled his fingers at me as if throwing an evil spell.

"I was no such thing. I saw bizarre shadows. I heard Vivienne's voice in my head."

"Not only your head," McTroy said.

I was about to protest further when Evangeline finally joined us.

"My heroes have gathered together again," she said, curling her lip amusedly.

"It is good to see you, Miss Waterston," I said.

"I am Miss Waterston to you, am I?" she teased.

"You are whoever you choose to be," I said, inclining my head.

"Oh, Hardy, I have missed you so much." She leaned in and kissed my flushed cheek.

"We have been apart too long," I said.

McTroy and Wu started along the path following Hodgson and Mrs Adderly.

"Yes, we have, but now we are all here. I cannot wait

to see what happens. These Adderlys are still waters, Hardy. They run deep. Strange giants swim in the depths," Evangeline whispered. She made a swimming motion with her hand, poking me in the ribs.

"Is it just Oscar and Vivienne living inside the mountain?"

She shook her head. "No, no. They have two grown children. Twins. Claude and Cassiopeia. And the household servants live here, of course, although I haven't been able to account for them all as they tend to come and go."

"Do the twins favor their mother or their father?"

Evangeline thought about this.

"Hmmm… neither, I'd say. But they are remarkable. What a spooky pair! When one is looking at you, it as if they both are. That's not exactly right. Suffice it to say, you'll see what I mean when you meet them. Let's catch up with the group now before they extinguish the globes and we are stranded in this dark wilderness alone."

I would have smothered the lamps myself if I thought that were true.

Instead, I offered my arm, and Evangeline seized it snugly.

7

THE DEAD ZOO

Nightfall Lodge
Sangre de Cristo Mountains, New Mexico Territory

Nightfall Lodge smelled of freshly sawed lumber. What had been made of mountain rock on the outside was made of mountain trees on the inside. *Here is a very rich man's cave*, I thought. It was not unpleasant. A painted buffalo hide hung on the wall. It depicted an Apache hunting party on horseback using bows and arrows to strike down a herd of bison. Zigzag-patterned baskets and black-and-white geometrically painted clay pots decorated the elegantly sparse room. The ceiling arched over us, supported with rough beams any bat would die to hang from. Granite fireplaces warmed the entrance hall. Despite its great size, the vestibule felt cozy. My face must have appeared quizzical, because Oscar answered the question I'd been asking in my head.

"I had them drill chimneys through the mountain," he said. "So we don't smoke ourselves out." He laughed, slapping me on the back. "You'll find one in every room. Viv hates the cold."

Two old but sturdy-looking servants appeared from the shadows of a hallway. The man took my bowler and coat. The woman attended to Evangeline. In a minute, each person in our group had a crystal balloon of warmed Armagnac in their hands. Quite smooth, and quite expensive I'm sure, certainly the best brandy I have ever drunk.

I sensed that Nightfall Lodge was shaped like half of a wagon wheel. The entrance was the hub, and various dark corridors led off like spokes of the wheel, or the hours on half a clock. Currently, a single spoke (twelve o'clock) was lit for our purposes.

"I'll spare you the grand tour. But I want you to see one thing before you go to bed," Oscar said. "Follow me." His boot heels echoed off the polished floor.

We followed him.

On either side of the hallway were alcoves, shadowy niches only partially illuminated by the corridor's lamps. Each alcove had a waist-high barrier with a small latched swinging gate. I could not help glancing back and forth into the gloomy nooks as we proceeded to our destination. Glassy eyes stared out from the dimness, unblinking. I counted more than a dozen watchers. Were these the other servants Evangeline mentioned? No. I tried to consider them more intently without breaking my prior pace or appearing to stare too obviously. But what were they, these contorted figures standing motionless among arrangements of plaster of Paris boulders, woven leaves, and paper mâché tree trunks?

The shapes became anatomies. I recognized a few but could not imagine them living here. Evangeline caught my hand as I reached for the next gate out of curiosity, though what I might have done after I opened the gate was a mystery to me. I gasped at my impulsivity. But I simply wanted to know more.

"It is so silent," I said. "Are they not chained? I mean, is it safe?"

Evangeline nodded.

I hitched my step when I spotted the tiger. I dodged away. Then a grizzly bear on the opposite side of the corridor reared up on two legs out of the darkness, his snarling pendulous lips and gaping jaws froze my feet in place. Had he lost his roar? Was he mute? His claws could decapitate Evangeline and me together with one swat. I lunged in front of Evangeline, blocking the ursine menace with my body and my stick.

But the death blow never came.

Oscar gazed over his shoulder at us when our steps ceased.

He turned and said, "Ah, Dr Hardy, I should have told you. I apologize. We are passing through my zoo on the way to the trophy room."

"But these creatures? How did you acquire...?"

"I shot them all. It is my artistry as a taxidermist that captures their fierceness so precisely that it stops you aghast in your tracks tonight. Do you feel awe? You should. Their innate power extends beyond their lives." He walked to where I had inserted myself between Evangeline and the bear, our backs exposed to the tiger stalking in the reeds behind us. "This bear I killed up in Alberta. That tiger who is about to break your neck came from a forest near Bandhavgarh Fort on the maharaja's game preserve, though she would much rather dine on a chital, or spotted deer, than you. There is one down the corridor, by the way. Just follow her eyes."

Oscar drew a line in the air from the tiger's alcove to the deer.

"Do you see?" he asked, playfully.

"Yes, I do."

"But what you do not see is that you have already passed a snow leopard, a black rhino, and a cape buffalo. Not to mention a Nile crocodile, a whole family of silverback gorillas, a jaguar and not one but two lions. You have already died a dozen times in this hall, Doctor."

He grinned and wagged his finger at me. "But you are no hunter. McTroy told me so. I asked you here for other reasons. You seek not the bloody-minded predator but the ancient wonders of the world believed lost to time. Discovering treasure is your desire. Is this true?"

I nodded cautiously, adding, "Historical treasures. I pursue knowledge."

"But of course. If not for wonders what would the world be?" Oscar paused, but when no one answered he said, "Quite boring. That is the answer, I'm afraid."

And he made a sad face.

He clapped his hands together, making a sound like a firecracker.

Everyone startled at the sudden noise except McTroy.

"Luckily, we have wonders aplenty. Now, come, come. You will have time to absorb the beauty of my dioramas tomorrow before breakfast, if you choose. The others will be here first thing in the morning.

We will meet in the trophy room and talk about our great adventure!"

"Others?" McTroy asked.

"Did you really think you were the only ones to receive a private invitation?"

"I reckoned we were," McTroy said.

"Well, you reckoned wrongly. After breakfast you will meet the teams."

"I don't operate with others."

McTroy was prepared to leave then and there. I could see it.

"Ha! McTroy, you misunderstand me. Your team is you and the friends you brought. I have my team. And there will be one more team. This is a healthy competition. We will all go out separately and do what we choose. The winner will take the prize. That is America, friend."

"You said we would be paid for coming here."

"And you will, you will. How successful you are determines your pay."

There was one thing that provoked anger in McTroy above all else, and Oscar Adderly had just found it: you did not mess with McTroy's money. But given that we were stranded, at least for the remainder of this night, at Nightfall Lodge, McTroy saved the battle for the morning.

"You don't trust your own skills?" Oscar asked.

"You're the man who should be worried about my skills."

"I fight the beasts when they come and not a moment sooner. Worrying serves nothing."

"One man's worrying is another man's examination

of probabilities," I said.

"Spoken like a true worrier, Dr Hardy," Oscar said.

"Oscar, are you insulting our guests?"

Vivienne pushed away from Hodgson at the far end of the corridor and wheeled herself to her husband's side.

Perhaps it was the exertion that caused a dewy sweat to glisten on her cheeks and an injection of color to invade her otherwise ivory paleness. Like a crimson hand, a mark appeared around her throat, but the look she shared with us crackled with electric excitement.

Oscar smiled down at her.

"A bit of manly gamesmanship never hurt anyone. It spices the meat of the matter. Don't you agree, gentlemen?" Oscar opened his arms in a grand gesture of conviviality.

"Spoiled meat needs the most spice," I said. "But I am no chef, myself."

"Get on with your pomp," McTroy said to Oscar.

"To the trophy room we go!" Oscar turned and walked away.

"Oscar is an incorrigible jouster when other men are around," Vivienne said, raising an eyebrow in disapproval. Yet, despite her objection, she seemed most interested in Oscar when he was behaving badly.

"I find that male jousting is an all-too-common occurrence," Evangeline said.

"Present company excepted?" I asked. "McTroy and I are not constantly sparring."

"You're more a swordsman where jousting is concerned," McTroy said.

"Thank you."

"Wu is still too young to compete in such games," Evangeline said.

"But I am learning," Wu said, sticking out his chest.

"McTroy? Your swordsman comment has turned in my brain. I take back my thanks."

"No need to apologize, Doc."

Evangeline said, "Does it ever bother you to live among these stuffed animals?"

"No more than it would any other woman," Vivienne said. "I think we should join Oscar. He will pout if we keep him waiting." She wheeled herself over to Hodgson, who asked her a question we could not hear. But she nodded exasperatedly and went on wheeling herself into the trophy room while he exited back the way we had come.

"He is a steely fellow," I said, as Hodgson passed us without as much as a glance.

"Good-looking though," Evangeline said.

"Do you think so?" I asked, surprised.

"I do," she said.

Here I assumed Hodgson had a disadvantage with women, being that he was of smaller than normal stature. Other men most certainly had teased him and acted cruelly toward him in public his whole life. I wondered what attraction Evangeline saw in him. But she had moved off to join the Adderlys, pausing only to pet the velvet antlers of the spotted deer as she went by.

"Do you find Hodgson to be handsome?" I asked McTroy and Wu.

They looked away and shrugged.

"His coolness of manner must be the key. The man

is confident. He has swagger," I said, brandishing my ape-headed stick. "No doubt he developed this attitude over time – as a defense."

"He has that Bowie knife and whip," McTroy offered.

I nodded slowly, not understanding how that changed anything. "What do you mean, precisely?" I asked.

"I don't know," McTroy said, tilting his hat back and scratching his forehead.

"Are you three finished? Or shall we start without you?" Evangeline called to us.

Our analysis ended, we scampered like hungry puppies at the sound of her voice.

Skull room. Antler room. Ossuary. Each of those names would have fitted our surroundings more than trophy room. Stacked buffalo skulls filled the wall behind us. A thicket of elk antlers took over two more walls. And windows looked out over the starlight-bathed icy peaks of the Sangre de Cristos. Vertigo spun in me as my eyes climbed the harsh crags. I felt like a man in a rowboat about to be crushed by a foaming, gray tidal wave. But the most disquieting thing in the trophy room was none of these. It was a cage. A twelve-foot square cube of iron bars.

Oscar unlocked it.

"What do you think of my jail? Be honest. Will it hold the so-called Beast?"

I was impressed with the cage, even if it shouted its high theatricality so that a deaf man might hear. "It appears the model of an oversized prison cell," I said. I grabbed the thick cold bars and gave them a pull.

"I'd dare to call it escape-proof. What do you think, McTroy?"

McTroy set his empty brandy snifter into the notch of an elk antler and left it there. "Ain't a cell can't be broken," he said. "That includes this one."

Oscar took this comment as a challenge. "Do you doubt the materials, or is it the workmanship you question? Because I assure you both are of the highest calibers available."

"I get paid to return men to inescapable places."

Oscar jerked the door open. "Would you care to test it?"

McTroy did not move.

"I have the keys," Oscar said, giving it a jingle. "Perhaps you have a fear of confinement? Some men do. It is nothing to be ashamed of. But we would never leave you in the cage. It is only for our amusement. Please, McTroy. Get inside. I'll pay you five hundred dollars. No? A thousand? One thousand dollars for five minutes locked in my cage. Do we have a deal?"

"I'll do it," said a woman's husky contralto voice.

We all turned to spot her in the corner by the last window of the row.

A young woman emerged from the Persian silk brocade drapery. Her wine-colored dress provided her camouflage, since the drapes were likewise plummy and dark, and her stillness rivaled the predators in Oscar's macabre zoo. She did not resemble either of her parents. Her heart-shaped face was far too exotic. The young Adderly's enormous amber eyes were spaced too far apart to be labeled conventionally beautiful, and yet what might have been unlovely in others was mesmerizing in Cassiopeia. She wore her sleek butterscotch hair shockingly short, cut like a boy's. But her shapely figure left no doubt as to her sex. No jewelry of any kind adorned her. She glided to the cage. I was surprised to see her walking barefoot. As she embraced Oscar one of her feet flexed up, revealing a sole as black as smoke.

"This is my daughter, Cassiopeia," Oscar said for our benefit. He held her face and kissed her cheeks. "The offer is only for McTroy, Cassi."

"But why can't I play. I would like a thousand dollars."

"Why do you need money? You have everything."

"I would go away. And seek my fortune in the world. I would roam," she said.

"Speaking of roaming, where is your brother?" Oscar glanced about the trophy room to check if his male offspring might be hiding there too.

"Claude went outside."

"Went outside *alone*? Does the boy have a wish to die? It is near midnight and cold and, in case you haven't heard, wild beasts are on the prowl."

"He'll be fine."

Oscar sighed. "How do you know that?"

"Because he always is," she said. While her father hung his head in disappointment, Cassi took the opportunity to grab the cage door and shut herself in. She rattled the door to make sure it had locked.

It had.

"I am a prisoner!" she shouted. Her laughter rang in the trophy room. I was sure no woman's laughter had ever been louder in that hunter's den. I hid my smile behind my fist, feigning a cough. But Cassi heard everything, missed nothing. Once I drew her attention, she laughed again, the full sound of her booming throughout the lodge.

"Who will save me?" she cried, widening her eyes at me in particular.

Her father produced the keys, and in his frustration fumbled them. Practically purple-faced with anger, Oscar lurched to catch the falling keyring, and kicked it instead. The trophy room's polished floor offered as much friction as an icy pond. The ring skimmed over to me.

I scooped it up with my stick.

The keys dropped into my hand.

In a few steps I stood at the cage. Cassi kept her chin tucked low and her eyes up. If I didn't know better I might've feared that releasing her would be a mistake – that this lively, odd young lady would enjoy nothing so much as to pounce on me. She smiled a sharp-toothed grin.

"Now if I let you out, will you promise to be good?"

She shook her head – *No*.

"Despite your answer, I'm opening the cage." I inserted a key, felt the heft of the well-oiled mechanism tumble smoothly, and with a decisive *chock!* the weighty door swung free. I stepped back. Cassi offered me her hand. I took it, and feeling the rough callouses on her palms, became momentarily distracted. She yanked me into the cage with her. Then she relieved me of the keys, tossing them far into the room where they slid under a towering mound of bison skulls.

"We are both prisoners now," she whispered in my

ear. Her breath felt warm on my neck, yet I shivered. Then she cried out to the others, "Whatever shall we do?" She slunk to the rear of our cage, dropping to the floor and curling her legs under her. There she reclined against the bars.

"Cassi!" Oscar yelled in dismay.

Vivienne appeared entertained by my predicament.

Wu watched with his mouth hanging open.

Evangeline looked cross, though I could hardly guess why.

McTroy said, "Stay locked up, Doc. It will do you some good."

Evangeline discovered Oscar's liquor cabinet and refilled her brandy. McTroy retrieved his glass from the antlers and joined her.

Oscar kneeled, peering into the bison skulls for a glimpse of his lost keys.

"Do you not have a duplicate?" Vivienne asked him.

He shook his head. "The locksmith mailed me two. But they are both on the same ring."

"We are locked in here for good! I shall need a blanket to sleep on for the night. Unless you are warm. What is your name, cellmate?" She patted the floor beside her. I sat down.

"Rom Hardy," I said. We shook hands. Again I was struck by the toughness of her skin.

"Call me Cassi, Rom. Are you very warm?"

"I am getting there," I answered truthfully.

"More importantly," she said, with a look of grave seriousness, "are you willing to share your warmth with me should the situation call for it?" She blinked, waiting for me to answer.

"I am—"

Chock!

Cassi and I saw Evangeline removing a pair of bent hairpins from the opened lock.

"You've picked it!" Cassi cried. "I *must* know how you did that."

"One of my talents," Evangeline said, replacing her hairpins. "I'll show you tomorrow, if you'd like."

Cassi jumped to her feet and nodded emphatically.

"She learned it from magicians," I said, afraid I sounded as disappointed as I felt.

"How marvelous," Vivienne said. "Did the magicians teach you much?"

"The Davenport Brothers? Oh, they were more dedicated to ropes and knots and putting musical instruments where you'd least expect them. Spirit-cabinet mediums – Ira and Henry were also frauds, of course. Their father was a policeman. They knew how to rake a lock. Nimble fingers, a bit of savvy, and the patience that comes with mature men. But I was the better picklock by the time we parted. I brought a lock to bed with me every night. Practice, practice…"

"I should love to hear your stories," Vivienne said.

I was brushing myself off as McTroy said, "Doc, you look like you lost your best friend."

"Yet you are still here."

"Aw, I didn't know you felt that way. You are the little brother I never wanted."

"Tears spring into my eyes – I am blinded with emotions." I tapped along the bars.

Cassi gave me a bewildered look as she left the cage.

"We are not brothers, and I see things perfectly well," I said.

But her focus had shifted elsewhere, to the trophy room's threshold, where a man entered, staggering and crashing into the liquor cabinet. He clutched his arm. Blood ran off his fingertips.

"Claude!"

8
A Dangerous Condition

"Claude!" Vivienne repeated her daughter's exclamation. "You've been attacked!"

"It looks far worse than it is," he said. "Might I bother someone to pour me a whiskey? My hands are sticky with this stuff." He flicked his hand and sprinkled us with blood. Then he appeared shocked at what he'd done – the gruesome splashes he'd made on everyone. The young man's face grew ashen. He teetered unsteadily. "Sorry about that. Can't get my paws clean." He swung his head loosely. "Who are all these people? Why do they tilt when I try to look at them?"

Cassi rushed to her sibling, holding him upright. She was strong. His legs had gone rubbery and were useless.

"Brother, you *are* hurt!" she exclaimed.

Claude laughed weakly.

I brought him a chair from a dining table behind the cage. "Here you go," I said.

"I do not recognize you. You must be a new friend," he said. "I would shake, but…?"

I helped Cassi to settle him into the chair.

"You smell of smoky fires, new friend," Claude said, pulling away from my jacket. "Or is it me?" He gave himself a deep and thorough sniff and ran his gory fingers through his hair.

"And you smell of the bottle," I said, wrinkling my nose.

"Claude is delirious with blood loss," Oscar said. "I'll send for a doctor."

"He's drunk," I said.

"I scraped myself on a tree… a tree, a tree… I did not see. That rhymes, doesn't it, sister?"

"What were you doing in a tree?" Oscar asked.

"Falling out of it, Father. Hitting all the branches on my way down."

"He has a long but superficial cut on the back of his hand. A small gash on his cheek. He might've knocked his head when he fell, but I think it's mostly whiskey at fault here," I said.

"Are you a doctor?" Claude asked me.

"Yes… of archaeology."

"Am I to be wrapped like a mummy? And buried in a pyramid?" The prospect seemed to alarm him and he clung to his sister's sleeve, leaving bloody smears.

"Mummies are usually not entombed in pyramids," I said. "We've only ever found parts. Robbers are the likeliest cause. Or the bodies of the pharaohs were moved as a precaution. But yours is a common misconception. That is why more Egyptian exploration needs to be done."

"Really? Where shall I be buried then?" Claude hiccupped.

I feared his drink would make a second appearance.

"In the snow, you fool." Oscar threw a fistful of napkins from the liquor cabinet into his son's lap. "You're lucky you didn't break your neck. Climbing up a tree? Laying out there in a snowdrift, freezing to death – that might teach you a lesson."

"Leave Claude alone," Cassi said, staring at her father coldly.

Claude, despite his inebriation, summoned the concentration to match his sister's glaring menace. I saw what Evangeline had mentioned about the twins' uncanniness: how they mirrored each other not only in physical traits (same height, coloring, bone structure, bearing, etc) but in attitude, and even synchronized movements.

They were like two bodies controlled by a single mind.

Vivienne wheeled herself over to Claude.

"Let me see you, dear. Are you certain I shouldn't ask Hodgson to fetch the doctor?"

Oscar stormed off, disgusted.

The twins swiveled around and watched until he vanished into the hallway. The tension eased out of them in a perceivable and collective sigh. Their eyes became droopy, as if thoughts of sleep occurred to them suddenly, concurrently.

Claude licked a trickle of blood from his wrist.

"Don't do that," Vivienne said. "It's revolting."

"It's only me, Mother," he said. "I taste like salt and Tennessee whiskey. There are worst things to eat, believe me, I know."

Cassi slapped his thigh, and he flinched and

attempted to bop her but she shifted away too quickly. He fell back into the chair, lounging with his lids closed and a soft burr in his throat.

"I'll bandage him." Cassi took her brother's arm and began to clean the wound with a lace trimmed handkerchief she pulled from her sleeve.

"How did you end up in a tree?" Evangeline asked.

"I wanted a better view. Climbing was the best way to get it. I didn't think. I just went."

"And that is why your father is so angry, Claude." Vivienne shook her head. "You know it is dangerous to be out on the mountain at night."

"What is it you wanted a view of?" Evangeline asked.

Claude half-opened one eye.

"The Beast," he said, growing more alert.

"You saw the Beast tonight?" I asked. "Right here, near the lodge?"

"A few leaps and bounds away... there's a ravine or two between us and it. But I saw something large and strange making tracks in the snow. The breath flew out its nostrils in two great plumes, like a dragon. I could see it breathing from a quarter mile off. I had a telescope in my pocket." He reached into his pocket and withdrew a brass tube and some broken lenses. "But I was too low. There was pine scrub in my way. That's why I needed to put myself at a higher elevation. I'm a formidable tree climber. Cassi will attest to the fact."

"Getting down is another matter," Cassi said.

"Thus, I am bloodied, drunk, and exhausted by my efforts."

"If what you said is true, I must tell Oscar

immediately," Vivienne said.

"Tell me what?"

Oscar reappeared, carrying soap and water, towels, and a roll of bandages. He passed the items to his daughter, who gave him a little smile signaling forgiveness for his previous outburst.

"Your son saw the Beast," I said.

"Where? What did it look like? Are you sure it was the Beast? Speak, boy."

"Give me a chance." Claude stretched and took his time relaying the same story he had told us to his impatient father. Oscar hung on his every word.

"To the north?" he asked, as he paced the trophy room. He approached the windows, and then he returned to his children. But he could not keep his feet still and was off again, this time lapping around to the far side of the cage.

"I think so…" Claude replied, languidly. "I hit my head and have grown fuzzy."

"You said 'to the north'. Is that correct? Yes or no? You do know which way north is, don't you? Damn it!" Oscar pounded his fist onto the table.

We all jumped.

Claude sat forward and grabbed his head. "You're giving me a terrible pain, Father."

"The Beast keeps to this mountain as of late… to my mountain. Those idiots gathered at the Starry Eyes can chase their tails in the hills around Raton. The Beast goes higher with each kill. If the Beast decides to move down, they will push it up again. It doesn't like to be seen, this one. That is our challenge. To probe every crack on this ridge until we drive it into the open."

A peculiar sound started then, like the whistle we'd heard in the Starry Eyes, only deeper and more richly toned. It did not pierce or shriek. The call was lonesome. But it made the hairs on my neck dance like variety girls. The howl – for it was a howl more than a whistle now – echoed in a nearby canyon. It was not close, but it was not far either.

McTroy, who had not spoken, walked to the windows. I watched as he cocked an ear toward the glass. The howl carried over the ridge. I felt it quaking in my chest. I'd swear I did.

"That's no wolf," he said.

"It is a trick of the wind," Oscar said, "piping through a fissure of stone, a hole perhaps."

"Have you heard it before? This howl we're listening to right now?"

Oscar did not answer, and that was an answer in itself.

"Wu, do you know this call? Is it any creature you've ever run across?"

Yong Wu shook his head. His parents were creatures of the night, and Wu's relationship with them brought him into contact with unusual beings: the living, dead, and in-between.

"Deep lungs... a lot of air... it has not taken a breath yet," Wu said. "It's big."

"It's wind," Oscar said again. "That's why it goes on so long."

"Look out the windows. No trees moving. What kind of wind doesn't blow trees?" McTroy gazed over the gray peaks, the pearly snow, and the sky like diamonds stuck in tar.

Evangeline knelt next to Claude's chair. "Did you hear the Beast? When you were out there tonight, hiding in the tree, did it call to you? Did it make any sound?"

Claude lifted his head as if to tell us something of great importance. His eyes were glazed, his mouth partly open. The breath between his lips, quick and sour, flowed so strong I could taste the flavor of it, like iron mixed with maple sugar. His body bent like a bow.

He vomited a puddle of whiskey onto the floor.

There was blood in it.

And a small lump shaped very like a bird.

Cassi threw a towel over his mess. Oscar called for the servants to clean the floor.

I whispered into Evangeline's ear. "I saw something in Claude's disgorgement. I think it might have been a finch of some sort. The colors were... difficult to detect."

Evangeline did not react as most women would. She raised an eyebrow and asked, "Do you think you could check it again?"

"The idea holds no appeal for me."

"Certain curses may cause a person to eject foreign objects. Vivienne is a witch. Her son may be the subject of an attack on a level not entirely physical. If you won't look, then I will."

She crossed in front of me, but I stopped her from proceeding farther.

"Very well," I said.

Claude slumped in his chair, his blanched countenance slightly improving, but a greasy sweat matted down his hair and darkened his collar; he'd closed his eyes again, and I could see them rolling around in their sockets. His hands were twitching too, as if he were receiving tiny jolts of electricity. Cassi added a second towel to soak up the whiskey. The smell did not seem to bother her much, but I felt my own gorge rising at the tangy acidic fumes. Yet I approached.

Using the end of my stick, I lifted a towel corner.

"Rom! Stay away, please," Cassi said. "Back... go back."

"Might I inspect the evidence of his... sickness?"

Claude moaned and twisted in the chair, drawing up his knees and hugging them to his chest. Sweat soaked his shirt, and I could see the knobs of spine. He was slimmer than his sister.

"Whatever for?" Cassi asked.

A good question. Perhaps an excellent one. Should I venture to say: *a possible finch*?

"I might offer him help. I think I spied blood. That can be a sign of a dangerous condition."

"But you are not a medical doctor," Cassi replied.

"True," I said, looking to Evangeline to offer me support in this, her line of inquiry.

"Dr Hardy saw what looked like strange meat. Perhaps your brother ate something he should not have?" Evangeline reached out to comfort Claude, but he wanted no human touch and drew himself into a tighter ball. He continued moaning. His hiccups had started again. "Water might do him some good," she suggested. "Would you like a sip of water, Claude?"

He waved her away.

The Adderly parents had drifted to the far end of

the trophy room. It might have been the smell or the embarrassment that propelled them there. Oscar was talking animatedly to McTroy, pointing to landmarks outside the windows in the silvered mountainous dark, and Vivienne engaged with Yong Wu. I guessed she was quizzing him about his knowledge of unusual creatures. *Child, where did you learn such things?* Wu seemed nervous. Vivienne determined.

I wanted to intervene, but the servants had arrived with buckets and mops.

"Strange meat?" Cassi asked. "We had roasted quail for dinner. I ate it too. So did my parents. I hardly think the birds were tainted, or we would all be feeling unwell." She smiled as she guarded the towels. "Really, Rom and Evangeline, I appreciate your concern, but you are overreacting. The situation is shameful enough for us. Claude drinks too much. He knows it. Our family knows it. I am mortified that you, as our guests, had to witness this untidiness. Claude is an irrepressible boy at times. We hope he will outgrow it. He'll be fit in the morning. You'll see."

"You dined on birds?" Evangeline asked.

"Quail, as I said. Father shot them. He never misses a chance to shoot things. You two should be on your guard while you're here." She laughed, making a light but mirthless sound.

Our awkward vying for a peek at Claude's vomitus ended when the servants bundled up the soiled towels and dropped them with a wet thump into a bucket, removing them from the scene. Steaming hot soapy water sloshed over the boards. I felt better even though we lost our argument. Evangeline did not appear chafed.

Claude requested the water he had earlier spurned.

"The howling has stopped," I said.

"It went quiet after he got sick," McTroy said.

"I still maintain that the wind plays a weird symphony on these peaks," Oscar said, but he did not pretend to believe what he said was true. "We have a hunt tomorrow. It is best we get to our beds, especially my drunken son, whose head will feel like a cannonball that has landed on his shoulders in the morning. But he will live."

"I may not live," Claude said, hiding his face.

We laughed. Cassi ran over and kissed his white bandage.

"I'm afraid we have a bit of a full house with more new guests arriving," Oscar continued. "Evangeline, you will have your own room, next to Vivienne's bedroom. Dr Hardy and McTroy will share a room. And your Chinese boy can sleep in the servants' quarters."

"Wu stays with me and Hardy," McTroy said. "Send someone into Raton for our horses."

"There are no spare beds. But he may make a pallet on the floor. I'll have my man bring an extra blanket to your room. The stable boy will collect your horses before dawn. I always find the hunt begins long before the hunt begins. Do you agree, McTroy?"

"I don't think about it."

That is how the first night ended. The Nightfall Lodge killings started the next day.

9

ORCUS

Wu and I took the beds. McTroy slept on the floor. Despite the hours of train and coach travel, and my exhaustion, I rested fitfully, tossing on my mattress – which was too soft, giving me the sensation of sinking into mashed potatoes – and fighting with my pillow, which was too firm and put a crick in my neck. I kept thinking I heard that howl again, but, when I sat up, it was always nothing. (Wind twisting round in the crannies of the pinewood paneling or strumming the cracks of the manmade cave which surrounded us. My own blood shushing in my ears. Or a dry, coarse rasping from where McTroy lay heaped against the wall like a half-shrouded corpse awaiting the coffin-maker.) Wu was a quiet sleeper. But that disconcerted me as well. I crept forth from my blankets and held the back of my hand above his lips to check if he was breathing.

He was.

So I climbed back into bed.

The logs in the fireplace crackled as they burned to embers. It was black as a tar pit in the room after that. Still I could not sleep. My mind teetered on the edge of dreams like a climber dangling from a precipice. The chasm of sleep yawned beneath me. But my mind refused to fall.

I heard the clop of hooves on the cobblestones. There were no windows to detect any natural light inside our section of the tunneled-out mountain lodge. I struck a match, lit a lamp – turning the wick down low – and checked my pocket watch, seeing it was just after three o'clock in the morning. Yes, still dark out. How did the sounds penetrate several dozen feet of solid rock? Did they snake a path to our quarters through the eccentric architecture of Nightfall? I had no answers.

Maybe I *had* fallen asleep and was dreaming this assortment of nocturnal disturbances.

But no, I hadn't.

Perhaps a few errant drafts of air were turning the whole house into a kind of elaborate instrument – wheezing in the corners, gasping little breathy puffs, and murmuring softly like patients wandering the halls of an asylum. Sometimes they cried, "*Oooooo*." Other times it was a dull, repetitive "*Uhuhuhuh*." Then they fell silent. My raft would drift down the river Lethe to the caves of Hypnos until they started up again, and I'd awaken bewildered, disheveled, and questioning things anew.

It was probably just gusts blowing down the fireplace flue, I said to myself. *Or rats. Yes, mansions often had rats.* Now there was a nasty thought: a hungry rat in my bed, searching under my blankets for a tasty morsel to chew on. I crossed my legs and had another nasty thought: might someone (Oscar?) be lurking inside a hidden passage in the wall peeping at the sleeping guests?

I was not sleeping. Not here. Not tonight.

I threw off my blankets. I was always imagining too much, thinking too much.

Why wouldn't my brain slow down when I begged it to? I was so very tired.

In response, my brain asked: *Isn't Oscar the owner of the Starry Eyes saloon? And didn't we escape the fire through a secret passage? And isn't Oscar's dead zoo solely for the watcher's pleasure? How different is it then for him to look at you, friend Hardy, instead of a stuffed hippo?*

I cupped my ears and listened. Faint sounds, far-off rooms – it was like reaching for objects just beyond my fingertips. Like a blind bat, I probed the semidarkness with my ears.

Then I clearly heard something that I recognized.

There is no mistaking the sound of a horse walking.

A single horse – obviously ridden by the stable boy who was leaving to collect Moonlight, Neptune, and Magpie: the horses belonging to McTroy, Evangeline, and Wu. I presumed McTroy had the forethought to bring a horse for me, although I hadn't asked him about it. Unfortunately, my last ride met an untimely fate in the Gila Desert. What if McTroy hadn't brought an extra for me this time? Would I have to saddle up two-to-a-pony with Wu? I suddenly felt the desire to ask McTroy immediately about my horse. Sitting up in bed, I leaned over to see if McTroy was asleep.

He was.

I sighed. I would not bother him. My question could wait until the morning.

Being the only one awake was a lonely prospect. Like being a ghost, I supposed.

How long I sat there in the dark I cannot say.

Then sound of the hooves on the cobbles came again. Clip-clop. Clip-clop. Clippety-clop.

Surely I had not fallen into a slumber sitting up? It was too soon for the stable boy to be returning from Raton, and certainly he would not have returned alone. McTroy's horses would be following, tethered in a line. I should be hearing a parade of iron shoes clicking on cobblestones.

I harkened more closely to the beats.

They matched the way a man would walk. Two-legged, rather than the looser, compounded sound of a horsey four-legged stride.

Two legs, yes, but hooves? No man has hooves.

The devil does.

Don't be silly, I told myself. Yet I knew the stories of witches summoning devils late at night. Wasn't Vivienne a witch?

I had to stop and think here.

Boots may sound like hooves. Might the sound be coming from inside the lodge?

That made sense. *Boots*, not hooves. *Inside*, not outside.

But I *had* heard hooves clicking on cobbles earlier. I was sure of that. And the cobblestones were decidedly outside. I was confusing myself. I shut my eyes to listen better. Does that even work? It felt like it helped… just not enough to satisfy my gnawing curiosity.

I tiptoed toward the door. I did not want to wake my roommates so I did not bother to dress. I wore my long woolen underwear and that seemed sufficient. My bare feet caught the stony chill seeping up through the floor. What kind of a madman builds a castle in a mountain?

I turned the doorknob and went out for a look.

Voices. I heard voices whispering. Who is it? What are they saying? What reason did any sane person have for being up and walking around at this hour?

Extinguishing my lamp, I felt my way along the wall and headed for the entrance hall.

I spied a glow in that direction. Faint, yellow, flickering – a candle.

Ahead of me – I heard the *Oooooo* and the *uhuhuhuh*.

Also I perceived not the clip-clop of hooves but a scratching. Yes, a definite scratching. More like claws than hooves. How many animals were traipsing in the hallways tonight?

The scratching moved on ahead of me.

I chased after it.

At the archway where the guestroom corridor intersected the entrance hall, I paused and peered ever-so-slowly around the closest wood beam. Its roughness dug into my cheek.

The entrance hall was empty.

But the candle-glow flared stronger. It was coming from Oscar's gallery of dioramas.

Warily I sneaked past the Indian woven baskets and under the painting of the Apache hunting party on the buffalo skin. Oh, the great buffaloes – we had murdered them into near oblivion. They were little more now than that pile of skulls in Oscar's ossuary. Our whole country would eventually turn into a pyramid of bones if we weren't careful. Look at the Egyptians... and the Sumerians and Akkadians before them... all the ancient tribes who inhabited this continent we call ours. Where had they gone? The way of the buffalo... I feared it was the way of humanity.

But enough with history!

Up! Up, Hardy! You are creeping in the dark. Stay in the present.

The candle stood on the floor in one of the dioramas – the pair of lions – and shadows lurched violently upon the opposite wall.

Two figures lay in the African grasses. I watched their shadows and listened to their now unmistakable cries. Cries of passion. Muffled but unable to be silenced. The shadows intertwined. A head thrown back, a torso twisted. A silhouetted leg kicking out in a spasm of pleasure. The figures melded and pulled apart. Pressed together again. I heard a low but clearly feminine chuckle, and a throaty growl. Then playfully loud kisses and more chuckling.

I slid my cold feet along the boards, inching closer.

Although I should have – I could not stop myself.

My brain ticked off the arithmetic of whom I might be spying on. I was an intruder on their privacy. But was this a private place? Not really, I told myself. And, more importantly, Evangeline was in Nightfall. I didn't even know where her bedroom was. But might it be her? And entangled with whom? Claude? Oscar? I shuddered at the thought. Yet she had every right.

Shamefully, I thought: *I am the lurker in hiding, the one who spies on others in the dark.* But that did not stop me. I flattened my back against the wall and edged farther along. The couple lay to my left beside their guttering candle. Their bodies cast weird forms on the wall. But distortions made it impossible for me to identify them, unless I turned my head into the gallery space and looked upon them directly in the diorama where they sprawled naked; yes, I could see a jumble of their clothes so near I might squat and steal them. But in the gloom I could not discern whose clothing it was. A gown, a robe, a silk nightshirt? I was not sure.

I detected a scent of roses, of wild fruit, clover, and licorice-flavored tea. Was it the candle or a woman's perfume? I did not get close enough to tell. The odor of a sulfur-based pesticide lingered near the lions. I assumed Oscar used a powder to keep his animal hides from being eaten by bugs. I would have to rely on my eyes and not my nose.

Turn around, the better half of me said. *This is not your affair, Hardy. Go back to bed.*

The lovers remained oblivious. They would never know if I looked in at them.

I molded myself to the wall and stuck my neck out... only to see the spiky branch of a fake thorn tree in front of my eyes. I crouched lower and tried again. This second attempt was blocked by a huge stuffed black dog Oscar had set on his African plain. I stretched out my arm to see if I might push the dog aside. As I was about to touch its fur...

The dog blinked.

Sad golden eyes, skin wrinkled in a frown, and a head the size of a fur-covered anvil – he looked rather disappointed in me. He opened his massive mouth. Out came a pink tongue. Hot damp breath flowed over my fingertips. His teeth felt very close.

"Oh..." I said, uttering an involuntary gasp.

I froze. My gaze switched from this gargantuan dog's face to my poor pale fingers.

I wanted to pull my hand away immediately but feared any abrupt action might provoke the bestial hound who looked at me balefully and cocked his head first to one side, then the other, as if wondering where this idiot with the pale fingers had come from.

"Why do you tempt my terrible jaws?" he asked me.

As you would be, so was I – taken aback by the voice of a talking dog.

"I- I- I..." Shall I cry out for assistance? Is it best to try and run? Can I fight a hellhound?

"Did you not hear me?" the dog asked.

"I did," I said. Was that proof of my delusion? A talking dog...?

"Can you answer?"

"I am sorry. I mean you no harm. It's only that... I'm a bit amazed."

"You were going to shove me. Were you not?"

"I thought you were stuffed." Surely this was a trick of some sort. But I dared not touch him. Proof was not worth losing a hand.

"Stuffed with meats?" he asked, licking his teeth.

"No, no, no... I thought you were like these other animals. Hollow?" I hoped not to offend him with any assumptions I had made.

"Ah, a forgivable mistake. But answer this, Undressed Man Who Smells Afraid, why do you wander this lodge at night alone?"

"I thought I heard things."

"I hear things too," he said, giving his colossal head a tilt, but never taking his toffee eyes from mine. "You wished to look upon the two coupling in the grass you cannot eat?" His dog brows arched up to emphasize his question.

"I- I- I..."

"I am the guard of this place. I guard all friends here."

"That is good to know. I am a friend too... *friend*... Do you understand me?"

"Why wouldn't I?" He stood up now on his stout, muscular legs. His huge head swung from side to side. His pointed ears flicked. "Do you hear something now, Undressed Man Who Smells Afraid?"

I turned and listened. Taking suggestions from a talking dog came more easily than I might have supposed.

"I hear what sounds like hooves on cobblestones, or maybe boots," I said.

"Yes, it walks on two legs. But it is not a man. I smell it. No man smells like this."

"I cannot smell anything. But tell me, friend, how is it that you can talk?"

"I need to go look for the walker. It is outside. But it wants to come in. That is not allowed. It approaches the bones room. Will you come with me?"

"Certainly, I can accompany–"

The dog did not wait for me to finish my reply. He stepped up to the gallery barrier, leaped over, and trotted down the corridor, heading for the trophy room. His claws scratched on the wood floorboards. It was the same scratching I had heard before. I stooped and looked deeper into the diorama. The lovers' candle remained, but their clothes, and the lovers, were gone.

I snatched the candle and caught up with the dog before I was left alone again.

The trophy room was freezing. The fire was out. I felt the frosty cold pushing at the windows. Where did the dog go? His black coat disappeared in the darkness. I was moving the candle about and illuminating the bones room, but I could not find him.

"Where are you?" I whispered. I was almost hoping to hear no reply. Then I could easily go back to bed and claim I had met up with a ghost dog, or a half-waking dream.

"Here," the dog said. He sat and watched the last window on the left.

I joined him, but all I could see was mountain, black sky, and our reflections in the glass.

"It's out there," he said.

"Are you sure?"

"It smells like dead things smell. But it moves fast when it wants to. I don't like it." He started up a low, menacing growl that made me shrivel.

"We are friends, you and I?" I asked.

He stopped growling. "I think so," he said.

That answer would have to suffice for now.

"Are you some sort of... forgive me for asking this... hellhound?"

"No, I am not a hellhound."

I nodded. "But you are most unusual. How would you characterize–"

"Be silent," he said. "It comes now. Blow out your candle."

I blew out my candle.

My eyes adjusted to the tenebrosity. The window

gave off waves of coldness like an ice block. I saw nothing in it. But I heard the hooves clicking, no longer on the cobblestones but on rock. It moved closer, stepping along the edge of the cliff. The dog was growling again, a basso profundo rumble from deep inside its barrel chest.

The Beast did not show itself bit by bit in the window, no. It was not there.

And then it was.

I jumped back. Every molecule of me wanted to flee.

The hairs on the dog's back stood up. In the splintery remnants of stars and moonlight, I saw his skin quivering, but he did not yield.

The Beast – gaunt and slavering, spittle running from its narrow chin – pressed its long face to the glass and smeared the pane with blood and drool. Its antlers spread as wide across as a bull elk's. The tips reached higher than the head of the window – each antler smooth and thicker than my wrist. Some points were stained with blood. Others shone white. The mouth was a toothsome grimace – red pink gray all running together like paint, with chunks of flesh stuck against the gums. Eyes like red ice. They did not blink but stared and stared. It seemed that I might die from looking at this thing. I could count its ribs, the arms all bones and tendons, it appeared to be almost without skin; but the skin of the Beast was pulled tight and gray as the night clouds. If it stood unmoving one might miss it among a landscape of trees. It raised a hand – the arm monstrously rangy, the hand like a human's stretched to a limit of extreme exaggeration; each bony finger tipped with a claw, six inches long, or more, and tapered to a knifepoint. It dragged its fingernails down the glass. Five furrows appeared.

I covered my ears.

The dog whined at the shrieking, scraping claws, and then growled so ferociously that I feared he might jump through the window, shattering the glass. There would be no barrier then–

Gone.

The Beast was gone as quickly as it had come. I never saw it bolt.

The dog lifted his nose. His ears were twitching. "It is running down the mountain. But it will come back. Not tonight. But soon," he said.

I touched the glass where the Beast left the five score marks on the other side.

"Does it scare you?" I asked. "Because it scares me…"

"I am thirsty," he said. "There is a jug of water next to my bowl in the kitchen. I will show you the way. If you would pour me some water, I would be grateful. Also, over there in that tall cabinet with the sweet-smelling liquor bottles, they keep smoked cow bones in a drawstring sack on the highest shelf. I would like one before I go to sleep. I have many things to consider."

The black dog carried the bone in his mouth as he walked me back to my room. I had lit the lovers' candle again in the kitchen. The flame fluttered. I was tired now. My eyes grew heavy. The dog dropped the bone to the floor with a clatter and pinned it there with his paw.

"Thank you for the bone, Undressed Man Who Smells Afraid," he said.

"You're welcome." I could see him, smell him, and hear him. "Are you real?"

"I am here, if that's what you mean. Everything is real, more or less."

He picked up the bone again and started to trot off. Scratch, scratch.

"Wait," I said.

He looked over his shoulder at me. His brow wrinkled.

"What is your name?" I asked.

He spit out the bone.

"I am called Orcus," he said.

"Goodnight, Orcus. I am Rom Hardy."

"Goodnight, Undressed Rom Hardy Who Smells Afraid," he said. Then he picked up the bone and walked out of my candlelight.

Feeling unsteady and completely exhausted, I retired to my room.

10
THE APIS BULL

"Doc, hey, you alive? Wake up," McTroy called out as he shook me roughly awake.

"What is it?" I asked, taking in the full measure of his grizzled, gray-hatted visage. "Let go of me!" I attempted to twist out of his grip. He hauled me involuntarily into a sitting position.

"You were sleeping down where the dead men go, Doc. I've hollered myself hoarse. I was starting to think you was snakebit, poisoned, or taken up in one of them trances."

I swept my pocket watch from the nightstand. It was six o'clock in the morning.

McTroy continued, "Wu's snuck over to the trophy room and back again. He says it's filled with maybe a half-dozen bad hombres. Old Oscar's itching to start his morning speechifying and that means he'll be laying out the terms of his reward for capturing the thing what's been eating the hunters and picking its teeth with their splintered bones. Drag on your britches, man. We've got business to conduct."

He threw my clothes at me, followed by my boots.

"Stop that!" I slapped everything aside.

I jumped up from the bed and picked my belongings off the floor. I pulled my boots on.

"Doc?" he said.

I was in no mood to entertain his rudeness before the crack of dawn.

"Hey there, Doc?" The bounty man poked my forehead.

"*What*?" I shouted, wheeling my arms around wildly.

He dodged the blows. "You're putting your boots on," he said.

"I know very well what I am doing. Don't be an imbecile. Get that light out of my face."

"Ain't you forgetting something?" he asked, shifting the kerosene lamp to one side.

"Yes, come to think of it, I am. I am forgetting why I left the comforts of my New York City office to be harassed by the likes of you before my eyelids have opened. I don't give a hot damn if Oscar is handing out gold nuggets the size of pawpaws to everyone who asks him nicely. I will get there when I get there. The Beast isn't going to be caged before breakfast, is it now?"

"I reckon not," he said.

"Then allow me to get dressed in peace."

"Can't do it, Doc," he said.

If, like a horned lizard, I might've shot blood from my eyes then I would've done so.

"Why?" I asked through gritted teeth.

"Because I am your friend and you ain't put on your britches."

I looked down from buttoning my shirt. He was correct. I also had omitted my socks and misaligned my top two buttonholes in my haste to depart.

"I had trouble sleeping," I said. I sat and slipped the boots off.

"Not when I saw you."

"No, before that... after we went to bed... you, Wu, and I... well, I could not fall asleep. The total darkness bothered me. And this bed... also, I heard odd sounds outside our bedroom."

"I didn't hear anything," he said.

"You were asleep. You didn't even wake when I left the room." I now recalled, with all due embarrassment, my spying on the mystery lovers *and* the highly improbable conversation I had with Orcus. What was I to make of talking with a hellhound? Nothing for now. I had seen the Beast! I was not sure how to broach these subjects with McTroy.

"Sorry, but you never left the room, Doc."

"That is where you are wrong. I saw wonders when I left this room." I combed my hair with my fingers, but a tuft refused to stay down. At the dresser, I filled a wash basin from a flowery porcelain pitcher beside it, dipped my fingertips into the cool waters, splashed my face, and wet my stubborn cowlick. In the mirror I watched it rise again. That would have to do. My cheeks had color. Properly attired, I knotted my tie quickly. "Hand me my stick, please," I said.

"You dreamed it, Doc. I'd have heard you go, if you did."

I pondered the possibility that I had been dreaming. The elements of a nightmare were all present. And no dog had ever spoken to me before in my waking life. When I dream, I do dream vividly. Had last night been nothing more than the product of an overactive mind and a strange bed? But any nagging suspicions soon fled. I had concrete proof of my stroll.

"It was no dream," I said. I pointed to the nightstand. "Observe the candleholder. Where did it come from? Answer: I found it on the floor of the lion's den in Oscar's gallery. 'When?' you ask, incredulously. When I went out in the wee hours to inspect the goings-on in this most strange lodge. I encountered things, McTroy. Significant things. It felt real because it was real. Mark me, sir. I know my way around the fantastic. Let's go to this meeting."

"That candleholder was here when we got to the room," he said.

"Was not," I said. I cracked open the door and breathed deeply. "I smell bacon!"

"You feeling up to snuff this morning, Doc?"

"I feel splendid. Exhilarated, in fact. Life is best when we are surprised by it. Now then, we shall endeavor to be surprised." I stepped past him and over the threshold.

"Whatever you say," McTroy replied.

And surprised we were.

The trophy room was a bustle of activity – manly activity – which is to say idleness, smoking, thrusting of chests, and thickly mumbled words of threat, braggadocio, or both. I spotted Oscar fixed in the center of business, expounding as he cut the end of a Havana cigar. Claude had a foot up on a window ledge with his back to the room. Smoke from his cigarette feathered the glass. It was the window where the

Beast had appeared. Intentionally or not, Claude was blocking the Beast's scratch marks from everyone's view. He massaged his temples.

Ah, the morning after a drunken night is a dry march through a blinding desert.

Of the other men, I recognized three: Pops Spooner, Billy the Kid, and a burly, bearded man in a beaver fur hat – they had all been at the Starry Eyes the night of the fire. The other two men were new to me. The older gent was an Indian, dressed in a fringed deerskin tunic and leggings, a mink poncho, moccasins, and two eagle feathers in his braids. He sat staring at the ceiling, only half-awake. The second man was a redheaded gunfighter. He wore a pearl Colt Lightning and sported goatskin shooting gloves. His right hand was missing two fingers. Red stitches marked their place. He holstered his pistol on his left side. His liquid eyes met mine and instantly moved to McTroy. The gunfighter smoked a meerschaum bulldog. He was looking at McTroy, smiling as he walked up.

"Haven't seen you around since… was it Dynamite Creek or Sully's Fork?" he said.

"Sully's Fork," McTroy said.

"That's right. I remember now. You still hunting bounties?"

"I am."

"Good for you. Get right back on the horse, as they say. Is she with your party?"

The gunfighter nodded at the archway where Evangeline had entered, pushing Vivienne.

"Yes."

"Introduce us, Rex. Show good manners."

Evangeline linked eyes with the red-haired duelist. She came over, extending her hand.

"This lady is Miss Evangeline Waterston. Evangeline, meet Gavin Earl."

Earl inclined his head and kissed her knuckles. "Charmed," he said. "If your wit exceeds your beauty, then I am in for a rare treat."

"Why, Mr. Earl, I was thinking exactly the same thing," she said.

"We shall not know disappointment this day," Earl said.

"The day ain't over," McTroy said.

"You're right, Rex. It's just getting started," Earl replied.

McTroy had an angry-looking rash climbing up the side of his neck. I cleared my throat and took a step forward.

"This is Doc Hardy," McTroy said. "He steals mummies from people."

"I do no such thing. McTroy jests. I am a scientist and historian. I studied in Chicago."

I gripped Earl's gloved, three-fingered hand. It was like touching a piece of machinery.

"I sketched a mummy's head once while I was at Yale," he said.

"Oh, Yale College is quite prestigious. What did you read there?" I asked.

"Old books," he said.

"What sort of old books?" I pressed him.

"The sort that made me flee New England." Earl shifted and cut our conversation short. He grasped Evangeline's fingers. "You've made this a worthwhile trip from Texas. Rex, I am so glad you're here to keep things from getting boring. Sully's Fork... that was quite a time. Forgive me. I need a word with my men."

He went to the group which included Billy, Pops, and the fur-wearing, long-whiskered fellow. Earl said something to Pops who snapped a look at McTroy and then gazed at Evangeline. He rubbed his bulbous nose and commented back to Earl. The two men laughed.

"What happened at Sully's Fork?" I asked McTroy.

"I don't want to talk about it."

"How do you know that man?" I said.

"He used to be my partner."

"Rex, you don't strike me as the partnering type," Evangeline said. "Is he as good as he pretends to be?"

"He collects the biggest bounties. We made money together in Texas."

"But you left and went to Yuma?" she asked.

"That's right. I went to Yuma."

"Why's that?" I chimed in.

"Because Yuma ain't Texas. Watch yourself around Gavin Earl. You'd be better off trusting a diamondback. He knows how to talk real pretty too. The man could sell sand in the Gila. Don't listen to him, either one of you. He's a devil."

"The more you say about him, the more intrigued I am," Evangeline said.

"Did he really attend Yale?" I asked.

McTroy nodded. "His family's rich. Shipping money. His story about leaving Connecticut is a lie. They *shipped* him out West. He killed a mayor in Kansas. You could fill the Grand Canyon with people he's stabbed in the back."

"Does he stab in the front too?" Evangeline asked, amused.

But McTroy was having none of her joke. "Watch yourself. He's greedy."

"We're all greedy for something. Greedy isn't the worst thing a man can be," she said.

"What is?" I asked her.

"Dull. I'd take greedy over dull any day of the week. Where's Wu?"

"Checking our horses," McTroy said.

"Oh, that reminds me. I was wondering if you brought a horse for me," I said.

"I thought you'd want to walk so you might get to use that stick of yours."

"I can't walk if you three are riding!"

"Calm down. I have a gelding for you. You'll get along," he said.

"What does that mean?"

"It means he doesn't get too excited. He's a thinker, like you."

"What's his name?"

McTroy grinned. "Jingle," he said. Evangeline covered her mouth and snorted.

"Jingle? Well, I suppose the horse didn't pick his name. I would never be a Romulus if I had picked mine. Prejudice is a terrible quality. I refuse to prejudge him."

"Hardy, you are the most fair-minded man I know," Evangeline said.

"When you speak of dull, I hope I am not that too. Last night I saw amazing things in this lodge. The sleeping hours hold mysteries. McTroy doesn't believe me. You may not either if I tell you. But I have proof, or at least corroboration of my account. Have either of you seen a black dog roaming the halls? You can't miss him. His head is bigger than mine." I put my hands up on either side of my head and moved them apart to show Orcus' size.

"That is no small accomplishment," McTroy said.

"Ha. Find the dog and I will render you speechless, bounty man."

I left him to his jibes.

Vivienne Adderly sat tall and straight in her chair. She smiled as she saw me heading in her direction. I don't know how an arrogant blowhard like Oscar convinced her to marry him, but I had to give him credit. She was a superior woman. And if she was a witch, so be it.

"You are looking tired, Dr Hardy," she said.

I dragged a hand across my unshaven face. "I sleep poorly in new places."

"Do you have nightmares?"

"What an odd question. Yes, I do. But what is worse is that sometimes I don't know if I am awake in a dark room or if I am asleep in dark dream. I have a restless brain, I suppose."

"Do you have any other restless parts of your anatomy?"

I paused, uncertain if I had heard her question correctly. "Pardon…?"

"Your feet? Do you sleepwalk by any chance? It is a trance state, and you are susceptible to trance states – as we have seen." She wheeled herself against my leg and crooked her finger at me. "Come down here."

I bent on one knee beside her wheel.

"You walked last night, didn't you, doctor?"

Her eyes were very big and appeared almost black to me. She smelled of incense.

"I don't know what you mean. I slept fitfully, as I said–"

"You left your room. Are you aware of that?" she said.

"I left my room!" I did what I could to act shocked. "How on earth did I do that?"

"You opened the door and..." She stepped her fingers up my arm and touched my chin.

"Heavens! How do you know this? Did you converse with me? I have no memory of it."

Vivienne nodded. "I did not talk to you. But I did see you. I have a crystal orb next to my bed. Last night the orb showed me you walking in the hallways. You went through the gallery and into the trophy room." She frowned and lowered her voice. "You were not alone, Doctor."

"Who joined me?" Here I played dumb, but I was also curious as to the extent of what she knew. Plainly, I suspected now that Orcus had reported my trespassing and our subsequent conversation to Vivienne. That was the likeliest explanation. The dog had told her everything. I paused to wonder which was more absurd: whether I wholehearted believed I had conversed with a canine or that I now questioned his discretion.

"I don't know. Nightfall is often busier after dark than in daylight hours. You were in danger last night, Hardy. I don't want to alarm you–"

"But you have!" I thumped my walking stick on the floor.

"I don't want to alarm you *beyond reason*. You must be cautious while you are here with us. Not everyone is kind. We have hidden natures. Do you know what I am saying? We guard a darkness inside us that we cannot control. The middle of the night is when the will weakens. Lock your door tonight, or better yet, I can move your room to one adjoining mine. If you wake, I will hear you. I am a light sleeper and reach my peak energy well after sundown. If you need somewhere safe from the horrors, I can provide that for you." She looked at me for a long time.

"I am lucky to have you watching me," I said.

"Watching is not enough," she said. "Consider what I've said. Your chance may pass."

I nodded solemnly and stood upright.

Cassi swept into the room and hooked my arm. She batted her lashes at her mother and danced me into a corner by her twin brother. Claude never even raised his head from studying the tip of his glowing cigarette.

"Was Mother seducing you? She seduces everyone, you know? Don't feel special," Cassi said. *Is she teasing me?* I asked myself. I must have seemed aghast.

Cassi laughed. "I've injured your feelings, Rom. I'm sorry. Perhaps I was a bit too forward and, maybe, accurate? I know you've heard all the rumors about Vivienne Adderly."

"Which rumors are those?"

"That she is a powerful witch. That she shares her bed with demons in various forms. That she vigorously entertains the devil himself?"

"I only heard the first part," I said.

"The second part is usually the best part. The first part is introductory, a bit like a lesson. The last part can be dangerous because it might turn sad, or end up leaving you quite unsatisfied. But the second part is what I like – the heart of things. You look as if I'm a raving madwoman. Try living up here with them and those terribly sad stuffed animals. See if you don't go a bit mad." She nibbled the edge of her fingernail.

Claude groaned something unintelligible as he lazily arched his back.

Cassi slapped him smartly on the head. He reached out a crabbed hand, only missing scraping her face by a few inches. She dodged, hissed, and kicked him hard in the leg. He winced and glared at her, but it was all in good fun. Shaken from his brooding, he brushed the cigarette ashes down the front of his suit and sauntered off to join the other hunters.

"What did he say?" I asked.

"Who knows? Claude's always chattering. Ooo! Will you look at this window? What happened here?" She traced the cold scratches with her nails.

"The Beast happened," I said. "You and I need to talk about it."

"The Beast scratched this window last night?" Cassi hunched toward the glass, studying the marks. "It put its hand… or paw–?"

"The claws were a sight! Bones – *long* bones compose the hand. Its feet are hooves. I heard them clip-clopping on the ledge. But we saw the claws clearly, Orcus and I," I said.

"Orcus?" she asked.

"Yes, he was here with me. We both heard the Beast. I have keen ears. We followed the noise to this room. The thing *appeared*. See the trace of demonic spittle on the window?"

"Demonic... spittle is it? This smudge right here? Yes, I see." Cassi looked as if she did not see at all. Confusion made her quite attractive, the way her brows curved and her lips parted as if she wanted to say more but could not decide how seriously I was to be taken.

I said, "Cassi, I would not joke with you. I'm not without humor. But this is a matter of life and death. Orcus saw it as I did."

"Orcus? My dog?"

"Do you not trust him?"

"I would trust him with my life."

"Well, then. There you have it. The threat is real. The question is: what do we do?"

Suddenly she roared with laughter. "Oh, Rom, you had me believing you. You really did."

"What did I say?"

She took firm hold of my shoulders, staring at me fixedly. "Stop it. You are too charming. I must admit that you are also exactly the remedy I so sorely needed." A quick kiss on the cheek sealed my perplexity. I was swirling in a whirlpool of emotions. Not the least of which was fear.

"Attention! Attention!" Oscar clapped his hands. "You hunters are here for one good reason. In case you have not guessed it, I will make things clear. We will form three teams for the hunt. The Beast is our objective. I do not wish the target dead. Before we talk of it, let's discuss your prize for a successful capture. Knowing the reward, you will heed me intently."

"What's he yapping about?" Billy whined to Pops.

Pops held a finger up to his lips.

Oscar continued his speechifying. "I know you came here for cash. And cash you may have, if that's your choosing. But I am offering a most unique prize. A piece of legendary status. Claude, wheel it in now."

"Poor Claude," Cassi said, hiding behind her hand. "The servants fled this morning when they heard that Father intends to apprehend the Beast and bring it home. Claude has been forced to work. See the strain on his face."

Claude tugged a thick rope attached to a rectangular platform with a wheeled base. His boots slipped, seeking purchase on the highly polished floor. The object lay secreted under a large canvas but it obviously weighed hundreds of pounds. Claude turned the color of a fine Bordeaux. The crowd gathered around the specimen. Claude touched the canvas.

Oscar said. "I will unveil it."

Claude stepped aside, sweeping his hair off his face and digging into his pockets for the materials to roll another cigarette.

"Good job, Claude," Cassi called out.

He snarled at her and parked himself on the window ledge again.

McTroy and Evangeline moved nearer the cloaked mystery. Yong Wu, whom I had not seen entering the trophy room, cautiously stayed back. When he saw me he lifted his shoulders in a shrug which I returned in kind. We waited for Oscar's revelation. Oscar enjoyed being at the center of all things. He had an insatiable desire for other people to envy him, to make them wish they had his wife, treasures, and trophies. It was not wealth he delighted in so much as inspiring other men's jealousy.

Oscar flung his half-smoked cigar into the fireplace and grabbed the canvas.

With a snap of the wrists he ripped it off.

"You may kneel if you so desire," he said.

"What the dang hell is that?" Billy said. "A goddamned cow?"

"Precisely! You have nailed it, my unschooled friend!" Oscar chuckled. "Dr Hardy, educate these heathens as to what they see."

I was taken aback. I was not too sure what I was seeing either. But I had my suspicions.

Oscar waved me in for an intimate look. "Come, come. Don't be shy. This is why you are here, after all. You are my expert witness. I will give you a hint. No, two hints. Let me see…"

I approached the artifact.

"The hints are *Egypt* and *mountain*," Oscar said.

The artifact reached higher than my chest. "May I touch it?"

"I insist," Oscar said.

It was warm as if it had been sitting in the desert sun.

"This is a golden bull. The Egyptian cult of Ptah worshipped the bull. They made idols to which they prayed and sacrificed. It is a large specimen." I peered at the metal. "Molded. But fashioned without extra decoration. It was made quickly, perhaps, in haste…"

I walked around the ancient idol.

"You are doing well, Doctor. Please continue," Oscar said.

"It is old but in excellent condition. The gold appears solid and not merely gold leaf."

"Correct again!" Oscar shouted.

"I would conclude, without knowing any provenance, that this is an example of an Apis Bull idol from the Egyptian empire. The Frenchman Auguste Mariette excavated near Memphis, at Saqqara, where he discovered the Avenue of Sphynxes and the Serapeum of Saqqara. Inside he found a burial place – a temple – dedicated to Apis Bulls." Who expected to locate a piece of Egyptian history in New Mexico?

"You have the *Egypt*. But what about my *mountain* hint?"

"I'm afraid I'm at a loss."

"Doctor," Oscar said. "What is another word for bull?"

Another word for bull?

"A calf is a young bull," I said.

Oscar said, "You have it, Doctor. Thank you."

"I have it?"

"Yes. This is not a golden calf. This is *the* Golden Calf."

"Mount Sinai!" I ran my hand over the warm, wavy gold of the bull's head. "From the story of Moses…"

Oscar recited the following passage from memory: "*And Aaron said unto them, Break off the golden earrings, which are in the ears of your wives, of your sons, and of your daughters, and bring them unto me. And all the people brake off the golden earrings which were in their ears, and brought them unto Aaron. And he received them at their hand, and fashioned it with a graving tool, after he had made it a molten calf..."*

"That's a damn lot of earrings," Billy said.

"You have found the Golden Calf of the Israelites?" I said to Oscar.

McTroy said, *"And Moses' anger waxed hot, and he cast the tables out of his hands, and brake them beneath the mount. And he took the calf which they had made, and burnt it in the fire, and ground it to powder, and strewed it upon the water, and made the children of Israel drink of it."*

"You know your bible, McTroy," Oscar said.

"The Golden Calf was destroyed," McTroy said.

"Yet there it sits," Oscar said. "Destroying it makes a good story. Could you throw away beauty like this? Imagine how tempting it would be to save it, in secret."

"Hey Doc, is it fake?" McTroy asked.

"I would need to study it further–"

"If it is real, Dr Hardy, what is its value?" Oscar asked, making a temple of his fingers.

"The Golden Calf is priceless, if authentic. It's the ultimate symbol of wealth and idolatry. The only other ritual relic of a similar magnitude is the Ark of the Covenant, which was also lost to time. Any Egyptologist would be a fool not to want them both."

"Lost to time," Oscar said. "But it's here for the taking, if any of you catch the Beast."

"What if we just want the cash?" Billy asked.

"Then $100,000 is the price I will pay," Oscar said.

Billy whistled and slapped his knees. "Damn!"

"What if we melt the statue?" the fat man in the beaver skins said. "What's it weigh?"

"That would be an insult to history," I gasped. "A travesty against knowledge!"

"Nearly two hundred pounds," Oscar said. "You'd lose money if you melted it. But once we make our exchange, I wash my hands of this golden bull."

"You don't want the Beast killed. What if I shoot it and it falls off the mountain or down into a crevasse?" Gavin Earl said. He lit his pipe and tossed the match to the floor. Oscar ground the match under his heel.

Then he said, "If the loss of the body is no fault of yours, you will be paid. However, I must verify the kill. There is no other way. If you choose to kill the Beast when capture is a viable option, you will be paid $10,000. I am the sole judge in this matter."

"What makes you the judge?" Billy asked.

"It's my bull," Oscar said.

"You offered the men in the Starry Eyes $10,000 for a capture and $1,000 for a kill. Why did the price change?" McTroy said.

"The men down in Raton are fodder," Oscar said. "They will neither capture nor kill the creature. They will pen it in, or drive it up the mountain toward us."

"How did you obtain the idol?" When Evangeline spoke, every man turned his head. She walked around the artifact. I knew she wanted the bull to be a part of the Institute for Singular Antiquities. What could be more singular than this? Yet she had a wily sense of business and a familiarity with the levels to which men lie for profit.

"I bought it," Oscar said. "The Golden Calf elicits strong feelings in the hearts of people. Some see proof of their God. Still others see—"

"Others see gold," Evangeline replied. "You have papers? Documentation of where the bull has been all these years?"

"I do," Oscar said. "Dr Hardy is free to examine them."

"I could get started immediately," I said.

Oscar smiled. "You may examine them when the Beast is in that cage." Oscar pointed to the iron prison within the trophy room. "Not a moment before... I am not here to host a symposium on ancient history, or to talk of lucrative business deals. Madam, I want to hunt."

Evangeline checked me in the crowd of men. She did the same with McTroy and Wu.

We three nodded.

"Then let's hunt," she said.

11
YOU'RE ALL GOING TO DIE

Jingle was a white horse with flecks of gray scattered like buckshot through his hair. I almost lost sight of him against the backdrop of snow. I hadn't been riding since our last journey into the Gila Desert, but, despite the promise of a sore bottom at the day's end, it felt good to have a strong animal under me. He had long thick lashes and a dark eye that minded me when I leaned in close for a talk. If horses smile, he was a smiler.

"There's a good Jingle," I said. "Let's not tumble today. Help me be better than I am."

He shook off a spray of glittering snow and stamped his foot.

I like to think we understood each other.

Wu rode up alongside me on his pinto, Magpie.

"It is a good day to ride," Wu said. "I don't like being cooped up in that house."

"I agree with you, Wu. Far better to venture out into the wilderness."

"The Beast does not worry you?"

"I saw him, Wu."

"You did?" Wu looked properly frightened.

"Last night he crept his way up to Nightfall. Let's say that I would rather hunt the creature outside than have it hunting me inside. McTroy thinks I was dreaming, and I suspect Evangeline might agree with him." I stared hard at an enormous brown mound yards ahead of us plowing through a snowdrift, sending up puffs of white and clouds of steamy exhalation. Alarmed, I pointed and asked, "Is that a grizzly bear?"

Wu nodded.

"It belongs to Dirty Dan. He's the trapper who's tracking for Gavin Earl's team. Dan lives in the mountains all year round. The bear is his pet."

"You cannot be serious."

"Oh, yes. It is not a very big grizzly. But still…"

The burly mountain man was checking his pack mule and his gear. He wore snowshoes and carried an oak staff for checking the depth of snow on the trail.

"What does one do with a bear?"

Wu shrugged. "McTroy said Dirty Dan is wanted for murders across three states."

Upon closer inspection, the man and his pet bore some resemblance.

Oscar addressed us from his stallion. "We have four trails. Copper, Bronze, Silver, and Gold." He indicated the locations of the trailheads. "The trails all branch off my road, the only road on this mountain. Each trail has a sign painted with its namesake's color. The Bronze Trail leads back down into Raton. We will not use it. The men of Raton will keep the Beast from going down, except perhaps for a snack. We will have him to ourselves. One team, one trail. You will hunt along your trail only on the first day. Vivienne will now draw random lots from her purse."

A smiling Vivienne, sitting in her wheelchair, held up a large purple silk purse, decorated with glittery-scaled dragons. On her lap was the fox fur blanket. The weather colored her face. She averted her gaze and plunged her hand into the purse like a girl searching for candies. A girl with a very sweet tooth.

"First draw is for my team," Oscar said. "Our tracker is Smoke Eel."

The gray-haired Indian who was snoozing at breakfast nodded in acknowledgment.

Oscar continued, "He comes from the Canadian Northwoods and may have special knowledge of our quarry. But it is too soon to tell how valuable his experience will be. Don't bother asking him what he knows, because he is a mute. Mind you, Smoke Eel hears perfectly well. He can write messages in the notebook he wears around his neck. Just remember, he works for me and me alone. He is not here to help you claim my prize. If I think his advice is worth sharing, then I will share it. Claude and Cassi complete my team. What's our trail, Viv? Pick a good one for us, darling."

Vivienne withdrew her hand and held up the gold card for all to see.

"Gold!" she said.

"Why can't we have the Gold Trail?" Billy said. "I wanted the Gold Trail."

Gavin laid a hand gently on his shoulder. "Be quiet, Billy."

Billy kicked a chunk of ice. He practiced his quick

draw versus a stunted pine.

"Very well," Oscar said. "Second team is Gavin Earl, Pops, Dirty Dan, and the Kid. What is their draw?"

Vivienne dug into the purple silk. The tip of her tongue touched her upper lip.

"Silver! A silver card!" She held it up high.

Oscar nodded solemnly.

"McTroy, that means you, Evangeline, the doctor, and Wu will take the Copper way."

Oscar passed out maps for each team.

"If you capture, wound, or kill the Beast, you will signal by firing three shots. *Bam! Bam! Bam!* In an equally spaced sequence. Sound carries on the mountain. Upon hearing the signal, the other teams will return promptly to the lodge. The shooters will also send a member of their party to the lodge with a marked map marked telling us your location. We will rally and transport the Beast, dead or alive, back to my iron cage. Then the prize will be paid in full. Any questions…? No? We are all very eager to start. Smoke Eel will ride out first. Good luck. Good hunting. And may the best team win!"

Oscar lifted his hand ready to wave the teams on their way.

I heard the scratching of nails on stone. A blackness moved swiftly along the mounds of shoveled snow bordering the walkway to Nightfall's doors.

"Ah, my hunting companion wants to join us," Oscar said.

Orcus trotted over to his master's horse.

"Where'd you get that devil dog?" Billy asked. "Hades?"

Oscar dug into his saddle bag and tossed a treat to Orcus.

"Orcus is an Italian mastiff bred from Roman bloodlines. He hunts anything from wild boars to bears. Absolutely fearless. But today he will have to be satisfied with guarding Nightfall. I am not leaving Vivienne unprotected."

The dog whimpered.

"I think he'd rather hunt the Beast," Vivienne said, laughing.

Then Oscar's wife made a low, gurgling sound as if she had something caught in her throat. She opened her mouth, but no sound came. Her face flushed as she tried to draw a breath. She pitched out of her wheelchair. Arms and legs flailed as she convulsed.

"Viv, my God!" Oscar said.

"Mother!" Claude and Cassi both shouted. They ran to her where she lay shaking uncontrollably, her leg braces chattering on the walk, her heels throwing gravel.

"She's having a fit," Pops said, climbing off his horse.

I dismounted and joined them.

Vivienne's eyes rolled up in her head, showing only ivory. Her hair had come loose from its braiding. Nuggets of grit and dirty ice balls clung to her. She'd landed face down and now rolled over onto her back. Her nose and upper lip were bleeding.

"Give me more to eat," she said. The voice was not her voice but that of a dead talker. "Give me more... give me, give me moremoremore..."

She writhed on the frozen ground.

"Viv, stop this. Grab her arms; someone help me."

Oscar tried to hold her kicking legs. She knocked him backward with a swift blow to the stomach that made him grunt in pain and struggle to draw another breath.

"Get something soft to put under her head," Pops said.

I took off my coat, tucking it beneath her.

She turned and licked my hands.

Her eyes showed nothing but whiteness. The veins in her neck bulged.

"Taste you, Doctor. Taste you and eat you," she said. She nipped at my fingers. I jerked my hands back. She laughed. "Eat you. Eat you. Eatyoueatyoueatyou–" Her teeth clacked together so mercilessly that I feared they might chip into pieces. This was not Vivienne Adderly. Some*thing* was using her body. She tore herself from Pop as he fumbled a needle from his bag, attempting to inject her. She raked black fingernails across his jaw. He swore. She rolled away. Then she went crawling on her belly. Claude and Cassi gaped in horror. Helplessly they watched her approach the horsemen. The horses retreated. She craned her neck, the muscles bulging. Her dress was shredding on the stones; her pale skin turned mottled. Despite her rolled-back eyes, she saw them. Giddy she was. Blood smeared half her face, staining her teeth crimson. It reminded me of the Beast glaring in the window last night.

"You are all going to die," she said, swallowing her own blood.

Billy the Kid stayed the farthest back. He put the pine tree between himself and the possessed woman. Dirty Dan's grizzly bear watched with dull beady brown eyes but did not come closer. Gavin Earl observed the scene coolly but made no move.

I tossed Vivienne's fox blanket over her. She clawed at it as if it were alive.

"I am so hungry," she said. She bit down on the fur, stuffing it into her mouth, straining in a futile attempt to consume it.

Smoke Eel stepped on the back of her leg. Feeling herself pinned, she twisted. He hit her with the butt of his shotgun. Vivienne's head snapped back. She slumped, motionless.

While she remained unconscious, Pops jabbed his needle into the globe of muscle below her hip. Vivienne's breathing fell into a deep, regular rhythm, her ribcage pumping like an exhausted animal that's been chased through the woods. Her eyes shut. She might've been having nightmares. But this was real and not as easily dismissed as a dream.

"You hit my wife." Oscar was sitting up in the pebbles. "You goddamned Indian bastard, I'll see you hang. I'll have you gutted and your entrails fed to my dog."

Smoke Eel took his pencil and scribbled in his notebook. He turned it for me to read.

"Not your wife," I read aloud for everyone to hear.

"Of course she's my wife. I've known her twenty years, you heathen idiot," Oscar said.

Smoke Eel wrote another note.

"Your wife on the outside. Not your wife on the inside," I said.

"A possession," Evangeline said. "Like her dead talks, only Viv did not control this. It invaded her. As a medium she is sensitive to such entities. To powerful malignant forces too."

Smoke Eel scribbled furiously.

"This lady speaks the truth. The spirit in your wife is evil. We must not listen," I read the written words, and then added a few of my own. "It is like a sickness that comes on suddenly."

"A sickness? She's been infected by an entity that wants to scare us?" Oscar said.

"That's possible," I said.

Cassi bundled up the bruised and unconscious Vivienne. Claude lifted his mother.

"Claude, put her in bed." Oscar turned to his daughter. "Someone from the family has to stay behind. Do you understand me, Cassi? You will have to miss the hunt today, I'm afraid. Stay with her. Your mother needs you."

Cassi appeared torn between the responsibility of acting as the dutiful daughter and feeling crestfallen for being left out of the day's events.

"I will make certain she remains safe," she said, nodding.

"Good girl."

She began to shuffle away.

"We can postpone the hunt until tomorrow," I suggested. "Vivienne is obviously feeling unwell. She needs rest and the town doctor. The Beast isn't going anywhere."

"No." Oscar regained his footing and dusted himself off. "Viv will recover. The best thing we can do is continue with our plans. The entity wishes us to slow down because it is threatened. We will go forward. Get back on your horses. My wife is my business. The Beast is yours. Find it. Let's go! Go!"

Oscar looked like a man who had lost his fortune and been run down by a stagecoach in the same day. He left for the Gold Trail with Smoke Eel leading him along the road. On Claude's horse, Oscar placed one of Smoke Eel's pages with a note telling Claude to follow. It was late morning by the time we filed out of Nightfall Lodge. The sun was climbing, offering light but little warmth. I was the last in line. I heard the doors open behind me and turned in my saddle.

When Claude came outside he had blood on him. The sun found the red stripe.

He did not seem to care. His face was a mask, his eyes without pity.

Claude rode in another direction, driving his horse up through the high rocks.

There is more the hint of a killer in him, I thought. He'll get bloodier. He wants this.

I was right.

And I was wrong.

12
GOOD DRAW

The copper-painted signpost stuck up from the rockpile like a fat lightning rod. There was a big black bird on it, maybe a crow; but the bird flew off before I could identify it, but not before leaving behind a streak of lumpy white deposit in its place.

"Wu, is it the Chinese who believe bird droppings are an omen?" I asked.

"Yes, we most surely do," he said.

"And what do they predict?"

"Birds."

I nodded with a false solemnity. It was good to see Yong Wu joking. He had endured much sorrow in his young life, and his resiliency inspired me. I tended to explore my wounds, never letting them heal, as if they were an unmapped country and I their devoted cartographer.

"Here is our trail," Evangeline said. "Do you think we got a good draw?"

McTroy had the map spread across his pommel. His mouth was shut tight and his eyes were slits. He was pondering. He looked up at her. "I don't see how it matters. The railroad lies to the northeast, but we won't go that far. There's a creek runs through our zone. That's good. But the Beast might be anywhere out there. Standing behind one of them ponderosa pines or huddled in its hidey hole waiting for after dark. I asked around town. None of the Beast attacks came before the sun moved into the west. I'd say daylight's about as safe as it's gonna get. And make no mistake, the Beast will find us 'fore we find it. But that don't mean we can't look."

Wu was visibly relieved at this information. He had been swiveling around in his saddle all morning, trying to catch sight of a monster. Any monster. Judging by his sudden jolts, he'd seen a few suspicious blurs creeping among the tree shadows and gnarly, snow-mottled rocks.

"What do you think it is?" he asked McTroy.

"I don't have an opinion. Not yet. I haven't seen it. Or even dreamed about it, right, Doc?"

I ignored his provocation about my night wandering and what I saw standing on the ledge in the lodge window.

"Yet you believe it is nocturnal?" I asked.

"Night privileges the ambusher. Predators take every advantage afforded to them. That's true for the Beast. And it'll be true for our rivals when they come too."

"Earl might sabotage us?" I said. "I hadn't considered him a threat."

"Start considering. He'll do what it takes to grab the gold."

"It's quite a specimen, that bull. I'll admit I was stunned to discover it here," I said.

"So, you think the idol's the real McCoy?" The bounty man remained dubious.

"Possibly," I said. "Oscar picked a good story. It's difficult to prove true or false. He's drawn to beautiful and unusual things. Like Vivienne. I could see him paying top dollar for such an object. It would hold a strange attraction for him. Parting with the biblical idol would be a genuine sacrifice. To him it would be a prize worth risking one's life to win."

"I want it," Evangeline said. "I don't care if it's biblical, mythological, or what-have-you. I'm not very biblical in case you haven't noticed. We write our own stories. Nothing is true but that power makes it so. Give me my dreams over your realities. The past is a rotting corpse. It falls apart when examined and stinks to high heaven."

I was flabbergasted. "How can you say that nothing is true? I am by practice no churchgoer, no godly man in the eyes of any creed, nor do I claim myself to be a believer. Yet the study of Egyptology builds upon authenticity. History must be vigilant against lies. It records the truth. However faulty the results, the goal is noble. Lies corrupt knowledge! We must have facts!"

"But, Hardy, you mistake me for a fellow Egyptologist. I am an occultist. What others call fancy drives me more than universal truths taught to you by dusty old men in dustier old classrooms. I reject them and their chalky dullness. Facts are not all there is under the sun."

"You are comfortable living with lies?" I said.

"If they are better lies, then I will take them gladly."

"And give them," McTroy said, smiling. He slipped a

whiskey bottle from his saddlebag and pulled the cork with his teeth. He offered the bottle around, but no one took any. He swallowed several times as he tipped it back. "I like you, Miss E. Sure you won't enjoy a drink with me this glorious morning?"

"I'll drink when we have something to celebrate," Evangeline said. She pulled off her glove and crossed her heart with her gloveless finger. "I promise."

She put the glove on again.

"I celebrate the morning." McTroy opened his arms and filled his lungs deeply with fresh mountain air. He plugged the bottle back between his lips and suckled it like a baby. The glass flashed blue in the sun. Then he wiped his mouth with the back of his hand. He corked the whiskey and returned it to his bag. Cardinals flitted through the pine boughs. A snowy valley dived sharply away to our right. The sunny brightness hitting the snow brought stinging tears to my eyes. I tugged my bowler lower and tried to look for tracks on either side of the trail. But all the pocks in the snow appeared equally indecipherable to me. I was like an illiterate leafing his way through the Sunday New York Times. Study though I might, any clear meaning evaded me.

I tried to concentrate on riding.

"McTroy, what do you know of Gavin Earl's team?" Evangeline asked.

"Murderers and scum."

"Care to elaborate?" she said.

"Pops ran brothels in lumberjack camps up north. Kept his soiled doves tame by making them slaves to opium. Rides a medicine wagon these days with the Kid. The Kid does some trick shooting. They con the local rubes and move on. Dirty Dan the Mountain Man butchered two families in their cabins. I'll not speculate on what he did *before* he killed them."

"How do you know so much about these men?" Evangeline asked.

McTroy reached into his coat and pulled out folded papers. He handed them to Evangeline, who read them and then passed them on to me and Wu.

"I got bills on them," he continued. "They're wanted men. These are famous fellas. Even if we don't find the Beast, I plan on collecting some bounties."

"You have no bill for Gavin Earl," she said.

"He's too smart."

"Does Earl deserve a rope and a tree too?" she inquired.

"What Gavin Earl deserves is a-coming for him," McTroy said.

"What about the one who calls himself Billy the Kid?" I said. "There is no wanted poster for him either. Perhaps that's because Pat Garrett killed the young gun years ago."

"He looks like Billy to me," McTroy said, matter-of-factly.

"You've met Billy the Kid?" I asked.

"Once at Hargrove's Saloon, the night he shot Joe Grant. I didn't witness the fracas. But I saw Billy there. Played cards with him. That's what he looked like."

"And our Billy resembles the real Billy?" I said.

"Yep. He hasn't aged a day since."

"Why didn't you collect at Hargrove's if he was a wanted man?" Evangeline asked.

"He was wanted in New Mexico Territory. I worked

mainly in Arizona and Texas. He never robbed trains or coaches. Billy's a cattle rustler. I had no cause to tangle with him."

"But we can agree Billy is dead. Everybody knows that," I said.

"What everybody knows don't mean a thing to me, Doc. Hard enough to know what I know and not get confused by it. Billy looks pretty good for a dead man."

I considered Billy's recuperative powers.

"Billy was shot at the Starry Eyes yesterday. A flesh wound to the ear. Pops sewed him up and injected him with a solution from a little green bottle. I think it was not the first time Pops repaired him," I said. "He seems fit this morning."

"Maybe Pops sewed him up after Garrett plugged him too. He's juicing him with an elixir that keeps the Kid sleeping outside the pine box hotel." McTroy rubbed his rough chin and smiled. "I hope I look as lively when I'm a goner."

"As an Egyptologist I appreciate your desire to leave behind a handsome corpse."

"I'm just not leaving it today, Doc."

Wu cleared his throat.

"Miss Evangeline, what happened to Mrs Adderley? Was she under a witchcraft spell?" Wu's voice might have deepened in the last year, and he had certainly sprouted, but he was still a boy inside after all, and he sought certain assurances that might provide comfort.

"Vivienne is a medium who opens herself to the spirit world. That makes her vulnerable to spiritual assaults. And she confided in me that she sometimes suffers spells – not of a witching nature but neurotic fits caused by the fall that crippled her legs," Evangeline said.

"Where did she fall?" Wu asked, wide-eyed.

"It was here. In these mountains. She ended up in a gorge. It was lucky she did not die, from what she told me. Oscar rescued her from the ledge. He climbed down a rockslide at great personal risk to bring her to safety. It's one of the reasons she puts up with him. He is her savior."

"Those things she told us were pretty awful. 'You are all going to die,'" Wu said.

"Perhaps she means eventually. You're all *eventually* going to die. That sounds less ominous." I did what I could to mitigate his dread. But I failed to put a dent in my own unease.

"Whoa, Moonlight."

McTroy stopped his horse.

Where Jingle was a mostly white horse flecked with gray imperfections that made me like him for his irregularities – those dots and foggy freckles were quite mesmerizing if you tried to trace a pattern, a bit like looking for figures in the stars – McTroy's Moonlight was a pure white mustang. Smallish and incredibly strong for her size, she had legendary endurance and an intelligence that bettered many men. She was a good-luck talisman for McTroy. He placed her high among his most valued friends.

McTroy swung out of his saddle, taking his Marlin repeater from its scabbard. He levered the gun and scanned the landscape carefully, keeping his rifle stock against his cheek. When nothing emerged, he crouched and inspected the snow at the trail's edge.

I hopped down from Jingle and joined him.

"What do you see?" I said. "Is it evidence of our elusive Beast?"

McTroy pointed to a line of tracks angling into a patch of thicker woods. The prints were large: four oval toe impressions and a rear paw pad. Taken together they were wider across than my hand, which I spread on the icy ground for comparison. I brushed snow from my palm.

"Mountain lion," McTroy said. "Walking, not running." He gazed over his left shoulder. "We're not half a mile from the lodge."

"Interesting, if not relevant to our chase. The Beast walks on two legs, McTroy, not four. Why are we wasting time looking for cats?"

"Because I don't want to be hunted by two beasts."

"Fair enough." I started following the tracks. "But it does strike me as unlikely."

"Hold off," McTroy said.

I had my head down staring intently at the impressions. I glanced up and saw them continuing for several yards, heading between a half-dead spruce and pile of pink boulders.

I walked on, ignoring McTroy's command.

"Shouldn't there be nail prints on the toes? Are you sure it's a kitty? Cats have claws. I don't detect any claw marks in the snowpack," I said.

McTroy did not answer. I straightened up and turned to see if he was still behind me.

Quick as a thunderstorm bolt McTroy wrapped his fingers around my windpipe.

"You don't see the cat's claws," he said. "You *feel*

them. They hook you like steel. Snap! Your neck's broke! Cat drags you off by the face. When she drops you, maybe you're breathing." He shook his head. "Don't matter. Puss lies there licking in the grass. Pretty sunset colors hit the treetops. Birds start singing. You are praying to God please, let me please make it out of this here mess alive. But, sorry son, it's over. You're ending up a stinky cat shit in them red pine needles."

He released me. Gasping, I leaned against a tree trunk. My temples pounded with the sudden rush of blood. I saw stars and flashing inky blots. I was dizzy, my vision blurred.

McTroy said, "Learn to pay attention. When I say hold off – hold off."

"You choked me," I said.

"To improve your outlook," he said.

"You are a tonic against optimism," I rasped as I massaged my tender voice box.

"The cat hides its claws until it needs them. Remember that, Doc. These aren't the freshest prints I've seen, but they're new. A day at most," he said. "Eyes open now. You hear?"

I nodded, wanting to batter him with my walking stick.

Wu appeared between us. I motioned for the boy to follow McTroy as he shadowed the cougar's trail deeper into the woods. "Do as he says. Be careful," I told him. Wu fell in line behind McTroy, who held his rifle at his hip as he moved slowly toward the boulder pile.

"Are you recovered?" Evangeline said.

She was looking down on me from Neptune's back.

"I will be fit to walk again shortly." I leaned heavily

onto my cane. My head ached.

"He doesn't mean to hurt you. When he's been drinking he acts without thought."

"You shouldn't apologize for him."

"He wants to warn you of the danger. It's what he knows."

"It's what he is," I said. "I was being foolish, of course. But he needn't throttle me."

From the direction of the pink boulders I saw Wu running toward us.

"What is it?" Evangeline said.

"Come quick, McTroy found something. He said to leave the horses here."

We three traced our way back over the puma tracks to find McTroy.

He waited under a medium-sized tree in a small stand of aspens. The golden leaves lit a fiery wall against the slabs of tombstone grays and evergreens dominating the scenery.

It was snowing.

"How beautiful," Evangeline said. In her long black sheepskin coat, she whirled around like an artist's model populating a Christmas painting. Ever at home, whether navigating in the Gila Desert or the manmade canyons of Manhattan, the woman managed to thrive. I felt the thinness of my city wools and wished I fit in better into this rustic scene. But, alas, I did not.

"The cat went up this tree. See the scratch marks," McTroy said.

Our eyes followed the torn bark scraped orange as if a hatchet had been applied.

"How high did it climb?" she asked. Looking up, she

held her floppy-brimmed hat to keep it from falling off backwards; her hair spilled out like champagne.

"Can't tell without going the same way, but looky here. That's blood dripped onto this tree trunk. There's more spilled here and here on the ground. The trail leads toward Nightfall."

"Was the cougar injured?" I asked.

"That's the strangeness, Doc. I'm not sure who the injured party was here."

"Is there more than one party who's been up the aspen?"

McTroy indicated with his rifle the tracks going to and from the aspen in question.

I saw distinct boot prints. They led away from the tree. No paw prints followed. When I looked back at McTroy he had a black mark on his shirt.

"You've got dirt on you," I said.

He pulled out the material and stared down like he was locating a spider.

"I see nothing," he said.

I shrugged. He brushed at his chest anyway, and his hand came away blacker than his shirt had been. I chuckled. My head was ringing from his throttling me, and to be honest I was still fuming and glad to see him in such a messy state. For some reason, my heart was pounding. I was hearing echoes coming at me from far off, not from any one direction I could point to but from all over at once. McTroy didn't seem to hear them. Evangeline had her arm draped over Wu's shoulders and was lending him a spyglass to see the farthest whitest peaks to our north. I thought maybe the altitude was doing something to my ears. It sounded like voices talking low, like I was eavesdropping on a private party. One voice might've been Gustav's from the saloon. A second sounded like the old-timer Billy had gunned down. I even heard a laugh, very faint like it was down in a canyon somewhere, that I could've sworn was Amun Odji-Kek, the ancient sorcerer I had resurrected from the sands of Egypt and pursued in the sands of Mexico.

I tilted my head and tapped each side like I was shaking out water from a lake swim. My head was on a merry-go-round when I put it straight again. At least the echoes had stopped. But I felt a slight buzzing in my extremities as if weak electrical currents were passing through me. It wasn't entirely unpleasant. Closing my eyes, I mistook myself for old New Yorker Rom Hardy sipping spirits at the Delmonicos'. But when I opened my eyes I was under-dressed Rom whose hind end was going numb in the Sangre de Cristos. I pumped my legs to improve circulation as I studied the cat's blood on the tree. I don't know why I cared one whit if McTroy had black stains on him. He looked like an ink bottle exploded in his pocket and he'd wiped it with his fingers.

"You've got the filth on your hand now... but it's your concern," I said.

"Doc, I'm clean as an angel here. You feeling put together right?" McTroy said.

"I'm fine," I said. "Do you suppose this is the tree Claude climbed last night?"

He went walking around the aspen saying, "To the back side of the tree is clean rock shielded by the branches. It won't hold a print. Our man in boots goes up from there, I reckon. The cat pursues. Starting where you're at. Then the boot man shimmies down, or falls... these ridges here, that was a hard landing. He walks away in the snow." McTroy squatted and pointed inside a footprint. "He's got a pebble caught in his left boot. See how the heel marks look different. His trail lines straight up to the lodge. The blood drops are on the same side as Claude's cut arm. It must be Claude going home."

"Where goes our cat?" I looked around, spotting no more prints.

"She flees by the rocky path whence the boot man cometh. Or she disappears."

"Could she be up there now?" Wu asked, craning for a view of the highest branches.

"How'd he get down? Did he slide past her?" McTroy said. "I don't see it."

He tipped his hat back. He fished in his coat pocket for a piece of jerky. He handed one to Wu. Evangeline and I declined. He started chewing loudly and shaking his head.

"It's an enigma," I said.

McTroy tore a strip with his teeth. It dangled from his lip. "It was a good headscratcher until your dictionary word went and ruined it. Still... two go up the tree, only one comes–"

McTroy did not finish his sentence. The crack of a gunshot sliced the air. The piece of dried meat flew spinning from his mouth. He dropped to the snow – his lip bloodied. We lay flat.

"Are you hit?" I asked.

"No, bit my damn tongue. But he nipped my

venison, the bastard," he said.

A second shot knocked a chunk from the tree. Bark shreds ticked off my bowler hat.

"Crawl!" McTroy said. "Get behind the boulders. Fast now. Go!"

The third shot anticipated our move, chipping away rock and spraying Wu with dust. Wu froze, knitting his hands over his head. McTroy crabbed over the boy and dragged him along by his jacket collar. Evangeline made the slenderest target, but I put myself between the shooter and her prone body. We squirmed into the shelter together. No other shots were fired. We sat there getting covered by the snow and listening. Finally, McTroy made a scouting trip.

He came back.

"They're gone," he said.

13
LICORICE & KEROSENE

"What do we do now?" I asked.

"Ride back to the lodge and explain what happened," McTroy said.

"Explain it to whom?"

"Oscar, I guess. It's his venture, his property and rules."

"He won't be there. He's out hunting the Beast like we are," Evangeline said.

"He'll be there. Three shots blasted in quick succession. That's the signal for cornering the Beast. He'll think we hit lucky paydirt. We'll have to tell him we didn't find squat and that the Silvers were sniping at us. Maybe he'll get the law involved." McTroy headed through the aspens to where our horses were tied.

"Do you really think so?" I said.

"No," he said.

"But there is a sheriff in Raton? If we needed to call upon the law for our protection?"

"There's always a sheriff. Citizens like a sense of order and civil society. I doubt Oscar cares much for town laws. He's his own king up here on the mountaintop.

He thinks he is, anyhow. Probably owns the sheriff.
I expect any protection we have lies here with our
irons." McTroy jiggled the Marlin rifle and dropped a
hand to one of his two Colt Peacemakers.

I carried no irons as a matter of principle. I preferred
logic, science, and laws. In my ape-head walking stick
was a concealed blade for self-defense. I knew Wu
had his own pistol now, a short-barrel version of
McTroy's cavalry sidearm, which the boy wore tucked
into a blue sash around his waist. Evangeline chose
for herself a California-bought, shiny, hammerless
Smith & Wesson Safety .32, carrying the pearly toy-
size shooter in her pocket. "I have a new lemon
squeezer in case we find ourselves baking a cake,"
she'd said, patting her thigh. Her comment had stirred
me in confusing ways while also putting me in the
mood for sweet treats. Thusly, I was the only member
of our ragtag posse unencumbered by manufactured
firepower.

A thought suddenly entered my head.

"No one was hurt today. What crime did the Silvers
commit?"

"Endangering the public. Shooting at folks is
unlawful even in New Mexico Territory," McTroy said.

McTroy's reply assured me. I often wondered if there
truly were laws in the West, or if they were rumors
carried by strangers from town to town, like gossip,
and worth about as much.

"Do you know for certain they were the ones who
did it? The Silver team? I saw no shooter." Evangeline's
eyes glinted teasingly. "Might you have a prejudice
against them?"

She made an excellent point. This topic of the lack of ocular proof irked McTroy. His stride widened and he sighed. "No, I don't have evidence. But they're the likeliest," he said.

We walked in silence a few yards, everyone trying to think of a good reason for someone other than the Silvers to shoot jerky out of McTroy's mouth and bully us into a rockpile.

"You figure it was Billy who did the deed?" I started speculating. "He has a quick temper. He already shot one man dead in town. Recklessness is his trademark. He lacks restraint."

"Might be the Kid. That was accurate shooting, and I don't know if he's capable. Trick shooting and people shooting are different. If my chin came away, I would say it was the Kid."

Evangeline stopped walking. "If, as you say, Gavin Earl shot at us, then two teams are heading back – Oscar's team and us. The Silvers get extra time on the mountain working their way closer to the Beast. That's exactly what they want. Why stand around for hours at the lodge complaining about them?" she said. "Instead, let's stay out here and keep to our plan. Search for signs of unusual activity. Build a hunter's blind. Lay bait... whatever. If we go now, treachery wins. I vote for not returning."

An excellent point countering McTroy's suggestion, I thought.

"Oscar should know who he invited to his mountain. If he wants, he can send Gavin's team home on the next train. This whole contest is a bad idea. Somebody's going to get killed," McTroy said, walking on.

We were almost back to where we left the horses when he broke into a run.

"Oh, shit. Them sons of bitches!" he shouted.

Wu went after him. His young legs surpassed his bounty-hunting mentor.

Evangeline had the disadvantage of her long skirts and tight coat, and I... well, I am not made for speed. I took her hand and together we climbed the final hill to the Copper Trail. When we arrived, red-faced and out of breath, Wu had his hat off and crumpled in his hand. He threw it down and stomped it into the ground. Tears brimmed in his eyes.

"They stole Magpie," Wu said. "All our horses... gone. I tied them to this spruce with the big gap in the branches. There's a bird's nest inside. I saw it when I put the rope around."

"Well, they're gone now," I said. "The horses, not the birds."

Wu looked in the gap and said the birds were gone too. This made him madder still.

"Everything's gone!" Wu threw fistfuls of crusty snow as far as he could into the woods just to watch them hit the trees and break apart. He grunted as he reached back and whipped his arm forward. His black hair fell into his eyes and his cheeks grew red and shiny as apples.

"Wu, we will get them back," Evangeline said.

"What if they kill them?"

"There's no reason to kill good horses. You know that," Evangeline said, combing his hair back from his face. Wu had little he could call his own. Losing anything pained him. I lifted his hat from the trail of dead needles, re-shaped it, and handed it to him. He put it on.

McTroy said, "We can follow them. Looks like they're keeping to the trail. One man snuck up alone. He's walking them in a line. Can't be the fat one with the bear. Dirty Dan had snowshoes on. If he smelled like bear, Moonlight would kick him in the equipment straight off. Pops isn't the creeping type. Besides he's too bow-legged to match these boots. Likely it was the Kid or Gavin. I'd put money on Gavin being the rifleman by the cat-scratched tree and the Kid swiping our ponies. They put thought into this. Jerking us around like dogs on a chain."

We walked in the snow following the hoofprints, but horses and people don't walk the same and our boots were wet and sliding on the round patches of ice or churning in the ankle-deep slush. The sun's glare cut through the pine tops and melted the horse tracks. We had a slippery muddy slog ahead. Walking was an effort. As the crow flies we were less than half a mile from Nightfall, but the Copper Trail meandered through the woods like a lazy prairie stream. We faced more than double that distance by backtracking. It was uphill too. I felt my legs burning. I was thirsty but my canteen was still attached to Jingle. Despite the cool breezy air I was working up a sweat. I wiped my brow with my sleeve, turning it dark. Then heavy clouds hid the sun like it was caught in a bag, but I was glad for the dimness. My hard squint loosened.

McTroy had grown silent and his jaws twitched every few steps like he was trying to crush a stone between his molars. He tipped his Marlin back against his shoulder, pointing the rifle at the sky with his hand still inside the lever. He retrieved another jerky strip from his pocket to replace the one he'd lost in the sniping incident. He offered it around again. This time Wu and Evangeline joined him. I was too thirsty to eat salted meat. I carried my pipe and tobacco pouch on me. I filled my bowl and had a smoke. I have found throughout life that the inability to quench one appetite is often soothed by indulgence in another. I expelled a sizable fog in my wake. Wu and Evangeline moved to the other side of the trail to avoid my pungent airy residues. McTroy maintained his pace, chewing and striding, checking our rear for creepers.

Smoking stimulates me; I quickly took over the lead. "They might just leave our horses someplace tied off," I said, encouragingly.

"If they're smart they would," McTroy said.

I heard my foot crunching snow before it touched the ground, then realized it wasn't *my* boot making the noise.

"Hold it right there, Doc Hardy, or your next step will be your last."

It was Billy. He'd leaned out of the pines and raised his gun hand, so I was staring down his Colt Thunderer, and it appeared like a war cannon. He was near enough I saw the inner details of the oiled barrel – a big steel zero – and imagined a bullet loaded snugly in its chamber. He'd shaken snow loose from the boughs when he shoved off his tree and a measure of white landed upon on his stooped shoulders and topped the Thunderer like sugar icing.

I puffed my pipe. I had nowhere to go where his

shot wouldn't get there first.

"What is your intention, Kid?" I asked, though his intention seemed rather clear.

"I aim to plug your hole with lead."

"Ah, you say you are no fan of discussion. Yet you choose to engage me in conversation rather than simply shooting me straight away. That is contradictory." I wagged a finger at my would-be assassin, hoping to distract him. "Perhaps you actually wish to talk with me, but you lack a strategy for initiating encounters which are not predicated on violence and the establishment of your dominating nature. Your gun is a crude tool for opening up a dialogue with those whom you find interesting and yet intellectually intimidating. Is this behavior sounding a bit familiar, Billy? Come now. Surely you see the irony of what's happening here."

Billy squirted tobacco juice on both of my boots. "Shee-it!" he cried. "You never quit talking. I swear it's a disease. You got it worse than ladies do when it's morning and you already paid and there's nothing left that hasn't been done twice or three times from the night before and your head hurts, but *here, have some more* they say as they dump words on you so you're a drowning man and their mouth is an endless bucket... No offense, Miss." He inclined his head in sincere apology.

"Oh, none taken," Evangeline said.

Well, I was taking some offense. It is rude to threaten people with murder and to compare a man or a woman to a bucket, especially if you are not related to them by blood. I did not think Billy's effrontery needed to be discussed in the moment, however, the timing being poor.

I implied my objection with stern silence.

"Billy, where are our horses?" McTroy asked.

"Horses?" he said, sneering. "Did you lose yours, pard?" He laughed and his boyish features pushed out like a fat man's belly. "Cuz I seen some pretty nice horses yonder in a swale *might* be yours. You can't make 'em out from here. They looked fine, those horses did. Heehee."

"I'm not your pard, Billy. But I am partial to the windy doc here. We got history in common, like you and Pat Garrett."

"Don't say that bastard's name. Just hearing it makes me mighty sore."

Billy shifted his gun to the bounty man. His jaw jutted forward, causing his neck cords to flare like fish gills. He was rattled and squirming in place as if he was getting ready to fly to pieces and pepper us with human shrapnel. The Kid came farther into the middle of the trail. His boots sucked up and down in the mud. He forked his legs far apart to keep from slipping.

"He's the man who popped your cork, ain't he?" McTroy said. "Fort Sumner as I recall."

"Goddamn, mister. Pat Garrett hijacks his friends in the dark. Do you sanction that?"

"Sounds a mite frosty for a friend," McTroy admitted.

"That's what I'm saying. It's like a cheat. Like tricking a person, shamming them when they don't expect it from you. It's a greasy way to lose a companion, I'll tell you. He gets hisself famous for doing a thing that should make people spit when they hear his name.

Pat Garrett shot Billy the Kid! Well la-di-da... it's Billy the Kid's name that sparks folks' eyes and lights their dreams. That's what legends do. Not backstabbing like barkeep turned turd-weasel Pat Garrett."

"Billy... Billy. Why are you listening to Rex? He's getting you riled up so you forget your purpose. Put your pistol back on the doctor. Let me talk with my friend." Gavin Earl approached from a blind bend in the trail. Dirty Dan and the grizzly bear were right there with him, side by side. I never knew bears could be so quiet. Dirty led a mule loaded with bear traps, extra snowshoes, and a Winchester rifle. Pops held back the farthest as if he didn't mean to mix with violent men but was only present to watch them do things to each other for his own jolly amusement. He was draining a wine sack into his gullet. He capped it and threw the sack high overhead to McTroy who caught it one-handed, drank, and spat out what he had in his mouth.

"Tastes like licorice and kerosene," McTroy said, spitting again.

"I make it myself," Pops said. "It's herbals and laudanum. I add alcohol for a kick."

McTroy motioned to pass the refreshment to Earl.

"Give it to Evangeline and your Chinese," Earl said. "It'll soothe their nerves."

They politely declined his offer.

"Dr Hardy, you want a taste, don't you?" Earl asked questions in a way that made you want to answer in the affirmative, as if he were a teacher helping you and yet marking grades.

"I am tired enough from walking," I said. "Laudanum might make me fall sleep."

"You're gonna sleep," Billy said. He was back to hating me for no reason.

"What do we have here, Gavin? You a horse thief now?" McTroy asked.

Gavin Earl smiled. He had a gold tooth like McTroy, only his was on the other side. "I came here for the bounty of riches, Rex. Same as you... the very same as you..."

"Same as all of us," Evangeline said. She trudged up through the gray slop and Billy was thinking of training his pistol on her, but Earl waved him off. "My skirts are soaked, and my feet are freezing. Are you playing games, Mr Earl? Or are you here to do business?"

"Can't I have it both ways?"

"Why don't we work together?" Evangeline asked. "The eight of us can catch this Beast and take Oscar's bull. He's the one pitting us against each other. It doesn't have to be that way."

"I don't like to share, Miss Waterston. My nature is selfish, greedy, and hard." He was proud of who he was. That was plain. He said evil things about himself like it was bragging.

"He's never liked having partners," McTroy said.

Gavin Earl smiled and nodded.

It was chills I felt looking at him. He was cold bathwater on a tin-skied January morning.

"Go and stand back where you were, Evangeline," Earl said.

"I will go when I am finished."

"You are finished."

"I do not need your permission to talk."

"Billy," Gavin said, "If she doesn't back up, shoot the Chinese."

Evangeline walked backward without taking her eyes off Earl.

"The lady cooperates," he said after she returned to her spot.

"What do you want, Gavin?" McTroy asked. "Is it that you'd like us off the mountain?"

Earl considered the question. Finally, he said, "I don't know if leaving solves anything. Not between you and me. It puts things off into the future. I've had you in my future for too long, Rex. I'd like you only in my past." That black goatskin glove moved down to his holster.

"I want to kill that talker in the derby first," Billy the Kid said.

"Drop the rifle, Rex," Earl said.

McTroy didn't move. The rifle was almost parallel to the ground. He'd levered it once, back when we were only worried about mountain lions. His finger rested on the trigger. Dirty Dan's bear wandered forward with his head swaying and his tongue poking out like it didn't fit in his mouth. His ears were golden and soft-looking. The hairs shivered in the breeze like tufts of brown cotton. He made a hoarse huffing sound as he came toward me. It was almost friendly. He yawned, and I saw teeth, orange and crooked. His tongue was like a tenderloin of mottled beef.

The bear stopped and sat down with a heavy sigh.

"Now the bear's in my way!" Billy said. "Tell your bear to move, Dirty."

"Bears don't always listen," Dirty Dan said. He

unhooked a tomahawk from his furs. McTroy threw the wine sack to Pops. Billy almost fired at him when he did that. He kept switching his gun from McTroy to me. I was mostly hidden by the bear though.

That was when the whistle started. It made my skin go bumpy. The bear picked up his head and sniffed the breeze. His skin was twitching like he had flies on him, but it was too late for flies. The whistle climbed higher, and Billy stuck a pinky in his ear. Pops looked around, high up in the pines because it sounded like a high-up sound, floating over us, flying tree to tree.

"That's what we should be chasing," Evangeline said. "Not a grudge between you two."

"I'm dropping the rifle," McTroy said. "We're going home."

"Go on then," Earl said.

When he talked I felt a cold flood come rushing down the Copper Trail. I was caught in the current but couldn't see a thing. It pulled at me like something big I couldn't escape. Like I was pinched in machinery that was chewing me up and there was no thinking being behind it.

McTroy chucked his rifle in the snow.

Before it hit the ground, Billy, who was aiming at me, pulled his trigger.

The bullet slapped into the bear. Billy yelled, "Goddamn!" The bear sat up and roared.

McTroy pulled his Peacemakers out of their leathers. They were barking fire.

He hit Billy twice in the center of his body. The fourth shot tagged him above his right eyebrow, putting him down. McTroy's third shot missed Gavin Earl.

Earl fired twice so quickly that it made one sound.

McTroy twisted like his name had been called from behind him in the woods. I thought maybe somebody was coming to save us. But no one was. Blood blossomed on McTroy's chest. It was right where I'd seen the black mark from before, the same dirty shape. Only now the mark was red. McTroy looked surprised. His Peacemakers pointed at the ground. He dropped them. Then following his guns, he fell softly on the dry pine needles. I hoped he might roll away and come up shooting.

But he didn't.

McTroy didn't move at all after that.

14
EVENTS TEND TOWARDS THE PECULIAR

Evangeline saved Yong Wu's life. I wish I had, but I was too startled by McTroy falling like he did, the unbeatable man beaten, and by all appearances dying for the second time since we'd met. My premonition of the black marks on his body unsettled me. They were coincidental, I tried to convince myself – after all, nothing had happened to his hand. I did not want the responsibility that went with knowing events before they occurred, particularly those of the mortally dangerous and peculiar varieties. I had precious little time to consider the scope of these recent developments. The disgruntled grizzly bear in front of me took up most of my attention. He'd been eyeballing me like I was the one who'd shot him. Might I convince him otherwise? He'd moved from sitting to standing, then dancing a slow jig, pedaling his front legs like he wanted to box me, or maybe he'd just grab my head and eat it. I'm glad Evangeline was there.

Wu's hand dipped to his blue sash and drew out his Colt pistol.

Earl might've killed him if the smartest, bravest

woman I've had the privilege to know didn't manage to block his target and twist the gun from Wu's hand simultaneously. She held onto Wu's wrist. He was crying hot tears and thirsting for quick revenge. She saved him from himself. He didn't know better. In the moment, he didn't care.

Earl took the gun from Evangeline.

"She saved your life, boy," he said.

"Rex wouldn't want you to die on his account," she said to Wu. "It's of no use."

Yong Wu sat on the ground, hugging his knees. He turned his face away from the bloody spectacle and stared into the pines, blinking away tears.

Evangeline's talking this way made the fact sink in that McTroy wasn't speaking for himself. Where Wu raged with emotions, I was as numb as the mountain. I couldn't accept that Rex McTroy might die. Or that we might soon follow him. We searched a mountain for a Beast and found our gravest threat in other men. Heroes made no difference. McTroy lost.

But was Rex McTroy dead?

Earl, thinking along similar lines, sought an expert's opinion.

"Pops," he said. "Check him." Earl hadn't put his gun away.

Pops waddled up with his Gladstone bag in hand. He must've stashed it around the bend. Given the present company, he figured somebody here would need doctoring. Walking past Billy, he glanced at the outlaw's fatal wounds. "The Kid's going to hate that hole in his head."

There's an odd complaint, I thought. Appearances

were the least of the Kid's problems.

"Do Rex first," Earl said. "Billy can wait."

Earl's order confused me. I couldn't imagine what difference it was going to make. These two patients were beyond any help but the miraculous kind. Dead is dead. Well, usually it is. It is true that I had encountered a few notable exceptions: revivified ancient mummies, Chinese vampires, and ghouls. None were strictly alive. But I'd witnessed Billy and McTroy cut down with my own eyes. I saw no supernatural factors in the vicinity that would change these facts.

Then I recalled the words Evangeline had said to me.

Facts are not all there is under the sun.

"What about my bear?" Dirty Dan said. "Puddin's suffering terrible. He ain't himself."

Puddin' groaned. Dirty called out, "Oh, my poor boy!"

The bear staggered to him for a comforting hug.

"I am no animal doctor," Pops answered. "You treat him, mountain man."

The fur-suited tracker mumbled in soothing tones to his ursine companion who seemed bored but kept contorting to bite at the new hole in his backside. Dirty Dan assessed the damage.

"Aw, it's only puckered under the skin," Dirty said, cheered by what he'd seen.

I don't know if he was directing his diagnosis to Pops or to Puddin'. But Dirty Dan snatched a handle of big ole bear flesh, choked up on his tomahawk neck, and used the blade to slice an exit for the spent slug. It squirted into Dirty Dan's fingers. He held it aloft like it was a gold nugget. "Hoorah! The worst's over now, Puddin'. You're good as new and pretty as a picture!" Dan rubbed his grinning, moony face in the bear's pot belly. The bear stood staring off to the side like he was shy about public displays of affection. His rear continued to bleed but not as badly as you might think. Then he settled in for a snooze, his chin propped on a boulder.

Pops kneeled at McTroy's side.

McTroy had an arm flung over his face as if he were napping. His motionless body lay twisted away from the medical man.

"Are you going to help him?" I asked.

"Some might call it help. Others would not." Pops grinned at me.

The latch on Pops' Gladstone was broken. The bag yawned when he placed it on the ground. I caught a whiff of menthol and… mescal? Yes, Doc Spooner collared a demijohn with a worm floating in it. I felt a certain well-earned queasiness around Mexican worms. The surgeon guzzled the straw-colored spirit, dribbling some off his chin into the overstuffed bag. He saw me watching in horror, winked, and – tapping the cork home with his palm – stowed it away. Out came a syringe with a glass barrel the same circumference as a shot glass. Clutched in his other fist, Pops had a bottle from his patent line of nostrums, liniments, and elixirs. It was a bright green glass to catch the customer's eye, or so I thought. But when Pops filled the syringe, I noticed the contents provided the glow – an eerie hue – akin to foxfire or the absinthe I'd seen on a bar shelf in New Orleans.

"Wait, Pops," Earl said.

He trained his gun on McTroy. He toed McTroy's arm away from his face, and then used his boot to roll the bounty man flat onto his back, wary that my friend was playing possum. I wished that he were, but his color was not that of a living man.

McTroy's eyes stayed closed; his mouth fell open. Snowflakes drifted in.

Pops touched my friend's neck. "He's not dead yet. But the reaper isn't far off, if you want me to let him bleed. I never used it on a live one before. The results are unpredictable."

"Will it bring him around?" Earl asked.

"I can guarantee that," Pops said. "It'll make a skeleton dance."

"And he'll feel pain?"

"Oh, yes. He's fresh, and his nerves are full of juice."

"Then stick him," Earl said.

Pops drove the nail-like needle into the base of McTroy's neck, towards his brain. He depressed the plunger and the thick luminescent liquid disappeared into McTroy.

"What are you doing?" Evangeline shouted. "Leave him alone!"

The men ignored her protests.

"Let me dig that bullet out of him while he's finding his way back to us." Pops dropped the syringe in his bag and rummaged until he found his forceps. Turning to McTroy, he poked his finger three knuckles deep into the bloody chest wound. "I can feel it. Your first shot missed?" Pops squinted at Earl.

"It drifted," Earl said.

The slanting snow fell faster as the wind picked

up. I buttoned my overcoat to the neck. I gripped my walking stick so hard I worried I might twist the ape's head off. If I charged these outlaws they would kill me. What would happen then with Evangeline and Wu?

Pops withdrew his red finger and went exploring with his forceps. His eyes were like a pair of glass balls dabbed with wet blue paint and a stroke of clear varnish. His pupils gaped: two snake holes. I wondered if I watched too long, would I see something cold-blooded slither out? These men were something south of human. I hated them.

McTroy's body convulsed.

"Damn it," Pops said. He backed out the forceps and tossed them bloody into his bag. "Mr Earl, hold his shoulders down, please."

Earl reluctantly pinned McTroy to the ground. Pops dumped his bag on the mud trail. He picked through the instruments – heavy scissors, pincers, a curved blade (rusted) that could only be called a scythe, and a saw! – until he found what he was looking for. It was like a long soda fountain spoon with a hook on the end instead of a scoop.

"Keep him from bucking," Pops said to Earl.

He began to probe the bullet wound in earnest. His tongue poked out of the corner of his mouth as he concentrated. Pops worked that fountain spoon like he was going for the last sweet drop of strawberry syrup at the bottom of his dish.

I turned grayer than the slush I stood in. The world grew watery as my vision darkened.

"Hardy, you are fainting," Evangeline said.

She came to me through the blurry periphery.

"We cannot let them defile him," I said. "But we are at their mercy."

"He'd better not puke. I hate the smell of a stomach turned out," Earl said.

Evangeline gathered snow, applying it to my forehead. "At the mercy of men is where I have lived my life," she said. "We watch and we remember. Our chance will come."

She loosened my collar and tried to get me to sit on a stump until the dizziness passed. But I would not budge. I feared I would black out if I tried to walk anywhere, only to awake to Pops poking his filthy fingers and tools into me. The coldness of the snow refreshed me. I cupped some in my mouth and sucked it.

"You have your color back," Evangeline said.

"If they plan to murder us, you will squeeze the lemon," I whispered.

She nodded and pushed her thigh into mine, so I felt the impression of her holster.

"Wu needs to run. He's better off out there, even if there is a Beast loose," I said.

"I'll help him."

"We will both help him," I said.

Evangeline looked tired. A smear of grime made a crescent on her cheek. I wiped it away. I touched my head to hers. "Rex is gone. But he rides still. He follows the sun."

She nodded again.

"They may desecrate his body, but they cannot soil the man's soul," I added.

"Goddamn! Get off me, you pop-eyed sawbones! I will chew your liver!"

McTroy, it seemed, lived.

I have never been gladder to hear another man's voice. But I feared this outburst might be a final flourish of activity before the inevitable end. He looked so awfully dead.

He punched Pops squarely on the jaw. Teeth snapped together; some broke. The surgeon grabbed up his bone saw from the pile of torture devices. He brandished it, but he was seeing stars, his eyes rolling in his head like spinning marbles. He tested his jaws to verify that they still matched up when he shut his mouth. Then his rear end dropped hard in the pine-needled mud.

Gavin Earl cocked his pistol, pressing the gun to McTroy's temple. "Welcome back, Rex. Now throw another punch. Go on, boss. Try me. I will empty your pig skull where you sit."

McTroy stared at his chest wound. "It burns. What did you do? Plug a chili in there?"

"Pops, will a knock keep the stuff from working?" Earl asked.

"No. It's a mighty powerful concoction."

Earl thumped McTroy on the top of his head with his pistol. McTroy lay back where he had been, dazed and muttering. The wound in his chest didn't bleed anymore, as if the elixir had stoppered the leak. Earl forced his boot heel under McTroy's chin. "It's Sully's Fork all over again," he said. "Only the boot is on the other foot. Or rather, *my* boot is on *your* throat. How does that feel, partner?"

McTroy sputtered indecipherable curses and clawed through the slush and mud until his fingers scraped against unforgiving rock. He grabbed Earl's calf, trying to push the weight off. For a mortally wounded man, he was fighting and full of vinegar.

Earl leaned on him. "Fair's fair," he said. "I want you haunted, Rex. I like you weak."

"I'll never be as weak as you," McTroy said. "You should've stayed at Sully's Fork where I left you."

"And you should've shot me in the head if you wanted me dead," Earl said.

McTroy reached up higher and dug his fingers into Earl's knee.

Earl cried out. He shot McTroy between the knuckles. McTroy screamed. Earl hopped off his neck, springing back quickly as a smile carved his handsome face into a hideous mask of hatred. McTroy rolled and cradled his hand against his bloody shirt. It sprayed the snow red. When he put it up to his face I saw through the hole. He tried to make a fist. And couldn't. More blood.

"I'm not going to kill you. Hell, I don't know if I could with Pops' green concoction zipping through your veins. It's better this way." Earl kicked him in the stomach. "Biblical."

"A hand for a hand," Dirty Dan said, snickering.

"That's right," Earl said. He turned toward Wu. "Let that be a lesson to you, boy. Your champion is a beaten man. McTroy thought he was better than me. He thought I would disappear because he knocked me down, ruined my shooting hand, and rubbed my face in the damned dirt. Over a bag of bounty money! He hurt me, boy. But I am back. Oh, yes I *am*!"

He kicked McTroy again and again. So wild was his thrashing that when his hat fell off, he didn't even notice. He gleamed with sweat. He tore a seam of his elegant sheepskin coat. He stomped on McTroy's legs and pummeled his ribs with unremitting blows. Too many for me to count. McTroy sighed and moaned like an old man on his death bed.

No one stopped the beating.

I could not judge how long it took. The sky, the ground, and the trees – all were painted the same sickly shade of gray. What could we do but watch? I feared any intervention would only draw more wrath and get us all killed. This poison had brewed a long while. Finally, Gavin Earl was out of breath. Panting, he suddenly looked at us as if we'd caught him rolling in the hay with a corpse. He smiled sheepishly, combing his gloved fingers through his hair. He found his hat in the snow. Putting it on, he tipped it to Evangeline.

"Miss," he said. "Good afternoon."

"Your horses are in the draw up the hill," Pops said, taking a friendly tone.

Dirty Dan hoisted Billy under his arm. He tossed the body over the mule. Pops brushed Billy's long oily locks, jabbing the needle in a gap above his spine, filling his skull with green elixir. Billy looked deader than any man I ever saw. Pops petted him. "Wild boys never learn."

"Storm's coming," Dirty Dan said, talking to himself the way hermits do. "Big one. I can smell it. The Beast wants a full belly 'fore the snow's too deep." Puddin' looked at the sky with his little eyes when he said that. Then he followed him. Snowflakes swirled on the Copper Trail. Any signs of the outlaws soon vanished. The sky darkened. The pines closed on us like a tunnel.

15
WOUND LICKIN'

We were alone with McTroy. Illness and injury can bring people closer together. But more often it raises a barrier, a fence you might see over but cannot cross. Pain is a country with a distant shore. You have heard of it, you have partaken of its goods, and even visited its coastal cities, but it's likely you have never traveled far inland and made it your home. Now your friend lives there.

I asked Wu to get our horses. He seemed relieved to go. The sight of the bounty man was pitiful indeed. Seeing him in his current condition could not help but mar whatever heroic thoughts you might have had about his character prior to the beating. Rex McTroy looked like a squashed bug. He seemed flat, partly embedded in the earth.

Snow continued to bury us.

Kneeling on the ground, I put McTroy's hat back on him, if only to keep the snow off his face. He gazed at me with half-lidded eyes as if he were passing-out drunk. He was breathing. He was alive at least. If I did not know better I would've guessed he was anesthetized by sleep, caught in an in-between land of waking yet still dreaming, trapped in that frightful nightmare place he could not escape. I lifted his coat and touched him.

"His ribs, I think, are broken."

He groaned, and I ceased my examination.

"They feel like a bag of snapped sticks. Miraculously, his hand has stopped bleeding. The bullet traveled out the wrist. See here?"

Evangeline nodded. "What about his chest wound? Let's have a look."

I carefully unbuttoned his shirt, peeling away the sticky blood-soaked material which had already begun to stiffen. There was a hole between his nipple and collarbone.

"Amazing," I said. "It appears to have sealed itself. There is a pink cork made of what appears to be healthy skin." I met Evangeline's eyes. "Are you familiar with this sorcery?"

"This is not witchcraft." She shook her head. "I don't know what this is. Pops doesn't seem capable of devising a method of flesh rejuvenation. It must be something he stumbled on."

"Or he stole it," I said.

McTroy mumbled unintelligibly.

"We will get you back to the lodge, friend," I said. "Sooner rather than later."

"Blllllaaa…"

"Don't try to talk. You have been severely beaten. You have also been shot. Twice."

"Daahaa…"

Wu emerged from the bend in the trail. He was riding Magpie. The other horses were in line behind him. It was encouraging to see their heads nodding through the white obscurity.

"Good job, Yong Wu!" I cupped McTroy's shoulder. "I am going to sit you up."

"Blaaa," McTroy said. His face was swollen. His lips plumped like two blood sausages.

"Evangeline, please take his other side. We will get him half way up, and then we will try to stand him on his feet. Move on my count of three. One... two... three!"

We bent McTroy into a sitting position. He hissed through clenched teeth.

"Blaaadaah," he grunted.

With his good hand he latched onto my coat collar and shook me.

"Do you think he might be trying to tell us something?" Evangeline said.

"He is delirious from being killed, brought back, and nearly killed again. His head is swimming with an unknown poison devised by a drug-addled drunkard and snake oil charlatan." I tried to pry his fingers loose. "I do not think he's coherent. This is purely a defensive reaction. It's natural. Like a pond turtle pulling his head inside his shell."

McTroy growled at me.

"Give me back my collar so I can help you," I said.

Wu jumped down from his saddle and joined us. We were variously standing, kneeling, and sitting in an oval of bloody snow. It smelled like the floor of a butcher's shop. The wind blasted hard little ice pellets against our bare skin. Although it was only afternoon, the sunlight faltered. Heavy clouds made the hour feel later than it was. It was the picture of bleakness. Time on a mountain was as hard to figure out as predicting the weather, or so I was learning.

When Wu was close enough, McTroy let go of me and seized him.

"At last! Oh now, release him! It's only Wu. You are making this so very hard for us."

McTroy's behavior was that of a madman. Lunging and grabbing. Spit-drooling. Unable to capture his thoughts in words. Who knew if Pops' elixir had irrevocably harmed his mental faculties? He had the strength of the mad as well. Wu was wincing under the power of his grip.

"Blaaa." McTroy's tongue clicked in his mouth. He gasped in frustration.

"He is saying something," Evangeline said. "I am convinced of it."

"You must calm yourself. We cannot understand you," I said to him. "Relax. Breathe."

I gave him an example of breathing. "In and out, you see? Smoooooothly…"

It must have been a scary thing for a boy to do, but Wu leaned in toward McTroy's battered, lumpen face. His de facto guardian pulled him nearer still and whispered urgently in his ear. Wu looked at first alarmed, then confused, and finally, absolutely terrified.

"He is saying 'blood,'" Wu informed us.

McTroy nodded vigorously, one red eye bulging. He tugged at Wu, bringing him in again.

The boy listened.

"Blood… bings? Brings! Blood… brings… blood brings beast," Wu said.

"My God," Evangeline said. "He's warning us. We haven't been paying attention. The Beast might've crept right up to us. Would we have even noticed?"

I quickly scanned the woods. What did I see? Virtually nothing. The shapes of trees. Shadows underneath them growing from the ground and filling the gaps like a black mist. The pale screen of snow falling, falling, quiet as feathers. I saw no living thing in the open except us.

"We must go at once," I said.

"Yeaaasss," McTroy said. "Blaaadaa. Beeessst..."

It took the three of us, and the valiant effort of McTroy, to hoist him into his saddle. He fell against Moonlight's neck, hugging her as tightly as a sailor holds the last floating beam of his ship in rough seas. We rode four across on the trail. Our horses' flanks nearly touching. McTroy bookended by Wu and me in case he began to slide off his horse. He seemed to have lost consciousness. Yet he and Moonlight appeared as one. McTroy was able to sleep in the saddle. He'd told me once that, if he could choose, he would die there. I only hoped today was not the day.

"We are not far from Nightfall," Evangeline said.

It was true of both our lodging place and the approaching hour.

I ducked under snow-laden branches sagging near the trail edge. To my right lay dense forest. To the left: a steeper downward slope of thinning timber, like a hound sleeping with its mangy, narrow hindquarters jutting into the air.

"I am sure we will make it," I said.

I was not sure at all.

Something was following us. I did not see it. But I felt it there. Watching. Stealthy. Keeping pace with our horses. Evangeline was feeling the same thing. She kept looking back.

"We've come a long way," she said. "The trail will join the road shortly."

"I hope so," Wu said.

"Do I smell the lodge's chimneys? The scent of roasted meats and hot cocoa?"

I injected this thought hoping it would bolster spirits. Nothing ahead of us looked remotely different than what we had already passed. The repetitiveness of the landscape was hypnotic. Disorienting. I understood now the danger of getting lost in these exotic high-altitude wilds. Never to return. To wander off the map was my sudden strong desire. I did not know why, or from where the strange temptation originated. I made a conscious effort to resist. The twilit hour stripped the stark geography of its colorful morning dress. We traveled among sticks and stones enrobed in white like minor gods awaiting a sacrifice. Our view down the mountainside was a pencil sketch of smooth mounds and sprigs of gnarly scrub; the rest might have been clouds.

It all seemed unreal, a fairytale scene where a wizard might appear in conversation with a winter ice queen or a mountain giant. Skinny evergreens slouched like disappointed elves. Everything lulled you as it lured you inward. *Go deeper*, it said. *Nothing too awfully bad can happen here. It's make-believe after all.* The horses' hoofs struck muffled drumbeats on the path. Even the majesty of the mountains – emerging between gusts – became no more than a diversion. Crags, cliffs, and walls of volcanic stone – along these precipices my mind strayed like a fool. With your senses compromised (I could smell nothing, for example), you become smaller. You think (wrongly) that you go unnoticed. This is the dullness that kills the deer chewing on a snippet of grass. The lion or the wolf springs. The deer dies. Bits of limp weed stuck greenly in its teeth…

Prey cannot afford daydreams.

I forced myself into the moment. Must keep my mind alert! I set my spine straight and pulled icy air into my lungs until they throbbed. I held it. Letting it go slowly.

I felt those watchful forest eyes. They made my heart skip.

Death. Was it death lurking in some terrible shape?

The horses kicked up little puffs of snow. Their manes whitened and became hard as carousel horses. It was difficult to lift my eyes without my lashes freezing together, locked in tiny crystal balls; our mouths steamed, no different than the animal engines we rode upon.

I turned around quickly.

Nothing.

But I sensed a presence out there. Stalking us. Whatever it was, the weather proved no obstacle for it. This thing lived in the weather. Used it. We were being hunted by a killer native to this place, at home in this harsh terrain.

"Do you see that?" Wu asked. "Look! There in the woods!"

We pulled up on our horses. Moonlight stopped on her own. McTroy slumped, oblivious.

A large form descended darkly through the timber.

"I make out no details," I said. My curiosity outran my fear.

"It is very tall," Wu said. "Long steps. Moving rapidly. What should we do?"

"Hold steady," I said. "Perhaps it will pass in front of us. Whatever it is…"

Evangeline wrestled with her skirts. Out came the silver pistol. She aimed it through the trees and pulled the trigger. Once. Twice. Loud and close by – I was momentarily deafened.

The form stopped. It turned in a circle, trying to locate us in the chaos of swirling snow and gunfire echoes.

"I have no range with this. Hand me McTroy's rifle," she said, pointing.

We had retrieved his Marlin after the beating. I slipped it from its scabbard.

"Are you sure this is wise?"

"Give me the rifle."

Evangeline handed me her small, hammerless weapon in exchange.

"The lever is cocked," I said. My ears were ringing still.

Evangeline shouldered the Marlin, tucked her cheek into it, and closed one eye.

The form was too tall for any ordinary man, though it walked plainly on two legs. It started up again, the long arms swinging, lurch-lurching along, still coming for the trail, not fifty yards ahead of us. If it continued, it would cut off our only route to safety. We would be trapped. The approaching Beast had a blocky bovine head and antlers like a stag's – but not the enormously expansive rack I had seen when it stalked the lodge's window ledge. I conceded the creature might appear more fearsome in the full dark. Or my sleeplessness had added to my terror. But that did not explain fully the marked change of appearance.

"Hold your shot," I said.

"Why?"

"I do not know…"

"I'll shoot as soon as it clears the pines," she said.

"Do as you see fit. I only suggest you might want to know what you are shooting at first."

It moved clumsily, smashing through the snowbank, knocking two wheelbarrows' worth of crusty snow chunks onto the trail. It was covered in brown hair. The upper body was massive and barrel-chested. It bent over stiffly, hands resting on its knees, winded and catching its breath.

Evangeline fired.

Missing her target (as it shifted suddenly) but shearing a branch near its head.

The creature crouched, pivoted to look for us, twisting not at the neck but at its waist. It appeared to have a hard time seeing. It raised its arms in alarm, then after some reconsideration, dropped them. When it finally saw us clearly, it cried out. This cry was not the piercing whistle we had heard earlier, but a low, chest-buzzing moan mixed with a gravelly roar. *Frustration* was the word I thought while hearing it. And pity. Why *pity*? This Beast on the Copper Trail was undeniably huge. I would guess eight feet tall, not counting the length of the horns. Yet I did not feel the same watery panic melting in my gut as I did last night. Where was the chill? The demonic red eye-glow? That slavering mouth?

It cocked its head.

Lifted its blunt chin.

Staring at something... behind us?

"The Beast is running away!" Wu shouted. It was true. The lumbering giant crossed the path, crashing into the snow-covered terrain, and headed for a gap between the rocks and trees.

I turned to see what it saw behind us–

The wildcat leaped across my vision and onto Evangeline.

Over the neck of Neptune they went together. Her horse – the poor frightened thing – reared up on his back legs and bolted away. Evangeline landed roughly. I heard the air go out of her in a rush. A crunching of snow and gravel as she somersaulted and came to rest flat on her stomach. The cat stopped its fall nimbly, landing on four large splayed paws. It loomed over her, covering her body with its own. Evangeline picked up her head in bewilderment, seeing one furry foot and then a second framing her upturned face. Snow stuck in her hair and there was a frosty pinkness on the skin of her cheek. Her mouth hung open in amazement. She looked as if she'd been pushed facedown into a whipped cream pie. Her eyes were frantic. Searching for the rifle, I realized.

But the rifle was out of reach. The collision had launched it some distance. I only saw the imprint in a snowbank. How deeply it sank, who knew?

This cat wasn't a mountain lion. How remarkable, I thought. Although I had never actually seen a mountain lion in my life, I knew what they were supposed to look like. I had read about them, perused drawings, even brushed my fingers through a rug that had once *been* a mountain lion. Perching over my millionairess occultist librarian partner was a predator of another stripe – or spot, as was the case.

A leopard?

I could not say for sure. Oscar would have known in an instant. Black spots bordered golden rosettes, at times filling them, camouflaging the cat's compact, muscular body. Many smaller dots dappled the face and neck. But this furry jigsaw puzzle was hardly an asset in New Mexico. Better suited for the jungle, which is where I suspected this animal belonged. Its underside was pale fur, like beer foam. At least two hundred pounds of menacing male feline – it just looked male, given its girth and swagger – exhaled a cloud of hot cat breath on the back of Evangeline's head, making her face flush scarlet.

"Hardy?" she said.

"Do not move, Evangeline."

"Would you please shoot this cat?"

"Any sudden movement may startle the creature into an attack. Besides, I don't have any weapon–"

"You have my pistol."

"I was going to say 'weapon skills'. I am no marksman."

"The noise may drive away the cat," she said.

"Or it may cause the thing to bite you. And drag you off."

I carefully slid from my saddle. Jingle was quite nervous. I did not blame him.

"Just shoot it!" Evangeline shouted.

The wildcat nuzzled the back of Evangeline's head. I gripped my stick and crept forward with deliberateness and caution. The jungle feline raised its head and eyed me coolly.

"I can kill the leopard," Wu said.

He had his Colt out and was pointing it at the cat's head. He had drawn his gun several times recently. None of them had ended well. I mentioned this fact.

"So, Wu, you agree this is a leopard?" I said, hoping to divert him from shooting.

"It looks very like a leopard to me," Wu said.

"But how would a leopard find its way here?"

I took another step closer. The cat flicked its tail.

Evangeline said, "PLEASE DO SOMETHING!"

"I am doing something." I waved my stick back and forth above my head. "The cat is now more concerned with me than with you. If I can draw it toward me, then Wu will shoot."

Wu cocked the Colt's hammer.

The leopard swiveled its head and fixed the boy with golden eyes.

"Oh no oh no..." Wu's hand started to shake.

I shook the ape's head of my stick near the cat's face.

The cat bared its teeth at me.

"Steady, Wu," I said. "Evangeline, carefully lace your fingers at the back of your neck to protect your spine. On the count of three I will strike at the cat's head. The cat should charge me. Wu, please empty your revolver into it. One... two..."

Then we heard a sound carried on the wind.

The cat looked away from me and stared up the Copper Trail.

And before Wu could pull his trigger, the leopard leaped high, ricocheted acrobatically off the trunk of an aspen, bounded through the snow-capped outcroppings and out of sight.

Trotting up the trail was an equally imposing and fearsome beast.

I called out my thanks to it.

"Orcus! I am so glad to see you!"

16
THE STRANGEST THING

Orcus watched the leopard disappear. Wu and I went to Evangeline. She stood up and turned away from me as she brushed herself clean of the mountain trail detritus. She had a small scratch on her cheekbone.

"That turned out better than I anticipated," I said.

I reached out to Evangeline, but she slid beyond my touch.

"You should have shot the cat," she said. "That would have saved me faster."

"You did not need saving," I said. "As is often the case."

But here I needed to leave my old friends behind to greet my new friend. I was not prepared to talk with a dog in front of them. Part of me wondered if Orcus *would* talk to me, or if our previous conversation had been a one-time telepathic interspecies communion. None of the Adderlys seemed aware of Orcus' talent for words. I began to suspect that he only talked to me. Why was I different? Perhaps my past mental connection with an Egyptian sorcerer had left certain channels open, which for others remained blocked.

Then again, madness must start somewhere. The mad hear voices. Was Orcus my first step toward an asylum?

I met the Italian mastiff up the path. He had paused to watch the gap in the scenery where the Beast and the leopard had fled; evidence of their tracks was quickly disappearing.

"Thank you, Orcus, for saving us from that leopard."

"It was a jaguar," he said.

So, our conversations were to continue. I was pleased, if also unsettled.

"A jaguar? I have never seen a jaguar."

Orcus furrowed his loose brow.

"Well, until now. How do you know it was a jaguar?"

"Because it was."

"We also encountered the Beast. It's been a busy morning. Our bounty-hunting partner is badly injured. How did you come to look for us?" I followed this by saying, "May I pet you?"

"You may pet me, Rom Hardy Who Smells Afraid."

Orcus closed his eyes and rotated his big anvil head, so I might scratch his ears.

"I did not smell the Beast," Orcus said. I felt the rumble of his voice through my fingertips. "I do smell your bloody friend. He has something strange in his blood that I do not know. Ashes smell this way after a very hot fire but not exactly... maybe a foreign spice is added... I was not out here looking for you. But I am happy I found you. That is enough petting."

I had been scratching rather vigorously. Orcus's fur was cold and warm at the same time. Rubbing him made me feel as if I were the one being soothed. "Why were you out in this storm?" I asked.

"The pups are missing. Oscar ordered me to retrieve them."

"What pups?"

"Claude and Cassi."

"Oh, I see. That is concerning. Oscar expressly told Cassi to stay with her mother."

"Oscar is my master, but he is not his daughter's. He is angry that she went out."

"You do not share his concern?"

"Oscar coddles them. The pups take care of themselves. Your friends are coming."

Wu and Evangeline had remounted their horses. McTroy lay across Moonlight. Jingle walked a few paces behind them.

"Might you lead us out of this blizzard?" I asked.

"Yes. It is easy. But the mountain grows more dangerous now."

"Because of the snow?"

"Many things make this a bad place. I like my life and do not wish to end my time."

"Neither do I. Ah, here is the rest of my hunting party."

We did not look like much: a boy, a disheveled woman, a half-dead man, and me.

Orcus ran ahead. But he stopped to check to see if we were following. His ears were pointed like stubby black horns.

"Demon dog," I muttered to myself, smiling.

Wu handed me Jingle's lead. I put my foot in the stirrup and climbed on.

"It seems that Orcus knows the way home," I said. "We should follow him, I think."

"Please give me back my pistol," Evangeline said.

I did as requested.

"Were you able to recover McTroy's rifle?" I asked.

"Wu got it."

"Excellent."

We spoke not another word until after we had re-entered Nightfall Lodge.

That was probably for the best.

Viv wheeled her chair to the edge of the bed where Hodgson the coach driver and I had set a limp McTroy. She looked drawn but otherwise fully recovered from her possession.

McTroy gave no indication of pain, or anything else. If he had not been breathing I would have thought he was a corpse.

"This is terrible... just terrible. How did it happen?" she said.

"He fell," Evangeline said before I could answer.

Her eyes flashed at me to keep silent.

Vivienne's face twisted in anguish. She knew the changes a fall could bring. Involuntarily she brushed the engravings of her leg braces. Then she grazed her fingers over McTroy's blood-soaked clothes.

Oscar rushed into the bedroom.

"Good God, he looks awful. Do you know Cassi is missing as well?"

"Is she?" I could not let on what Orcus had told me.

"Ran out looking for my team, I suppose. Claude never caught up with us. But he is gone too. The morning has been a disaster all around. Did you manage to spot the Silver Team while you were out?"

"No," Evangeline said.

I gathered that she had decided we would not share the truth. Details of our run-in with Gavin Earl and his men might derail the entire hunt. And McTroy's humiliation was best kept as private as possible. I quietly agreed with my sponsor on that point.

"Evangeline said he fell." Vivienne gripped her husband's hand and brought it to her cheek, then kissed his knuckles.

"He's been shot in the hand," Oscar said.

"His gun went off," Evangeline said.

Oscar opened McTroy's shirt, checking underneath the bloodstain. "This blood is fresh, but these wounds look weeks old. They are already healing."

"McTroy is a scarred man," I offered from my position in the hallway. "He is as tough as they come."

Oscar nodded, but his face remained perplexed. "I'll call for a doctor as soon as this storm ends. We'll make sure he is patched and able to travel before we deliver you to your train."

"Train?" Evangeline said. "We aren't leaving."

"What?" three people said at the same time.

My shock was greater than Oscar's or Viv's.

Evangeline went on. "Accidents happen. McTroy will recover here in your wonderful home much better than he can on a jostling train. Or even in Yuma. If you'll allow us to continue the hunt…"

"Certainly, you are welcome to stay for as long as you like," Oscar said.

Viv agreed. "That is a wise decision. Hodgson will help me clean him up. Then we'll move him to the room adjoining mine. I always put Claude and Cassi there when they are sick. You may be surprised, but I am a good nurse. There are remedies beyond scientific medicine."

"Thank you both," Evangeline said.

Then, changing the subject, she asked, "Who fired the three shots?"

"The Silvers," Oscar said angrily. "I think they used the signal falsely. Although I'm glad Orcus found you, it was not his mission. He was supposed to locate my children. I've sent him out again. But the weather is making things difficult."

The main door to Nightfall banged shut and echoed down the hall.

I was the first to arrive in the vestibule.

Cassi was placing her Remington rifle in a cabinet beside the door. She unwound a long maroon woolen scarf from her face and startled when she saw me, half-hidden in the shadows.

"Rom!"

Her father stormed past me. "Where were you? You left your mother alone."

"Is she well?" Cassi said.

"Yes, but that is not the issue."

"I stayed with her until she appeared herself again."

Oscar huffed in frustration. "Did you not recognize the three-shot signal to return?"

Viv and Evangeline joined us to hear Cassi's response.

"Hello, Mother. It is quite a crowd in here," she said. "To answer your question, Father, I did make note of the signal. But I stayed out on the mountain."

"Why?" he asked.

"As you may have guessed, I didn't follow the Gold

Trail. Instead, I went looking–"

"Why weren't you on the trail assigned to you?" Oscar said.

"Father, if you stop interrupting me, I will explain everything." Cassi then paused to see if he would break in again.

Oscar folded his arms across his chest.

"Very well," Cassi continued. "Father, you and your guide friend, Mr Smoke Eel, rode to the Gold Trail as I expected. I was going to do my best to catch up with you. Really, I was. But I spotted Claude riding higher up the mountain! Not at all where he belonged. He was following none of the trails. Now that shouldn't surprise anyone who knows Claude. He is his own compass. But given Claude's illness and injury from last night, I was worried about him. I felt it was my sisterly duty to chase him down if I could."

"And did you?" Oscar asked.

Cassi hung her coat on a wall peg. She removed her boots. The cold had added the most attractive rosiness to her complexion. The red of her lips, the brassiness of her curls, all her coloring and everything else about her seemed to pop and crackle with renewed energy.

"No. My horse was too slow. Or I do not possess the recklessness of Claude when it comes to driving an animal up a slippery slope of ankle-breaking holes. I lost him. Then, in quick order, the snow began to fall, the wind to gust, and I lost myself. Oh, I knew where I was in general terms. I had not strayed far from Nightfall. Direction wasn't the problem. But I had trouble finding a safe track down. When I finally came to the road, I must have been confused because

I crossed it without realizing that I had. Then I saw the strangest thing."

"A jaguar?" I said.

Cassi looked a bit horrified.

"Nooo… I saw Gavin Earl and his team in pursuit of a rather large and unusual quarry…"

"The Beast!" Oscar clapped his hands, causing us to jump.

Cassi smiled. "I can only assume that's what it was. They were very excited and did not notice me. Though the fat man's bear raised its nose in my vicinity. I'm wearing vanilla and musk perfume, with a hint of cashmere." She held out her wrist to me and I sniffed it.

"Warm and inviting," I said.

Smiling, she closed her eyes, opening them slowly like a cat.

"What happened with the Beast?" Evangeline asked. "Did they capture it?"

"I don't think so."

Cassi failed to elaborate further.

"Is that it? You *don't think so*?" Evangeline took a step closer to us. "What happened?"

"Oh, I realized I was lower than the road, so I backtracked and sure enough there it was–"

"With the Silver Team and the Beast?" Evangeline asked. "Did you see where they went?"

I thought Evangeline might throttle Cassi if she did not give a suitable answer.

"The men grew angry. The quarry had slipped through their net. There was shouting and cussing. Words I've never heard before. I will have to ask you about those, Rom. The Silvers went down toward the creek. They weren't in the Silver Trail area at all, I should mention. It was on your patch, Evangeline and Rom. Copper Trail. But I didn't see you anywhere."

"I'm just glad you are home," Oscar said.

"It was brown," Cassi said.

"Pardon me?"

"The Beast. I saw it sort of sneak around the Silvers. It hid behind a rock pile. I got a good look. It was brown. Like a cross between a buffalo and a buck. It had buck antlers and a big buffalo head. It was a tall fellow. I didn't have the heart to shoot at him. He seemed almost frightened."

"Most unusual," Oscar said. "I wouldn't think the Beast is afraid of anything."

"I thought so too. That's why I left it alone. Storms do confound things. I only wish Claude wasn't still out there in this blizzard."

But then the door opened again.

A flurry of snowflakes blew in like confetti.

Claude stomped his boots and brushed the gathered snow from his shoulders.

"What? Is it a party? Am I late for the festivities?" Claude stepped to the side to let Orcus in. "Get this dog a meaty bone. He practically dragged me home."

Cassi hugged her brother more emphatically than I would have expected for so short a separation. He seemed embarrassed by her enthusiasm. "Did you presume me dead? I was only losing myself in nature. Storms are exciting. It's a waste not to enjoy them."

I found Orcus and gave him a good scratch.

"You seem to have made a new friend," Cassi said.

"I hope I have," I replied.

McTroy had torn away his shirt and left it in the bedroom, so he was bare-chested when he walked among us. His torso was stained red but the bruising of his face and limbs had faded to ugly dark yellows and winey purples. His eyes were cold, glittery. He was barefoot. His hair stuck out at strange angles, glued in place by his own gummy, red-black blood. His mangled right hand was empty and twisted out of shape like a tree root, but his left hand held a Colt Army pistol, with the hammer cocked.

"Where is Gavin Earl?" he said.

People were torn between the shock of the gun and the savage-looking man himself.

"Not here," I said. "His gang's out on the mountain. Are you feeling better?"

McTroy nodded. "I need whiskey."

Oscar brought him a bottle, newly opened. We watched him drink it.

All of it.

17
CLUE TO THE GREEN ELIXIR

"I feel nothing," McTroy said.

I stepped forward. I took McTroy gently by the elbow and led him back to our room. The others stayed put in the anteroom to Nightfall. I heard a collective sigh of relief as we exited their company. McTroy tossed the empty whiskey bottle over his shoulder. It clunked and rolled along the floor. The pistol jutted from his left hand, pointing down the hallway. He sweated profusely.

"You've had a hell of a day," I said. "And you are scaring everyone, I'm afraid."

"Doc, I'm not right in my head. I feel hollowed out. I hear echoes inside me."

"Drinking that bottle of whiskey was questionable."

"It usually is. But listen to me. I don't feel the liquor. I'm not drunk. Either Oscar waters down his own booze or there's something mighty weird going on with my functions."

I led him into our room and shut the door behind us.

"I'd feel better if you gave me your gun," I said.

"I'm keeping it," McTroy sat on the edge of his bed. He laid his pistol on the blanket.

I pulled a chair in front of him and sat down.

"The back of my head hurts," he said. He rubbed the base of his neck.

"That's where Pops injected you. Do you remember any of it?"

McTroy shook his head.

"I see stars," he said.

"You were shot in the chest. The wound was mortal. Pops injected a vial of an unknown solution into your... well, I imagine it went straight into your skull. Rather than bleeding to death, you came back. So, if nothing else, Pops saved your life. But I don't think he was being kind. Earl only wanted to save you in order to prolong some sort of plan for revenge and further torment. He pummeled you until he was utterly spent. You killed Billy. Do you recall that? You shot him through the forehead. Billy the Kid number two is dead."

"I see stars like I'm flying up in them. Real stars and the blackest night... it goes forever."

McTroy ran his damaged hand over his face. Then he stared at its deformity.

"Earl did that too," I said. "He put a gun barrel between your fingers and..."

McTroy tried to close his hand, but the fingers moved stiffly, pinching like a claw.

"I can't shoot with this."

"I think that was the idea. I take it you gave him a similar wound at Sully's Fork?"

"Sully's Fork ain't worth talking about. I'm thirsty.

Hungry too…I could eat and eat…"

"You need to rest for now. Why don't you try lying down?" I lifted his legs and helped him get settled on a stack of pillows. "There now. That's comfy." Quickly I slipped his gun into my waistband as I covered him with the blanket.

"I'm seeing things. I'm not ready to be with the world."

"What sorts of things?"

"Before I left our room I saw a bat fly out of my ribs. It's cold, but I'm in the desert someplace. I mean, I know we're here outside Raton, but I'm in the desert too. The heat doesn't get to me. It don't feel hot enough for what I'm used to. I shut my eyes. Still I see things. It's like I'm in a tight little box and can't move a muscle. I smell dust and camphor. But I'm in the desert too. How can I be in all these places, Doc? They did worse than kill me. They made me crazy."

McTroy looked up at the ceiling as he talked. He pulled the blanket under his chin.

"Soon you'll feel better. Why, earlier today you were dead! You're much improved."

"Don't take my gun," he said.

So, even in his delirium he had noticed. "I think until you are in a clearer state of mind–"

"Please, Doc. What if they come for me?"

I turned and pushed the chair into the corner. While my back was to McTroy, I opened the cylinder and spilled out the bullets into my hand. I slipped them into my vest pocket.

"I'll leave the pistol on the chair over here in the corner. How does that sound?"

"You need to find out what they did to me, Doc."

"I will do just that."

"Thanks for leaving my gun."

When I closed the door, I pressed my ear to the wood. I heard McTroy get out of bed and take the pistol from the chair. Then I heard him sink back onto the mattress.

"So many stars… how am I going to find my way home?"

After that he was quiet.

The anteroom to the lodge had emptied except for Wu. He looked up at me with profound concern. McTroy's disturbing appearance had shaken the boy. He was smart and knew that McTroy should be dead. Wu's parents had turned into vampires some years ago. He feared undeadness as much as death itself. I had no illusions and understood that Yong Wu admired the bounty man much more than he did me. What did I have on my side except bookish habits, a love of ancient cultures, and the exceptional memory required to tell long-winded adventure stories? Rex McTroy on the other hand was a gunslinging, hard-riding catcher of evil men. It was no match. However, I had qualities McTroy did not. I brought calm, logic, and critical observation to the table instead of bullets and bravado. I was a thinker, a man of science and the future as well as the long-ago past. Wu needed me. So did McTroy in his current predicament. I thought Evangeline valued me as a friendly partner in adventure, business, and wherever else that may someday lead us. But where had she gone off without me?

"Wu, you are exactly the person I was looking for. McTroy is resting. Uneasily, I should add. But we need to conduct a bit of clandestine investigation. Are you up for it, young man?"

"I am, Dr Hardy," he said. Wu stood at attention.

"Excellent," I said. "Do you know where Miss Evangeline is?"

"She went with Mrs Adderly. They were talking about conducting a *Seis Ants* tonight. But I don't know what six ants can do to help us. They must be magic ants."

"Seis... you mean the Spanish number six... Six Ants, you say?"

"Six magic ants. That's what they were talking about. The Seis Ants might tell them where the Beast hides here on the mountain."

"Might they have said 'séance'? That is a French word for a sitting, or meeting, where the dead are contacted. Vivienne is a medium, as you know. She goes into a trance and seeks out the spirits. That spooky talk she had with Gustav the hunter at the Starry Eyes was a kind of séance."

"Oh, yes. That must be it." Wu colored with embarrassment at his misinterpretation.

"I wonder with whom they want to speak? Never mind. Let's get busy with our own inquiry. Come! We must act quickly before the Silver Team returns to the lodge."

Wu followed me outside. The storm provided us a degree of privacy in our search. I had seen a niche cut into the mountain, right around the bend from Nightfall's doors. It was wide and shallow and had only a low gate guarding it, which we discovered was unlocked. Inside the niche I found what I was looking for: Pops Spooner's medicine wagon. His horses had been unhitched and stabled, watered, fed, and safely sheltered from the harsh elements. They were corralled at the other end of a cave-like pocket, munching hay and watching us. The wagon was left alone. Wood chocks were stuck under the wagon wheels to prevent the vehicle from rolling away. I closed the gate, gazing out into the snow, looking for any signs of human, or inhuman, activity. I saw none. From the higher vantage point of the niche, perched on a lip of stone overlooking the tree-studded valley below and the opposing ridge, the storm appeared like a white fog. Almost serene, certainly mysterious. I wondered what terrors were lurking out there.

"Wu, we need to search this wagon and see if we can find anything that gives us information about the eerie green elixir Pops used on McTroy. It healed his wounds and revived him. But it has left him altered. I fear if we do not deduce the origins of this solution, McTroy's condition may deteriorate. He is hallucinating already. His mood is suspicious and unpredictable. That concoction is responsible. Now let's see what the charlatan surgeon keeps in his cupboard."

The front end of the wagon sported a padded bench seat, a footrest, and a short awning to keep the sun and rain off the drivers. There was no access to the interior. The sides of the wagon were identically painted with jaundiced letters: *Doc Spooner's Famous Elixirs and Potent Remedies*. The dry wood siding had faded to the color of old sunburn and it felt rough under my palm. But the painted letters were fresher. The sulfur-yellow pigment had cracked but hadn't begun peeling. I used my ape-headed walking stick to tap the boards and see if any seemed loose or fashioned to hide a trick door. No, they were tight. At the back of the wagon was where the real action happened. The rear step extended to create a small platform whereupon Pops Spooner might ascend above the crowd to hawk his dubious wares. Pops lacked the charisma of a born peddler but he was amiable enough to charm a gathering of eager dullards. I imagine he sold his goods mostly to loggers and miners. Here were tired, uneducated men, often worked to the brink of death, with a life's accumulation of aches and pains and a taste for stimulating intoxicants. If anyone said they cared about their troubles they would listen. Even the wariest would not be skeptical for long if Pops told them what they wanted to hear. Miracle cures! Hah! Most remedies I've come across are no more than alcohol masked with exotic flavorings. The stranger the taste, the better the sales – a shot of spirits improves a person's mood if not their afflictions.

I climbed up the step.

Two doors and one large chain, looping like an ouroboros through the handles. Locked with a padlock.

I pulled on the lock and found it secure.

Wu was studying my problem-solving. "McTroy would shoot the hasp," he suggested.

"Would he now?"

"Miss Evangeline might pick it with a pair of hairpins. She has a skillful touch."

"Yes, she would, and I'm sure she does. Quite a resourceful woman."

I lifted the lock, studied it. Weighty. The chain links

were as thick as my bent little finger when I held it up side-by-side for comparison. I leaned in for a closer inspection. The doors looked dusty, cobwebbed in the corners. My nose nearly pressed at the doors. I smelled them.

"What are you going to do?"

"Hold this lock," I said. "Out here to the side as far as it will stretch."

Wu grabbed the padlock with both hands and pulled the chain taut.

"Keep pulling," I said. Employing a two-handed grip, I raised my stick above my head.

Wu shut his eyes as he prepared himself for the assault.

Then I rammed the ape's head through the brittle, rotting door.

I inserted my ebony cane into the gap and broke out the softer wood surrounding the door-pull. The hardware soon dangled by its chain. I flung the doors wide. Upon gaining access I immediately started sliding out drawers and flipping open cabinets. Using my stick like a silver-headed hammer I smashed the glass display cases, discarding their contents willy-nilly, tossing them to either side as I continued searching for clues to the green elixir that vexed my friend.

"How did you break through the door so easily?" Wu asked, astonished. He poked at the crumbly edges of the boards I had ripped out.

"Dry rot," I said. "Pops comes from the Northwoods where things are damp and fungi grow in abundance. The doors smelled like musty old blankets. That powdery substance looks like ordinary dust but is actually fungal spores. Those webs are too. The chain and lock were strong, but the wood it clamped together was weak. Help me examine these compartments."

"What are we looking for?"

"I'm not sure. But I suspect we will know it when we find it. Think green."

Wu pulled out trays of brown glass bottles and crates of clear, corked jars. We found ointments, unguents, liniments, tonics, creams, suspensions, tinctures, and nostrums of every ilk. There were dried herbs tied in bundles or sealed in cans. I put my nose in them, and once I recognized the scent I tossed the plant materials on the ground outside the wagon. The liquids took me longer to sort. I identified opium, cocaine, corn liquor, tequila, and a small barrel keg of spiced rum.

I was amazingly thirsty. I lifted the barrel and found it to be better than half-full. I opened the spigot and splashed a decent portion into the cleanest vial I spotted. After a cautious sniff, I drank a few swallows, drying my mouth with my coat sleeve. The rum tasted charred, and heavy on the star anise for my personal taste, but good. Part of me wanted to stop the search, sit down for a spell, and see if I couldn't drain the contents of the barrel a great deal more. But I resisted.

"There's nothing here," I said. "No sign of the green elixir Pops has in his bag."

Wu hopped down off the wagon step and walked beyond my view.

"Interesting!"

"What is it, Wu? Are you seeing something out there?" I refilled my vial.

"These drawers and cabinets can't go all the way

to the front. The deepest ones on the bottom might, but not those on the top." He struck the outside of the wagon. "There's a space inside this wagon we haven't reached yet."

I followed the sound of his knocking.

"A secret compartment? Yes! Any medicinal agent that rejuvenates the mortally wounded would require a special hiding place to discourage common thieves." I set aside my empty vial and tore open the top cabinet, hauling forth stacks of papers. Advertising handbills. Receipts for bulk ingredients. Formulas and recipes for various fraudulent concoctions. But none referred to the eerie elixir that heals gunshot injuries in hours and brings men back from the threshold of death. I threw the papers behind me and watched the swirling gusts of wind inside the rocky niche build them upward like a paper tornado and sweep them out over the gate and down the steep, icy mountainside. I tipped over a crate of unlabeled jars, spilling the breakage on the stone floor. I stood on the upended crate, peering into the hollow of the empty cabinet. I saw a rectangle of fresh, unstained pine at the back. I probed it with the tip of my stick. Hitting the pine barrier made a hollow sound.

I tried driving my stick through the wood, with no success. It was new and solid.

"There must be a catch, a lever of some sort that will gain us access to the inner cell."

"I'll go under the wagon," Wu said. "What am I looking for?"

"Some mechanism that can be reached from the edge of the wagon. Pops isn't going to contort himself like an acrobat or venture very far underneath. He'd want a discreet but simple release. He'd trip it by feel. A small, unobtrusive thing that draws no attention even from a curious observer."

Wu's muffled voice came to me through the wagon's floor. "Might it be an iron ring?"

"It very well might."

"I see a ring. It hangs under the step where the driver climbs down from his seat."

"Give it a good hard pull, Wu. Let's see what happens."

I lit a match and stuck my hand and then my face in the top compartment. Watching.

Waiting.

Wu pulled the ring. We both heard a smooth metallic *ka-chunk*, like the sound of a heavy key turning over, triggering a mechanism that draws back a stout, oiled bolt.

The back of the compartment slid upward. The pine terminus was gone. Stale air blew out, flickering my flame as it tickled my eyelashes. The air smelled of camphor and spice. I pushed my arm in deeper. My eyes squinted into the dusty cubbyhole.

A green thing stared horridly back at me.

"Good God!"

I retreated quickly and bumped the top of my head, stumbling off the crate, losing my balance, and nearly pitching over the rail and falling off the rear platform.

Wu scrambled out from under the wagon and met me at the door.

"Did it work? Did we find a clue to the green elixir?"

I nodded, while gingerly checking my head for blood. "You look. I swear I can't trust my own eyes since we have arrived on this cursed mountain."

I tossed him my box of lucifers.

Wu leaped upon the platform and rushed onto the overturned crate. He had grown taller during our months apart; desert life agreed with him, but he still had some inches to add in his maturity. Luckily Pops Spooner was a short man. The cabinetry was designed to his proportions. Wu's hand reached the secret chamber's opening, and, standing on the crate, the boy could easily peer inside. He struck a match off the corner of a half-open drawer overflowing with empty vials.

"I warn you, Wu. Prepare for a shocking sight," I said.

Wu plunged his hand into the shadowy compartment. His head plugged the cramped opening as he strained to see inside the hidden chamber.

"Is it a cabbage?"

"I think not. Look closer."

In my mind's eye I saw it again: two eyes trapped under a shimmering green layer of–

Wu went up on his tiptoes. The crate tipped perilously as he shifted his weight.

"A crystal? It shines like a green gemstone, Dr Hardy. But it is so big…"

I went to him and placed my hand lightly on Wu's back. My face pressed into the crevice. I smelled the odor of camphor and a spice I could not identify. And another layer of odor, like old ashes in a fireplace. The space was too small. It was awfully dark. Wu's match had burned out. I could not get enough air in that sealed up wagon. My heart thumped in revolt until I retreated. Walking to the edge of the platform, I sucked in a lungful of cold blizzard blasts from the side of the wagon. I felt dizzy, unsteady. My sweaty hands kept sticking to the frozen iron railings. But at least I could breathe. My sight cleared. So too did my thoughts. Perhaps earlier my imagination had gotten the better of me. Certainly, I had not seen a gemmy crystal when I gazed in the compartment. No. Nor any putrefying cabbage. My vision was of something much stranger, and much, much worse. Should I take another look?

"I can touch it with my fingers," Wu said from behind me, his head buried in the wagon's dark, smelly recess. "It is soft. Not a gemstone at all. Soft like jelly... I feel a cool burning in my fingertips. But it is not bad. I touched an octopus once at a fishmonger's stall. It was like this."

"You had better stop touching. Just to be safe," I said, turning around. I heard a hollow rolling sound from inside the nook. Wu had both of his arms shoved into the cubbyhole. His narrow shoulders worked back and forth as if he were wiggling something free that was lodged inside.

"I have it! I think I can get it out."

Brave boy! Braver than I!

"What does it look like? Is there enough light sneaking around your body to see? Because I thought I saw something very different from what you said you saw." I chuckled at my apparently erroneous first impression. "I probably shouldn't tell you this now, but I swore I thought I saw what appeared to be a slime-covered, bald, and somewhat teardrop-shaped–"

"There!" Wu said. He withdrew his slender arms. His upper half flowed from the hole as if he were being poured out. In his hands he held the prize.

"It's a head!" we both shouted.

To Wu's credit he did not throw the gruesome discovery as far away as possible. Instead, he stretched out his arms rigidly and screamed. I like to think I did not scream. But what I like to think is often not true. Together we ran, jumping off the platform and bolting to the rear of the mountain niche. This change of location did nothing to calm us. After all, we had brought the drippy, oozy, oval source of our terror with us. At the back of the niche we changed direction, following the curve of the alcove, passing the startled horses, and then pivoting on the slippery floor, our boots skidding, and heading for the blizzardy mouth of the grotto and the only way out.

I halted. I seized Wu by the blue sash he wore like a belt. "Wu, listen. Stop." He struggled to pull away as I dragged him backward to the rear of the wagon.

"Let go of me," he said.

"This is an important find. We cannot risk losing it... if only for McTroy's sake."

"You take it then," he said. "The cool burning is in my fingers. It's creeping up my arms! I can't feel my hands. I... I... I can't drop the damned thing. I think it blinked at me when we were running. This head... It's alive!"

He offered the head to me. Green slime coated his bare hands. The alarming color was more chartreuse than shamrock, and rather than suggesting a specimen of the natural vegetable world, it seemed highly odd.

Otherworldly. Wu's wrists and elbows dripped with the odious gel.

"Blinked, you say?"

Wu nodded. He turned his face away from the horror in his hands.

"Let me study it."

"No! Take it. Please take it."

"You say you cannot feel your hands."

"I can't!"

"Well, if I take it and I can't feel my hands, then we are two handless investigators. I think that would be a disadvantage to our mission. I will remove it in the fastest and safest way possible. Hold still and let me have a good look. Who knows, it might be dangerous to remove it from your grip altogether. Or even impossible, for that matter."

"Ooohhh… don't say that," Wu said. "I don't want this green thing on my hands forever."

"I'm sorry. You are correct. Wu, we must stay calm." I dug into my pocket.

"What is that?" Wu said.

"My pocketknife," I said. I opened it with a snicking sound.

"I am going to try an experiment here. Close your eyes. I promise not to hurt you. Tell me if you feel this. Again, I won't hurt you. Believe me. I am being very careful, Wu."

"Ooohhh… just do it already…"

"Here we go…"

18

THE FLESH DRAWS

"You are telling me that you feel this? Yet you do not have any sensation when I touch, say, here…?" I moved the dull edge of my pocketknife from one location to another.

"That is correct," Wu said.

"Interesting…" I inserted the point of the knife through the gelatinous ooze. "And what about riiight… now?"

"Ow!" Wu winced. "That is very uncomfortable."

I retracted my knife. Leaving Wu standing at the back of the wagon, I went inside. Rummaging through Pops' supplies, I found a wad of cotton, wiped off my blade, and put it back in my pocket. I dragged a drawer full of miscellaneous instruments out to the wagon's platform with me. I had prodded the severed head's upper left eyelid. I didn't tell Wu that when I did that I saw it wince too. Exactly as he had. The reactions twinned.

"We have a most intriguing situation," I said. "When I touch you anywhere on your arms from the crooks of the elbows to the tips of your fingers, you say you cannot feel it. Yet, if I touch anywhere on the head that you are holding, you claim it is sensitive, even painful. Somehow your nervous system has merged with this foreign body, or body *part*, and it has numbed you near the point of contact while extending your peripheral response into its domain."

Wu whimpered at my findings. "What can we do, Dr Hardy?"

"That is the question, Wu. I wonder what would happen if you tried to put it down. Climb onto the platform with me. See if you can roll it off your hands onto this retractable shelf." Pops must have used the shelf to mix remedies on the spot for customers. "Your arms must be getting tired."

"I can't feel them. I don't think I can bend them either." Wu's face began to twitch and I sensed he was going to cry but was doing his best to keep his tears bottled up. He chewed his lip.

"Wu, stand right there, over the shelf. I will attempt to push the thing out of your hands."

"Good. I like that idea very much."

What should I use? I dug into Pops' drawer until I found a pair of long metal tongs.

"These will do the job," I said.

I clamped the tongs through the green jelly onto the sides of the head.

Wu yelled. "I feel them! Do not squeeze, Dr Hardy! What if my head rolls away?"

"I am stopping." I pulled the drippy tongs away from the head. "It is quite fascinating, really. I absolutely wish you were not in peril, of course. But the sympathetic connection between you and this unknown entity is remarkable. The head is not green. Do you see that? I think it is gray. When I open up a gap in the gel I observe the actual color. Then it re-seals. It appears green because this viscous gel has a glowing tint. I wonder if it's plant-like, an algae maybe. It might contain chlorophylls and use photosynthesis for its energy. It's not very light in this alcove. But it's much darker inside the medicine wagon. Have you noticed if the head has gotten progressively slimier the longer we've had it out of its compartment?"

"I wasn't paying attention," Wu said. "I've been too horrified."

"That is one reason you are lucky to have me here. I can maintain a scientific distance."

"I wish you wouldn't."

"Oh, it's no trouble. What I am wondering is if the slime is the real culprit."

"What do you mean?"

"If the head exudes this sludge, this viscid mucus, as a defensive protection against predators. You cannot feel yourself where you are attacking the head – that is how the head would see it from a protective angle – and anything you do to harm the head, feels like it aggrieves *you*. It's quite a deterrent keeping you from inflicting further damage."

"But the head is cut off," Wu said.

"Ah, but it still works to some degree. It blinks. It oozes. It seems to be sending telepathic signals into McTroy's brain. To this we can attest." I had my pocketknife out again. I was using it to pry the lid off the rum barrel. After some fussing, the lid popped free.

"I have an unorthodox idea, Wu."

"You have so many, Dr Hardy. Maybe you should get Miss Evangeline," Wu said.

"Nonsense. It would take a long time to explain all this to her. Who knows how the head might be knitting its nervous system into yours as we speak! We must act. And if we succeed in fixing this matter, there is no reason to tell her what happened."

Wu sighed. The strange bald head inside its encasement of verdant muck sighed too.

I set the slightly less than half-barrel of rum on the platform at Wu's feet.

"Move your boots apart a bit," I said.

"What are we doing?"

I brushed at a few nonexistent dust specks on Wu's shoulders. Then I grabbed him firmly by the biceps.

"This!"

I forced his locked arms downward and plunged his hands (and the green-gray head) into the barrel of liquor. Then I quickly hauled up on his armpits. The head had detached from him. Wu smelled like a sailor on shore leave, but appeared none the worse for the experience.

"Can you feel your limbs coming back?"

"Yes! Like tiny needles sticking me. I can move again." He smiled, showing me his elbows and wrists bending. His fingers worked like a pair of giant, pale, excitable spiders.

We had but a short interval of celebration. As I tilted over the barrel of rum to observe the stream of bubbles popping on the surface, an angry outcry from the other end of the wagon jolted us.

"What are you bastards doing in my wagon?"

Pops rounded the platform. His face was red from the cold and his glasses were fogged. He dropped his Gladstone bag in shock. Spittle flew from his lips. "Vandals! Thieves! I will see you suffer for this crime, the both of you. Age is no excuse. I offer no second chances."

I straightened my spine and stepped down off the platform toward him. Wu stayed behind me.

"Bold charges coming from the mouth of a faker and poisoner. But lying is the least of your vices. Have you been playing God too, Pops Spooner? You experimented on McTroy."

"I saved his life." The surgeon was baffled by my accusation.

"Saved it so Gavin Earl might hurt him more."

Pops shook his finger at me. "But I saved him regardless. He'd be dead if I hadn't."

"He wouldn't have been shot at all if not for your gang," Wu shouted.

"Boy, you best learn to respect your betters," he said.

"You are his elder, but no better," I said. "Wu is ten times the man you'll ever be."

Pops surveyed the destruction of his medical props, where they lay scattered off the back end of the wagon. He shuffled through the wreckage of shattered glass, spilled rum, and boot-trampled herbs, shaking his owlish head. "This all costs money! Do you know how mean a man gets when you take money from his pocket?"

"What about when you sell him impotent potions? Quackery? You defrauded people."

"They had a choice. Every one of them could've

walked away. I took no coin that wasn't offered to me freely. I sold hope to the hopeless. Who can say what benefit my cures had?"

"I can. They had none," I said.

Pops removed his glasses and polished them with a soiled handkerchief. "You will pay for ruining my wagon. Oh, yes. Since you have no inclination to give me any gold, I will take my restitution in another form." Pops set his hands on his hips and smirked. His teeth were jagged, and as multicolored as flint corn. "I demand the punishment of your flesh." He giggled and wagged his tongue at us. "It might be worth my loss of stock to watch you twist in agony."

I knew then that Pops had enjoyed Earl's whipping of McTroy. There was a sickness that ran deep into the roots of this so-called medical man. Pain entertained him.

"Doc Spooner," I said, "you carry no weapon. I think it would be unwise of you to engage in a physical battle with me and Yong Wu. We don't wish to hurt you. Any damage we did to your wagon occurred during our search for the nature of the elixir you injected into McTroy. We're trying to save our friend. Cooperate with us, and we will tell the law to spare you when the time comes for your gang to answer for their depravity."

"The law?" Pops laughed. "Oh, you are far from home, Dr Hardy. There's no law here."

I had hoped that my warning might have swayed him.

"There is law in Raton. And where there are no lawmen, there are good people who stand against men like you. Now step aside, and let us pass. Wu, grab the barrel."

"That's my rum!"

"Not anymore it isn't."

Wu placed the lid on top of the barrel and hammered it with his boot heel. He hugged the barrel to his chest and fell in line with me. Pops still blocked our way. I swung my cane out in front of me.

"Pops, this is my last warning. You won't be able to stop us from leaving."

"I don't need to stop you," Pops propped his aging backside against the wagon's frame. He hooked his spectacles around his ears and grinned at us. There was a crack in the left lens that split our view of his eyeball. It made him look like he had three eyes embedded in his face. "Because Billy will," Pops said. "Nail 'em, Billy. Nail 'em both good."

Coming in from the blizzard, Billy the Kid carried a pistol in one hand, a rifle in the other, and a black bullet hole cratering the center of his forehead. He walked unsteadily, dropping his feet as if he were wearing iron boots. His stare pegged us, but his left eye kept rolling up into his skull. It was like part of him wanted to check and see if he had any brains left. There must not have been much. I'd seen a good portion blown out onto the snowy trail hours earlier: a steaming spray of hot red soup swimming with gray lumps and gritty chips of cranium.

"Draw me down, dare dogs. I'll cur you 'fore the hour that kills," Billy said.

Instead of emitting a menacing growl, or a silence that chills the marrow of men's bones, Billy burped loudly. His slack mouth hung open. Spittle, like a broken kite string, floated off his lower lip, vibrating sympathetically in the wind-strewn cavern.

"You are the house in Billy Kid's town. Know it," he said. Adding, in a whisper as cryptic as it was disturbing, "Me show yellow."

The rolling eye returned, bloodshot. The spittle thrummed but did not break. He raised his pistol, pointing it with alarming accuracy at my face. I don't know if resurrected Billy was more dangerous now than he had been before, but it occurred to me in that very instant what we were dealing with was likely the *twice* resurrected and authentic outlaw, William H Bonney, Kid Antrim, born Henry McCarty Jr in New York City, baptized in Manhattan, and killed in Lincoln County, New Mexico, by Sheriff Pat Garrett, his former friend, in 1881. Billy scratched the bloody, matted, sandy mop of hair under his sombrero with the hammer of his Winchester '73.

"Now Billy," I said. "Be reasonable. Pops has been using you. You're an experiment."

"He won't hear your lies, Hardy. Billy knows his friends," Pops said.

Billy began singing, *"Darling, I am growing old, Silver threads among the gold, Shine upon my brow today; Life is fading fast awaaay…"*

"What do you hope to accomplish by killing the two of us?" I asked Pops.

"Oh, nothing. But it sure will feel good. I might bring you two back with my elixir. Put you to work on the medicine wagon. I could always use extra hands to post my advertisements."

"Is Billy an automaton? Does he understand anything?"

"The flesh draws!" Billy shouted. He cocked the

hammer of his Colt.

"Billy understands just fine. He knows without me he'd be wormfood in a graveyard. This way he's having fun times. McTroy set him back with that head shot. But give him time."

The gunfighter sang out of tune, *"Never, never winter's frost and chill; Summer warmth is in them still... Silver threads among the gooooooooold..."*

"No head shots, Billy. Hit 'em in the belly. Let's watch these fools bleed," Pops said.

Billy lowered his aim.

I felt as vulnerable as if I had been stripped naked. How could I stop a bullet with a stick? I had no doubt I would soon be lying on the cold floor of the niche with my life force leaking out of me... then darkness descending like a cloud of flies... next, the sting of Pops' needle piercing the base of my neck. My only concern was getting Yong Wu out of this predicament. If I rushed Billy, that might cause a surprise big enough for Wu to dash around the wagon's other side and run for the lodge. It is hard to fight one's animal instincts for survival. My feet felt cemented.

"Billy," I said. "Would you rather fight like gentlemen of old?"

I drew the sword secreted inside my walking stick. The blade was razor sharp. I slashed the air between us. Billy's eyes followed the distracting motion, but his weapon never wavered.

"Lurp?" he said.

At least that's what I thought I heard. Confusion contorted Billy's face. His body lifted up off the ground, reaching so high that the ceiling of the alcove dented his sombrero. He fired his pistol wildly. Then he fired his rifle before dropping it. Bullets ricocheted around the enclosure.

Billy's boots kicked helplessly in the air.

A high-pitched whistle drowned out his screams. A claw burst through his chest. Warmth splashed me. It was as if Billy had dived into a summer pond. Everything was suddenly wet. I turned to see Wu, who was likewise splattered. He wore a slick red mask of Billy's blood.

"The Beast! Get under the wagon! Now, Wu, crawl! Crawl!"

Pops stood shaking and awestruck. The color drained from him.

The Beast opened its claw. Billy's ribs cracked apart. Blood gushed from the Kid's mouth. He was still screaming – screaming and firing his gun spasmodically – when the Beast reached around with its elongated arm, knocked the weapon from his grip, and sliced his face off. The skin landed in one piece at Pops' feet. It made a horrible wet, smacking sound. Pops jabbered to himself. Kneeling in the broken glass from his bottles, he groped for his Gladstone bag – he fumbled it open, rising up again unsteadily, holding a scalpel in his tremulous fist.

"Stay away from me!" he yelled.

The Beast smashed Billy against the wall. The Kid's body left a man-sized red print. Then the Beast flung him to the floor. Wu and I were under the wagon. Billy's faceless head slammed down right in front of us. His bad eye popped out of the socket. His teeth chattered together incessantly. The Beast stepped on his denuded skull. Billy's good eye bulged only briefly. Bone shattered. The Beast's hoof pressed flat. It was making a gurgling noise deep in its throat. It took me a moment to realize that the sound was laughter. The Beast found this amusing.

"No, no, no! Get back, you monster," Pops said. His legs staggered in hasty retreat.

Pops slipped on the spilled rum and landed on his back. Moving quicker than I imagined him capable, the surgeon flipped onto his stomach and spidered underneath the wagon.

The Beast used a claw-nail to scrape up Billy's cranial leftovers. We could not see it, but we heard licking and the soft musical humming of the creature's delight. It ate the rest of the Kid.

Pops said, "Maybe it'll attack the horses next and leave us alone."

"I wouldn't bet on that. Raton has plenty of livestock. The Beast prefers humans."

Pops considered this. His weak, grizzled chin bobbing as he tried to outthink the eater. He was drenched in fearful body sweat and to say he smelled worse than a goat is insulting to goats.

He pushed his scalpel at me.

"You're going next," he said.

"What?"

"You heard me. Get out from under my wagon. I'll take your eye if you don't."

I had my cane blade inches from his torso but I supposed he was too afraid to notice. We had no time to debate which of us might grievously harm the other in a battle to see who might be consumed first. The decision had already been made.

A claw skewered Pops' ankle. The Beast dragged him out from under the wagon. He tried to dig himself into the floor. But stone doesn't yield. He left scratches though, ten little white lines etched into the rock. Not that it would've made any difference but he forgot to take his scalpel with him. In the final tussle he wrapped an arm through one of the wagon wheels. The Beast yanked and a spoke snapped. So did Pops' forearm. It wasn't any quieter after that. They might've been flying. We heard windy noises. Blunt impacts. Sucking liquid crunches like a man shoveling mud into a washtub. Pops' voice echoing, bouncing around the alcove. The horses were shrieking, kicking at their corral. The Beast's high-pitched whistle covered it up – mostly.

Mostly. But not all of it. Pops talked to God for perhaps the only time in his life.

"OPLEASEHELPMEOGODPUUUHLEEEZZZZZZ!"

God didn't help.

I put my arm around Wu's shoulders. I was surprised to feel the rum barrel at his side.

"Wu, my young friend, we're going to make a run for it. Out the front end of the wagon, right there. It's only a short distance and we're clear of this niche. I bet you can jump that skimpy gate. It's a blizzard out there. Easy to hide. Hard for the Beast to follow. And a fast runner like you…? You keep the mountain wall on your right. Around that first bend is the door to Nightfall. Run. Leave the barrel with me. Keep your head down. Don't stop until you're inside the doors. Scream until everyone comes to see what you're yelling about. Don't let Miss Evangeline come out here. I don't want her to see this. Now I'm right behind you. When I slap you on the back, you move. Ready?"

Wu nodded.

I gave his shoulder a squeeze and then I slapped him hard on the back.

"Get moving! Run!"

Wu shot out from under that wagon like a cannonball.

Well, I'd lied to the boy. It wasn't easy to hide. The Beast was faster than any boy.

I wasn't following him either. At least not yet I wasn't.

On all fours I wriggled out from my hiding spot. Cane sword in hand I looked around, waiting to be swept up in claws, thrashed and skinned alive. But I would slow the Beast down and give Yong Wu a chance to make it back safely. My heart was a hammer in my chest. I was breathing like I was the one running for my life. I circled around to the rear of the wagon.

Nothing.

I looked high into the rocky dome of the alcove.

Shadows, yes. But none loomed so large as the Beast. I thought about what I had seen since Billy was taken. This was the Beast from my night with Orcus watching at Nightfall's windows. Not the clumsy, moaning, bovine-headed creature lurching through snowdrifts on the trail. Here was the slaughterer of Raton's hunters. A thing that felt no fear of any man that walked the earth.

But where had it gone? And where was Pops?

I did my best not to step in the bloodstains of

resurrected Billy. But it was impossible. The soles of my boots were sticky. There was a single bone in the corner, tossed away against a wall. It was a long bone, likely one of Billy's legs. It might have belonged to Pops though. I did not let myself be distracted by the grisly spectacle. My gaze I kept up high, swiveling my head like an owl's. The horses appeared terrified but physically unharmed. Their corral remained intact. No, the Beast was not interested in killing animals. Except for one: man.

I had no doubt that Pops was dead. But where had the Beast fled with him?

I circumnavigated the wagon. Ready to fight. Prepared to die.

The Beast was not here.

At first, I felt better. I squirmed under the wagon one last time and retrieved the barrel. As I backed out it occurred to me that if the Beast was not here it might be just outside the niche. I might have sent Yong Wu running into a deathtrap.

I hoisted the barrel under my arm. I marched out into the blizzard. Before I could leave I had to open the gate I had advised Wu to jump over. I saw his sliding boot marks in the snow on the other side. He'd made it this far. Good. Maybe we had gotten lucky. Or Wu had.

I stepped through the gate. Dragging it shut behind me, I heard the voice.

A husky, wet voice it was. Slow-talking, enunciating every syllable. Like language was something it had learned quite recently, and the acquisition was a point of great pride.

"I let the boy go," It said.

I expected to see the red eyes, the slavering jaw of killing teeth.

I saw only snow. Snow falling in a thick curtain just outside the edge of the stone shelter.

"Who goes there? Who speaks to me?"

"You know who I am," It said.

"You are the Beast."

"Some call me that. I do what beasts do and cannot reject the name given to me."

The voice seemed to come at me from more than one direction. It was to the right of me. But also to the left and farther off. I felt it in my head and filling my senses. It buzzed my bones.

"Show yourself," I said. My eyes darted, looking for any sudden movement. I wished I had a lantern or a torch. The palpable dark was like a monster itself.

"Do you really want that, Doc-tor? Isn't it easier to talk this way?"

Snow masked the darkness of the mountain. I saw only what was directly in front of me. Snow clinging to me, to my face. Air changing to fog as it left my lips. My words, my breath disappearing. I pointed my blade at snow.

"I- I don't know what I want," I said.

"That's better," It said.

"No, I do know. I want you leave this place."

"I was called here. I go where I am called – if I want to. When I want to leave, I'll leave."

"Who called you here? I don't believe it. No one desires... something as dreadful as you."

"Tsk...tsk, Doc-tor, you're going to hurt me talking like that. I'm acting friendly to you. When I might have, oh, pulled out your guts and peeled your skin off like a dirty white glove."

"How can you speak if you are a beast?"

"Do you talk to dogs, Doc-tor? Or, rather, might I ask if they talk to you... hmm?"

So the Beast knew of Orcus too. How long had it been watching us? Did it spy on us within the interior of the Adderlys' mansion? I had thought we were safe inside, at least.

"You seem to know me well," I said.

"I wish to know you even better. These dark mountains are a lonely place. But I live across dimensions. The woods are my home. Where you find remoteness, you'll find me. Would you like to travel, Doc-tor? Do you want to see things no man has seen? I can take you from this dull rock. I'm tired of it. And so bored. Let's go, you and I, and have new adventures together."

I dared to step closer to the rim of the alcove.

"Why choose me, Beast?"

"That's close enough, Doc-tor."

I froze mid-step, and then gently let the toe of my boot touch the ground. The wind howled. The red eyes glowed ahead of me. Not up high where I expected the head of the Beast to be, but lower, level with me. The ruby-bright eyes were lit from within. I could not look away. I did not chance to shift my body. Or step forward or back. The Beast was so close. It might sweep out a long-clawed hand and open my throat. My breath was stuck in me. I felt as if I might faint.

"Why are you killing men?" I asked, finally.

But the eyes were gone. I walked to the edge of the mountain. I gazed into the snow churning clockwise in the abyss like foamy, black ice-waters flowing into a deadly whirlpool. I was suddenly shivering. I clutched my coat tight, tucked my chin, and returned to the lodge.

19
ONE OF US

Before I made it back to the lodge doors, two things happened to change the course of the evening and subsequently our investigation into the Beast of Nightfall Lodge. I have always believed that life is chaotic as a rule and serendipitous on rare occasions. Hindsight provides the only indication of which type of event one is experiencing at any moment. In a shorter formula: things only make sense when they are finished. Often they never make sense. I do not intend to say that life has no meaning. But meaning is imposed rather than implicit. We must question everything, always; we are thinking creatures for a reason. It is what we do best. I am forever on the search for patterns and clues from which I can deduce facts. Despite my thudding heart and the watery, boneless way my legs wished to buckle under me as I rushed from the scene of my encounter with the Beast, I could not ignore the appearance of evidence. I saw clues – there were several of them just outside the niche. I left the path twice.

It was, as I have stated, quite dark.

The moon had been stuffed away behind a cloudbank. The stars too.

I had my cane-sword in my right hand. The rum barrel rested in the crook of my other arm. I was trying to follow the path. Snow blew over it, but it was still recognizably the smoothest, flattest portion of ground. I suppose a blind man might have wandered too far to the outer border and walked off the mountain. I didn't. But I was surprised to see someone nearly had. Rather, they appeared in the process of doing so as I approached. First, I worried it was the Beast. But it was too small, too stooped over, and it seemed to be holding its head in its hands.

"Ho, there! Get back from the precipice!"

The figure spun on me. I saw it was not holding its head but a pair of binoculars. The figure had been looking out into the storm, at the opposite ridgeline, despite the fact that visibility was nearly impenetrable.

"What are you doing?" I brandished my blade.

The figure came toward me but did not answer.

"Answer me, or I will run you through." I might have done just that; my nerves being frayed as they were. I held up the blade, hoping the figure might see I was not making idle threats. Still, I received no answer. The figure wore a furry hood and a thick coat of the same animal skin. He pulled off his hood and I saw why he had not answered.

"Smoke Eel, is that you?"

The guide nodded. He opened his mouth as if to speak (which I found rather strange in a mute), but then he fumbled inside his coat and removed the notebook he wore on a string around his neck. He used his teeth to pull off his mitten. He had a pencil stub in his pocket. He began to scribble in the notebook. He flipped it around so I might read it.

"It's too dark. I can't see," I said. "Look, let's get inside. There are dangers afoot."

He shook his head. Then from under his coat he produced a lantern. He struck a match and lit the wick. You could tell he had some experience lighting things in the wind. When the lantern glowed, he held it out with the notebook for me to read.

DID YOU SEE THE BEAST?

"Yes, I did. At least two men are dead. Well, Billy the Kid is dead. Really, really dead this time. Pops Spooner is missing and very likely dead. Did you see the Chinese boy run this way?"

Smoke Eel wrote. He turned the notebook around.

NO. NOBODY BUT YOU.

"Got it. I need to check on the boy. He was going to the lodge." I started off, but Smoke Eel grabbed my sleeve. He tipped the lantern back along the path, casting a patch of light closer to the mountain than where I had passed. He pointed with his pencil and tried to pull me along.

Back to the niche.

"No, you don't want to go back there. I'm not going either."

He pointed and clamped onto my elbow.

"You want to show me something?"

He nodded.

"I'll go. But not where the wagon and horses are. Do you understand me?"

He nodded again.

I let him lead me over to what I'd call a significant piece of evidence. Between two rows of snow-covered boulders was a second path, hidden from the main one. It was narrow enough for only one person to pass at a time, and going that way required a bit of climbing. No trouble in the daylight under more normal circumstances, but not something I was going to do on this night.

"I'm not going there," I said. "I thought you said you didn't see anyone?"

He wrote on his pad.

I DID NOT SEE. I HEARD. MOANING. I THOUGHT SOMEBODY WAS HURT.

Here I worried that the "somebody" involved might be Yong Wu. That the Beast had attacked him along this second pathway, parallel to the one we'd walked together. I snatched the lantern from Smoke Eel and entered the path. I couldn't let go of the sword or the rum barrel, so I hung the handle over my sword grip. There it swung. Flashes of lamplight made the landscape seem to tilt like the deck of a ship. Growing dizzy, I slipped over loose stones and lost my footing, tumbling sideways, before a pair of boulders caught me. A vise-like pain struck through my pelvis. Panicking, I nearly dropped the rum barrel. The last thing I needed was a severed head covered in iridescent green slime gushing out and making a proper mess.

Smoke Eel hauled me onto my feet again.

Bruised, if not broken, I pressed onward.

"I need to see if the boy's body is here. Help me look," I said, limping ahead.

He scratched out a message.

I LOOKED. NOBODY HERE. BUT YOU NEED TO SEE.
"See what?"

He took the lantern and swung it low.

Footprints, a neat track of them. A man's boots. I bent and inspected them. They went toward the niche and back out again. I'd smeared some of the tracks when I tripped but the rest were preserved. They were fresh enough to still be visible. But the storm would soon erase them. The "going in" prints had more snow filling than the "going out" tracks did. I didn't understand why they bothered Smoke Eel so much. He indicated that we had a bit farther to go. I wanted nothing more to do with the niche on this particular night. But I supposed if the Beast wanted me in its belly, that's where I'd already be. As it turned out, Smoke Eel only wanted to walk a few feet farther. He stopped and nudged my arm. Then he pointed.

The tracks ended well short of the place where the horses and wagon were.

They didn't go off in another direction. But they changed. There were signs of a great commotion in the snow. The boot tracks spread apart, as if a man were standing, waiting for someone to pass, or for something to happen. All around those last prints the snow pushed against the rocks. Smoke Eel brought the lantern to one side. Scratch marks. Deep ones. They were not made by human hands. Five claws dragging against the stones. Frozen dirt dug up and flung around. Great chunks of icy, hard ground pried up and overturned. I couldn't have done more to deface the earth with a shovel and a pickaxe. The ground was too hard, you see.

And there was some blood. Not much. But a single mark like a brushstroke from a clumsy housepainter. The color leaped out very red in that sandy lane of whites and tans.

"I see," I said. "You followed the moans you heard, and found this?"

Smoke Eel nudged me again and smiled to show I'd gotten things correct. Then he raised his lantern a little higher. The light was not so strong but it cast farther. He stretched his arm but didn't want to walk over the disturbed ground. I saw what he wanted me to see. There on the other side of the scratched up snow and dirt lay a pile of clothes. I went straight to it and picked up a pair of men's long johns, a wool shirt, and a pair of riding trousers. Men's clothing. High quality. Torn to shreds, so their size was difficult to judge. The undergarments had animal hairs stuck to them. The shirt and trousers too, though not as much.

Dark gray-black hairs like the Beast's.

Smoke Eel wrote in his book furiously.

IT CHANGED. FROM A MAN.

"You think the Beast is a man?"

Smoke Eel wrote.

YES. ONE OF US.

I nodded as I unbuttoned my coat and stuffed the clothing inside.

"We'll go and tell the others." I started backing out of the narrow passageway. I had no room to turn around with the barrel. My blade clanged against the rocks. I was feeling claustrophobic jammed in this narrow crag. *Death chute is more like it*, I thought.

I didn't notice Smoke Eel writing another note until

he pushed it into my face.

YOU SHOULD BE CAREFUL WHO YOU TELL.

ONE OF US = THE BEAST.

BUT WHICH ONE?

"Yes, that is the key question." Despite the numbing blast of the blizzard winds, I was glad to leave the cramped passage. "I know who I plan to talk to first," I shouted over the storm.

Smoke Eel scribbled another message

REMEMBER. TRUST NONE OF THEM.

NO ONE IS SAFE.

MAYBE NOT EVEN YOU.

He had the lantern hanging between our faces. I read the note and looked into Smoke Eel's steel-blue eyes. He stuffed the notebook down into his layers of furs. He blew on his fingers and put his mitten back on. As he lowered his light, I regarded the sawed-off shotgun holstered to his thigh. His mitten rested on the pistol grip. He could cut me in half with one pull.

A blue-eyed Indian guide.

Trust no one, I thought.

Good advice.

20

A CHESHIRE GRIN

"Let me understand you. You're asking me if I change from a man into the Beast? Do I have that correct? This is too much. Is everyone hearing what Dr Hardy is saying?" Claude's voice climbed higher. "It's a joke, right? You're playing some sort of cruel, awful prank on me. Ha! Well, I appreciate humor. But yours is in poor taste, Hardy."

Claude Adderly reclined on a tufted gold velvet divan in front of a roaring fire. The orange flames threw warm tiger-stripes over his body. He had a whiskey glass in hand. Empty. He wore a silk robe. His hair was combed back wetly; the rows of the comb's teeth still showed. He had bathed since returning from his ride. I smelled the musky soap he used. He lit a cigarette.

He put the cigarette between his lips. His hands were shaky. He had dark rings around his eyes like an insomniac. After a few puffs of tobacco, he started clapping.

"Bravo, Dr Hardy." He talked around his cigarette. "You take first prize among fools. Father! Get the doctor his treasured Apis Bull from ancient days. But really, no one has more bull than the doctor does. Am I right? You're positively full of it. Don't be greedy now."

"I only want to ask you a few questions," I said. "If you answer them satisfactorily, then we can all rest easier. You will be vindicated. I'll gladly apologize for any insult you've felt."

I had tried to carry out my interrogation privately. I asked Evangeline and Wu (thank God he had returned safely and was in the process of forming a posse to aid me when Smoke Eel and I came through the door) to be present, along with Oscar and Vivienne. Cassi overheard our conversation and insisted on being included. Smoke Eel lingered on the perimeter of the discussion. I wanted him there. He was a witness, the first one to discover the shredded clothing.

"Answer the doctor's questions, Claude. You have nothing to hide," Oscar said.

The long, trying, murderous day had made everyone tired and irritable. I knew my accusations would fail to endear me to the Adderlys. But I saw no other way. Oscar had a cigar in hand. He'd also been drinking. Now he perched for a moment on the arm of a well-worn leather wingback chair. He could not bring himself to sit down fully. He had been pacing the length of the room ever since I told him of my intention to confront his son. I told them Billy was dead and Pops was missing. Vivienne backed her wheelchair against the wall, as if she expected a physical brawl to break out. And it might well have, if not for Cassi. Claude's twin sister did not treat me as an enemy or a joke. If anything, she acted as though she hoped we all could still be friends.

"Rom isn't charging you with a crime," she said, gliding near her brother's seat and bumping up against it with her hip. She reached out, ruffling his hair with her fingernails.

Claude ducked forward to escape her. Lank locks fell down his forehead. He left them there. Smug, bored, and spoiled rotten – and yet the greatest aura he gave off was fear.

"I have no authority," I admitted.

"And I have no compelling reason to submit to your grilling. In my own home!"

"Claude, darling," his mother said. "Talk to us. We are your family."

"Huh! You don't act like a family. You with your starcharts and occultist literature. Communing with the spirits of the dead or whatever it is you do locked away in candlelit rooms at all hours of the night. And Father... Father has his safaris and expeditions. He'd pay more attention to us if he could shoot us and stuff our carcasses for his morbid little jungle dioramas."

"They are not all jungle scenes," Oscar said. "You know that. I am an avid explorer. It's in my blood. I have invited you to join me on multiple occasions. You steadfastly refused."

"I've no desire to sit in a tent, shivering with malaria. Hearing *Bwana* this, and *Jefe* that out of the mouths of the fawning local villagers is not my way of enjoying a tramp in the woods. I'd rather go to Paris. Or London. I want cities. Joy! People! Slaughtering exotic fauna doesn't set my heart racing."

Oscar grunted with disgust.

"That is unfair to your father," Vivienne said. "He is

a pioneering naturalist. Whether you agree with him or not, your father is an artist. Without his collections many animals would be lost to history, unknown to museums and the general public. He loves his animals famously."

"He loves the dead ones he can control and play with like toys. *His* animals – that's more correct than you intended. He wants to possess them. Only they don't have any say. Do they…?"

"Enough!" Oscar roared. He slammed his fist down on the desk beside him, making the pens and ink bottles jump. "You will answer Dr Hardy's questions." Oscar shook his white-knuckled fist at his son. "Afterward, you may leave this house. If we are no family to you, then go!"

"Father!" Cassi cried. "You don't mean that."

"I mean every word. Claude feels he is better than we are. So let him prowl the globe until he finds others like himself. I have given you and your brother everything. Maybe now is the time for you two to make the leap. Seek your own fortunes. You might find the world is less kind than you think. You want joy? You'll be lucky to get survival." A cylinder of ash dropped from Oscar's cigar. He stepped on it, grinding it into the Persian carpet. I don't think he perceived what he had done, either to his children or his rug. "Dr Hardy, ask away. Claude will comply. If nothing else, your inquiry has revealed to me a schism in my own household. Begin, before I lose my temper and throw the lot of you out on your asses into this stormy night."

"Yes, well… thank you," I said.

I was feeling much less sure of myself now that I had the floor. My frozen coat and trousers had begun to thaw. I saw a puddle spreading under me on the boards. I stepped away from my leakage. "Billy the Kid is dead."

"Obviously," Claude said.

"What I mean to say is that the man we knew as Billy the Kid is dead. And he was, in fact, Billy the Kid. Pops brought him back from the dead with a bright green glowing elixir that he injected into his brain. But the revivified Billy is also dead. Dead for certain. I saw the Beast crush his head flat. And then... the Beast ate him."

Claude started laughing.

Cassi covered his mouth with her hand. He nipped at her. She bared her nails as if to gouge out his eyes. But while she was playing to break up the awkward atmosphere of the room – an awkwardness I delivered and still had more in supply – Claude was genuinely unnerved.

Everyone stared at me. Even Wu, who knew the truth of what I related. Claude pulled a queer, elastic smile stretching his cheeks like a mask. His mood had altered from a sense of personal outrage to barely controlled mania. He bobbed his head along with my every word.

"Yong Wu is my witness," I said.

Wu cleared his throat.

"Yes, I saw what Dr Hardy has told you."

"Thank you, Wu." I started to feel a confident wind gathering in my sails. "The Beast grabbed Pops and, from the sounds we heard, he is also a fatal victim of the Beast." I decided to omit the part about the Beast talking to me. "In my retreat to Nightfall I ran into

Smoke Eel who told me he had found something along a second narrower path, closer to the mountain."

"The goat path," Claude interrupted. "Sorry. That's what we've called it since Cassi and I were children. Go on. Your tale is captivating me. I am a great fan of the mysterious and macabre. Poe has nothing on you, Dr Hardy." Claude smashed the stub of his cigarette roughly into a black onyx ashtray atop a carved stand shaped in the image of the Egyptian goddess Bast, the feline deity, daughter of Ra, the sun god, and wife of Ptah, the craftsman god of re-birth. The onyx dish balanced on the tips of the cat's ears. She was intricately carved rosewood with gold flake eyes. Claude nearly knocked her over.

The logs in the fireplace collapsed, sending up fiery sparks and unraveling tentacles of smoke that drifted through the iron grate. The wood statuette distracted me. I thought I heard it purring loudly but no one else reacted to the sound. Claude rolled himself another thinly-twisted, abysmal-smelling cigarette. His whiskey glass, tucked between his knees, glinted in the firelight.

"Will anyone pour me a drink?" he asked, not bothering to glance up from his rolling. He licked the cigarette paper. He had a very long, very pink tongue. Why hadn't I noticed that until now?

Cassi appeared beside the divan with a crystal decanter. She refilled his whiskey.

Claude shot his big eyes up at her and blinked slowly. Then he smiled a Cheshire grin. It was too wide, that smile. His teeth were like tusks, pressing down against his lips. Without breaking his connection with his sister, he swept a long, silky arm at me.

"Your question, Doctor," Claude said.

"Pardon me," I said.

"Ask me if I am the Beast."

"Oh, I wasn't there yet."

"I know. I'm skipping ahead." Claude sipped his bourbon. The purring – I was hearing it. Definitely. I looked at the statuette. It seemed less wooden now and more like a real cat, covered in shimmery hair. The eyes were alive, watching me coldly. Claude watched me too. I backed away from the divan. Claude swiveled, crouching on his haunches. He was covered in hair too.

"Rom, are you feeling all right?" Cassi asked.

Evangeline came to me out of the shadows. She put her arm around my shoulders. She touched the back of her hand against my forehead.

"He's burning with fever," she said. "Help me get this damp coat off of him."

"It is not a fever," I said. "Do none of you see Claude's teeth? They are horrible."

As they shucked the coat from me, I fell with it to the floor. Fainting has never been a manly quality in literature or in life. That held true for this occasion as well. I peered through the space between Evangeline and Cassi to spot Claude tearing at the divan cushions with scimitar claws. His jaws opened and his throat was like a train tunnel.

Oscar leered at me through a cloud of cigar smoke.

"I have had worse fevers," he said.

"What is wrong with my teeth?" Claude asked.

"Get him up and onto the couch," Evangeline said, taking charge.

Claude (who appeared restored to his human state)

and Oscar seized my armpits and ankles, depositing me on the couch. It was not torn up as I had envisioned. Claude's smirky attitude had dissipated. If he did not seem quite as caring as his sister he was at least aiding in my revival. He waved an embroidered pillow at me and tried to give me a sip of his whiskey.

"You were changed," I said to him. I pushed the smeary glass away.

"So you have said. Repeatedly. Rest up and you can accuse me in the morning."

"Bast," I said. "The cat changed too. It was alive... purring..."

"Hardy." Evangeline unbuttoned my shirt. "You are hallucinating. This is fever talk."

I propped myself up on the cushions. The ashtray, the Bast wood carving – it was normal.

"No! You will not dismiss me so easily. I am not hysterical," I said.

"He's acting like a damned madwoman," Oscar said. "He's the one we need to watch."

I grabbed the onyx ashtray and threw it at him. It smashed the window. Snow poured in.

Evangeline, Cassi, and Claude – together they restrained me.

I was weak. My head spun.

"Smoke Eel? Smoke Eel, tell them what we found. Look on the floor with my coat. I have the shredded remains of a man's clothing. Smoke Eel found it outside. There were tracks. Boot prints. They stopped abruptly. Whoever made them clawed up the frozen ground... Tell them!"

"Smoke Eel, is any of this true?" Oscar asked him.

The guide came forward cautiously. He went over to my coat on the floor and looked inside the folds. He wrote in his notebook. Turning the pages toward Evangeline to read.

But I saw them too.

NO.

THERE'S NOTHING IN HIS COAT.

I NEVER FOUND TRACKS.

"He's lying! We found them. He is lying!"

And in my struggles the exertion overcame me. I felt a dark liquidity pooling up from underneath me. The trophy room flooded with darkness. My head sank. Black pools rising. The howl of the wind in the shattered glass... the firelight flickered like the devil's own tongue. Smoke tentacles wrapped me tight and squeezed me down hard into the divan's soft cushions. Vivienne was the last thing I remember seeing. Her face calmly observing me from the shadows.

As I went under in utter blankness.

My consciousness obliterated.

Like a dying star...

21
MAD MEN

I awoke in a rush. All my senses snapping into focus instantly. I sat up. I was in bed, naked but for a sheet. There was a pitcher of water on the nightstand. A bowl with a washcloth soaking. A half-filled glass. My head ached. I filled the glass all the way and drank it down. Then I did the same twice more. I had the most unquenchable thirst. I stopped, fearing I might make myself sick drinking so much water so quickly. The room, my bedroom at Nightfall, was dimly lit with a low-burning oil lamp. I smelled herbs and noticed an oily residue on my neck and chest.

I thought I was alone.

"You look like mule shit that's been stepped in. Paler than a drowned witch too. Though maybe I shouldn't be talking so loud about witches," McTroy said.

He tipped his chair forward, away from the wall, and dropped into the circle of light.

"It's good to see you," I said. I rubbed my fingers on my chest. My skin tingled.

He nodded toward the door.

"We're locked in."

"You cannot be serious!" I jumped up from my bed. Winding the sheet around me like a Roman toga I proceeded to the door. I jiggled the handle and discovered McTroy was right.

"This is absurd. You and I are the only two people I fully trust right now."

"Ain't you being a little harsh on Evangeline and Wu? They're our partners in this affair."

I stalked my way a short distance back to the bed and sat on the mattress.

"I wish I could trust them. I mean I do trust them. But I don't know if *they* are them."

"Doc, I can't tell you how much I've missed the way you talk. Now can you explain it to me so a person might understand? Ever since that concoction squirted in my head I get fuzzy thoughts, though I'm starting to feel better. Part of me is still in the desert somewhere bakin' under the sun and almost freezin' while I do it. But the boxed up part of me is gone now. I'm floatin' and feelin' pretty fine." He hiccupped, smiling his gold-toothed smile as he scratched his overgrown chin. "My thirst is cut down. The world's looking a lot more charming than it did a few hours ago, I'll tell you that."

"You're drunk!" I gazed in his bleary, bloodshot eyes. I smelled his stale breath.

"Don't see how that's possible. I ain't been out of this room. They locked me in right after you left. Then they opened the door only long enough to dump your butt in that bed. They stripped your clothes off. Viv perfumed you like you were a dancing girl. I was too damn beat to care. But now that you mention the liquor – I do feel pleasantly lubricated."

I stood up again, attempting to walk around the bedroom as I was puzzling over things.

"Of course! The head is in rum. You, McTroy, therefore are submerged in rum. Or the head you are connected to is sunk in spirits. The desert part of you must be associated with the headless body. It is a three-part, triangular connection between you, the severed head, and the headless desert body, which we have no idea how to locate. I suppose that Billy also felt this bonding, if you will. That explains why Pops kept the head sequestered from the outside world by locking it inside the inner sanctum of his medicine wagon. Everything is becoming clear!"

McTroy sat with his arms braced on his knees. He wore faded long underwear with holes worn through the knees and elbows and a sprinkling of patched moth holes, poorly sewn, that resembled closed, puckered eyelids.

He grinned.

"Doc, I can't believe I'm saying this. But you're making even less sense than usual. Now go back further and explain what the hell you're talking about. 'Cause I ain't got nothin' better to do for one. And for another, it seems important. Whose head is where now?"

"Viv stripped me?" I asked, just realizing what he had said.

"Naw." He waved me off.

I sighed with relief.

"It was her and Evangeline together. But it was like they done it a thousand times before. There wasn't no joy in it. A pair of grim night nurses. Like nuns. At least they weren't giggling."

I turned up the lamp. "I suppose it is too late to feel any embarrassment."

"Your bare ass meant little to them." He patted me on the shoulder in an attempt to comfort me. "They thought I was sleeping and left me alone," he added. "For what it's worth."

"I don't know what to make of that," I said.

"Viv did some strange talking and put her hand on your head. Then they was whispering and conspiring. Weaving all sorts of witchy schemes. I didn't know if they were fixing to ride you or cook you in a stew." McTroy fetched my water pitcher and drank deeply from the spout.

"You're accusing Evangeline of witchery?"

"She's never hid her interest in the spooky arts. But this was flagrant."

"I see."

"I can't say the prospect of a woman being a witch tamps down my interest. Not entirely."

"So you are interested in Evangeline... romantically speaking?"

"I never mentioned romance. Calm yourself. I'm saying the idea, not the doing of it."

"Theoretically, you mean?"

McTroy snapped his fingers and shut one eye tightly. "There you go, Doc. I knew you'd know the word. Theoretically being most of what you do." The rum-soaking made him turn philosophical. "I don't rule out witches as acquaintances. That's all I'm saying. I'd dance with 'em, you know? Walk with 'em by the river in the moonlight. These are fine women we're talking about here. Friends of ours. Why, think of all we been through with Evangeline. She's our partner. But I'm not exactly calling for a preacher to marry us in the mornin'."

"That is good news." I meant it sincerely.

"Oh, they drew something on your forehead with a bowl of blood and a shiny black feather. Might've been a crow's. But I wouldn't make a big fuss about it."

"What?" I searched the room for a mirror. There was none. I tried to see my reflection in the lamp glass. "Is it still there? What does it look like?"

"Well, lemme see…"

I craned my neck forward and handed McTroy the lamp.

"I don't need that light shoved in my face." He pushed my hand away.

"Well… is the sign there? Perhaps you were only dreaming. You've been drugged, which is not insignificant. And, as far as I can tell, you are drunker than usual."

"Hold still." He seemed to consider my forehead for a long while.

"It's there," he said.

"Oh mymymy–"

"And it's definitely blood. But so what? Woman paint themselves up to act fancy. Why wouldn't they fancy you up too? You was like a doll to them. A plaything. They was poking at you. Under the blankets it looked like they might've been pouring water on your nether parts."

"My nether parts…?"

"It's likely harmless. Like plucking a dead chicken. You can't hurt a dead chicken."

I grabbed the washcloth and was about to wipe the bloody mark away.

McTroy seized my wrist. "Don't do that. What if it's important? Even if they're witches, they're smart witches. It's a biddy little thing you wouldn't even know you had if I didn't say."

"What does the symbol look like?"

McTroy tried to describe it with no success. He said triangles, then a circled star. When I attested to my confusion, he licked his finger and drew the shape with his spit on the dresser.

"A pentacle," I said, sitting back on the pillows, gathering the blankets around me.

"Is that bad?" McTroy tried the door handle again. It was still locked. He hit the door with his shoulder and knocked the butt of his Colt Army above the keyhole. Nothing happened.

"I believe so. But, on your suggestion, I will leave it until I know more."

"There, that's the smartest thing you said yet. What's this I hear about a head in a barrel?"

I told him everything that had transpired since I last left him.

"Where's the rum head at?" he asked when I had finished. "Did you lose it?"

I shook my head. "Out there. I set it down when I came in. I believe Wu took it for safekeeping. No one else knows its significance."

"You think Smoke Eel might be in league with the Beast?"

"It's possible. He is certainly showing a degree of deception. I know those torn clothes were in my coat." I found my luggage and changed into a fresh suit. My boots waited by the door. As I sat to put them on, I remembered another crucial piece of evidence. "Remember the human tracks we found under that tree. The one with the panther scratches etched in the trunk?"

"The tree where Claude fell," he said.

"That's it. Well, you showed me how those boot prints had an imperfection because there was a rock stuck in the wearer's boot heel."

McTroy nodded. "I noted it."

"The tracks Smoke Eel showed me had that exact peculiar marking. It was the same man both at the tree and lurking outside Nightfall Lodge last night."

"Claude," he said.

"It had to be. That is why I confronted him."

"I knew that boy had killer instincts. But how is it that a man changes into a Beast?"

There came a knocking at our door, followed by the quiet, yet audible, insertion of a key into the lock. The door cracked open a few inches as the person with the key struggled to free it from the old locking mechanism, which likely hadn't been used in years. McTroy drew his pistol. I remembered then that I had taken the bullets. I searched in vain for my walking stick, but it was not in the bedroom. I put up my fists. McTroy slid behind the creaking, oaken door.

"You're up," Evangeline said brightly. She carried a lit candle.

"Stay away, witch!" I shouted.

Evangeline frowned. "Are you ill?" She scanned the room. "Where is McTroy?"

In that instance, McTroy slammed the door and seized her in a bear hug.

"Bruja, I have you. Enchant us no more." He grunted and picked her up.

At first startled, Evangeline's expression soon altered.

"Have you two been drinking?" she asked.

"He has," I said.

She spotted the pistol in McTroy's hand. "Are you planning to shoot me?"

"Why? Have you hexed my bullets?" McTroy said, as his arms tightened. He aimed his pistol haphazardly at the wall and pulled the trigger. The hammer clicked on empty chambers.

"Ow! Let go of me! Or I will cast a spell you won't soon forget."

"You have already. See what you did to my forehead." I lifted a few stray hairs. "You stripped me and smeared me with... with... magical ointments. I may not be myself anymore."

"Hardy, if I could do that I would have done it long before tonight."

"See! You admit it!"

Evangeline shifted her hand, bringing the candle's flame under McTroy's hairy wrist.

"She burns me!" he cried. "The witch burns me."

He released her, jumping away and knocking over the chair. His legs tangled with the chair legs and down he went. He fell next to the bed, striking his head remarkably hard on the floor going down and again on the footboard as he attempted to rise. Then he was silent.

"What brand of wickedness do you wish to inflict upon us?" I said to Evangeline in hushed tones. I stiffened my resolve. "Is it unholy?"

"Depraved acts and vile things... that's what I'll do."

She spread her fingers and held them out rigidly. The nails were incongruous pink shells from the depths of some malignant, corrupt sea. Her green agate eyes became the devil's kaleidoscopes, flashing their enchantments even as they shucked the very soul from my body.

"Spare us," I said. "Remember, we were once your friends."

"Spare me," she said, dropping her hand. "Locking you up was a mistake. I told Viv as much. But she thought you needed protection. Now you've gone and become mad. It didn't take very long." She placed the candle on the dresser. "Is your fever gone?" She touched my cheek.

Overthrown by her powers, I nodded. "I think so."

Evangeline rinsed out the washcloth and dipped it into the bowl. She began cleaning the symbol from my forehead. "Viv is very worried about what's been happening. She put this pentagram on you to keep the dark forces from entering your mind." She tapped me above the eyebrows. My gaze darted into a bare corner. "You *have* been seeing things? Things other people do not see?" The kindness returned to her face. How could I have suspected her of evil?

"Yes. And the dog, Orcus, talks to me in my head. Oh, the Beast came to me outside. We spoke as well."

She dropped the washcloth in shock.

"You talked to the Beast? What did it say?"

"It asked me if I wanted to be its traveling companion. To see things across dimensions." I opened my arms slowly until they were wide apart. "Dimensions," I repeated.

She looked quizzically at me. "The Beast is a changeling. It's supernatural and more dangerous than any wild predator of the forest. I'm not sure how it got here. But it may not be the only changeling in this house. We have work to do. Is your lunacy finished for tonight?"

"I think so," I said, blushing. "Wait, no. I must tell you about the head in the rum barrel and why McTroy is drunk although he has had no spirits to drink."

Evangeline sat on the bed, sighing.

"Continue," she said.

After I finished my re-telling of the discovery Wu and I made of the elixir's secret ingredient, Evangeline eyed me curiously. She picked up the rag from the floor, tossed it in the bowl, and pressed her clenched hands into her dress.

"Where is the head now?" she asked.

"I think Wu has it."

She nodded and stood.

"Good. Your news is much to digest. But I have more. Claude has left Nightfall. Oscar refuses to venture out and search for him. I told Cassi and Viv that we will go after him. They are beside themselves with fear for him, and they asked for our help. Claude's likely heading for Raton. It's only a few miles."

"But the storm…?"

"Has nearly blown itself out. Claude is on foot. He can't have traveled far. But I'm afraid he won't make it down the mountain alive. Weird, sinister forces are aligned here at Nightfall."

I thought about the torn clothing I'd found and the prints that likely matched Claude's. The Beast's long sinewy arms and its red, red eyes. I saw in my mind's eye what it did to Billy.

"What if Claude is the Beast? Smoke Eel was lying. I had a vision. I saw Claude change into a monster."

Evangeline sized me up. She dusted my lapels. Snugged my tie.

"You have had a traumatic evening, Rom. If Claude is the Beast, then we will slay him and claim the reward," she said. "If he is not, we will bring him home." Her soft lips parted, revealing her teeth. *Will she kiss me?* I wondered.

Evangeline's eyebrow arched. "Did you say Orcus talks to you?"

"I did."

"You are a strange man, Rom. But I take you at your word."

McTroy moaned and sat up.

"Are you ready for a hunt, Mr McTroy?" she said loudly as she stepped back.

"I need bullets," he said. His unruly hair crackled electrically and stood on end as he rubbed the bumps he'd received. Despite a large tear in a seam under the arm of his longjohns, he appeared no worse after his fall. "Can't kill a damned Beast with only good intentions."

"Then I shall remove all hexes from you. Get up and get dressed. We'll leave at once."

Out the door she rushed, taking the candle with her and spilling wax on the threshold.

22
The Wendigo Hypothesis

I LIED TO PROTECT US. I TOLD YOU BE CAREFUL.
YOU DIDN'T LISTEN.

Smoke Eel turned his notebook around and wrote
more.

"I don't know why you lied. But the fact that you
discredited me was no favor," I said.

I was bundling myself up for the trek down the
mountain road toward Raton. Oscar still refused to
accompany us. He was a stubborn, iron-willed man.
Those qualities may have served him well in the bush
or braving the sweltering slog of a months-long jungle
expedition, but it did nothing to help him as a father.
Despite his unwillingness to go after his prodigal son
personally he was persuaded to aid our efforts. He gave
us proper winter gear, including a horse-drawn sledge
and a huge red Morgan stallion to pull it. Smoke Eel
argued against our going. Oscar quit the discussion,
stalking off to the trophy room with his box of Havanas.
Now the Indian guide tried to explain away his betrayal
of our mutual findings. He tugged at my arm.

I WILL SHOW OSCAR THE RIPPED CLOTHES. I

WILL TELL HIM. BUT NOT THE OTHERS. YOU DON'T KNOW WHAT YOU ARE FIGHTING AGAINST.

"Well, what is it? I have seen it firsthand. I can tell you it is no grizzly bear, wolf, or wildcat. It is a supernatural being. Much more like a man in its thinking than an animal."

He flipped to the next page.

IT IS A WENDIGO. OJIBWE AND CREE AND OTHER PEOPLE KNOW IT. NOT THE WHITE MAN. IT IS A SACRED CREATURE. EVIL SPIRIT. A MONSTER WHO EATS MEN. IT LIVES IN THE WOODS. BUT SOME MEN CHANGE INTO WENDIGOS TOO.

"You must tell Oscar. This is his hunt. He's put everyone in jeopardy," I said, stunned.

HE KNOWS.

"What? How could he? He seemed very skeptical of the supernatural when we arrived."

HE KNOWS. HE HIRED AN INDIAN TO CATCH INDIAN MONSTER.

I considered this. Smoke Eel had lied before. I certainly wasn't ready to trust him now.

"Does the Wendigo live here in New Mexico? Is it native to this territory?"

NO. I DON'T KNOW HOW IT CAME. BUT IT IS HERE.

"An indigenous monster uncommon to this area suddenly shows up and starts slaughtering hunters. It just so happens that one of the world's most famous hunters lives on the same mountaintop. And he hires you as an expert and guide. He wants to study the thing and then stuff it just right for a museum. Maybe one with his name over the door? It would be the capstone to his career. But I'm not sure I'm buying what you're selling, Smoke Eel. Why did he keep this a secret from us? If Oscar knew, then why send us out with incomplete knowledge? We acted at a great disadvantage. This is a competition. Knowing the monster is half the battle. We were almost guaranteed to be killed."

The guide looked at me as if I were a greenhorn. He didn't know whether to pity me or laugh in my face. I'll admit to a certain degree of naiveté when it comes to treachery.

THE MAN WHO CAPTURES WENDIGO WILL BE FAMOUS. OSCAR TIRED OF WAITING. ANGRY. HE SAW IT AND NEVER SHOT. WENDIGO TOO SLOW FOR OSCAR.

"I've seen the Beast, and it is not a slow thing."

Smoke Eel shook his head in frustration.

MORE HUNTERS MUST DIE. OSCAR WANTS MORE BLOOD = BIGGER NEWS. WENDIGO LEAVES HUNTING GROUNDS SOON. PRIZE HUNT SPEEDS UP KILLINGS.

If what Smoke Eel was saying were true then Oscar Adderly was a special kind of bastard. I had too many questions for the Indian guide to answer and no time before we left to rescue Claude from his ill-advised tantrum and solitary hike through the snow-filled canyon into Raton. McTroy had loaded his Colts and Marlin rifle. Evangeline wore a trapper's hat made of rabbits and she had a bow slung across her chest and a quiver of arrows. Wu put something on the sledge: the rum barrel. I needed to go. And I wasn't sure anything Smoke Eel told me was going to change the mission we were embarking on. Though now we had a clue what the Beast might be: a legendary creature, a mythical man-eater who roams the woods. The cannibal demon.

But I had another question.

"Smoke Eel, might there be more than one Wendigo?"

ONE WENDIGO. MORE FEEL ITS SPIRIT. TAKE IT INSIDE. ALWAYS HUNGRY.

"I don't understand. The Wendigo possesses men?"

Evangeline called me to the sledge. McTroy and Wu were already on board.

Smoke Eel was writing frantically. He scratched out a message and started again. Snow fell on the paper. He smeared the writing as he wrote. The end of his stubby pencil broke, and he threw it down in anger. He tore the last page of the notebook, pressing it in my hands.

ONE WENDIGO. MANY MAN-WENDIGOS. TOO LONG WITH EVIL MAKES U EVIL. MEN CHANGE TO MONSTERS. EATERS. ALL PART OF SAME. EVIL STAY HERE TO WANDER IS DEATH THE BEAST WILL TRICK YOU MAKEURUNCRAZY STAY!!! NIGHTFALL HUNGER IN THE WOODS FEEDSELFASTFAST DANGERURALLINDANG–

The Indian was determined to hold us back. His motives were unclear to me. I crumpled the note in my fist.

"Hardy, we are leaving without you if you do not come now," Evangeline shouted.

I walked away from Smoke Eel. The sky had cleared but it was still black night above us. Stars studded the cracks in the clouds like silver flecks in a coal seam. The wind had died. Powdery snow drifted from the treetops. They were heavy-laden, bending earthward. My steps creaked. The air was almost too cold to breathe unless you took small sips or pulled it through a woolen scarf. It was silent. Everything I saw appeared clean-edged, cut from tin. Icicles like wavy glass teeth. My friends were loaded in the sledge; exhalations fogged their faces. The Morgan horse stamped, ready to pull. I turned back to see Smoke Eel shutting the doors to Nightfall. I heard him bar the doors. Viv and Cassi were too upset to watch us leave. They wanted Claude back but feared we might perish. Guilt kept them back. Evangeline said Viv wasn't speaking to Oscar. Cassi wanted to join us. But her mother forbade her, begging her not to double her sorrow.

"I cannot lose both my children tonight," Vivienne had said.

Cassi remained with her mother.

Oscar sent Orcus with us to locate Claude a second time in less than a day.

The sledge had two benches. Evangeline and McTroy took the front. Evangeline sat tall with the reins in her hands. McTroy rested his rifle across his knees. Wu and I climbed into the second seat. Orcus jumped in between us. His furrowed look of concern bothered me.

"What did Smoke Eel want with you? He was agitated," Evangeline said.

"He spoke of Indian legends. Evil spirits. He may be right. But I know for a fact he is also a liar. I hear his arguments with a high degree of mistrust. He would have me doubting my very self." I stroked the dog's neck. "We'll guard the rear. With Orcus on our side, who will dare to challenge us?"

Orcus peered at the road. His tongue lolled from the side of his jaws. Ears sharply alert.

"I brought the rum we found," Wu said. He kicked lightly at the side of the barrel between his feet and winked at me.

"Excellent, Wu. You are as resourceful as you are brave. I hope my feverish antics did not distress you too much. It has been a long day after all. But I am feeling much better."

Evangeline clicked her tongue at the horse and shook the reins.

With a jolt we took off down the hill. The sledge's blades sliced through the snow.

"It's like a big sled," Wu said. "I have never been sledding before."

"Then you are in for a treat," I said.

The tall pines and scrubby white-wigged trees flew past us in a blur.

"Can you see Claude's tracks?" I shouted.

McTroy pointed. "He's dead center on the road. Heading into town like we guessed."

"Then we should have him in our company soon," I said.

I saw the moon appear. Like a snowball impaled on the jagged gray fence of the ridgeline. A ragged scrap of cloud soon blindfolded it. The road grew darker, curving deeper into the bottom of the canyon. The Morgan knew the way to town. He moved with confidence. His harness bells jangled merrily. I looked back and saw a smudge of shadow streak across the road and into the trees. It vanished so quickly that I wasn't sure it had been there at all. But a puff of icy crystals sparkled, dancing in the air, floating down from where they had been kicked up, like dust. We were gliding too swiftly for me to register any tracks, only the grooves we left in our wake. The hairs on my neck began to prickle. A scaly, snaking fear slithered against my spine.

"Dr Hardy, do you see something?" Wu asked. His voice carried a note of anxiety.

I smiled. "Looks like a fairytale. The woods are filled with ice magic."

Wu seemed happy with my answer. He settled back into his seat.

Orcus tilted his head at me.

"Did you see anything?" the brutish mastiff asked.

None of the others heard him. But I did.

"A dark something-or-other sprinting out there. I can't be sure," I whispered.

The dog looked over his brawny shoulder.

The horse brought us round a longer curve. Sword-like the sledge cut through high drifts.

Whump. Whump. Whump.

I used the excuse of wrapping my arm around Orcus to glance back again.

"There! To the right. See how it goes?" I said, nudging him.

A bounding shadow, like a river of darkness, flowed just beyond the spaced-out pines. I saw it pouring over rocks. Disappearing. Then dodging deeper into the woods. An erasure of the snowy whiteness more than anything else. An absence where one shouldn't be, where a moment later I spied the clear outline of boulders, but for an instant earlier, something flashed in front of the rocks.

Formless shadow. So fast. How could anything be so fast? We were outpacing it still.

Orcus stared off, following the direction of my outstretched arm.

"I missed it. Might it have been a deer?" he said.

"That was no deer," I said.

"A deer?" Wu asked, twisting in his seat. "Where is it?"

I thought I spotted antlers. An elk? But it did not run like an elk or a deer.

It was gaining on us.

I felt as if it could overtake us at any time if it chose to do so.

Orcus turned his nose up and sniffed. I grabbed hold of Wu's jacket collar.

"You're choking me," Wu said, making a face.

"Sorry there, Wu. Midnight is such a chilly hour. Come closer to the dog. Get warm."

"But it's after midnight," he said. "It is very, very late."

I said, "Soon the sun will climb those peaks. In the daylight, nightmares look foolish. That's why they come in the bedtime hours when our attention slackens and we are most vulnerable to suggestion. Oh, how they creep like poison ink. As our minds sleep, we soak up their permanent stain... our unknowing bodies relax... and their dinner bell rings. Bite, bite, bite."

I snapped my teeth together without thinking.

"Hey, Doc, what're you telling that boy?" McTroy asked. "Ghost stories?"

I looked at Wu whose mouth dropped open in an approaching wave of panic.

"Don't listen to what I say," I said. "My imagination always gets the better of me."

Orcus adjusted his position. The weight of him crushed my knee. He was keen on something he'd caught the scent of, ahead of the sledge in a flat treeless area where water must collect in the warmer seasons. A big rock sat there like an altar. Blanketed in white. There was a black flag staked out on the rock, by the side nearest the road. Orcus's jowls quivered. I thought he might leap out of his seat.

A torch rose from behind the rock.

The black flag turned red.

It was no flag.

It was blood… splashed blood that had melted the snow ran red over the rock. It steamed.

The torch moved around the rock. A big man was holding the flame. He studied the blood. Evangeline pulled on the Morgan's reins to halt the sledge. There was no fast stopping on this icy road. The sledge slowed and we headed for the rock where the blood and the man met.

McTroy shot his Marlin rifle once into the sky.

Then he levered it and aimed it at the man.

"Stop right there. Keep your hands high."

The big – no, he was huge – man was bundled for walking in the cold. I don't know if he heard what McTroy said. But he didn't listen. He cocked the arm carrying the torch back and hurled it at our horse. The torch pinwheeled through the air. The Morgan pulled us off the road trying to keep the fire out of its eyes. The blades of the sledge clashed with boulders. I heard the sledge cracking apart. We were turning over. I reached for Wu and found that he and Orcus were gone. The rum barrel banged against my ankle as it rolled out of the bench footwell and spilled over the side into the road. A whiteout wave of snow broke over the top of us, temporarily blinding me. I held fast to the sledge.

The vehicle abruptly stopped; I did not.

I was catapulted into a field of alternating blacks and whites. I hoped, against the odds, for a gentle landing. Pine branches reached for me greedily until they gobbled me up. I shut my eyes.

Flying–

Until I wasn't.

Cold crunching and evergreen smells: the sound of my battered body being slugged with cudgels and mangled by prickly jabby, tar-sticky pines. I tasted soft green needles on my tongue. I came to a stop, alone in a stand of pines.

Out of the corner of my vision I saw the huge man by the rock.

The blood inspector. Our torch-thrower. He looked like a giant.

A jaguar had him in its mouth and, with great effort, was dragging him away.

23
GIANTS & JAGUARS

When I say giant I do not mean a fabulous creature
that hates beanstalks and grinds men's bones to make
his bread. What I mean is a circus giant: a man of
extraordinary height and proportions that boggle the
mind. That is who I saw struggling with the jaguar.
Now I noticed something about this jaguar. It was all
black, not spotted. Its figure was leaner and suppler
than the first jaguar we had encountered on our return
along the Copper Trail. This was not the same cat that
had knocked Evangeline from her horse.

The predator took hold of the big man's neck and
shook him, dislodging his wooly hat and unraveling
the scarf that covered his outsized head. The man
looked rather grisly at that moment. His face dripped
with blood; an ear the size of my palm dangled by
a thread and he grimaced in the manner you might
expect of someone who was being throttled to death.
The giant had colossal hands and he used them
to pummel the jaguar's head. This did not faze the
creature, who bit down harder on the poor fellow and
gave him a twist that caused the man to moan in a

low, bellowing voice. It was a pitiful noise.

The wildcat pulled the giant through the snow, actually lifting the upper half of his lanky, though wide-bodied, opponent. Victim would be a truer term. The giant slugged his fists into the cat's fur. The cat blinked and looked annoyed. The man wore round glasses. The lenses were cracked now, and the wire frames bent all to hell. They slipped from his beakish nose. The giant tried to reach them as they were tumbling down his chest but the cat dragged him another few yards closer to the woods. It was a sad sight to see: this wounded man raking the snow for his shattered spectacles. His lengthy legs flailed. I once saw a man electrocuted accidently in a lab experiment back in Chicago during my college days. It's the sort of thing one never forgets. Convulsions and gritting teeth. A constant uncontrollable tremor racking the body. The giant writhed like that student.

I spied the edge of the woods up a short hill. The jaguar couldn't reach the summit with its quarry, although not for lack of trying. The giant had given up or fainted. Either way, the flapping of his elongated limbs ceased. He grew still as felled timber. His unfocused eyes remained open but his face relaxed. It was smooth and blank, the color of river clay. He had a heavy simian brow and a lantern jaw; his profile would've been difficult to hide behind a shovel blade. Saliva bubbles ran pinkly down the corner of his mouth into his collar. The jaguar struggled with the weight of him, easily in excess of four hundred pounds. In a fit of vexation the jaguar twitched its jaws, snapping the giant's neck.

Only then did it let him go.

The cat circled. From the cage of pine branches I watched the coal-black feline panting. Muscles rippling, tense, ready to pounce. The torch the giant had thrown still sputtered. Cat's eyes matched the flames. If it turned into a warlock I would not have been too surprised. Such was the ritualistic atmosphere in the canyon bottom during this peculiar pre-dawn sacrifice.

No fog formed above the giant's lips.

The cat and I reached our conclusions at the same instant: the giant was dead.

And if it could dispatch a giant, what would it do to my friends and me?

I shivered at the thought.

The jet fur of this black jaguar carried an oily sheen. Despite the terror it inspired, it was quite beautiful. I only wished there were bars between us.

So, I *had* spied a nocturnal stalker running behind the sledge on our way down the road from Nightfall. The panther had looked rather like the Beast out there lurking in the snowy cage of trees. I wasn't wrong to think a hunter was pursuing us.

Two jaguars. I hadn't expected that. This had to be the work of Oscar. I wondered if he had caught these cats in a South American jungle and released them up on the mountain. He had to know they were here, living in the shadows of Nightfall Lodge. Maybe he hoped to spread their species in the Southwestern territories. Maybe they were his mistake.

The black cat slunk across the icy road. It padded along in an urgent jog. Smoky amber eyes agleam, head bowing down and mouth open, its thick black tail trailing like a hook.

I looked at the overturned sledge. My head was only now clearing enough for me to put aside my panic and wonder about the health of my friends. I dared not call to them. My shout would bring the jaguar right to me. Or, worse, perhaps the creature might shift into a frenzy of killing, tearing apart the sledge riders, the Morgan horse, and any living thing in its sight. I kept quiet.

The horse began to blow and squeal at the approaching cat. He was down on his side, not off in the ditch with the sledge but on the edge of the road. His traces were twisted tight, and there was no way for him to escape his straps. He craned his neck to keep an eye on the cat.

But the cat was not interested in him.

I crawled on my belly out from under the pine branches.

When I propped myself up to see if I might locate the cat amid the nearby rocks I ended up sliding down the embankment and ramming into the sledge. It made quite a racket. The Morgan yelped and snorted at me.

"Easy there, boy. I am friend, not foe."

I scrambled onto my feet. The sledge tipped onto its right side, and when I poked my head into the seats I found no one. I didn't know whether that was good or bad. If they had been thrown in the crash they might be dashed upon the rocks. Maybe they fell out before the impact.

I peered over the top of the sledge.

In the ditch the black jaguar sniffed at a body. It was

not a woman, nor did it seem short enough to be Yong Wu. The cat was licking it. I saw blood in the snow. Red arches.

It has to be McTroy, I thought.

Desperately I searched for a weapon to save him. What did I have? A pocketknife? I opened the small blade. It was nothing. At least I could cut the horse's straps while I thought of a better way to help McTroy. Freeing the horse might fluster the cat and scare it off. Buy me some time. I started sawing at the leather. I worked by feel.

The horse sighed, looking back at me.

"Loose soon," I said. "You're on your own to run for it after that."

"Hardy," a voice whispered to me. "Get out of there. There's a panther about."

I looked for Evangeline. I knew it was her voice calling my name. "Where are you?" I said to the dark.

"In the rocks, behind you," she said.

"I'm saving McTroy," I said. "First the horse, then I'll help him."

"What?"

"I must save McTroy. The cat is about to feast upon his flesh. Do you have a weapon?"

"Hardy, you don't need a weapon. Crawl back here."

"I'm not about to fight a jaguar with a penknife," I said. "McTroy is unconscious."

She said, "McTroy is crouched right beside me. So is Wu."

McTroy said, "That's right, pard. I got a rifle. But you won't use it, I know. Just tell me where that cat is. It creeped into the ditch, but I ain't seen it since."

He waved the rifle to show me where they were hidden.

I was cold and bruised but alive and sawing the last piece of leather keeping the horse attached to the sledge, and thinking: if Evangeline, McTroy, and Wu were behind the rocks, and the giant lay dead on the other side of the road, then... who was in the ditch?

Bloody and tongue-bathed by a murderous black panther?

I'd cut about halfway through the strap when I felt it snap apart.

The Morgan rolled and bolted toward Raton. Hoof beats echoed in the canyon. I listened to them recede and my heartbeat took over as the loudest thing in my ears. I duck-walked to the back of the sledge and popped up to glance over the bent runners into the ditch.

I had seen many odd things in my adventures. Mummies revivified after millennia in a tomb, train-robbing ghouls, hopping vampires, and worms as big as silos. But never had I seen what lay in that ditch bleeding in the Sangre de Cristos.

I might say it was a man.

It had two arms and two legs. The general shape of a man, and surely it was no woman because it shivered in the snow: naked, gray in the cloudy moonlight, half-yellow by the dying fire of the giant's torch.

I might also say it was a cat.

All over its body it was covered in thick fur. The pattern of the fur matched the first jaguar we had seen on the mountain. This jaguar-man had more than fur to aid his classification. His arms ended in paws and claws rather than five fingers. But it was his head most of all that filled me with fright. The bones of the skull retained a jaguar shape, but they were moving, collapsing, closing like a furry fist, and the pain of the transformation was obvious. Despite my terror, I felt sympathy for the creature who was both cat and human. His fangs stuck out well below his chin. (The lower half of his face was shrinking faster than the top.) I watched as his teeth retracted into his gums. His long, pink tongue withered.

He saw me now. Which of us was more afraid I cannot say. He could not move while in the transformative state. It was paralyzing to the victim. His wide, flat, black nose pinched and turned pale; whiskers receded. Every hair quivered. His facial structure rearranged. I detected the faint grinding of cartilage and bone. He was thin enough that I might've counted his ribs. The sharp contours of his hipbones weren't very different from the rocks on either side of the ditch. His gold eyes were the last to change. They dimmed and dimmed. His teeth were chattering. He must've gained some control over his movement at this point because he drew his knees to his chest and rolled onto his left side.

Deep lacerations gouged his back. The wounds oozed blood. Red pooled under him.

"Go, Dr Hardy! Leave me!" Claude said.

"My God, what can I do for you?" I said. I leaped over the sledge, not thinking about my own safety or the whereabouts of the other jaguar. "That black cat has shredded you, old boy."

Claude laughed.

"I need to get you a blanket. We must return to Nightfall."

"No!" he screamed.

"You will die," I said. I shouted for Evangeline, McTroy, and Wu.

"I should die," he said. "Death would be better."

"Where are your clothes?" I asked.

He said nothing.

Evangeline gasped when she saw the state of him.

McTroy found a blanket in the sledge. He wrapped him up and lifted him. McTroy swiveled around. "Where's that damned black cat?"

"Cross the road," Claude said. "A cave... through those trees... I keep things there."

"But the panther...?" Evangeline said, hesitating.

"Is gone," Claude said. "Ran off. Hardy scared it."

Had I?

McTroy hoisted Claude over his shoulder. The four of us walked up the hill, passing the dead giant, and found the cave entrance.

I lit a match and we went inside. The cave was a jagged gap between two conjoined volcanic outcroppings. At first it was no wider than a pantry door but after twelve steps the passage expanded like the inside of an Esquimau igloo. I lit more matches. Claude had used the domed space for some time. He'd put down an old army cot. Covered it with cigarette ashes and a waterlogged copy of *The Wolf Leader* by Alexandre Dumas. Milky starlight and snowflakes shifted in from the fractured ceiling. A battered upright traveling trunk stood at the foot of the bunk. There was a drawstring bag on top of the cot's thin blanket. Jackets and capes hung from railroad spikes hammered into the gray walls. An overturned crate functioned as a table. I fired up the lantern sitting on it. Broken bits of glass glittered at the far perimeter of the rotunda floor. Shards and bottlenecks. Despite the frigid temperature the room stank of whiskey and stale tobacco smoke. It smelled inhuman too: an ammoniac stench of cat piss, rotting meat, and blood.

There were gnawed bones.

I did not want to look in case they had once been people.

McTroy put Claude on the cot.

Claude coughed. "Whiskey," he said. "In my bag. I need it."

McTroy loosened the drawstring, uncorked the bottle he found. He passed it to Claude.

Claude upended the whiskey, spilling liquor. After several swallows, he slowed and nuzzled the glass bottle against his cheek. Evangeline opened the trunk. It split apart into two equal compartments, each containing drawers. She pulled them out, one by one. I heard her quick intake of breath, a suppressed exclamation of surprise. She returned with a change of clothes.

"The bleeding won't stop," I said. I took my hands from Claude's back. The sledge's blanket had soaked through. I replaced it with the cot blanket. My hands were wet and slipping.

Claude said, "Someone please roll me a cigarette."

"Where's your shag and papers?" I asked, wiping my hands on my trousers.

"In the sack where this was," Claude said, taking another swig from his bottle.

McTroy tossed me the sack.

I dug out the tobacco. I pinched up some shag and

started to roll.

"Don't really know what I'm doing here. More of a pipe and cigar man," I said.

"Give it to me," Evangeline said.

Her delicate fingers moved adroitly. She licked the paper and rolled a perfect cylinder. She put it between her lips. "Match?" she asked me.

I struck one, and she drew at the fire.

Then she placed the cigarette between Claude's lips. He inhaled smoke. Eyes closed.

"Sorry for knocking you off your horse," he said to Evangeline.

"Then why did you?"

Claude shrugged. "Cats are curious. You smelled good."

His wounds leaked through the blanket. A man has only so much blood in him. He wouldn't be awake much longer. We'd never get him to Nightfall. I wanted to be respectful. But I had a question that needed answering.

"Ask away, Hardy. You're itching to know what the game is." Claude's hooded eyes half opened. "You deserve as much. Candor, I mean. You're an honest man, aren't you?"

"Yes," I said. "At least I try."

Claude nodded. "Thought so... I can smell them... me being a werecat. Haven't smelled many though–" He coughed and there was blood. "I was born this way. Mother's family is very, very old and a bit... ambiguous... she's not like me. Viv's all woman. Her father was a werecat. Thrown from the cathedral walls after too many *ciudadanos* went missing... They killed him in Mérida, forcing my grandmother and mother to flee to France."

He sighed. Removed the cigarette. Looked at it. He tore the soggy red part off. He spit the blood out of his mouth. His cheeks hollowed out as he sucked at the tobacco. Smoke trickled from his nose.

"Who wounded you?" I said.

"A fucking bear. That fat shit's grizzly. I was on the road. Coming here to change. I can do it when I please, you know. It's not moon-related or any bullshit like that. I saw the leader, Earl, and the fat shit. They had the giant on the ground. They were going to kill him. *Frenchy-something* they were saying. It was about money. I was getting closer. Then that damned bear–"

"What happened to the bear?" McTroy asked.

"I tore out its throat."

"Who was that giant man?" I said. "Why was he out there when the sledge came?"

Claude shook his head.

"No clue," he said. "Earl and Trapper Dan the Hatchet Man ran off with him after I fought the grizz. There's a hunters' shack back there. They must know about it. Probably waited out the storm inside. They had that giant scared. Maybe they sent him to check on the bear. He didn't have a gun. I heard the sledge and I needed help. Boy, that giant was surprised to see me."

Claude dropped the bottle. The glass shattered.

"Ahhh… shit. That's all I had."

"Where's the Beast, Claude? What do you know about the Beast?" I said.

He didn't answer me. He still had the cigarette. Staring at the lantern, like he saw figures inside it. Dreadful figures. I touched his shoulder. "Hey, Claude… tell me about the other jaguar."

McTroy stepped up to the cot. "He's dead, Hardy. We need to get out of here."

24
FRENCHY'S FRIENDS

"Where is Yong Wu?" Evangeline said.

McTroy and I shut Claude's eyes and wrapped his corpse in the blankets. We moved the cot to the back of the cave, tucking his drawstring bag beside him. The news of his death would damage his family enough. They didn't need to find him naked, mauled, and gaping into the void of eternity. Whatever they knew of his feline transformations, there would be guilt at losing him.

"McTroy, Hardy, have either of you seen Wu? He's not here."

"He was here a few minutes ago," I said.

"Was he?" Evangeline asked. "I can't seem to recall his presence in the cave."

"Did he stay on the lookout?" McTroy said. "The boy's got sense. He wouldn't wander."

We three exited Claude's makeshift tomb.

Wu was nowhere in the passage through the gray volcanic monuments. Outside the cave the night was fading. The sky turned from charcoal to ashen in the east. The snowy ground glowed whiter. I could see more of the trees and the road climbing up to Nightfall. The giant lay quietly on the ground, a toppled statue spattered with red paint, and missing most of an ear.

"Wu!" I shouted. Then I noted another among our missing. "Orcus! Wu!"

"He is nowhere," Evangeline said as she returned from crossing the road to the sledge.

"Neither is the dog," I said. "I don't like this one bit."

McTroy studied the tracks. The snow was a chaos of prints, both cat and human.

"Here's where Claude the jaguar passed after fighting the bear," McTroy said.

"Puddin'," I said.

"What're you saying, Doc? Is your stomach growling at a time like this?"

"Puddin' is the grizzly's name. Dirty Dan mentioned it after Earl kill– after he shot you."

"You got to be shittin' me. Dan named his bear Puddin'?"

Evangeline and I confirmed the ursine creature's moniker.

"Dan was fond of his pet. I suspect he'll be furious that it has died," Evangeline said.

"Losin' your killin' partner tugs at the heartstrings," McTroy said.

He did not appear to be joking.

"How do we know it *is* dead?" I said.

Evangeline said, "Claude *ripped its throat out*. I think that's how he phrased it."

"But what if he was wrong? A wounded grizzly? Is there anything more dangerous?"

"The Beast for one. That black jaguar would be another. Not to mention our human hunters. I'd say this mountain is full of dangers." Evangeline waited for my rebuttal.

I had none.

"Puddin's dead," McTroy said.

"You're certain?" I asked.

"I'm lookin' right at 'im."

McTroy had backtracked Claude's jaguar prints around a pile of broken slabs that at one time or other land-slid down the mountain face. They looked like crude ancient tombstones. Plowed from the earth, jumbled, and capped with snow. On the far side of the pile, Puddin' the Bear in his death throes had bled buckets over them. It was ghastly.

McTroy nudged the bear with his boot.

"Claude judged correctly," Evangeline said. "Most of the throat is missing."

"Puddin' died quickly," I said. "The animal didn't suffer. Blood loss is euphoric."

"Which is more mercy than you'll have."

Dirty Dan emerged from the pines. He seemed half tree himself. With boughs fastened to his furs and even a little cone-shaped headdress. He'd smeared pine tar on his bare skin and pressed on handfuls of fallen needles and a few unlucky pinecones. I had mistaken him for a stout evergreen tree. But this tree lumbered toward us with a murderous glare. He had a tomahawk in his right hand and an old-style flintlock blunderbuss pistol in the other.

Odd fellow, I thought to myself. Regardless of the bear, Dan marched to his own drum.

"Ho, there, Dirty D," McTroy said. "We didn't kill your friend."

"You kicked him. I saw you do it."

"He is dead, Dan. I don't think he cares." McTroy meant this as a comfort.

"I'm killing the lady first. Then the schoolteacher. Then I'm gonna kill you for good, McTroy." Dirty Dan pointed the blunderbuss at Evangeline. "I loaded this with buckshot and rusty nails. Your pretty face won't be pretty after I'm through." He sneered. His teeth were like mollusk shells. I smelled his breath at ten paces. But I could not stand his gross inaccuracies.

"I am no schoolteacher," I said. "I'll have you know I am an Egyptologist, you buffoon."

"Doc, does it matter?" McTroy asked.

"Yes, it does!"

"Quiet yourself, teacher. I always hated teachers." Dan swung the blunderbuss at me.

"For Godsake, perhaps that's because you failed to pay attention," I said.

"To what?"

McTroy reversed his rifle and struck Dan squarely in the face, breaking his nose. Dan stumbled. Fired the blunderbuss. My shoulder moved as if I'd been shoved rudely. I felt a stinging like hornets and saw blood seeping through the holes peppering the sleeve of my coat.

"Ahh," I said. "I am shot."

McTroy hit Dan again – a quick chop under the chin – and the evergreen-disguised trapper flopped. McTroy kicked the flintlock pistol away from his hand. He bent and took the tomahawk. Kneeling at Dan's side, he raised the war ax to cleave his skull.

"McTroy! Stop! Do not kill him," I said.

Evangeline cautiously approached the bounty man. He kept the tomahawk overhead.

"Rex? He is no threat. Let's bind him before he wakes," she said.

"The stars! I am made for the stars!" McTroy blinked rapidly. His arms trembled. But still he did not lower the tomahawk. "I kill and I feed. I eat. I will survive this. Who is here? Why? Let me go to the stars."

I sat clumsily on the stone slabs. I was feeling lightheaded, foggy. My arm burned, and my mitten was full of blood. "He is having a conversation, I believe. McTroy is more than one entity. He is beyond himself. He is many things right now."

"I am alone. But not alone," he said. "I want to be one. Not these who fight themselves."

"Rex, give me the tomahawk." Evangeline moved so he might see her.

He braced a hand on Dan's bulky chest. Something in him was about to butcher Dan.

"Kill him, it says. But I am for the stars bound. In the desert, I dream. In the mountains... I drown... yet I wither. When will I be whole? For the stars I should be," he said. "Not here."

Evangeline took the tomahawk from McTroy.

"You saved us again," she said.

"We will not kill him today," McTroy said.

"That's enough. Both of you get away from him," Gavin Earl said.

He had Wu. Had him locked in a chokehold. A pistol pointed to his head.

McTroy was kneeling in the snow. Arms hanging. Face blank.

He never looked at Earl.

"Get him up. You, Egyptologist, come along. We're going to the shack," Earl said.

"Why?"

"Because I'm cold and tired. And I need to figure out who's who on this rock."

Evangeline helped McTroy to his feet.

I joined them. Holding each other up, we walked.

"What about him?" Evangeline pushed her chin in the direction of Dirty Dan.

"Is he dead?"

"No," she said.

"Then I guess he'll wake up with a goddamn headache. Now move," Earl said.

The shack wasn't big, more shed than shack. Rough pine logs and a stovepipe chimney. We couldn't all fit inside. Gavin Earl stayed in the doorway, on the other side of the threshold. He pushed Wu at Evangeline. There were two small windows without glass. The shutters were open to let light in. The air turned blue now, and you could see things that were hidden a while ago.

"How do you know Frenchy?" Earl asked.

He hadn't slept. He looked older than he had a day ago. His eyes were red like he was scared to blink. I wouldn't say he was panicked, but his confidence had taken a blow or two during the night. It made him more reckless. Fidgety. I thought he might kill us right there in the shack. Group us up and *BANG BANG!* It wouldn't have been hard. McTroy walked like he was asleep. Wu was terrified. I am no fighter. Only Evangeline posed a problem. Earl didn't know it, but she was the one he needed to worry about the most. Did she have her hammerless pistol?

"We don't know anyone named Frenchy," she said.

"You're lying. I don't have time for liars. The giant told me everything."

"We didn't know the giant. We only saw him die."

Earl's eyebrows arched. He hadn't seen the giant's body lying outside the cave. It was behind the rock pile. I tried to figure out just what he knew and what he didn't. I couldn't.

"Who killed the giant?" he said. "Was it McTroy or Ole Dirty?"

"Neither. He was killed by a black jaguar," I said. I watched to see how Earl reacted.

"The spotted cat?" he said.

"No," I said. "All black."

"So, there're two of them?" He scratched his jaw with the knuckles of his black-gloved hand, the one missing fingers.

"The spotted jaguar is dead," Evangeline said. "Puddin' killed it. They inflicted mortal wounds on each other. They're both dead. Listen, we don't know what's going on here. But if we work together, we might live. Sitting here in this shack is stupid. The Beast is going–"

"The Beast is the one thing I do know about. Lie to me again, I'll shoot the boy." He pointed at Wu with the barrel of his gun. "I won't hear any more Beast talk from you all."

McTroy slumped against the wall of the cabin. He would've hit the ground if I didn't get underneath him and pin him to the logs.

"What's wrong with Rex?" Earl asked. His eyes glinted with delight.

"Pops' elixir," I said. "He isn't the same since then."

Earl smiled. "Death's a bitch. She likes to gnaw on you when she gets hungry. Are you folks hungry? Because I'm starving. Last night during that blizzard, I got to thinking I might shoot that bear myself and slice off a couple of nice big, juicy steaks. Roast them over a hot fire. Just to hear that fat drip and sizzle. What I wouldn't do for chicken leg. Hey, China Boy, you got legs like a chicken?"

Earl laughed and licked his dry lips.

"I know what you said, but the Beast is what we're here for," Evangeline said.

"Wrong! Gold is what I'm here for, Miss Waterston. The Beast is a fraud. A con, a hoax. Frenchy's cut you in on the deal. I know he has. And Frenchy and all of Frenchy's friends are going to Hell. I'm sending them there personally. If that cat hadn't killed the giant I was going to put a bullet in his gut and let the wolves take him home. Something took my horse and Dan's pack mule during the night. They didn't even make a sound. It was like they were snatched up in the sky. Wolves, Dan said. But I don't think he believed it. No sign of blood. We didn't hear a pack yelp or howl. That's why I sent the giant out to look for Dan's bear. Wildcats or wolves, I figured a big catch needs big bait. Something was going to eat that tall sonofabitch, I reckoned. Now you can wear the suit,

Doc. But nobody's going to mistake you for a Beast? Are they now?"

Earl laughed again.

"We don't know what you're talking about," I said. "Who is Frenchy?"

"Oh, sure you do. It's like Frenchy planned it. His giant friend goes running around the woods. Too far for anyone to take a decent shot. He blows that skinny brass whistle and makes some curious tracks. Then one of you claims to have plugged him and say he fell in a crevasse. The others swear to have witnessed it. Old Oscar pays the shooter in gold. When you get far enough away from Raton, you split it up. It's a good plan. I'll grant you that. Hell, I might've joined in with you. Only I wasn't invited in on the game. Now your Beast is dead. So, it looks like Dr Hardy is the new Beast. Or maybe McTroy. Say, he'd be perfect. He's died once already. Let's try the costume on him and see if it fits. I always told Rex he should join the damn circus."

Evangeline and I exchanged glances. Earl sounded as if he'd gone mad in the woods overnight. But some of what he told us fit together. He went around the cabin, stopping to poke his pistol in one of the windows. He was knocking up against the logs. Carrying a heavy object that scraped and thumped along the outer log wall. Back in the doorway, he dragged the object out from under a moldy canvas. Antlers. The rack was sticking out of a headpiece. He reached down and hauled up a long-faced, sad, bulbous buffalo head. He tossed it at me.

"Put that on McTroy," he said.

"He's barely awake."

Earl fired a bullet into the log above my head.

I looked inside the buffalo head. It wasn't really a buffalo head. Even I could see it had been shrunk some. The inside was cleaned out and smelled of sweat and hair oil. The antlers were not the bison type, but likely came from an elk or a mule deer. There was no skull inside the skin. So it was much lighter than it looked. The inner top was a sturdy helmet with leather straps and a chin buckle. The rest was a mask made from buffalo hide. It had changes to the outside to give it a weirder, more fearsome aspect. The eye cutouts were set high and close together, to fit a man-sized face. The teeth glued into the widened mouth, in a hideous rictus, came from a big breed of dog or maybe even a wolf. While still propping up McTroy I fitted the mask over his head. He moaned in the dark.

I'd heard that moan before. Or something very similar to it. The giant had worn this. He was the Beast we saw crossing the Copper Trail, the creature Evangeline had taken a shot at and missed. No wonder he acted as if he had trouble hearing and seeing. Cassi said she saw a brown Beast sneaking around the Silvers. That was the giant too. A circus performer. An actor playing the role of the Beast. And this Frenchy person had put him up to it.

"Don't forget the whistle," Earl said.

He threw the brass whistle on a long chain at me.

"I'll blow the whistle. He can't." I put it to my lips.

Earl nodded. "And I'll howl through this megaphone." From under the canvas he produced a conical circus ringmaster's bullhorn.

I blew. A harsh high-pitched shriek filled the cabin.

"Louder, louder, Dr Hardy."

I filled my lungs and forced my air into the whistle. The noise was piercing. Like the Beastly whistle, or close enough that it would be hard to distinguish any differences in the mountains, where rocky surfaces and their echoes altered loud noises. Evangeline and Wu covered their ears. McTroy shifted, taking some of his weight off me. Standing on his own two feet. I blew and blew until Earl waved at me to stop. He howled into the megaphone like a lovesick wolf. I'll admit these instruments might have produced the noise we heard at Nightfall.

Earl put down his horn. "Pops and Billy wanted to head back to the lodge. We'd lost sight of the Beast – I mean, Frenchy's giant. The storm wiped out the tracks. So, we split up. Dan and I stayed low in the canyon. We'd go as far as the road and then circle back if we didn't see anything. But we found the giant right here in this shack. He cried like a woman when we kicked in the door. Dan's bear couldn't fit, but Dan could. He had his tomahawks out. And the giant screamed, practically knocked himself out standing up so fast he hit the ceiling. Dan said he'd skin him right here if he didn't talk. And he would have. The giant doesn't speak much English. He's a French Canadian too. Just like Frenchy. They met up in the circus. Now we couldn't get the giant to explain everything, because he was pissing his drawers and he doesn't know the words to tell us what we're asking him. We took him out of this closet and thumped him around in the snow. 'Frenchy made him do it. Frenchy lied to him too.' Then Dan's bear gets into a brawl with a spotted wildcat, and we pull back. The giant's yelling, '*La bête sauvage*! *La bête sauvage*!' He tried telling us the Beast was real. He'd seen it out in the woods. That's why he was quitting. After the storm he was leaving for Raton. Screw Frenchy."

"We had no part in this," I said. "The giant is correct. I've seen the Beast. The real thing, not this giant in a costume. Smoke Eel thinks that any one of us might be capable of turning into a Beast. He says that his people believe in the Beast as an actual living demon. But people under its influence lose themselves. They act as the Beast does."

Earl stared at me. I thought he might kill me.

But he said, "Smoke Eel told you this? Did he write it in his little notebook?"

I nodded. "That's exactly what he did. I found shredded men's clothing outside Nightfall. I thought it might belong to a man who changed into the Beast. I don't think that now. But Smoke Eel warned me not to follow the road. He thought the Beast was one of us. But changed."

"Smoke Eel? He's your expert?"

Gavin Earl began to laugh harder than before. He reached into the cabin and snatched the beast head off McTroy. He chucked it out into the snow. He slapped me on my wounded arm, and I nearly screamed with pain. He grabbed the whistle and looped it around his neck. He leaned out of shack, blowing it. The canyon filled with echoes, like one long cry. He spit the whistle from his mouth.

"Oh, Doc," he said. "You're a bigger fool than me. I can't wait to tell Billy and Pops."

I didn't inform him that he'd have to wait a while to talk to them.

"Tell them what exactly?"

"Smoke Eel is Frenchy. René 'Frenchy' LaFarque. He's pulling the strings. Oscar's phony Indian is a Canuck confidence-man. He dyes himself with iodine and carrot juice. Ha!"

Earl blew the whistle again. Then he threw it at me.

In the distance, we heard the whistle answered. Loudly, clearly. Not by an echo. It cut through the flesh until we felt it vibrating inside us. Drilling into the bone. Getting stronger and stronger until the shack rattled and a fine, woody dust rained down from the joints, like sand.

All our heads turned toward Nightfall Lodge.

25
SNOWMELT

We trudged out of the shack together to go and check on Dirty Dan. He was gone. There was a big, sandy crater in the snow where he'd fallen, and tracks leading off into a deeper part of the woods at the creek bottom. The woods gave him ample cover, and the water would keep him from losing his bearings. Gavin Earl marched us back to the road, then, without a glance toward Raton, uphill toward Nightfall Lodge. He was determined to get a share of the golden bull for his troubles. He declared the Beast a con game in its entirety. Oscar was a fool blinded by his grandiosity. Earl refused to listen to my tale of talking to the Beast. I think frankly he found my credibility somewhere south of a village idiot. The chilling high-pitched whistle that had answered his call he attributed to another metal whistle like the giant's, a spare, no doubt in the possession of Frenchy LaFarque (alias Smoke Eel). Earl didn't worry about us as long as we kept walking, in a line, with him behind us. He holstered his pistol and lowered the brim of his hat against the glare of the morning sun.

The temperature was rising. Brilliant melting ice glittered in the mountainside like cut diamonds; the frozen melt shone like veins of wet silver. Everywhere was the sound of dripping, trickling water.

The wind had turned warmer. I loosened up my coat. My arm had stopped bleeding. I could move it, but a sizzling pain coursed through me whenever I did. Otherwise, my wound settled into a dull throbbing ache. I helped McTroy unbutton his sheepskin jacket and open his collar. He was sweating; his skin felt clammy, sickly. He remained sluggish, and though present in body, his mind drifted elsewhere. In the barrel and the desert.

"Keep going, friend," I said. "We'll rest a spell when we get to the top."

McTroy stared straight ahead. But he walked. He'd stopped talking except for fragments that meant little to me. Picking them up and trying to make any sense was fruitless.

"White fire," he said, as I unknotted his scarf. "My ship is stranded. I am a prisoner."

"You are a free man, McTroy. The most free I have ever known."

"White fire in my eyes," he replied. "I can't see the stars."

"Yes, that's only the snow melting on the road. Watch that you don't slip on this ice."

But he wasn't talking about the brightness of glinting snowmelt. I asked him to take the lead. Even though he was stunned, he was the fastest walker among us. Evangeline trailed me with Wu at her side. I overheard them talking about his turning up missing when we entered the cave. She asked him his whereabouts.

"I went to get the rum. McTroy must have the barrel. Mr Earl was looking at the sledge, and he found me there. I couldn't run away. He said he'd shoot me in the back if I tried."

"That's not your fault," she said.

I turned. "Did you find the barrel?"

"It wasn't there."

"It fell out up the road, here when we started our skidding." I glanced back and forth, ditch to ditch, but if the barrel had rolled off either side it might be under snow or between rocks. In any event, I couldn't spot it. "What about Orcus? Did you see him, by chance?"

Wu said he hadn't. But he'd gone straight to the sledge. It wasn't long after that Earl had him by the collar, sticking a gun to his neck, telling him he'd kill him if he called out for help. He asked where we were. Wu said the cave. He'd take him there. Fearing it was a trap, Earl was reluctant to follow. He decided to take Wu back to the shack and tie him up. Keep him as a hostage, something to barter with if negotiations were to develop in the future. Before they reached the shack, Dirty Dan's blunderbuss exploded. So they circled back and watched us.

A black head popped up from the ditch. At first, I feared it was the panther. But it was Orcus. His ears were pointed but he was keeping low, avoiding Earl's sightline from farther back in our marching line. He chuffed once at me. Earl likely wrote off the sound to our boots scraping.

"There's a good boy," I whispered. "Glad to see you alive. You best hide from him."

I jerked a thumb to show I meant Earl. The sun had him blinded. All I saw was the top of his hat. His knees rising and falling as he followed in our footsteps.

"He's nasty," I said. Drawing nearer to the dog's position, I saw he was hunched over something. "What've you found there?" The dog eyed me and gave another friendly grunt.

Then he took off for the woods, bounding through the snow, and soon he was only a dark shadow flitting between trees and heading for home.

I paused, scanning the ditch.

Here was our rum barrel. The lid was off. The head lay face-down in a small drift. The smooth back of its gray head like a wet, lumpen stone. I might've easily overlooked it had I not known what it was. The ragged sawed end of the stump gave it away, a wrinkly sock with a hole.

McTroy had continued to walk on.

I jumped into the ditch.

"Whoa, Egypt," Earl shouted. He fired a shot into the air.

"I'm only recovering lost gear," I yelled back.

"Climb out," Earl said. "And you better not think you can outsmart me."

I rolled the strange triangular head into the nearly empty barrel.

"What big eyes you have," I said to the severed cranium. "A little mouth. No ears."

I retrieved the lid from a nearby rock and slapped it down. Lifting the barrel overhead, I felt a searing jolt from my wound and blood once again drooling into my armpit. Nevertheless, I gritted my teeth and started up the side of the embankment.

"It's rum. A bit of spirits to warm ourselves," I said.

Earl pointed his pistol at me. "Stop."

I obliged his request. "May I set this down?" I was out of breath. My arm ached.

He nodded, and I carefully set the barrel at my feet.

"How do you know what that is?"

"It's ours. It fell off the sledge. Spiced rum. Not very much of it left, I'm afraid. It spilled over there on the rocks. Smells like a sailor's breath. But there's a few inches left in the keg. Worth saving, I'd say. Don't worry, I'll carry it."

"If it's only rum, then drink some," Earl said, suspiciously.

The prospect of drinking the potion in which the monstrous head marinated was unthinkable. If he recognized Pops' rum barrel, he wasn't saying so. A barrel is just a barrel after all. And even if he did suspect I'd stolen it, he had no knowledge of the hidden additive.

"I... It's very early in the morning for a drink."

"I won't tell your mother. You haven't got a wife. So, drink up."

I swallowed dryly. "I am not a good imbiber on an empty stomach. Weak intestinal constitution. And I am famished, as you said you were too. Mountain air, I suppose. It makes a body hunger. I will have a long drinking session in front of the fire at the lodge, I promise you."

Earl cocked the hammer of his pistol.

"You'll drink it now. Or I will put you in the ditch where you found it."

"Fine," I said. "Fine! Make a man drink against his will. It takes a sober man to walk up this mountain. Don't blame me if you have to carry me." I lifted the barrel and twisted the spigot.

Nothing came out.

"It's frozen," I said.

"Try tilting the barrel toward your mouth. Get under it, Doctor Egypt. You've got it shifted the wrong way. You act as if you're kissing a rabid fox. Think of sweet Cassi Adderly."

Earl shot at my feet. The bullet perforated the end of my boot.

"Don't play me for a fool," he said. "I am no Dan."

"I'm drinking it," I said, checking to see if my toe was still there. "What do you think I have here? Explosives? Cobras perhaps?"

I could not force myself to drink the rum. I felt it sloshing loosely inside the barrel, circling the bottom dregs. I also felt the head tipping on its chin like a child's spinning top, rolling around. I imagined the forehead pressed into the staves, mimicking by own.

As I closed my eyes and prepared to fill my mouth with wretched green-slimed poison, the barrel was suddenly snatched away.

McTroy had it.

He put his lips to the spigot and drank, spilling rum down his grizzled, hollowed cheeks as he sucked the barrel's liquid mysteries greedily into his belly.

"Save some for later," I said, as I turned off the spout.

Gavin Earl was satisfied.

"Rex always loved his liquor. Take up thine cross and walk, pilgrim."

McTroy propped the rum keg on his shoulder. He recommenced trudging.

I waited to see any effect rescuing the head from the drift or guzzling the head-spiced rum might have inflicted upon him. His step was sprightlier. And a vague smile curled his lips.

"You are better?"

"I can see," he said. The distance in his voice had vanished. He was McTroy again. "It was like a thick cloud on me before. That rum hits the curative spot." His pace quickened.

"I am not certain that Pops told any of his crew about the, ah..."

"Secret ingredient?"

I nodded. "If Pops revealed what it was that brought Billy the Kid back from the dead, then why wouldn't they steal it? No, Pops was a cagey operator. I think Billy knew. But none of the other Silvers do. Now we are the holders of the key to revivification."

"It's nothing to be happy about," McTroy said. The sun threw spears of light over the peaks. Despite the windy knives that whittled our flesh, it was an inspiring sight to behold. We might have been Greek gods ascending Mount Olympus. Bedraggled, tested, wrapped in glory.

"Would you rather be dead?"

"Not my choice," he said.

"But if you had a choice?" I insisted.

"I'd keep it out of my own hands. Death has rules. There's no cheating without a price exacted in return. We shouldn't be cooking in the Reaper's kitchen," he said, and then spit.

"Don't you mean the Beast's kitchen?"

Before he could respond, we spotted a rider on the road. Coming down from Nightfall in the melting path left by the sledge: a speeding horse, the rider trailing smoke. It was Oscar. He rode alone. A cigar clenched in his teeth.

My first thought in seeing him was that he did not know the fate of Claude. Who would tell him? I was not volunteering. My second thought was what Smoke Eel had said about Oscar: he set us up to be sacrificed so that he could be more notorious for slaying the Beast. Was it true?

"McTroy," Oscar called out as soon as he recognized him. "Did you find my son?"

"He's not on the road. His tracks turned to the woods at the canyon bottom."

Oscar absorbed this information. None of it a lie in a strict sense.

He said, "Claude can take care of himself. I need everyone up at Nightfall. Vivienne has taken ill. Visions grip her. She talks to the walls. Screams out the warnings of the dead in breathless unfamiliar voices. I cannot control her. She wheels through the rooms, knocking into furniture, as if she is looking for someone. Yet the dead surround her, it seems. I fear she may be lost to me. I tied her to her bed. She raves about the Beast. Did you hear the thing whistling?"

"We did," Earl said. "But was it really the Beast? Or is a trickster more likely."

"I cannot say what the nature of it is. But Vivienne told me the Beast will come to Nightfall tonight. It will break down the doors and slaughter all who are present in the house. She predicts this emphatically. She says we must get out. Flee to Raton until the hour of the Beast passes... It enters my own house... and she tells me to run away!"

"What do you say?" Evangeline asked. The news of Viv's breakdown upset her. Yet I could tell she was divided in her feelings about the best course of action for us to pursue.

"I say tonight the Beast will be mine."

Oscar flung the burning stub of his cigar as he inspected our exhausted group.

"Now is no time for faltering. Where is the sledge? Crashed? What of my Morgan? Never mind. I can buy new horses. I will send Hodgson down here with the carriage. The road is open enough. We must prepare." He passed a canteen to Evangeline. She and Wu drank and gave it to me next. A flask from inside his coat he tossed to Earl. "Where are the woodsman and his bear?"

"The bear died. Natural causes." Earl nipped at the flask. "Dan's run off, inconsolable."

"Grief is a funny thing," Oscar said. "I've never seen the point of it."

I cringed at his callousness.

How hard will your heart turn when you hear news of your son? I wondered.

Oscar jerked his horse around and spurred it toward Nightfall. His dark coattails flapping and the hoofbeats' muffled drumming leaving us... leaving me feeling more barren than before. I like to think I am no coward. I suppose most men do. But the nightly promise of the Beast did nothing to make me walk any faster. Wu

joined arm in arm with Evangeline. Earl offered his
flask to McTroy. When McTroy extended his hand, Earl
pulled the flask away and laughed.

I would like to say I never wished ill of any person
beyond a normal twinge of spite. But frankly, if the
Beast were going to tear apart any of the remaining
members of this hunting party and devour their
smoking hot innards while the devoured individual
observed the eager, lip-smacking devourer emptying
their body cavity of strings of offal, organ tubes
unbundled and consumed like fat blood sausages from
a butcher's case – I hoped it would be Gavin Earl.

This appallingly macabre daydream oddly made my
mouth water. My stomach gurgled.

"Something warms your thoughts, Dr Hardy?" Earl
asked.

Jauntily, he threw the flask at a spoon-eared
jackrabbit hopping between two stumps.

"I only pray we find our reward, each accordingly."

"Me too, Doctor Egypt. Damned Smoke Eel will
regret his schemes. I'll skin his iodine hide. This night
holds promise for revenge. And I'll fetch my reward
one way or another."

"I hope so," I said. "Sincerely, I do."

Under a slate canopy shaped rather like a question
mark we waited out of the wind for Hodgson to
bring the coach. The snow continued to melt under
a climbing sun. A small cataract spilled over the
canopy. Stepping through it we'd entered a space of
dampness and moldy leaf matter. But the wind was
kept out. The smell of the place was not altogether

unpleasant but it did suggest mice. A few darting motions near the ground confirmed rodent life. There were boulders to sit on.

Gavin Earl retreated to the back of the question mark and lit his pipe. He had regained his bravado, which had crumbled a bit during the night. I think losing his horse and the pack mule disturbed him. Did Claude take them for a fright and some quick meat? I wasn't sure he had the time. It wasn't wolves. The Beast, a real Beast – not Frenchy's giant in a buffalo mask and elk horns – that's what had Earl shaken, whether he realized it consciously or not.

Men weren't the masters of this mountain. To comprehend that loss of dominance was more than many could tolerate. It filled them with dread. I had never made much of dominating over things in life, other than my books; mastering a theory here and grappling with an unwieldy concept there. I only felt I was top dog when I walked the ancient ruins of a dead civilization. I brought it back to life in my mind. I imagined myself transported. I cheated time. In my own way. What greater destroyer is there than Time? I flitted back and forth between the present and the past like a warlock. But I always knew I was more of a sly, crouching margin creeper – like these mice we had scared away – than a chest-thrusting bully with a gun. Finding out I could be eaten at any moment was nothing new to me. The world is an open maw. I danced between the teeth. Mousy Rom Hardy.

I found a boulder as far from Earl as I could. I lit my own pipe. Using my knife, I cut a strip from the tail of my shirt and folded the material into a square.

Carefully, I peeled away my clothing to check my wound. It was gory mess under there. I stuffed the square against the worst of it and fastened myself back up.

Evangeline joined me inside the shelter.

McTroy stayed outside, sitting on the rum barrel, staring at the sky. Squinting into the sun. What was he seeing up there? I worried about him. His crippled hand was like a dead crab stranded in his lap. He'd taken it out of his fur mitten and smacked it against his thigh absently. He could learn to shoot with the other hand. In time. But it was a reminder of his own mortality: the day Gavin Earl killed him in a gunfight in the woods high above Raton. He'd never be the same man. Not inside. Even if we got him squared away with the peculiar, almond-eyed decapitation he now sat upon.

Wu hit him with a snowball. McTroy turned slowly from his sun-gazing. With his good hand he packed a handful of snow and launched it at the boy. Wu raced over the road and lay in the ditch. He stacked his munitions in a pyramid like cannonballs.

Evangeline cleared her throat.

I turned as if I hadn't been watching her for the entire time out of the corner of my eye.

"Oh, it's you," I said, scooting over so she had room to sit beside me.

She smiled.

Maybe she did know I was watching her. Maybe she was always ahead of me.

"What are we going to do about Cassi?" she said, quietly. We were far enough from Earl that he couldn't hear.

"What do you mean?"

"Hardy. You know," she said. She lowered her chin, and her eyes were cool green.

I shrugged and scratched my ankle. "Telling her about Claude? I suppose I'll do it."

"Not only about Claude. About herself – that we are aware."

I said nothing. I gazed through the cataract. The clear mountain water falling like rain.

"She is the black jaguar. In the cave, I found her clothes on the other side of the trunk. They both used the cave when they were changed. Who knows what else they did together. It is a lonely place here on the mountain. Nightfall must've seemed like Devil's Island to them. You can't blame them entirely. In isolation people do strange things they would not do otherwise."

"Like turn into werecats?"

Evangeline waited for me to go on. But I had no more to say.

She said, "Cassi will take Claude's death badly. I am unsure of how she will react. In the end, she's a predator. Unpredictable."

"More than you?" My pipe fizzled. I knocked the dottle out and repacked it. "We don't know for certain that she is the black cat. It might be… just a big jungle feline that Oscar brought over to give his Claude a companion when he changed. I won't rush to judgment. If she is a werecat, what difference does that make? She's still a strong young woman. She has qualities, good ones."

"Hardy, she can't leave here. That's probably why Oscar built this retreat for them. Is she going to live in

New York? Think about it. Part of her is wild and will always stay that way."

"Are there no cats in New York?"

Evangeline's smile was sad. She rolled herself a cigarette with Claude's supplies.

"You took those?" I said.

She shrugged. Claude wouldn't be needing them, would he? "Have a light?"

I struck a match. She cupped the flame, turning into it like she would a kiss.

"I like you, Hardy." Her lips pressed tight. She had a pink scrape on her cheek. Her hair fell over one of her eyes and she didn't bother to brush it back. Her coat opened into a long "V" that dragged on the ground; its bottom drenched, muddy. She stretched out her legs. Her burgundy boots were pointy.

"Let's get married then," I blurted out. "We're business partners already. It wouldn't be that difficult. We enjoy the same things. I am devoted to you. And you are... friendly toward me."

Her look of shock would've been comical had I not been the one asking the question.

I gazed out at McTroy.

Wu had hit him with so many snowballs that the front of his coat was white. He was sun-gazing again. His hat tipped onto the back of his head. His mouth hung open. The falling water from the melt on the canopy shone like a wavering mirror, but I could not see myself in it. I only saw him through it. In the gaps.

Evangeline took my hand. I turned back to her. Sorry I had said anything.

"I can't give you an answer to that question, Hardy.

Maybe another time, another place."

I nodded. "That is an answer."

Mice skittered in the leaf litter. They made tiny crashing sounds.

A hawk cried out. McTroy shielded his eyes from the sun. He followed the raptor as it glided thermals above the canyon. I couldn't see the hawk from where I was. A knife-like shadow passed over him quickly. Wu waved at someone up the trail and came running, shouting.

"The coach is here!"

Evangeline stood. Dropping and crushing the cigarette under her heel.

"We'd better go," she said.

"Yes, an excellent idea," I said. She took my elbow.

We stepped through the falling water together.

26
WHO WILL EAT WHOM?

I don't know if places are capable of going insane. I hadn't felt anything the first time I rode up to Nightfall in the coach, but this time was different. Or it might've been me. Maybe I had changed. I couldn't help but look around and wonder if the mountain was real. Were the trees really trees? And all this wet, sloppy snow seemed somehow put there by design, arranged for a purpose. What caused this estrangement? Certainly I felt disappointed that Evangeline had not accepted my proposal. But that alone would not make my skin turn to gooseflesh. No, it was an alteration in atmosphere. Almost like a switch in the weather. But instead of rain or snow I perceived malevolence. A palpable violence that touched me as physically as raindrops would. What was even worse was that I seemed to welcome the corruption. Gleefully.

Hodgson arrived surlier than the last time we had seen him. Perhaps he'd had enough of the Adderly dramatics, or maybe the oddities and various monsters were getting to him. His black caterpillar eyebrows twitched and he sucked the chill air through his teeth, like a man who has something to say but can't say it and stay employed for very long. McTroy climbed up into the driver's box with him. Hodgson bristled. McTroy grabbed the dwarf's double-barrel shotgun from its scabbard and pulled back on the hammers.

Click-click.

McTroy stared ahead without uttering a word. He put the rum barrel beside him in the box.

Hodgson swore under his breath and barked at us to climb aboard. Gavin Earl went up top too. There wasn't any room in the front bench so he sat cross-legged where the luggage was usually secured. He wanted to keep an eye on McTroy. His former partner made him nervous, even though he'd killed him once already.

As I was saying, I don't know if places lose their grip on sanity, but this mountain gave me the most horrible case of jitters.

I won't tell you it was alive, but evilness cloaked it like a fog.

There was real fog too. At least, I'm assuming it was real. The rising temperatures coaxed a mist out of the snowy ground. Everything was wet, wet, wet. I felt it on my face like a clammy hand; it didn't grip or slap but lay there coolly, oozing a vile residue that wouldn't rub off. It stuffed up your nose. Put a film over whatever you were seeing. I caught myself smiling for no reason as I took a window seat. I tried not to speak because I was afraid I'd jabber like a monkey.

Oh, this was not right. Not right by any stretch of the imagination.

Evangeline, Wu, and I sat side-by-side like school children at church.

I giggled and covered my mouth to hide the outburst. Evangeline flicked her gaze over me quickly and then looked out her window again. But Wu, who sat between us, studied me. I wanted ever-so-much to slam his head into the floor of the coach. To stomp him until he slid under my boot like a bag of damp laundry. Damn Chinese. Orphan rice-eater. Who was he to look at me with those dark little eyes?

I gasped.

What was wrong with me? I cared for Yong Wu like a brother. Even a son. What were these prejudices vomiting into my mind? I dug my fingernails into my palms and stuck my face outside the coach. But the air... the air was bad. It had an awful rotten smell. Like seepage from a sewer. I breathed through my mouth so as not to smell it. Spoiled meat. Chunks of bloody chewy flesh covered with hair... human hair. I stuck out my tongue and brushed it with my fingertips.

Nothing.

I was so hungry. I might eat anything. I bit my fingernails. Too hard, tearing too deeply, and the skin bled and so I sucked my own blood. The salty morsels. Saliva leaked from the corners of my mouth. My fingers slipped in and out while my teeth rasped against them. Yummy.

Wu whispered to Evangeline.

I snapped my face at them. Didn't she look succulent? The boy would be an appetizer.

Who am I?

I scoured my brain but could not recall my name.

I nodded at them. They made faces at me. Were they afraid? Or did they plan to eat me?

Who are they?

Meat. They are meat for my table. The coach floor is my table today. They are prime cuts of steak. Ribs to pick and suck the bones. The juicy bones. Organ meats are sweet and rich if not overcooked. Rump roasts are delightful. These two don't need much seasoning. Or cooking for that matter. Good the way they are. Fresh. I smelled her fats. The boy had lean, tender cuts. He'd go first. Maybe she'd join me in my meal. Then I'd get her too. Bend her supple neck back and…

I opened the coach door and threw myself out.

"Hardy!" Evangeline screamed.

I hit the road. My perforated shoulder slammed into the ground. The pain was unspeakable. But it broke the spell of whatever had descended over my soul. The eater spirit.

Wendigo.

I rolled several times. Finally I lay on my back in the slush. The ruts from the coach wheels jammed under my back. I saw fog above. The dark wedge of the mountain looming in the background. The sun was a lamp wrapped in thick cotton gauze. My muddy clothes smelled sour.

The wound in my shoulder howled. New blood gushed from my sleeve.

The coach had stopped. Evangeline, McTroy, and Wu stood over me, concerned.

"I am not dead," I said. My chin was bleeding. I felt a lump on my forehead too.

"Why did you do that, Hardy?" Evangeline said. "You might've been killed."

I groaned as McTroy helped me to my feet.

"Easy, pard," he said. "Give yourself time. Your eyes are still spinnin'."

"Evangeline saw me. She and Wu recoiled from what I had become. A monster."

"I don't know what you're talking about," she said. "We saw no such thing. I was resting with my eyes closed, in fact. Wu had his head on my arm. No one was watching you."

Wu took my hand. He and McTroy led me back to the coach. "Dr Hardy, I swear I did not see any change. You only looked a little sad. But sometimes that is how you are," Wu said.

I stumbled. The ground tilted, rushing at me. McTroy straightened me up.

"We need to get you mended," Evangeline said. "You've lost blood. It's making you lightheaded. You're confused. Can you walk up these steps?"

I willed my leg to rise up onto the coach. McTroy boosted me into the passenger compartment. Wu had gone in the other side. He caught me before I could topple over. I sank against the upholstery. I was sweating, bloody, and mud-spattered. The cut on my chin hurt.

"Too bad he lived," I heard Gavin Earl say. "We might've stuck a spit through him and turned him over a bed of coals. Better than a hog. That's what the cannibals say." He cackled.

I grabbed Evangeline's hands as the coach took off again.

"There is an evil here. Invading our minds. Smoke Eel said the Wendigo influences those who are around him. They become like the Wendigo. It is happening right now. The way I saw you and Wu just a while ago… it was unspeakable… I was possessed. I might've hurt you."

Evangeline caressed my cheek. She pinched it lightly.

Then harder, so that I winced.

"Who will eat whom, Hardy?" She grinned, showing her teeth that had grown too sharp.

Wu poked me in the belly. His eyes glowed red.

"I get the liver. Please, may I have the liver, Miss?"

27
ODDITIES

I rolled away from them, pulling my coat tight around me. If I believed in God I would've prayed. Instead I concentrated on keeping my mind clear. I counted back from a thousand. I hoped I would not have to fight them off. But they were rocking in their seats, whispering and occasionally tapping me with their boots or leaning over me to smack their lips and chuckle.

The boy and the beautiful independent woman I loved.

When the coach pulled up to Nightfall, I grabbed the vehicle door and exited. Orcus was standing off to the side of the path at the edge of the fog, watching us disembark.

Evangeline and Wu climbed out behind me. Innocent and quizzical, returning my haunted gaze.

"Hardy, you are pale. Let us walk you in," she said. Wu reached for my arm.

"Get away from me. I'll do it myself." I backed away from them, walking sideways through the doors of the lodge, like a fearful crab scrabbling across a beach at low tide.

Evangeline pulled Wu away from me.

"We will let you get settled inside," she said.

McTroy did not seem affected by the Wendigo influence. I supposed this was the result of the elixir and his telepathic connection to the inhuman severed head. Whatever it was, the mental bond it created with McTroy prevented the Wendigo from invading him, running a sort of interference. Take your luck where you find it. I asked McTroy to help me stay on my feet. He tucked the rum barrel under one arm and gave me the other for support.

Gavin Earl rushed into the lodge and disappeared down the hallway toward his room.

In the entryway, Oscar greeted us. He'd shed his coat, and his shirtsleeves were rolled back. He carried a hammer and an inch-thick pine board. Four ten-penny nails stuck out from between his thinly pressed lips. He spit the nails into his hand.

"Good. Now that you're here, you can help me board the windows in the trophy room."

"Where is Cassi?" I asked. "I need to speak to her immediately."

"She's either with her mother or in her bedroom. I haven't seen her since I got back. Say, you're bleeding profusely. I have a medical field kit. McTroy, can you sew him?"

"Not with this." He held up his disfigured right hand. "Evangeline might though."

"Excellent. I'll fetch it for her. When you've finished, I'll be in the trophy room."

"Where is Smoke Eel?" I asked.

"Gone up the mountain. Above the fog. He's

scouting. It's why I hired him."

You may have hired a confidence man, I thought. *He tried to convince me you're a heartless striver who would use us as bait to make a bigger name for himself. At the very least, you do not know him like you think you do. Or you are the best actor in the world...*

Oscar left to retrieve his medical kit. After handing it over he strode down the hall past his stuffed animals. He was a man with purpose.

So was I.

"I want to see Cassi," I said to McTroy. "Then we need to talk to Viv. If she's communicating with the dead, she might tell us where the Beast took Pops. Through Pops, we can find the origin of this green elixir head. The Wendigo spirit is heavy here. It had hold of me when I jumped from the coach. Evangeline and Wu were under it too. They talked about eating me. We'll be at each other's throats literally if we don't get a handle on this."

McTroy scratched his beard. Revivification had slowed his thinking but not dulled it.

"I don't figure somethin'," he said.

"What's that?"

"If Earl's right about Smoke Eel, if he's this Frenchy LaFarque... then he ain't no Indian."

"So...?"

"Well, he's the one who filled you in on the Wendigo spirit and its ways. Who's to say that ain't phony too? A pretend Indian ain't no expert on Indian evil spirits. Maybe this thing we got here ain't a Wendigo at all."

He pried the lid on the rum barrel and peeked inside, sniffing.

"I see your point. But then what is the Beast?"

McTroy shook his head, and I heard a sloshing in the barrel.

Evangeline came in with Wu. I scrutinized their demeanor. When I was satisfied that I saw no cannibalistic hunger in their eyes, I asked them to help me search for Cassi.

"Are those medical tools in that bag? We must treat your wound. You're weak. A fever is the last thing you need," Evangeline said, taking the kit from me. I acquiesced. I was feeling queasy and my legs had begun to tremble. My vision blurred.

"Take off your coat. Lean against the wall if you are dizzy," she said.

Wu and McTroy went to fetch Cassi. McTroy had the rum barrel under his arm.

"Bring Vivienne here as well. We will need her," Evangeline called after them.

"For what?" I asked as she used a pair of silver scissors to divide my sleeve.

"We're going to have a séance."

Evangeline finished dressing my shoulder when McTroy wheeled Vivienne into our bedroom.

"Wu and I are going to see if Smoke Eel is back. If he is I'll make sure to watch him. Make sure he doesn't try to run for it. He may have already flown the coop," McTroy said.

"Be careful. He cannot be trusted no matter who he is," I said.

McTroy nodded and left.

Vivienne did not appear as wild and incoherent as

I expected from her husband's description. Or it was possible that my assessment of how disturbed a person needed to look to be deemed irrational had shifted here at Nightfall. I surveyed all those present. If any of them had entered the Institute for Singular Antiquities office in Manhattan a week ago, I likely would have bundled them off to a hospital for medical observation and a strong dose of sedatives.

"You've been shot!" Vivienne cried out.

"Only with a blunderbuss. Evangeline got all the foreign bits out of me." I scooped up a collection of lead balls, two bent nails, and several fragments of gravel. I dumped them into my hostess's upturned palm. She inspected them with a mixture of fascination and disgust.

"My word, she dug those out of you?"

I received back the objects of my profound discomfort and put them in my watchpocket. Artifacts, you know. "Oh, Evangeline is an excellent excavator. I shall take her on my next field expedition. She has a keen eye and a delicate touch. And persistence. I only screamed once."

"Twice," Evangeline corrected me. "But to your credit the second was more of a yowl."

I slipped on a clean shirt and began buttoning it, slowly, one-handed.

Evangeline finished the job for me.

"Viv, Oscar tells us you've been having strong impressions from the other side?" Evangeline was best suited to this rather sensitive probing. I only hoped that Vivienne would be as cooperative as I had been. It took all my concentration to keep my mouth shut.

"It's been awful. I can handle one spirit at a time. Typically, I direct the encounter. These intrusions have been assaultive in nature. No sooner is one spirit filling me with its energy than I am pressured by another and another. They are crowding through the door. But I am the door!"

"Who are they?" Evangeline asked.

"I remember only pieces. That is unusual. Usually my connections remain quite clear."

"Do your best." Evangeline sat opposite Viv, their knees almost touching. "I am worried that if we cannot make sense of your recent dead talks Oscar will tie you to the bed again."

Vivienne rubbed her wrists. I saw purple welts. But she quickly adjusted her sleeves.

"I think they were the Beast's victims. All those poor men, the hunters. I know Gustav was there. He's the one I spoke with at the Starry Eyes. But there were new voices. That man with the spectacles, the bald one with the medicine wagon... he spoke to me."

"Pops?" I said. Evangeline shot me a glance. I coughed into my fist.

"Yes, he was there. And Billy the Kid. He was furious but hard to understand."

"His head was smashed to a pulp. That might account for his hostility and poor communication. Ah!" Evangeline screwed an unseen fingernail into my thigh. I gestured for Viv to keep talking. "Sorry. I will say no more. No interruptions from me. Do continue. Please..."

If Viv had not been so exhausted and perturbed I think she might've asked us exactly what we were about, why were we interrogating her, and where did our authority lie. But she was frazzled and out of sorts. Her dark hair had come unpinned, streaming out in all directions like electrical charges. Her cheeks were pale, as always, but now they appeared drawn and hollow, as if she were losing vital juices and being literally sucked dry. The blaze in her eyes had not dimmed. To the contrary, it seemed an inferno burned in them. Here was a woman using every ounce of energy she had to hold herself together and to keep from running mad. Oscar had made her sound hysterical. But she was not acting disproportionally excited. She was fighting insanity appropriate to the level of bizarre stimulation sprouting around her.

If invisible spirits spoke to me in great numbers, would I not rave? I had been touched by the Egyptian sorcerer Odji-Kek and I was now sensitive to forces which had flowed around me for years, yet passed unnoticed. It was as if a man who had never seen lightning were transformed into a lightning rod. Vivienne Adderly had made a study of her sensitivity. She had honed and developed it into a set of peculiarly alarming skills. How much more energy did she attract than I? What dark forces struggled to control her mind and cast her into an abyss of absurd speculation and unending delirium?

"May I ask you if you saw Claude on the road?" Viv smiled queerly.

"We did," Evangeline answered with minimal detail.

"How did he look? Was he still angry, or happy to be away from Nightfall?"

"Angry at first. But Claude was at ease when we

left him. Wherever he travels, part of him will always remain at Nightfall. He takes a part of his family with him, like a legacy."

"I thought I heard him," Viv said. "Among the dead voices. A mother knows the sound her children make. I couldn't be sure. They're all talking at once. But I thought…"

I hoped at this point that Evangeline would not go any farther. Viv could not withstand the verification of her son's death. I think she knew, even then. But she did not want to know.

"He told us about your family inheritance. Your father's persecution in Mexico."

Viv's eyelids fluttered. She gripped the armrests of her wheelchair and watched us. "His murder, you mean? Claude told you about that? Ahh, well, the cat is out of the bag, then. Yes, my family has old bloodlines. Oddities are bound to creep in. Have you told Oscar?"

"We've told him nothing," I said.

Viv's body visibly relaxed; her shoulders slumped forward and her jaw dropped.

"Thank God. I can't imagine what he would do if he found out."

"He doesn't know?" Evangeline said, shocked.

Viv shook her head.

"The changes don't begin until adolescence. For Claude it came late. He was a perfectly normal troublesome little boy who took great pleasure in irking his father since before he could speak a word. But no bodily transformations. Not until last year. If Oscar finds out about this, well, he will call it a curse. It would embarrass him. Oscar hates to be embarrassed.

It's only a matter of time until he learns the truth, I suppose. Nightfall has been an easier place than most to hide my family's heritage. That's why I insisted he build it. We had money. Oscar knew all about that. It's why he married me, to fund his excursions around the globe. He's famous now, but he wasn't when we met. Ambition was what he had. He was awfully handsome and bold. I think I loved him the moment we first danced... it was summer in Newport, Rhode Island..."

"What about Cassi?" I asked.

"Of course she knows. She and Claude are as close as any twins I've ever–"

"That's not what I mean. Is she...?"

The bedroom door burst open.

It was Wu.

"Come quickly! Miss Cassi has been attacked by the Beast!"

28
RIPPING

"Where is she?" I asked.

"McTroy took her into the trophy room," Wu said.

We rushed down the hallway. Evangeline pushed Viv, and Wu and I ran ahead of them. Coming through the anteroom, I saw the trail of bright blood on the floorboards. My heart sank.

Cassi lay on the divan near the fireplace. McTroy stood over her. The blankness on his face might have looked menacing to a stranger but I knew that he was worried. This knowledge did nothing to comfort me. I would've immediately bolted to her side if not for the presence of a second figure at the divan. I assumed it would be Oscar Adderly. But the bandana and black braided hair with the twin eagle feathers told me that the man in the deerskins was Smoke Eel. I approached quickly but with caution in mind.

Cassi lay with her eyes closed under Smoke Eel's mink poncho.

"Is she… you know?" I asked McTroy.

"She's alive. But the better part of her left forearm is gone. Ol' Smoke said he found her about an hour ago. Half hanging in a crevasse."

"She was outside? What took so long to get her here?" I gazed at the guide.

Smoke Eel wrote in his notebook.

TAKES TIME TO GET DOWN A MOUNTAIN. IN THE FOG. I WAS ON LOOKOUT FOR BEAST. I CARRIED HER. LUCKY I FOUND THE GIRL. SHE'D BE DEAD.

"Wu and I spotted him above the lodge. He had her over his shoulder."

Viv wheeled herself up to the edge of the divan. When she could maneuver no closer, she pushed up with her arms and raised herself up on her braced legs. She stood for a moment, finding her balance, and then sat on the end of the couch, rubbing her daughter's wool leggings.

"She's so cold. Dr Hardy, slip her boots off."

I pulled the muddied boots from her feet. They were large boots for a woman, although perhaps not for a female werecat. I noted scuffs in the leather, creases, and weathering marks. I turned the pair of boots over in my hands and set them on the hearth to dry out.

"Yong Wu," Viv said. "Will you build up that fire? I want it roaring."

"Yes, Mrs Adderly." The boy removed the cast-iron scrollwork screen and added logs.

I was not finished with Smoke Eel, although I did not feel the full conviction of my previous hot anger toward the man.

"Did you see the Beast?"

He shook his head. And scribbled.

I HEARD IT. THE WHISTLE.

"Well, there is more than one way to make a whistle," I said, remembering the giant's brass whistle

Gavin Earl had thrown at me. And that horrid mask merging buffalo, elk, and myth. A monster conceived in a circus. "What makes you sure it was the Beast that attacked her?"

SIZE OF THE BITE. AND I TOLD YOU I HEARD WHISTLE.

Wu dragged the fire screen back in place. The logs were catching fire. Smoke floated into the trophy room. Wu waved it away with a photo album of Oscar's North American excursions.

"She is coming around," Evangeline said. She poured a glass of brandy. And she brought a stack of Indian quilts to cover Cassi. What was left of Cassi's arm was folded across her chest.

Cassi moaned, tossing her head side to side.

"Away… Stay back… I will jump."

"Cassi dear, mother is here. You are home, safe and sound." Viv sounded unsure herself.

McTroy had tied a tourniquet above Cassi's elbow with his belt. Her lower arm was bandaged in a scarf that I knew was his. Blood soaked through the fabric.

"I will jump," Cassi said again, weakly.

She opened her eyes. They were so enormous. Too big almost. Honey-colored. They stared with a warm intelligence and made me feel undeserving of being watched so thoughtfully.

I smiled at her.

"Rom, have you saved me?"

I did not know how to answer her. "I did my little part. It was Smoke Eel and McTroy who brought you home. Wu helped too," I said. "But you shouldn't have been out in the fog."

She did not seem to recognize that we were not alone.

"But you would've saved me if given the chance," she said. "By yourself, you would have."

"I certainly would. You are worthy of saving."

She smiled a toothy smile.

"Do you have nightmares, Rom?"

I looked around at the others a bit flustered. I felt the color climbing in my face. The heat of the fire was intense at this point. And the smoke drifting into the room had gotten worse. It reddened my eyes and made me cough.

"I have nightmares from time to time," I said.

"I had a terrible nightmare. About the Beast. I was going to kill myself."

"Now don't say that. We found you. For whatever reason, the Beast did attack you. But the good news is that it could have been much worse. You escaped with your life. You took a wound to your left arm. But I'm certain we can fix you up. What were you doing outside?"

Cassi frowned.

"Outside?"

"Yes, you were on the mountain above the lodge. Smoke Eel found you at the edge of a crevasse. Do you remember?"

"I sleepwalk," she said. "Mother was hearing voices. We put her to bed. I went to nap. Claude is gone. He went away, and I don't think he is ever coming home again. Father is awful to him. I went to sleep and I had that creature chasing me in my dreams through the fog. I couldn't see where to go. I couldn't run because

I couldn't see. Then it bit me! I couldn't believe it. But it bit me and it shook me like I was nothing. A page in a book. Made for ripping. I was going to jump into the crevasse and kill us both because that would teach the Beast a lesson. But then I..."

She seemed to lose consciousness. I grasped her good hand and felt the rough skin of her palm. The tough pads of a werecat, I realized. Evangeline had to be right. Claude was a werecat. So was his twin. They kept their extra clothing in a trunk in a cave down the road. They ran through the woods and they killed things together. Who knew what else they did during the long days and nights with their paralyzed mother and oft-absent father. What would be worse, Oscar away in a jungle or a far-off forest hunting exotic trophies for his dioramas or Oscar at home, lounging about his stuffed animals, smoking his Havanas, and dreaming he was someplace else?

"Where is Oscar?" I asked the room.

No one knew.

"He wasn't here when we came in," McTroy said.

I looked at the half-boarded windows. The fog pooled beyond the glass like gray milk.

The fog was leaking into the room from the edges of the windows. It was getting inside.

No, not the fog.

Smoke.

The fire was burning, but the smoke wasn't going up the chimney. It was billowing back into the room. Plumes of gray smoke rose to the ceiling and collected there.

My coughing turned to choking.

"Something is wrong with the fireplace," I said. "Get water."

I pulled the iron screen off.

McTroy kicked at the logs. He grabbed a poker and poked it up the chimney.

"There's something stuck in there," he said.

It was too hot for him to stand amid the enflamed logs. Evangeline ran to the fire and dumped a pitcher of water onto the conflagration, which hissed and smoked even more, sending bitter ashes into the air as well. Smoke Eel grabbed one of the wool blankets from Cassi's lap and attempted to smother the flames. The wool began to sizzle, giving off an unpleasant odor like burning hair. The smoke reduced. Wu returned from the kitchen with a sloshing bucket of water and doused the wooly logs, leaving quite a smelly mess. But we could breathe. Evangeline opened one of the boardless windows, and the smoke gradually found its way out. McTroy prodded up the chimney with the poker again. Then he tossed the poker aside and thrust his hands up into the bricked chimney. He seized hold of something and with a bit of struggle managed to free it from where it had been jammed rather snugly. The burnt logs clattered and one or two rolled into the room. McTroy heaved the blockage onto the Persian rug.

"It's Pops!" Wu cried out.

Or half of him.

I had avoided studying the smoked corpse too closely. But the boy was correct.

Pops had been ripped in two, lengthwise. We had the right side of him, one arm, one leg, and as luck would have it, his entire head. He was obviously quite deceased. And naked. Smoke blackened his skin. More so the top half of him, which led me to believe he had been stuffed down the chimney headfirst. Or, I suppose for the sake of argument, rammed feet first up the chimney. Though that seemed pretty unlikely. His hair had been burned off completely, including his eyebrows. He appeared singed and altogether like a poorly executed Christmas ham.

"This is a gruesome discovery," I said.

"Agreed," Evangeline said.

"He looks mighty different without his clothes and burned up like that," McTroy said.

"We all do," I conjectured. "But it is he. I am having a particularly ghastly idea. Do you suppose there is any compounded elixir in his satchel? We may not need to talk to the man in the spirit realm if we can stir a last gasp or two out of his crisped remains."

"How did he get in there?" Wu asked, gazing into the chimney mouth.

"Not by his own accord," I said. "I think it is fair to assume the Beast put him in as a practical joke. Or perhaps this was an attempt to smoke us out of the lodge. But our fire-building revealed the trap early. Who knows? But we can take an advantage here."

"Excuse me," Viv said. "But where is my husband? He isn't, you know…" She pointed in an upward fashion and looked intently in the direction of the fireplace hole.

McTroy crouched in the place of wet ember and damp stinking wool.

"I can see sky. There's nobody else up this here smokeshaft."

Cassi sat up, opening her eyes fully and focusing first on the room and then on the charred body of Pops.

"Oh my. I thought my wound was grievous. But is that a man?"

"Indeed," I said. "It is formerly Pops. Now the Beast's leftovers. I hope you are not too disturbed by the sight of him. Should we cover him up?"

Cassi considered the question.

"No, I am fine with it."

She fell back on her pillow.

Viv said, "She has fainted."

"What is that putrid stench?" Gavin Earl said. He entered the trophy room and went straight for the liquor cabinet. He had changed his clothes, and I noted extra bullets tucked into his gunbelt. The last remnants of smoke sucked out the open window.

"It's your partner," McTroy said.

Earl craned to see what lay upon the Persian rug.

His face wrinkled in repugnance. "Which one?"

"Pops Spooner," McTroy said. "Billy's dead too. The Beast took both of them."

Earl nodded and drained two glasses of bourbon before speaking.

"There is no Beast," he said.

Smoke Eel shook his head in disbelief. Earl spun from the cabinet, walked over to him, and grabbed one of his braids. Before the Indian guide could stop him, Earl wrenched the plait.

"I have scalped your Indian," Earl said.

He held up the wig. Both braids were still attached to the red bandana in Earl's hand. Before us stood an utterly bald man whose darker pigmented skin ended in a line just north of his forehead. The skin of his pate was as smooth and white as a peeled onion.

Smoke Eel turned purple with rage, stomping his feet, and shouting.

"Crisse de câlisse de sacrament de tabarnak d'esti de trou viarge!"

29
SOURCE-WENDIGO

"What does that mean?" I asked.

"It means I'm not invited to Frenchy's house for dinner any time soon," Earl said.

"You bastard!" LaFarque said. "If the Beast does not kill you, I will."

"Curb your outrage, con man. We are the ones who should be damned angry with you. But the charade is over. Your giant friend is dead in the woods. We have your costume and sound effects. This farce is at an end. I will hold Oscar to his promise to pay me when I capture the Beast. Here is the Beast, or the thinking part of the Beast scheme. I am taking home that golden bull. The rest of you all can fight over the scraps and a train ticket home. Where is old Oscar?"

"Stupid, stupid fool," LaFarque said. "We are in *la situation dangereuse.*"

"Is Gavin right?" Evangeline asked. "Is the Beast a hoax? Who murdered those hunters?"

LaFarque said, "It is true that I wished to trick Oscar. My compatriot, Jules le Géant –

who you tell me sadly is dead – together we planned

to take Oscar's money. But we hurt no one. I am here thinking Oscar was seeing things, a man caught in his own imaginary games. So yes, we played along. But I experienced the real Beast. I heard the piercing cry which no whistle can imitate. This *femme*, Cassi, she has a bite in her arm… did I do that? Ask her. No. She was in the grip of this thing before I saved her. I know the Indian legends. The Wendigo spirit is here. Someone invited it. It is infecting our souls. I feel it gnawing in me. I have thoughts I never had before. Devouring thoughts. I am a *loup-garou* in my dreams. But worse. I kill to kill. I eat knowing I am forever empty. But I do not care. Ask Dr Hardy. He saw the Beast. He feels it too."

"I have seen a Beast I cannot explain," I said. "It was surely no man. No disguise could do what this creature did. And it talked to me. I think it is not of this world, this dimension where we perceive the world. But it travels through our plane of existence. Monsieur LaFarque, you told me Oscar used our hunting party as bait for the Beast. That he knew it would likely kill us. But he did not care as long as he made a bigger name for himself when he captured it. Is this true?"

The con man hung his head and spoke without looking at me.

"No. I was worried you and McTroy would kill Jules. I was waiting for him the night you saw me with my spyglasses. The storm was not a thing we expected. But I did find those torn clothes. I believe the Beast transformed from a human host. The Wendigo possesses one of us. That person is a source-Wendigo. Others fall under the spirit's influence. But only one changes into the monster completely. If we kill that person, then the spirit will leave the mountain. All those who are under its spell will be free once the spell is broken. But make no mistake. This evil thing was invited here. It was called to walk among these trees and stones."

Cassi groaned. Her wounded arm slid from her lap and struck the side of the divan.

She screamed in pain.

"We will take Cassi to her room and lock her in," I said. "It is too dangerous to bring her down the mountain road until we know the identity of the Beast who inflicted this injury. Wu, you and I will put Cassi in Vivienne's chair and bring her to her bed. McTroy, stay here and make sure no one leaves. Evangeline–"

"Vivienne and I will prepare for the séance," Evangeline said. "If you agree…"

"I do." It did not matter if I did or not, she would proceed as she pleased. "McTroy, will you need anything to assist you in guarding the trophy room?"

"Nope," he said.

He handed Hodgson's shotgun to Evangeline and rested his hand on his revolver.

I looked hard at Earl, who was the one gunman I knew could match McTroy's skills.

"Don't worry, Doctor. I am fascinated by this investigation of yours. I can't wait to see what happens next." He lit his pipe and reclined against the wall, amused and lethal.

"I will return shortly," I said. The room had gone absolutely frigid with the fire out and the window open. "Perhaps another fire is in order? It is going to be a long night."

"Longer still if we don't find Oscar. I'm not sure what's going on up here anymore. But I'm not leaving until he pays me my money," Earl said.

"Then you had better hope he is not the source-Wendigo," LaFarque said.

The thought had not occurred to me. But now that the seed was planted, I feared it would grow and overcrowd my reasoning. Where was Oscar? Why would he challenge us to a hunt where he was the hunted? An arrogant monster might see us only as food, not adversaries.

"Who's to say you're not this thing?" Earl retorted. "What better way to hide your identity than by creating a masquerade of that which you really are. I vote for you, Frenchy."

LaFarque hissed and threw his hands up in the air. "I would eat you first, bastard!"

"Enough," Evangeline said.

She stepped between the two men. McTroy was smart giving her the shotgun.

"I know that I am not the evil spirit," I said. "If one of you is this Wendigo, or whatever you are, be forewarned. We will find you. You are outnumbered and outgunned. Now Wu, help me move Cassi to the chair."

Cassi did not rouse as we transported her in Vivienne's chair down the long shadowy hallways of Nightfall Lodge. The wheels hummed. Her head twisted to one side, and when I adjusted her position, she made a low, gentle rumbling sound and rubbed her cheek against my fingers.

"Wu, when you found Viv, was she still tied to her bedposts?"

"No, I don't think so."

"So she might've been able to leave her room?"

"I guess so," he said. "Are thinking she is the Wendigo?"

"She is a dabbler in black magic. And she is sensitive to the spirit world. Her family has a long history of shapeshifting. How far is a werecat from a Beast? I make no direct accusations, Wu. Not under these dire circumstances. But she might've been able to slip out of the lodge and attack Cassi, and then return to her bed before you and McTroy fetched her. That night I saw the Beast in the lodge window, I might've smelled Vivienne's perfume in the animal gallery."

"Then she *is* the Wendigo."

"We cannot be premature in our conclusion. But the Adderly family does live on this mountain where all the attacks on Raton's townsmen originated. Who else was even here?"

"LaFarque might have been, and we don't know when Gavin Earl really came to town."

I opened the door to Cassi's bedroom. Wu pushed her inside.

"That is what is so insidious about this affair. We stop trusting each other. Everyone hides a monster inside. That is what we come to believe. We are the monsters. It eats away at us."

I turned down the blankets on Cassi's bed. Wu went around to Cassi's legs and I scooped my arms underneath hers. We lifted her onto her bed. Even though I am quite uncomfortable with the sight of fleshly trauma, I unbound the scarf from Cassi's left forearm.

"Wu, take these matches. Light the lamp on the nightstand and bring it to me."

The scarf was soaked in blood. I dropped it into a painted bowl on her dresser.

"Let me have that light." I turned the wick on the lamp higher. "Go and find towels. They must be with the sheets in one of the linen closets. Cut them into strips for bandages."

Wu left on his mission.

I forced myself to inspect Cassi's wound.

The sudden intake of my breath did nothing to alleviate my lightheadedness.

LaFarque was correct. Something with a huge mouth had stripped most of the tissue from the lower half of her arm. Skin, fat, muscles – all were missing. Except for the two white bones which were not broken but upon which I could discern deep tooth marks. Her wrist and hand remained intact. The Beast must have clamped down on her when she raised her arm to defend herself. A Raton doctor would surely need to amputate. If Cassi lived through the night. I loosened the tourniquet only a smidgen. The vessels near her elbow began to pump fresh blood.

"Achh, I'm making quite a mess of you, poor Cassi."

I retightened the knot.

"Rom, you are here. In my bedroom," she said, smiling mischievously.

One might've mistaken her hooded eyes for an effort at seduction if one did not realize it was languor and the shock of almost dying from substantial blood loss. Her paleness surrendered none of its distinctive allure. If anything, Cassi looked more beautiful to me than she ever had.

"We will fix you," I said.

"And if I cannot be fixed?"

"Don't talk that way. It could be worse."

"How, Rom?"

"You know how. You are still among the living, Cassi. That is the best chance at improvement, I believe. The alternatives are far from reliable and have dubious side effects."

"Claude is dead," she said.

"We don't need to talk about that."

"But he is. I feel it. Or what I feel is his absence. He is missing from me."

I looked at her for a long time. She had the most pleasing way of never breaking one's gaze without any underlying feelings of awkwardness or hostility. I swam in her honeyed stare.

"I know what Claude was. We witnessed him changing."

"Where did he die?"

"In the cave. It was like he fell asleep, very tired. He had a last drink. And a smoke."

"So you've visited our cave. It was rustic but private." Her tear-filled eyes stayed on mine. "Are you afraid of me now, Rom?"

I shook my head. "No more than I was before."

She laughed softly.

"Read me a bedtime rhyme from that book on the top of the others," she said suddenly.

She indicated a sizable volume on her bookshelf.

I picked it up and held the cover near my light. Gold lettering on black leather.

"*Odd & Ghastly Rhymes for Frightening Young Children.* Are you serious? This is what you want to hear now?"

She nodded in an exaggerated manner.

"My favorite," she said. "Read 'An Eerie Alphabet Rhyme'. Start with 'C'."

"Here we go. Just a few lines and then you must try and sleep."

"This will help. I promise," she said.

I cleared my throat and began:

> "'C' is for Centipede asleep on your cheek.
> Stir and you'll wake her. Those legs! Shriek!
> 'D' is for Dung Beetle rolling 'round her ball.
> Strong little scarab – she gives it her all."

"Oh, I do like dung beetles. They are scarabs, you know? The Egyptians loved them."

"I knew you'd like it. Keep the book. It's my gift to you. You see, I know you, Rom. Even though we've only just met. We are kindred spirits, you and I. Won't you take me away? I want to go with you to the city. Or to some far-off country, I don't care. I get lonely on this mountain with only my family. Now that Claude is gone I will lose my sanity. Mother immerses herself in her charts and esoteric books. Father has his trips and sews his trophies to remind him of his past adventures. Where are my adventures? What is my story? When will it begin? Take me with you, Rom. Please. I will be good, I promise. I am awfully good when I am good. The bad part of me might be something you learn to love as well. Don't you need a little badness in your life, Rom? Unpredictability. I see in your face that you are lonely like me. Evangeline will never be yours. She is good and, well, exciting to you. I like her. But will she ever ask you to be with her like I am asking you?"

I put the book down on the blanket.

With her good hand, Cassi took up mine. She pressed her lips to my knuckles. I felt her hot breath. Her kisses were damp on my fingers, and she licked the inside of my wrist playfully. She whispered something I could not hear. When I leaned closer she kissed me on the lips. It was quick but not without bolts of energy. The back of my head felt as if it were lifting off.

She is too young for you, I said to myself.

Although she is a woman, I answered, and not *that* young. She needs you too much, I said. *You are not in need?* A voice in me barked back.

She is a werecat. You are an Egyptologist.

Wu returned with the towels.

I took my hand back.

Cassi closed her eyes.

"She is still asleep?" Wu asked.

"Yes, she needs to rest. I hope to talk to her in the morning. We have much to discuss."

I dressed her ravaged arm and turned down her lamp.

Though the pain must have been incredible, she did not move the whole time.

30
COLD GRUEL

When Wu and I returned to the trophy room we discovered the space transformed. Evangeline had ordered LaFarque and Earl to place the only round table in the room near the center, beside Oscar's cubical Beast cage. Viv told her where to locate a black tablecloth embroidered with stars. After spreading the cloth, McTroy could not seem to keep his fingers from tracing them. A stout red candle sat in a stand before the only place without a chair; this is where Viv would seat herself and conduct the séance. Viv steeled herself for the task, drinking a small pour of brandy from a cordial glass. I noticed she had put her back to the windows that still showed the mountain.

I pulled Evangeline to the side.

"Has Oscar appeared?"

"He hasn't," she said. "Viv isn't asking about him. I don't know if that's good or bad."

"Place an empty chair for him. I will go out to the stable and see if I can find Pops' medical bag. If he has any elixir left, that's where it is. I want to use it on him. Maybe Oscar went outside."

"Because he is the Beast?"

I shrugged. "We are all susceptible to the Beast's influence. It is best the others stay together here. That way everyone is being watched. If behaviors alter, early intervention is a must. Tie the person up, or, failing that, you have McTroy."

"What if he is the one under the Beast's control?"

"I trust you still have your pistol under your skirt."

She smiled. "I will shoot to incapacitate, not kill."

"How very kind of you," I said.

Then to the others I raised my voice. "I am going to see if I can find Pops' bag out in the enclave. I will go alone. If I do not return in thirty minutes, assume I have met with an unfortunate end. Conduct the séance. Find the Beast's lair. Stop the source-Wendigo."

"Why do you get to go?" Earl asked.

"I have spoken to the Beast. Perhaps I may again. In any event, I am expendable."

No one disagreed with my logic.

Evangeline took the shotgun from the table and handed it to me.

She said, "This is about as foolproof as it gets. Pull one trigger and one barrel shoots. Pull both and that's all the firepower you'll ever need. Aim in the general vicinity of your target. Good luck."

Under normal circumstances I would refuse such a weapon. But these were not normal circumstances. I took the shotgun and walked down the hall of dioramas. Here were the lions to my right. I had spotted the lovers entwined in their grassy habitat. I had smelled a perfume that reminded me of roses. Plugging any combination of participants I could imagine into that tryst left me dry-mouthed. But they were real. I wasn't sleepwalking, and it was no dream. As I opened the front door, I heard a scrabbling of nails on wood behind me.

"Are you going for a walk?" a deep voice said. Orcus peered up at me and cocked his head. His stubby black tail wagged.

"Yes, would you care to join me?"

"A walk turned down may never be offered again," he said.

"Then let's be off."

Orcus and I took the path. The fog had thickened to a cold gruel. I could see no farther than a few steps in any direction. The mists swirled and eddied in our wake. The walk seemed much longer than I remembered it. I held the shotgun out in front of me as if I were offering my enemies a loaf of freshly baked bread instead of death.

"Do you smell anything unusual?" I said.

Orcus lifted his nose and took a few deep sniffs. His ears twitched.

"We are getting closer to the horses. Master Oscar has passed this way."

"Recently?"

"Hard to say. But I think so."

"Did you know that Claude was a werecat?"

"Yes, but he never tried to eat me. I knew him since he was a pup."

"And Cassi?"

Orcus stopped. He looked toward the foggy right. Out there, not very far, the ground ended abruptly in a sheer drop. The plunge was as deadly as it was obscure.

I felt as if I were already falling, awaiting the impact of pines and boulders the size of small apartment houses.

"What is it?" I whispered.

"I hear things moving," the dog said.

I crouched and pointed the gun. My finger feathered the triggers. "What sorts of things?"

"Your tongue for one."

"Sorry."

The mastiff stiffened his neck.

"It walks on the snow. In the trees, branches moves. But there is no wind."

"Might it be an animal? Rabbits or, say, a single young unimposing deer?"

"In the fog it might be anything. I can't see through fog. It's big. Two legs."

Orcus considered this noise a bit longer. He started trotting along again.

I stayed where I was. Eyes fixed on the gray boiling vapors.

"We should go," Orcus said.

"Is the two-legged thing walking away?"

"No. That is why we need to hurry. It is coming. The fog makes it leery."

I quickened my step. Soon the outline of the mountain and the darker impression of the alcove emerged from the mists like the prow of a damaged ship. A slender figure came at us, pausing, and extending its arm. I touched the triggers but feared the spray of lead would hit Orcus. The dog ran ahead of me into the mouth of the horses' niche. I thought Orcus was springing onto the long-armed devil in the misty haze, but then I heard a loud human voice.

"Who are you?" it asked me.

Oscar.

"Dr Rom Hardy, Egyptologist," I called back.

I lowered my weapon.

"Get in here," he said, impatiently. "I almost shot you with my elephant gun."

Oscar had donned a sheepskin vest and a knitted cap. I was happy to see him. He had no overt beastly qualities I could discern. He seemed invigorated by the intensification of our ordeal. Oscar was not to be mistaken for a likeable man, but he possessed a level of self-confidence I envied. There was no room for doubt in his worldview. He knew the facts that he knew. He sought out other facts which interested him. Everything beyond that scope was useless information. It was a tidy philosophy if nothing else. He anticipated my question, answering before I could ask it.

"I came to check on the horses. I thought the Beast might slaughter them to keep us from leaving in a hurry. But, as you can see, the horses are fine. Why are you here, Hardy?"

"Pops' medicine bag has something in it I need. You should know that Cassi was attacked. The Beast caught her when she was out on the mountain above the lodge."

"What was she doing up there?"

"Sleepwalking."

"Is she hurt?" he asked.

"She will likely lose her arm." I watched to see his reaction to my blunt delivery of the tragic news. His expression revealed strain but little in the way of tenderness.

"A person can live without an arm. We must finish this tonight at all costs. I have to capture that creature. I'll send Hodgson into Raton tomorrow for a doctor. Hardy, help me load these boards into that wheelbarrow. We didn't have enough wood inside to seal all the windows."

"I need to find the bag first," I said.

"It's by the wagon. Let's get going. I don't like the feel of the mountain. I've hunted enough big game to know when a predator is lurking around. The Beast will strike as soon as it sees we are vulnerable. Timing is the key. I don't want to miss it."

I found Pops' bag where Oscar said it was. Inside was one vial of the glowing green elixir. I pocketed the potion. I also found my trusted ape-headed walking stick where I had dropped it during our confrontation with Pops and Billy. The great naturalist and I loaded the wheelbarrow with a dozen boards (and my stick and shotgun); we whisked them back through the fog (I did the whisking, Oscar the elephant-gunning), and we followed Orcus to Nightfall's heavy doors.

Surprisingly, Oscar didn't object to the séance. But he insisted we finish fully boarding the windows and the front doors first. It didn't take us long. After the last nails were pounded home I found myself feeling more secure that I had since arriving at the lodge. It would take a great deal of force and time to break through the boards. Oscar, McTroy, LaFarque, and Gavin Earl were all experienced hunters, and, frankly, extraordinary killers. Evangeline and Viv's séance would soon lead us to the Beast, I was certain. Now I was not neglecting the fact that one of my housemates might be the Source-Wendigo, as LaFarque had suggested. But I thought it just as likely that LaFarque was wrong. He'd heard an Algonquin legend. But what did a white con-man circus performer know about Indian spirits? The Wendigo – or Beast, or whatever it was that killed the hunters, tempted me in the dark, and cast its contagion over the mountain like a malevolent pall – might be an abomination completely unconnected to any of us. Demons don't need men to live.

It came here for a reason.

We may never know why.

We only had to send it back.

Or cage it.

31
SHOTGUN SÉANCE

We sat in a circle and joined hands around the black table. Fogbound. Barricaded. Staring at a lit red candle; its flickering light was our only illumination. The darkness gathered around us. The charred partial remains of the surgeon lay across the table like a roasted carcass waiting for the carving knife. If we had been floating at the bottom of a chasm, or tumbling through the outermost planets of the solar system, it would not have felt any stranger than it did. My head ached dully from lack of sleep and a growing pressure mounted behind my eyes.

Faces.

That is what we were to each other.

A ring of masks in this order: Vivienne, and to her left around the circle – Oscar, Evangeline, McTroy, Earl, LaFarque, Yong Wu, and me completing the circle with my sweaty hand in Viv's.

The candlelight wavered. In this yellow, trembling pool we began our descent.

Viv said, "I call to the spirit of Pops Spooner. We have your corporeal self before us. We can put you to rest if you help us. But we have questions first. Enter your body. Speak."

I released Viv's hand and stood. I took the syringe from the table. The elixir in the glass barrel cast its own eerie light. I shot the full cylinder into Pops' skull, entering through the top of his spinal column as he had done to McTroy on the trail. But it did not stir.

I refilled the syringe.

"That's the last of it," I said as I plunged in the spike. We watched.

There! Did the skin along one cheek quiver? Yes, I believe so. I saw a blackened tooth I did not notice before my administering the potion. A shivering of the limbs, almost imperceptible. But I could swear–

The hand of the surgeon slammed on the table and his bloodshot eyes met ours.

"Pops, do you hear me?" Viv asked.

"Aaagrrhlahfff…"

His cracked lips peeled back. His tongue protruded, as sooty as a blacksmith's thumb.

"Give him water," Evangeline said.

I lifted the pitcher from the side table and poured water directly in his cooked maw.

"Yassssss," he said finally. His wet burned head smelled… indescribable.

I sat in my chair and rejoined hands with Wu and Viv.

"Do you know where you are?" Viv asked.

"In Hell."

"Your soul has not yet left this earthly dimension. You are at Nightfall Lodge."

The encrimsoned eyes rolled around, taking in the sights.

"I need to ask him about something," I said to Viv.

She nodded for me to take my turn at questioning.

"Pops, this is Rom Hardy. Wu and I discovered the secret ingredient to your elixir."

"Th-thieves."

"Yes, well, regardless of that. We have it. I want to know where it came from."

Pops' mouth worked as if he were chewing a tough chunk of beef.

"D- d- desert. I found it in a shipwreck."

"A shipwreck? In New Mexico Territory? You'll have to do better than that."

"P- Peeecos River and Salt Creekkk... not a water ship. Airship. Took the wagon out by John Chisum's Jingle Bob Ranch. Right before I dug up Billy. I found maybe a balloon. It was silver. In the silver was the Pilot. I cut his head off for a souvenir. He didn't stink. The buzzards stayed away. Soon as I put him in the wagon he started to slime up. Green as foxfire. I tested it. You know it was a special slime the Pilot made. Heh-heh. Old green devil. I'll keep him, I said."

"How does it work?"

"Hell if I know. I keep the head quiet or Billy goes whacko."

I nodded. Something else occurred to me.

"I injected you with the elixir. Are you... in communion with the Pilot the way Billy was, and McTroy is?"

Pops thought about it.

"I don't feel like nothing but Hell."

"Very well then. My questions are finished."

Viv squeezed my hand. I had done well, not breaking

the contact with Pops.

"Pops, do you know where the Beast lives?" she said.

"Right here, I reckon." He licked at the drenched tablecloth.

I poured more water on him.

"Is there a lair or den where the Beast retreats when it is not in the woods?"

"Goes inside."

"Please explain. We don't understand you." Viv was polite but firm with him.

"Lady, I watched the damn thing eat me. It stuffed my corpse in a tree crotch. Comes back later to drag me around the mountainside and cram me into that chimney flue."

"But where did it hide?" I asked, interrupting the conversation.

"Inside. Up in the body of a host. It shrunk down after. I was dead, what did I care."

"Whose body?"

"You're so smart, you figure it out, thief. I told you. Don't matter to me. I hope it kills and eats you all. I hope you watch it eat each of your chums and it scares the shit out of you and then it kills you like it did me. I am in Hell, boys and girls, and I'm waiting to climb up your sweet little asses as soon as you get here to join me. It's flamin' hot. My skin is blisters and pus. My ass smokes like a fine seegar. You're gonna feel rows and rows of teeth tear at your hide. I'm laughing thinking about how it's gonna look with all you going at once like a damn meat grinder, a-grindin' and a-chewin' aw Hell yes–"

McTroy shot Pops in the head with his Colt Army.

Pops had half a skull now to match the half of everything else.

I wiped Pops' brains off my jacket. There was a smoking bullet hole in the tablecloth. McTroy seized the remains of Pops' ankle and hauled him off, hurling him into the corner where clattering buffalo skulls tumbled over him in an avalanche of bones.

"I didn't need more from him," McTroy said. "Let's carry on."

Viv was shaking. She had kept up her strength through the first interview of our session, but I wondered how much more she might endure. The longer we sat together at this table the more she looked at her husband. She was pleading with him silently. He was uncommunicative. He glanced away or simply stared down at the section of cloth in front of him as if waiting to be served his dinner. Evangeline nodded at her to go on.

Viv took a deep breath. Her gaze fixed on the flame.

"I call now to the dead spirits who roam around us. I am your instrument. I invite you to speak through me to this group. We are not here to harm you. Miss Evangeline will ask you questions. Answer her using me as your conduit. We do not judge you. We wish you only peace. Help us to defeat the evil which plagues this mountain. I feel you standing behind me. Speak."

Viv's voice dropped into a deep bass.

"*Où est le chat? Le panthère?*"

Evangeline said, "He is not here. You are safe. The doors are locked against intruders."

"Jules? Is that you, *mon ami*?" LaFarque said.

"I am here, René," the giant answered through Viv. "But I am gone too."

"Our game did not work as I planned. We knew the risks."

"Yet you sit here. I am sleeping in the snow forever. You always had the better risks."

LaFarque's face collapsed. His chin quivered. Tears streamed down his cheeks.

"You are correct, Jules. But what can I do now? Nothing..."

The giant did not reply.

Evangeline asked, "Did you see the Beast?"

"I am the Beast," Jules said.

"I told you so," Gavin Earl said. "Where is my gold? I'm finished with parlor tricks." He let go of McTroy. He drew his pistol and pressed it to the temple of LaFarque's head.

"Do it!" LaFarque shouted. "I do not care if I live. Kill me. The Beast will still come."

Gavin Earl had no scruples about putting a bullet into LaFarque. I braced for the shot.

"But I am not the only Beast. There are two. I was an actor. The other is *le diable*."

Viv's face appeared to lengthen. Her shoulders squared up. She swayed in her chair.

Jules said, "I saw it behind a tree. You were there, gunslinger. Chasing me. But snows were falling. You did not see it. But *le diable* saw you. Red eyes. *Plusieurs dents* like a *loup-garou*. I tried to hide. I work all my years in a circus with wild cats. Then one kills me. Ah, life."

Earl lowered his revolver.

"Where did the Beast go? Did you see its den?" Evangeline asked.

"*Non.*"

Viv's head switched from side to side as if she were hearing something we could not.

"You lied to me," Jules said. "*Les chats* are here."

Viv's body slumped forward as if she had been shoved hard from behind.

"Jules, don't go. Not yet," Evangeline said.

But when Viv lifted her face and smiled, it was not Jules.

"The happy family gathers with friends. This is the worst party ever. Where's my sister?"

"Claude?" Oscar said. "How could you be here? These people are dead."

Viv let go of Oscar and me so she could clap. "Bravo, Father, you solve another mystery of the world. And for this one you did not need to leave the comforts of home. Can someone please get me whiskey? Evangeline, roll me another cigarette. Your last one tasted the best of any I've had."

Oscar was watching Viv. But he was seeing Claude, and it tore at him. I cannot say if I saw guilt in his features, but regret was there. He'd miscalculated. Never did he expect Claude to die, nor did he think the news would reach him by so shocking and circuitous a route.

"Was it on the road? I thought you made it to town. Who killed you, son? Let me know, and I will take my revenge. I promise you. No one kills the son of Oscar Adderly and lives."

"It was a bear, Father. A dead bear that loved a fat

man. If I could've bet on a million ways I might've died, that's one I never saw coming. You should get Cassi out of here. Far away from this. Rom, she loves you. Has she told you yet? She told me. But there's nothing a boy can do about that. Especially not a dead boy. Being a ghost may be more boring than being alive."

"Oh, Claude," Viv said, in her own voice. "Please forgive us. Your father asked me to invite that evil spirit here. He said it would be a challenge. He wanted to fight a real monster. To cage a myth. He asked me to open a portal. And I listened to him."

"Viv, be quiet," Oscar said.

"No, I will not."

She addressed her son again, "Your father read some legend on a monolith in the Canadian woods. Ancient, older than the tribes that live there now, or any in recorded history. Far to the north, where he sought the polar predators. He copied down the words and symbols. He asked me to find out what they meant. I found nothing. No record of them anywhere. So I asked the spirit to come to me, unknown. To show itself. Night after night, I opened myself to… anything that happened to be passing in the cosmos. This spirit traveled from a long way off, across dimensions forbidden and immeasurable, loathsome spaces impossible to navigate. Yet it came to me. When it knocked, I let it in. Gustav was right. The Beast is a demon. I brought it here for your father to hunt."

"The Wendigo," LaFarque said.

"No, not a Wendigo," Viv said. "Just wickedness. Pure evil greed and hunger. The Beast with No Name."

I was outraged. *They had invited the Beast to Nightfall!*

It was all for Oscar's sport. A reckless experiment to augment Oscar's self-regard. He wanted to catch a myth and in doing so to make himself a legend among men. The carelessness of these people appalled me. Viv clearly felt guilt. I could forgive her. Perhaps she acted out of love for her husband.

But Oscar! He had invited us here because he provoked a fight with a force he could not conquer alone. We were expendable hired guns.

I felt a violence growing in me, a desire to attack.

As Vivienne named the unnameable Beast I grew numb from the soles of my feet, up my legs and trunk, until like a man slowly dipped into a tank of gelid slush, I sank beneath the surface and froze. My ears filled with a cold burning. My eyes refused to blink.

I was too cold to think. All I could do was watch. Paralyzed – utterly immobile, I thought with an onrushing panic. But no, my lips still moved. I did not move them. But something did. An invading intelligence played a tune upon my vocal cords and formed my mouth around its forced words.

"If I wanted a name I would give myself one," It said.

32
FROM TIME TO TIME

"Are you in Rom Hardy?" Evangeline asked, to my escalating horror.

I – the Beast – laughed such a vile, corrupt snigger that I was repulsed by my own sound-making. Yet what could I do but sit there, mute in my private expressions, the puppet of a more powerful entity which occupied me as if I were solitary room in a cheap boarding house.

"Rom and I are together," It said.

"Is Rom the killer we have sought?"

"No!" Wu shouted. "I saw the Beast when it took Billy and Pops by the wagon. Dr Hardy was with me *underneath* the wagon. He was in New York when those hunters died."

"The boy speaks the truth, though rudely out of turn." It, not me, began to crush Wu's hand in our grip. I wanted to yell STOP! But nothing happened. Wu squirmed, wincing in pain.

The Beast released him. Wu clutched his bruised hand and slid his chair away.

"Respect is important. I am your elder by several

thousand thousand millennia."

"What do you want?" Evangeline asked.

"Only to eat. I am hungry. When I am full, I will go. Is that not fair?"

Oscar shifted in his seat. I could see – so I am sure the Beast could as well – that the clockwork of his mind was pondering ways to lure or impel me into his cage.

"If Rom is locked up, I will seize your wife's body. The physical is only one way I manifest my power. I could go into you too, Oscar. Would you like that? I might stuff you like you stuff those poor exotics in your collection. I collect things too. In my belly. Ah-ha-ha-ha…"

There was a loud pounding on the front doors. It sounded like a fist, then two fists beating against the wood. The percussive sound echoed in the halls like the shuddering, banging chambers of a large, irregular, sick heart.

"Who could that be, I wonder?" It said.

The demon spirit infected my perceptions. I ached with hunger. Hunger for raw meat, the bloodier the better. If I could bite something made of flesh and sink my teeth into it and rip, then I would feel better. My mind suggested this to me. Suckling a fresh wound would slake my thirst.

"Why are you here?" Evangeline asked.

"I was invited, as the mistress of the house told you. Oscar needed company."

"What would make you leave, Wendigo? Do you demand a sacrifice?" LaFarque asked.

"This clown needs more time to bake," It said. "He looks a mite pale at the top."

LaFarque slumped at the jibe. He touched the pate of his head and wiped the sweat.

"You will see me in my glory, clown. Then tell me if I look like a buffalo perched on the head of an oaf. I will lift you on my antlers and take you high in the sky. I will burn you with cold and heat. We will speed together through the pines. Then I will crack your bones and suck the marrow. I will shit you out, LaFarque. Flies will lay eggs in the waste your mother birthed."

"That is quite an insult, Frenchy," Earl said.

He turned toward the Canadian con man, but his move was merely an act of distraction, hoping to divert the attention of the Beast. Because the next thing he did was swiftly pivot, bringing his revolver up over the edge of the table.

He shot me in the face.

Or he would have if the Beast's reflexes did not take over from mine.

I dodged to the side. The bullet plugged the wall behind me. I smelled the gunpowder. My ears rang like bells. The pummeling on the door grew louder, more insistent. The wood cracked and splintered. But to me it sounded a long way off. A dull thumping that traveled to my ears through waves of fluid. The Beast spirit was in me, but I felt sunken in it. Down at the bottom of a gloomy, murky tank.

The red candle flickered.

I saw the stains. Black smudges like the ones I spotted on McTroy before Earl attacked him in the woods. But these new marks were more numerous. I saw them on everyone seated around the séance table. Wu's face was a smear of charcoal. Evangeline looked as though she wore a black ribbon around her throat. Oscar's face stopped below his upper lip. Inky splotches wrapped around all the others' bodies like the soft limbs of an enormous cephalopod.

I was the only one clear of the markings.

Like a man who has held his breath under water well past the point where his consciousness functioned properly, I teetered on the brink of lucidity. And like that same man, once he is dredged up from the depths into the thinner element of air, I gasped and filled my lungs again, and again. The spirit had vacated me. The cold was gone. My possessor had fled.

"Hardy?" Evangeline asked. "Are you...?"

"I am me."

"Where did it go?" Oscar asked. "It didn't leave, did it? I mean, not entirely. I am so close to winning this game."

I wanted to throttle the man.

"Do you hear that crashing on your door like an elephant butting its head? I expect that is where you might locate your Beast manifesting. Open the door and stand there, Oscar. See if you can drive it into your cage. Maybe if you ask it will enter. When you requested its presence on this mountain it showed up. You have a knack for invitation. That's why we're here after all."

McTroy and Earl approached the front door. The boards held. But we could hear the hacking of wood and the feral grunts that followed each tremendous blow. Claws, I thought.

Claws.

"Save your bullets until you see it," Oscar said.

He had dragged his favorite wingback chair from the trophy room to the entryway. With one knee planted deep in the seat cushion, he balanced his elephant gun on the top back rail, bracing his other leg on the floor. "Let me try for a hobbling wound first. A clean shot to the leg with this should do it. I will cripple the thing. But I want it taken alive."

"Who cares what you want," Earl said.

He and McTroy took up positions in the corridors on either side of the entrance.

"Doc, you get that coach gun. Wait in the trophy room with Wu and the women."

"I can stay here with the men," I said to McTroy.

"I know you can, but if the Beast rips us in no time, where would you rather be?"

Oscar tossed me the keys to his cage.

"If the creature dispatches us, lock yourselves in the cage. It is Beast-proof."

Nightfall's entry shook with every new assaultive strike. Nails shrieked as the creature outside rammed the doors.

"Go, before it is too late," LaFarque said. He followed me into the diorama gallery. From the lion's exhibit he removed a long Maasai spear and a red and black shield made from stitched water buffalo hide. "The old ways are sometimes the best, eh, Monsieur Har-dee?"

"If you know how to use it," I said.

LaFarque hefted the spear. "Throw it, no?" He smiled. But I saw only doom in him.

I felt better with the shotgun. Yet I was as much a gunfighter as LaFarque was a Maasai warrior. How does one kill something that is not of this world? I knew no strategy for dispensing with demons or cosmic travelers who hunger insatiably for the meat of humankind. Did anyone? If we killed the main spirit, would we be rid of it? This was no Wendigo. But did the same rules apply?

"Evangeline, what do you think about getting inside that cage?"

"I think not," she said.

"Oscar says it is Beast-proof. We are to secure ourselves in there."

Wu pushed Viv's wheelchair to the cage's door. I unlocked the cage. They went inside.

"I will fetch some pillows and blankets. A pitcher of water. We might be in there for a while if things do not go our way." I passed the provisions to Wu through the bars.

"Dr Hardy? If the Beast gets in the house, what will stop it?" Wu said.

"We will find out. But for now, we make ourselves hard to eat. Hiding can be noble too. Let the Beast worry about getting us out of the cage, rather than us worrying about *it* getting in."

"But can't it just wait?" he asked.

I considered the smart boy's conundrum.

Stepping around to the cage's door, I handed over the rum barrel with the green head inside. Wu took it from me and placed it in a far corner of the cage. He used it as a makeshift stool, sitting down to further philosophize about our deteriorating situation. I stepped inside the iron cube and crouched beside him, putting my arm around his shoulders.

"Wu, you ask very good questions. That is half the battle in life," I said.

"Thank you."

I tried giving him a comforting squeeze.

"You can't answer my question, can you?" he said.

"No, I cannot."

Viv lifted her head. "Listen. The pounding has stopped. Did the Beast break in?"

I sprinted to the hall and peered around the corner.

"The door is intact. But the siege has, for the moment, ceased. Perhaps the creature tires."

A loud crash sounded, not from the entry, but from behind the cage. Glass shattering. Then again, another explosion of breakage. The steady clawing of the boards over the windows commenced with urgency. The Beast was huffing and grunting with exertion.

"It is trying to enter through the windows!"

These last boards we had taken from the alcove were not as thick as the first Oscar used. The wood was dry, splintery. After only a couple of sharp blows I saw gray light spill from between the cracks. It was still light outside. I had forgotten what time it was. Evening twilight. The cool, damp air of the foggy mountain flowed through the crevices in these flimsier boards. Each cleaving strike created a gap, another gray slit, like ghostly eyes opening to observe us in our misery. The rush of cool air was nothing short of panic-inducing. Was that a knifing claw prying apart the boards? A hooked fang inserted and pulling back, cracking a long board in two and flipping the broken board fragment out over the ledge and down the mountain.

We have but moments, I thought. Moments to live before the ripping starts and the stains I saw in black are spouting red blood. My premonitions would not come true if I could help it. We had to kill this thing.

I saw the shotgun on the floor.

I am no murderer. No man of violence. But I cocked back those twin hammers and inserted both barrels of the coach gun into the gap where the newest hole appeared. With no further consideration, I pulled both triggers. The barrels issued a mighty roar. The shotgun recoiled hard into my shoulder. I stumbled back.

No scream from outside. Only the quiet fog. And an echo of the blast I caused.

A heavy body lay upon the ledge. I could not look at it.

Turning away, I watched the men from the front door defense rushing in.

"I have slain the Beast," I said. "I had no choice."

McTroy was at my shoulder. Laying a hand there and urging me aside. He surveyed my damage. I sat heavily upon the floor, sliding the emptied gun away from me as far as it would go.

"Is it over?" I asked, knowing the answer, for I had glimpsed the hideously hairy form.

"I think not," McTroy said.

"What do you mean?" I got up and joined him at the aperture. "Look at this beast."

"Doc, you have slewn Dirty Dan."

"No, that's wrong."

"He's slewn all right. I know slewn when I see it."

"The word is slain. Are you sure it's Dirty Dan?"

"He is both slewn and slain. And, yes, it is Dirty Dan, as far as I can tell. Though you did remove a majority of his face."

"Good God."

"The blast tossed his brain out on them rocks. There's no head to him, really. Looks like something went over there. Teeth? If you squint, you can picture how he looked when he had a head, which wasn't that great. But that's the bulk of him. Dropped him where he stood. He was using his tommy hawk to chop at the windows. Crazy fella. Probably still mad about his bear."

"Please, say no more. I'm feeling unwell. Was it quick?"

Earl, Oscar, and LaFarque took turns peeking through the fissure at the trapper's corpse.

"You shot him not even a minute ago. Here he lies, deader than Caesar. I'd say that's damn quick," Earl said.

"He was an ugly bugger, and this did not improve his looks," LaFarque added.

"I'm sorry," I said.

"Hell, Doc," McTroy replied. "You can't be blamed for how ugly a feller is. He lived with it his whole life, I imagine – well, his whole life up to the point where you shot him in the face. At least you spared Dirty Dan the Hatchet Man having to go another day with that mug." He spied through a gray rift, wrinkling his nose. "He smells bad too – as bad on the inside as on the out."

I dry-heaved.

"We all murder people from time to time," Gavin Earl said. "Dan was among the worst there is. Don't let it get to you. Lots of folks are safer because he's buzzard meat and red snow."

"Gavin is a true bastard who murdered me. But, Doc, when he's right, he's right."

Earl acknowledged McTroy's compliment.

"Doesn't make up for Sully's Fork," Earl said.

McTroy held up his crab-like crippled hand. "If killing me didn't do it, nothing will."

Earl walked away from us.

Despite the words of encouragement I felt no ease in my conscience.

Evangeline said, "Dan might have been Beast-influenced. His rage was either murderous, or both murderous and cannibalistic. You did the right thing, Hardy. For all the best reasons. That is what heroes do. Take your time with your feelings of grief. But never regret saving your friends from harm. Do not allow self-reflection to derail you from our task. The Beast lives."

"Can we kill it?"

"I don't know," she said. "But it's our only chance at surviving."

She was right, of course. Her assessment of the sanguinary event with Dan helped to quell my turmoil. I might've spent the rest of the waning hours of the day probing the depths of my guilt, but we had work to do. The Beast had to be stopped.

We re-boarded the windows with the scraps we had. Oscar allowed us to sacrifice his dining room table for our fortifications. When the trophy room was sealed, we talked of inspecting the destruction Dan had done to the doors, but the matter proved irrelevant.

For no sooner had we finished the windows than the doors were breached.

The Beast entered Nightfall Lodge.

33

THE BEAST'S KITCHEN

But we could not find the Beast. You would think something of that size and ferocious demeanor would be obvious from the start. We had evidence of its passing. The doors were gone. Exploded out into the night. Hardly a shred of wood left on the doorstep. Daylight left the mountainous ridge bleak, desolate, and stark, but the fog stayed. It smelled of musk and iron blood. The cloven hoof prints of the Beast dappled the slush on the path. It was hard to read them, impossible for me. But McTroy and Earl conferred about their meaning. LaFarque lingered in the doorway with his spear and shield. Oscar kept his elephant gun at the ready. But he was impatient. It was wet outside. The anteroom showed watery prints and scratches where the Beast had walked, but the steps went no farther into the home.

"It took the doors off and then left? Is that what you're saying," I asked.

McTroy said, "That's how it looks. Dan made a damn mess of the snow when he was out there chopping things. The rocks aren't holding much for us to read. But it didn't come past here." McTroy pointed to the gallery that led to the trophy room where we all had been.

"Maybe it sensed a possible trap," Evangeline said.

"Or maybe it plays with our minds," LaFarque said. "An attack on our psychology."

"For whatever reason, it has chosen to remain outside. In its familiar habitat. It lures us," Oscar said. "You talk about my invitation to the monster. Well, it repays me with an offer to visit. But I for one will not accept. Let it come here. Out there in the dark we are more vulnerable."

"We should at least check the perimeter. It might smell Dan's body. As impossible as it sounds, that may be scrumptious bait for this eater," Earl said. "McTroy and I will go."

"You will?" I turned to my partner.

McTroy nodded. "Earl and I can do it. It won't take long. Just a little scouting mission."

The former partners stepped out in the fog.

Within a minute we could neither see them, nor hear their footsteps.

"Separation seems a bad idea," I said. "We should all be together." I had a horrible thought. "Cassi! My God, we have forgotten about her in her bedroom."

Viv said, "She should be kept out of this. The Beast did not go down that hall. So she is safe. Safer there than with us if the Beast returns."

"No one is safe," Oscar said. "That rule applies in every land. But I agree with my wife. What good is it to bring the girl here? The Beast will come for us if it comes at all."

"What about Hodgson?" I asked.

"Hodgson?" Oscar looked surprised.

"Where does he live?"

"Hodgson lives in Raton. At the Ram Hotel," Viv said. "He manages the books as well as our stables."

"But the night of the storm, he was here," I said.

"There's a spare room for the servants to sleep. More of a closet, with a cot," Oscar said.

"Where is it?"

"Down at the end of the bedroom hall. Past Viv's room. All the way at the end."

"And is Hodgson there now? Did he ignore this commotion?" Evangeline asked.

Oscar shrugged. "After he returned with the carriage I told him he could go. I assume he went back to Raton with his horse. I didn't see it in the stables. What is your concern with the dwarf?"

"Everyone is a suspect," I said. "What if Hodgson is the Beast?"

"Then the Beast would be four feet tall," Oscar said, smirking.

Viv wheeled her chair away, rolling into the gallery.

"She has a soft heart for the little deformity. He's a good bookkeeper from what she tells me. And he has a way with animals. But he is not the Beast." Oscar stared into the fog.

"I think I hear something," LaFarque said.

"I heard it too," Oscar agreed.

"A moaning." The con man took up the spear and shield and ventured to the doorstep.

He hoisted the spear the way warriors do in paintings. The shield hooked to his arm.

"Do you see anything? McTroy and Earl?" Oscar called out.

"No. Only this pea soup fog." He walked out farther. Wisps of fog slid around him.

"And the moaning," I said. "Is there any more of that?"

LaFarque stood up straight. "I hear nothing. I see nothing. I am coming bac–"

He was gone.

"LaFarque?" I said.

Oscar shouted, "LaFarque! LaFarque!"

But there was no reply.

"Look! There in the fog. Some movement," I said.

"LaFarque! Can you hear us?"

Oscar's question was answered by the spinning shield that flew out of the fog. Then we heard a high-pitched screaming. The whistle of the Beast – moving left to right, right to left. Up high into the tops of the pines it went, from the bottom of the canyon it shrieked, then above us. I would have said it was riding in the clouds.

"I am burning! Burning!"

"That's LaFarque," Oscar said. "The Beast has him in its claws. It runs him through the woods as it said it would. He is killed. The man is as good as dead. Taken from right there. I still see where he stood when it snatched him."

"Burninggggggggg…"

We listened as the Beast played with LaFarque like a cat does with a wounded mouse.

I asked Evangeline to take Wu back to the trophy room with Viv. But Wu insisted that he stay. The boy could make his own decisions. He was old enough. But

I would have left if I felt I could. We saw LaFarque's face once, popping out of the fog too high to be standing on his own feet. More than fifteen feet off the ground. He looked sunburned, but it was too dark to tell much.

The broken Maasai spear fell from the sky, landing with a clatter on the doorstep.

We never saw LaFarque again.

"It's been more than an hour," I said. "What should we do? Go after them?"

"That's a mistake," Oscar insisted. "It's luring us out there. You saw what happened to the Frenchman."

"Canadian," I said.

"They're dead. The same as LaFarque. This Beast is really something. Horrible, yes. But you have to admit, there's something to be admired in a predator that can pick hunters off like sheep standing in a field."

We had moved into the cage. Even Orcus joined us. He slept on a large pillow at Viv's feet. Wu tapped on the bars with his fingertip. We didn't bother to try and block the doors. The fireplace was dark and the lodge was freezing now. We had our coats on. The cage door was open a few inches. I still had the keys in my pocket. If I shut the door it would lock. Unlocking it required a bit of contortion involving my wrist, but it was possible. I left the door open just in case. What if McTroy returned and needed to get inside quickly? I sat next to the door and watched the gallery hallway, waiting for any sign.

"Rom?"

It wasn't anyone in the cage saying my name.

"Rom? Are you here?"

It was Cassi. I saw her walking slowly, barefoot. Her arm bled. She had taken off the bandages and the tourniquet was loose. She bled on the floor and her face was pale as the fog.

"Cassi, we are in the trophy room," Oscar called out.

I exited the cage.

"Where is everyone? Where is Rom?"

"I'm here. Right here." I went to her. She was cold as a corpse, as if she'd come in from outside. Had she been sleepwalking again? She was dressed in different clothes than when I had left her asleep. The nightgown she now wore, a simple shift, was splashed with red. She'd absently touched her hair and that too had become encrimsoned. Holding her I quickly became covered in blood. "We need to fix your bandages. You are badly wounded. Let me take you to the cage and you can rest there safely with us."

She collapsed in my arms. I picked her up and carried her.

Wu swung the cage door wide and I put her on the pillows. Orcus moved off and went to guard the hallway. I pulled the cage door shut and felt the heavy lock engage.

"You are safe," I said.

"You love my daughter," Viv said.

"I– I do not know what love is, I think... but... I think I may love her, yes..."

"She is like Claude," Viv went on. "You know what I mean?"

"Yes, we saw her. We saw... saw her when she was like Claude," I said.

"Twins are all alike," Oscar said. "But she's better

than Claude was. Stronger."

Viv refused to look at her husband. The cage seemed very small, and cold.

Footsteps. Footsteps in the hallway.

"Someone or something is coming," Wu whispered.

Oscar propped his elephant gun on the crossbars of the cage. He aimed for the gallery.

"Should we call out?" Wu asked.

"I think Cassi could be happy with a man like you, Rom Hardy. The right man can make a sad woman less so. He can transform her life from grays and blacks to color. We never know where love is until it finds us. Do you think she is beautiful? I do. She was the most beautiful baby. Her brother fussed and cried. But Cassi was the quiet one. Always watching. You could see her thinking. Her soul is old. She is less impetuous than her brother was. But you will have to watch her, Dr Hardy. She has moods like all sensitive people do. Then she is unpredictable…"

I wanted to hush Viv, but it didn't seem to me that she would listen.

I looked over her shoulder at the gallery.

"Look at her poor arm. Maybe the changing will heal her. It does sometimes you know. Wasn't it worse before? They said her arm was almost gone when they found her. I see a deep wound. But the flesh repairs itself in time. She will have scars. This family has scars."

"Who is in my gallery? Name yourself," Oscar said.

I glanced from the gallery to Cassi's arm. I expected Viv to be wrong, but the arm did look improved. There was still a chunk of flesh missing. A semi-circular incision where the teeth went in took something away.

I had Cassi's head in my lap. Her head felt warm, almost feverish. As I looked at her wound, I saw her arm bone lengthening. Her face stretched forward into a feline snout. Next the black hair. It did not grow gradually, but all at once, in a flash. She grew claws, and a tail curled out from the pillows.

I was fascinated, horrified, but most of all heartbroken. Cassi was no monster to me.

"Ho, in the trophy room! It's us. McTroy and Earl."

The pair of gunmen stepped out of the gallery.

Oscar lowered his rifle. Wu took the keys from me and unlocked the cage door.

"McTroy, we thought you might be dead." He ran to the bounty man.

The trophy room was dark. We had one lamp in the cage and we'd left the red candle burning on the table. Gavin Earl picked up the candle and brought it to McTroy.

"We'll eat the boy first and make them watch," Earl said.

McTroy twisted the keys from Wu's hand. They fell clattering to the floor. "I get to pick the next one," he said.

When he bared his teeth, it was a terrible thing to see. The gold tooth he had sparkled in the candlelight. His grizzled jaw opened wide. Glinting eyes from under the brim of his hat showed no remorse for anything he had done or ever would do. Wu screamed. But McTroy had him fast by the arm. He wrestled the boy over to the round séance table. And flung him on top with such force that the air left Wu, and I worried his back might be broken.

"Not much meat," Earl said.

"We'll have more courses, friend. Grab the whiskey and bring me a bottle."

"A bottle for you and one for me," Earl said.

"Or more, or more, whatever the cabinet provides is ours. I am dry and empty."

"Dry as the desert where I lay blind and motionless," McTroy said.

Earl frowned, and then laughed.

Evangeline reloaded the shotgun. "Do not let that door shut, Oscar. Or we are trapped."

Oscar put himself in the door. His elephant gun lay over his arm.

"Shall I shoot them?"

"That is what I am planning on doing," she said. "Save your shot for the Beast."

"Where is it?"

"I'm sure it will appear soon."

Cassi's transformation did not proceed all the way to full panther. She was half-woman still, and half-cat. Her eyes fluttered open. I felt her purring in my lap.

"You see how she likes you, Doctor," Viv said.

"Evangeline? Cassi is turning into a panther. What do you suggest?"

Oscar gaped. This was all too much for the great hunter to bear. He staggered from the cage, avoiding the table where McTroy and Earl struggled with a kicking Wu. Keeping to the wall, he found his way into the gallery opening. And he left.

"One's getting' away, pard," Earl said.

"We got plenty more. And where's he going to anyway? If we don't catch 'im here, we'll nab 'im on the road."

Earl pulled a knife from his boot. "What's the best way to skin a boy this size?"

"I'd say hang him by the head and pull down."

"But where we gonna hang this one? By the damn chandelier?"

Cassi rolled off my lap. She stood on two legs, but hardly like any person I'd ever seen before. Her motion was silky. Her dark furry legs crept toward the bars. Evangeline snapped the shotgun closed and pulled back the hammers.

"Don't shoot Cassi," I said.

"I wasn't going to."

"Why not?"

"I think she will fight those men better than we can."

"Excellent point." I pried open the rum barrel and, using my mittens, I lifted out McTroy's rum-soaked telepathic contact. "Sorry for this." I took the head and rammed it into the bars.

McTroy let go of Wu and grabbed his skull.

I banged his contact's head repeatedly into a crossbar, and I ran the forehead along the bars like a mallet along a xylophone. McTroy fell to the floor, writhing.

Cassi left the cage, crouching into a pocket of shadows. She darted under the table. Earl screamed and leaped away, grabbing a bloody slash in his groin. Wu seized the opportunity to flee back into the cage. Unfortunately, in his fright, he pulled the door closed, locking four of us inside.

"Wu, the keys," I said.

He understood now his mistake.

"See if you can reach them," I said as I continued to bash the severed head into the floor of the cage with alternating side blows to the bars. McTroy had gone from thrashing about in agony to curling up in a protective fetal ball.

I looked up in time to see Cassi bolt into the gallery.

Wu's arm was too short to reach the keys which McTroy had torn from his hand. Being a resourceful and adaptive youngster, he stripped off his boot and sock and attempted to clutch the key ring with his toes. But he lacked both length and dexterity. However, Evangeline did not. Her toes clasped the keyring and she recovered them. She was about to unlock the door when a scream from the gallery caused me to ask her to suspend our liberation until more facts came to light.

Oscar's elephant gun fired.

Another scream, like the first, began but was abruptly cut off – giving way to a sloshy wet gurgling like rain traveling out a noisy gutter spout.

McTroy lay still. Gavin Earl leaned against the wall with his back to us, self-judging the severity of his very private wound, while striking match after match and swearing quietly.

Oscar walked in from the gallery.

His lower jaw was missing.

We knew where it was because the Beast followed him into the room and placed its bloody prize on the table beside the red candle, which had burned down but still provided enough illumination that everything was appallingly, dreadfully, and almost clinically clear.

34
WOUNDS

Red ice eyes. The antlers looked even bigger indoors than they had by the window that night. Saliva dripped from the teeth. But what I noticed was the chunk of flesh missing from the Beast's left forearm. She'd bitten herself. I don't know if Cassi did it when she was sleepwalking, like she said, or if it was a devious trick by the Beast to throw us off her trail until she could get us where she wanted us for a final feeding. Either way, it worked on me. Maybe my mind couldn't comprehend how a woman who might change into a werecat might also change again, or keep changing, into a hungry, insatiable, cosmic creature far more powerful than I had ever been or ever wished to be. Cassi was cursed from the start. Doubly cursed to be the victim of her father's lust for fame and her mother's craving for occult knowledge. Oscar was more to blame than anyone. He'd started it. He'd pushed it. He tried to control it, cage it, and finally to kill it.

She took his elephant gun and snapped it in two.

We found the pieces in the gallery afterward.

He'd fired at her after she changed into her Beast

form. Snuck up from behind and blasted her at her back. But she wasn't hit. No harm done. Oscar left a mighty hole in the stone wall of his castle. The Beast didn't follow Oscar's rules. She turned on him and grabbed his chin. Stuck her thumb in his mouth. Then she flicked her wrist.

Oscar, in a daze, pulled out a chair and sat at the séance table gargling blood.

Cassi – I don't want to call her the Beast anymore, because, despite her second transformation, part of her was still a young woman who laughed and loved... who loved me... I wished that we could go back in time before all this happened, before Oscar asked his wife to call a demon into their home. Before his daughter became that demon's host. It wasn't possible, but I wanted to meet Cassi when she was only Cassi.

But she was never only Cassi.

She spotted Gavin Earl mumbling in the corner and put her antlers in his back and lifted him, shaking him with his head caught up in the chandelier. He was dead when she wrenched him from her prongs.

She threw him in the cold fireplace.

Her breath made long plumes of smoke in the frigid room.

The Algonquin people say their Wendigo smells like decay, like dead bodies. Their story is a warning against cannibalism in hard winter seasons, a frightful tale to keep the children close to home and prevent wandering too deeply into a dark wood. In general, it teaches people not to prey on each other. Not to consume your neighbors or yourself just because you've gotten a taste for something that's not on the menu. That's probably overly simplistic and wrong on my part. Like LaFarque, I am no Indian. But what I'm saying is that this advice is good. But it does not apply to my story of what happened at Nightfall Lodge. Because Cassi did not smell like death or decay. She smelled like nothing. Like the cold wind, like ice, like a Beast That Has No Name.

There was no lesson for me.

I learned nothing.

Cassi started for McTroy. He was coming awake. The evil spirit influence wasn't on him anymore. I don't know if I knocked it out when I battered the green moldy head, or if Cassi stopped what she was doing to him. I don't even know if she could stop it. Or if it just arrived with the entity that took up residence in her and spread itself over the mountain like a plague.

But it was with killing in mind that she bent over my friend. Her claw snapped off his buttons. She checked his flesh the way a grandmother thumps a gourd in the fruit market. He was going to die in front of us. I couldn't stay silent.

"Cassi, please don't hurt him."

The Beast... Cassi stood to her full height and approached the bars of the cage.

"Doc-tor, are you speaking to me? I thought I heard you."

"Yes, I'm asking you to let my friends go. Stop what you're doing here."

"Why?"

"I am at your mercy. We are all at your mercy. There is nothing for you here. Is it possible for you to move on? You told me you are a traveler."

"I cross dimensions. Time is not the same for me."

"Can you leave, and can Cassi stay?"

"No, we are one now."

"I am begging you please not to kill us. You told me that you can go where you please when you want. If this is true, then I ask you to choose to leave now."

The Beast shook its head. There were pieces of clothing and moss in its antlers. Its fur stuck together in clumps because blood had dried there.

"What if I go with you? You told me it is lonely where you are. I will keep you company. If you are bored, like you say, I will listen to all you have to teach me. I am always talking, so conversation is not an issue. I am interested in old things, wise things. And you are the oldest, wisest intelligence I have ever encountered. Leave my friends and take me."

The Beast grabbed the bars on either side of my face and pulled them apart as if they were licorice whips. Then Cassi lifted me out of the cage. My feet didn't touch the ground. She turned away from the others.

"I will show you what no man ever sees, Rom. I will make it so you do not lose your sanity despite the magnitude of unearthly designs. Do not be terrified. I feel your heartbeat. Come with me through the gateway of endless tomorrows. We dare to dream this now together."

As I had carried Cassi in her human body on this same night, she cradled me in her arms and walked toward the gallery. "The woods are cold. But I will warm you, Rom," she whispered.

Evangeline pulled the triggers of the shotgun.

Blood blinded me.

I thought I was dead. I knew darkness. I fell through the abyss, not knowing if I would ever wake again. Not caring, if truth be told. The darkness welcomed me as few places ever had.

A list of wounds, their treatment, and the results. For the record, and to the best of my memory:—

Hodgson returned in the morning from Raton, where he had indeed gone after Oscar dismissed him. His affection for Vivienne, and hers for him, no longer stayed secret. They were the lovers I snuck up to in the lions' diorama that midnight when I first talked to Orcus and saw the Beast in the window. Besides being a gifted horseman and an excellent bookkeeper, Hodgson proved to be a proficient student of the occult. Later a teacher of the same highest quality. The Ram Hotel was rebuilt as a school for female sensitives, like Vivienne. It remains in operation to this day.

Vivienne Adderly was never the same woman after losing both of her children in the tragedy at Nightfall Lodge, but she found relief in escaping her oppressive husband and freely acknowledging her love for Hodgson, whose first name is Erasmus, but who I will always think of as stern Hodgson. Still regarded as one of the three most gifted sensitives west of the Mississippi, Viv has mentored many mediums and students. She and Hodgson retired from the Ram School of Mediumship, turning over the reins to their twin daughters, Agatha and Eudora.

Unbelievably, Oscar Adderly did not perish from his grisly wound. His disfigurement required multiple surgeries from the finest medical teams in America and Europe. In the end he fashioned his own prosthetic lower jaw from a combination of wood, silk, and dyed leather. He never regained his speech and wore a black notebook on a chain around his neck in the manner of Smoke Eel's disguise. Oscar continued his expeditions for several years after the murders. However, his health deteriorated after his separation from Vivienne who, despite their catastrophic break, continued to be the sole heir of his collections (she did not need his money; her family had more than he did). Oscar lived at Nightfall alone for five years. He maintained a small staff, but, like Hodgson, they lived in Raton. Oscar committed suicide on his sixtieth birthday. He jumped into the same crevasse from which he had rescued Vivienne years before. His suicide note, pinned to an elk antler in his trophy room, read: I DID THIS. He named the crevasse and asked that his body not be recovered. It never was.

The Apis Bull which the Copper Team was awarded proved to be a fake. It was melted down, and the gold went into the coffers of the Institute for Singular Antiquities, where it was spent.

Rex McTroy and Yong Wu left Nightfall Lodge with the head in the rum barrel. They rode out into the New Mexico desert where the Pecos River and Salt Creek meet in search of the star man and his shipwreck. It is their story to tell, and not mine. But I will say they returned to Yuma with an empty barrel, and McTroy suffered no more afflictions attributable to psychic links.

Romulus Hardy, Egyptologist, and his partner in the Institute for Singular Antiquities, Evangeline Waterston, took a terribly long train ride back to Manhattan together. You know the rest of that story, Evangeline, so I will not bore you with it. There's my story. How did I do?

Variation on a Monster

New Year's Day, 1920
The Waterston Institute for Singular Antiquities
Manhattan, New York City

"You have the best memory of anyone I've ever known, Hardy," Evangeline said.

Her silver hair was an enchantment to me. The late afternoon light was catching it in the best way possible. People who don't know Evangeline Waterston often call her *distinguished*. But that does not scratch the surface. It makes her sound old, outmoded, like a nice formal building people eat lunch in front of when the weather is pleasant. She is so much more than that.

The woman lives!

"Thank you for the compliment," I said.

"But," she started. "You have a fault in your recollection. A blind spot. As I suspected, you have blocked a key piece of information out. Or, to be more precise, you've written it to make it more acceptable to you. Less painful."

"I hardly know how the mountain adventure at

Nightfall Lodge could be more pain-filled. I still have trouble lifting my shoulder on cold days like this from that blunderbuss wound Dirty Dan gave me. But it is almost worth it to tell people that I have a blunderbuss wound at all."

I chuckled.

Evangeline took my glass, walked over to my liquor cabinet, and poured.

"This must be bad! You've even got me to the point where I might say I've had too much, too early in the day. It's not even close to fully dark yet."

She lifted a framed photograph of me from the cubby next to my whiskey. "I've always adored this picture," she said, handing me the glass.

She showed it to me, though I knew it better than my own face in the mirror. The face in the mirror changes, but this sepia representation never does. It was the boardwalk. I wore a linen suit, so it must have been July or August. I forget months, sometimes exact years. This was two decades ago. He had a stick in his mouth. No leash. The idea of him on a leash was absurd.

"Orcus loved the beach. He could walk for days," I said.

"He was a good companion to you."

"I think he felt guilty about leaving the lodge that night. He knew too much. His loyalties were divided. Whom to protect? Whom to attack? He went for a walk instead. Spent the rest of his life trying to make it up to me. Oscar wouldn't have him. Said he failed to guard the house. What a bastard Oscar was. I buried him in the park, you know. Orcus, not Oscar. Took my shovel and buried him one midnight in Central damn Park. I was like a reverse resurrectionist."

I sipped my whiskey deeply. I was better than half-drunk. Old dogs do break your heart when the memories start coming at you from all sides. But it's a good kind of pain. Sweet, really.

"Abandoning Orcus wasn't the worst thing Oscar did," Evangeline said.

"No." I searched my pockets for my pipe. "No, no… Where is my…?"

"It's right there in the ashtray."

"Huh! I *have* had too much. Are you trying to lure me into a compromising position?" I swirled my glass and raised my eyebrows.

"Isn't that your fantasy?"

"A-ha, Touché." I relit my pipe, but it even smelled awful to me. I put it down. "What were you criticizing about my memory? I thought I did quite a good job considering the passage of time and how confusing the whole Nightfall situation was."

Evangeline sat close to me.

"Hardy, I need you to listen. This will be hard. But the truth is often that way. I'm going to tell you what you got wrong. I don't know if the violence erased your memory, or if you did it consciously. But you've held Cassi's death against me for a long time."

"Oh, *pshaw*! That isn't true. You and I are on good terms. There's no one I admire more on this earth. I know what you did. There was no other way in your mind. I can see that."

"Cassi was not walking you out the door to live with you in some cosmic relationship for two lonely souls. She was a monster. Maybe not at first, she wasn't. The werecat part of her was predatory. That is natural. But the Beast in her was *un*-natural. This isn't a love story, Rom."

I stared at her.

I said, "I understand that she was in some minor way your rival. You had turned down my proposal. I was vulnerable, yes. Some men would call me weak. Fair enough. But Cassi and I had a strong connection from the moment we met. I'm not forcing you to call it love–"

"She wasn't taking you out of the lodge to run away with you, Hardy. She was going to eat you. I shot her when she opened her mouth around your throat."

I swallowed the last of the whiskey. We sat there together in silence for half an hour.

At last, I got up. I was as ready as I ever would be. I fetched my ape-headed walking stick from the ceramic stand near the door. Then I turned and met Evangeline's eyes. "I have something to show you. Are you coming with me? Or am I to do this alone?"

"You don't have to do anything alone, Hardy. I am here for you."

"Then let's go."

We took the stairs slowly, which is the only way I take stairs these days.

Together we crossed the large exhibition hall. In the back there is a door marked *Storage*. Storage in a museum often houses the greater part of the collections. Items rotate for public viewing, but most things are in boxes, or drawers, or they sit on shelves getting dusty.

Like old men.

At the back of the Institute's main storage room is a second smaller room to which I have the only key. I have visited this room once before, two weeks after Oscar Adderly died. He'd shipped me something before he wrote his last note to the world and jumped to his death in that crag. The shipping crate had a card attached. A hasty message scribbled inside.

SHE IS YOURS NOW

Nothing on the billing told me what it was. I only knew it came from New Mexico. And it was large. Very large. Although when I pried off the front of the crate, I didn't really expect to see what I did. He'd kept it up there on the mountain with him for years. I picture Oscar working on getting the features just right, the way they were at Nightfall when we were last together. He'd become a recluse. His face scared people. The adventurer was a hermit.

I turned my key in the door and opened it.

Evangeline grabbed my hand. I felt her trembling.

"There she is. Oscar did a fine job, I think. He got the eyes right."

Red ice.

Red ice...

Acknowledgments

Thanks to those who ushered the Beast into this world: Ann Collette, agent and guide; the Angry Robot Gang of Marc Gascoigne, Lottie Llewelyn-Wells, Penny Reeve, and Nick Tyler, plus cover wizard Dan Strange. And for my friends along this rugged journey: Gary Heinz, Bob Tuszynski, Ross Molho, Pat Howard, Greg Wolf, and the Novel Approaches posse. Lastly, to my family, who keep me safe from storms and light my lantern in the dark woods; and to Lisa, my best partner and true love.

UNDER THE
PENDULUM SUN

A NOVEL OF   THE FAE

JEANNETTE NG

Two Victorian missionaries
travel into darkest fairyland,
to deliver their uplifting
message to the godless
magical beings who dwell
there… at the risk of losing
their own mortal souls.

*Winner of the Syndney J
Bounds Award, the British
Fantasy Award for Best
Newcomer*

*Shortlisted for the John W
Campbell Award*

UNDER THE PENDULUM SUN by Jeanette Ng • PAPERBACK & EBOOK
from all good stationers and book emporia

The INSTITUTE *for* SINGULAR ANTIQUITIES

FURY FROM THE TOMB

"A master of the unsettling."
— PUBLISHERS WEEKLY

S.A. SIDOR